FINAL
HARBOR

FINAL
HARBOR

★

Harry Homewood

McGRAW-HILL BOOK COMPANY
New York   St. Louis   San Francisco
Düsseldorf   Mexico   Toronto

1 2 3 4 5 6 7 8 9 B P B P 8 7 6 5 4 3 2 1 0

LIBRARY OF CONGRESS CATALOGING IN PUBLICATION DATA
Homewood, Harry.
    Final harbor.
    1. World War, 1939-1945—Fiction. I. Title.
PZ4.H766Fi   [PS3558.045]   813'.5'4   79-24174
ISBN 0-07-029694-4

Book design by Marsha Picker

AUTHOR'S NOTE

All the characters in this novel are fictional. There was no intent to limn any person, living or dead. Those readers who served in submarines in the Pacific in World War II will notice a certain chronological compression of some events, a device the author felt necessary for the purposes of the story.

Grateful acknowledgment is made to Clay Blair, Jr., whose monumental work on the role of the United States Submarine Navy in World War II entitled *Silent Victory* (published by J.B. Lippincott Co., Philadelphia and New York, 1975) served to refresh my memory.

This book is dedicated with profound respect to the memory of the 3,508 officers and enlisted men who died in the sinkings of 52 United States Navy submarines in World War II, some of whom I had the pleasure of serving with before their deaths.

It is dedicated also to those submariners who lived through the bitter and dangerous years of the submarine war against the Empire of Japan—in particular to Lieut. Comdr. Joseph J. Sibley, USNR, who was the personification of the ideal submariner, in war or peace.

PROLOGUE

There were no gestures of tenderness, no soft words of love when she was conceived. Those would come later when men lived with her, rode her, cursed her and finally came to love her.

The conceptual couch was built of drawing boards and the fetus was a thick stack of blueprints labeled "Fleet Submarine Work Order SS/58903-6431-171/39-41."

She was midwived by Navy Yard workmen dressed in grimy work clothes as the world convulsed in agony; as Poland reeled under the invasion of Russian and German troops, and England, fearful but unafraid, lashed out with a declaration of war against the invaders.

As she grew from a long stretch of gaunt circular ribs of steel to the smooth, deadly sleekness of her finished shape, Finland was overrun, Norway fell and the Low Countries drowned in the riptides of war that swept across Europe.

She had no name. That would come later when a bottle of champagne would be broken over her bulbous nose. Until that day she would bear the generic name given to all submarines—"The Boat."

In time the Navy sent a man to command her. Later he was joined by other officers and a cadre of Chief and First-Class Petty officers.

These men grew with the Boat. They watched the Navy Yard workmen install the intricate systems of oil, water, air and hydraulic lines that were the arteries of the Boat. They traced the myriad webs of electrical circuitry that were the Boat's nervous system and they watched as the Boat's propulsion systems were installed, four huge diesel engines for running on the surface, two immense storage batteries for propulsion while submerged. In bow and stern the Boat's weapons were installed, six bronze torpedo tubes in the bow, four in the stern. With their knowing hands and eyes the men who would be the Boat's living heart watched her as she was formed and learned all her concealed parts before they were hidden from view.

The work went on under a blizzard of newspaper headlines that told of the war in Europe. As the men learned the Boat they came to respect the long, sweet reach of this underseas warship that was to be their home in time of peace, the weapon they would wield if the war raging in Europe should come to their shores.

This is the story of the Boat and the men who took her to war in the far reaches of the Pacific Ocean against the forces of the Empire of Japan, a war which would claim of those who fought in submarines the heaviest casualty rate of all the branches of the United States Armed Forces.

CHAPTER 1

Far back in the mists of time, 320,000,000 years ago on the geologic time chart, huge predator fish and reptiles swam in the warm seas that covered much of the Earth. Of all the toothed horrors that swam in those Devonian Age seas and in all the seas down through the eons of time, only one great predator survived virtually unchanged, except for a reduction in its size to accommodate to its reduced food supply—the shark.

From the time when man learned to wage war on the seas he yearned for the ability to strike his enemy unseen from the safety of the depths of the sea, yearned for a weapon that would be as deadly as the dreaded shark.

He invented the submarine.

The night air was thick and soft, heavy with humidity. Occasionally a land breeze drifted across the sea from the dark bulk of Borneo, the wind bearing on it the faint trace of wet vegetation, the smell of land. In the darkness of early night the U.S.S. *Mako*, Fleet Submarine, prowled Makassar Strait, her camouflage paint dull and blotched in the starlight.

Just aft of the submarine's open bridge Capt. Arthur M. Hinman kept his solitary night watch on the cigaret deck, his short legs braced against the slow roll of his ship. The ship's Executive Officer, Lieut. Comdr. Mike Brannon, a plump man with a studious manner, stood in the cramped bridge space with the Officer of the Deck and the quartermaster of the watch. Above the four men three night lookouts perched in the steel webbing of the periscope shears, searching the horizon through night binoculars.

For as long as man has gone to sea custom had dictated that the man who commands a ship must stand apart from those who serve under him. The custom is well founded; by the law of the sea and nations a ship's captain has the power of life and death over his crew. He is their judge and jury and, if necessary, their executioner. Command at sea is one of the loneliest of all professions.

That ancient custom had changed somewhat in the peacetime submarine service of the U.S. Navy. The change had come about gradually as the submarine grew more and more complicated. The demand for intelligent, highly skilled sailors to man the increasingly sophisticated ships had led to a form of special camaraderie among submarine crews and their officers that was based on the respect each man held for the skills of other crew members. But as the submarine captains took their ships to war, inexperienced in the grim game of fool's dice they must play with the enemy's warships, untested except in peacetime war games, the ancient wisdom of a Captain's need for removal from his crew was recognized. The decision to be bold or cautious, to attack against heavy odds or to evade, rested in the mind of only one man, the submarine's Commanding Officer.

Lieut. Comdr. Arthur M. Hinman, USN, Commanding Officer of the U.S.S. *Mako,* was ill-fitted by nature for the solitary role of a ship's captain. Hinman was a gregarious man with a consuming fondness for practical jokes that had been nurtured in the small Iowa town where he grew to manhood. His bubbling sense of humor, his love of an elaborate practical joke, had earned him a demurrer in his official record which read, in part:

This officer, while highly qualified in all respects, has a weakness that must be considered whenever assignment to

a critical job is contemplated. Ensign Hinman often suc-
cumbs to an impulse to exercise what he calls a "country
boy sense of humor," often to the detriment of his work. If
this habit persists removal from assignment to sea duty or
even termination of his service might have to be considered.

The stigma had followed him throughout his early career, effectively slowing him in his struggle for increasingly responsible assign-
ments until it was announced that he had become engaged to the
daughter of a highly regarded Admiral. The Admiral was not noted
for his sense of humor or his tolerance of anything that was not
strictly Navy regulation. His paternal blessing of the fiancé of his last
unmarried daughter was taken as irrefutable evidence that Arthur
M. Hinman had at last outgrown his small-town fondness for jokes
and games and had become a serious Naval officer.

The Admiral's daughter and Arthur Hinman made an odd
couple. He was of medium height with the muscular body and feline
grace of the middleweight wrestler he had been at the Naval
Academy. She was taller than he by several inches and lean, a
flat-chested girl-woman with an ungainly stride she never quite
learned to adjust to her consort's shorter legs. Long before Arthur
Hinman had appeared on her horizon other young and ambitious
officers with an eye to the promotional advantages that would be
theirs if they took her as a wife had looked her over and passed her by
in favor of a woman more feminine, less sharp of tongue.

Hinman saw something in Marie the others had missed. He
appreciated the steel and flint of her character. He recognized that
her caustic tongue was a defense weapon, employed because she
lacked the outward attractions of most women. He sensed the deep,
throbbing capacity for physical passion that resided within her spare
body and he found a joy in the elfin spirit she had kept so well hidden
from her father, the Admiral. Their union was consummated in a
curiously sensual night a month before they walked from the chapel
at the Naval Academy beneath an arch of swords held by Hinman's
fellow officers. The marriage developed into an enduring and pas-
sionate love affair that in time became the envy of other Navy
officers—and their wives.

The marriage of the Admiral's daughter and Lieut. Comdr. Arthur Hinman ended in noise, fire and blood on a sunny Sunday morning when the pilot of a strafing Japanese dive bomber zeroed in on a car he saw approaching the chapel at Hickam Air Field. Marie Hinman and two other Navy wives in the car died on that Sunday morning, December 7, 1941, at Pearl Harbor.

The news of the Japanese attack against Pearl Harbor reached the U.S.S. *Mako* at sea, two days outbound from Balboa, enroute to the submarine base at Pearl Harbor.

The news of his wife's death and her burial was given to Captain Hinman an hour after *Mako* had made its way past the wreckage of the Navy's Pacific Fleet, the ship's crew standing at shocked attention to honor the memory of the thousands who had died on that flaming Sunday morning.

The Navy Chaplain who had taken Captain Hinman to one side on the dock had difficulty telling his tragic news. Captain Hinman wasn't listening to him. He was looking, standing on tiptoe, searching for Marie's head above the crowd of people on the dock. And then the impact of what the Chaplain was saying had hit home. He rocked back on his heels, his eyes veiled, his face grave. He stared at the Chaplain for a long moment.

"Please stand by, Padre," he had said. "I have work to do. My ship, you understand? When I have taken care of my ship's needs I want you to take me to her."

The Chaplain had nodded wordlessly and watched Captain Hinman as he walked over to Adm. Chester Nimitz and saluted and then began to talk, a ship's Captain engaged in ship's business with a man who had also been a ship's Captain and now commanded a fleet. When Captain Hinman had finally saluted the Admiral and come back to him he nodded his thanks at the Chaplain for waiting and got in the Navy car the Chaplain had called for. He said nothing on the ride to the cemetery where the remains of hundreds of the dead had been hastily interred. He stood for a long time at his wife's grave, marked only by a painted number on a plain white wooden cross. Then he had stepped back, saluted crisply, executed a smart about-face and marched back to the car. He said nothing in the car and when the Chaplain stopped the car on the dock alongside the *Mako*

Captain Hinman got out and then turned and bent down to speak to the Chaplain.

"Thank you, Padre," he said quietly, "I know it has been hard for you, too." Then he had wheeled about and strode over the narrow gangway to his ship's deck, took the salute of the deck watch and disappeared down the Forward Torpedo Room deck hatch.

The Executive Officer coughed discreetly and the sound carried back to the cigaret deck.

"Damn it, Mike," Captain Hinman said, "if you want to talk to me come back here. Don't just stand there."

"Figured you might be thinking about something, Skipper," Brannon said. "Ship's captains are always supposed to be thinking deep thoughts, aren't they?"

"You have to stop thinking every once in a while," Hinman said. "Go crazy if you don't. What's on your mind?"

"Tomorrow morning is on my mind," Brannon said. "As per your night orders we'll be in position to dive at zero five hundred. We'll dive on a course due west into the harbor mouth of Balikpapan. That way the sun should hide the periscope if anyone's looking for us."

"Someone will be looking for us," Hinman said. "That's the name of the game. We're going to have to go in as close as we can. The Staff in Pearl wants to know exactly how many oil tankers are loading in that harbor, what other kind of shipping is in there. We might have to go right into the mouth of the harbor from the way that chart looks."

"The chart isn't all that good," Brannon growled. "It's old, damned old! The channel is marked for depth but off to the south of the channel it only says possible shoaling. There's a river comes down about there and I suppose it drops a load of silt. I just don't know how much room we've got once we're out of the ship channel and to the south of it. If I may suggest, sir, we might lay off a day submerged and watch, see what comes out. That way we might be able to get an idea where the deep water is south of the channel."

"No," Hinman said. "Anything that comes out of the harbor is going to turn north, not south." He nodded as he saw Brannon jerk his head toward the after end of the small cigaret deck and he walked back to the rail and stood with his back touching the barrels of the twin 20-mm machine gun that was mounted in the center of the cigaret deck. Brannon joined him, his voice a low murmur.

"Chief of the Boat said to tell you that he and Ginty have finished modifying all the exploders in the torpedo warheads, sir. He says they'll explode only on contact now, the magnetic circuits have been disconnected. I shouldn't stick my nose in your business, sir—" his voice trailed off.

"It's a good Irish nose," Hinman said. "We've been friends a long time. Stick it in."

"Well," Brannon began. He looked up at the stern lookout who was standing in the periscope shears, his elbows braced on a pipe that ran around his lookout stand, his hands holding his binoculars to his eyes. Brannon's voice dropped even lower.

"I'm worried, Skipper. The Bureau of Ordnance says that no one, not a ship's captain, not even the experts in the torpedo shop on the Base can touch one of those Mark Six exploder mechanisms. The Chief and Ginty have done more than touch them, they've taken them apart and modified them!"

"On my direct orders," Captain Hinman said.

"I know," Brannon answered.

"You know how many torpedo failures we had on our first patrol," Hinman said. "Nothing but failure! Nine fish that ran hot, straight and normal according to the Sound man and passed under the targets as they were supposed to do and not a one of them exploded. Then eight more that we fired to hit the targets and they ran as they were supposed to run and nothing happened! Then the two we set to run at two-feet depth and they hit the side of the target and just sank! The damned exploders don't explode."

"That doesn't change what BuOrd says," Brannon's voice was stubborn. "You, the Chief and Ginty could all be hauled up in front of a General Court-Martial when we get back to Pearl and they take the fish off and find their damned exploders have been tampered with!"

"You're assuming we'll have torpedoes left aboard to turn in at Pearl," Captain Hinman's voice was dry.

Brannon shrugged his meaty shoulders. "It would seem likely we will. The patrol orders tell us to observe and give a detailed report on the shipping in the harbor at Balikpapan and to report on the size and course of any convoys that leave the harbor."

"So other submarines to the north of us can have first crack at the ships!" Hinman growled. "Those damned bureaucrats at Pearl Harbor want their old friends, the Captains with three full stripes, to get the first crack at the ships so they'll get medals and promotions! I'm the youngest commanding officer in the submarine fleet, did you know that? They want to make sure the older skippers get the targets.

"I know what the patrol orders say. I'll obey the orders. I want your plot laid down so I can go right into the mouth of the harbor if I have to. You let me worry about everything else."

"I know my Irish nose is too big," Brannon said mournfully, "so I'll stick it in some more. You're not only my Captain, I consider you to be my friend, and this damned exploder business has me worried!"

Hinman reached out in the dark to put his hand on Brannon's shoulder and then he thought better of it and pulled his hand back.

"I know how you feel, Mike. We both know there's something wrong with the design of that Mark Six exploder. We both know it's never been properly tested. But the BuOrd people and the Staff at Pearl are going to keep on saying that the submarine captains are missing the targets rather than admit they've given us a defective weapon. Every captain who has complained about the exploders has had his ass chewed out! Hell, Donaho in Flying Fish damned near got a General Court for telling those dummies at Pearl what he thought of their exploders—and what he thought of them!" He drew a deep breath.

"I intend to follow my orders to the letter. I will observe the shipping in the harbor and report what I see. And then, by God, I intend to carry out a sentence in the patrol orders you seem to have forgotten. It reads, quote and unquote, no attack on enemy shipping will be carried out unless conditions are most favorable and the chance of enemy reprisal minimal.

"If there is enemy shipping to be attacked then the conditions are going to be favorable! If Chief Rhodes is right about what's wrong with those exploders and if he and Ginty have corrected that error, then by God, we're going to end this exploder controversy. once and for all!"

Brannon turned toward the bridge. "Very well, sir. We should be about three miles due east of the harbor when we dive."

"Not 'about three miles due east,' Brannon. My night orders say we will dive exactly three miles due east of the harbor mouth."

Brannon was busy at his chart in the Control Room, sliding a set of parallel rulers across the harbor mouth of Balikpapan when Chief Torpedoman Gordon "Dusty" Rhodes stopped beside him.

"I gave him the word, Chief," Brannon said in a low voice. "I told him that he had laid himself, you and Ginty open to a court-martial but he says it doesn't make any difference. He's going to shoot all the fish we have and if we get hits he feels this will end the argument about the Mark Six exploder, that they'll have to modify the exploders."

"I didn't think we'd be doing much shooting this patrol," Rhodes said. "I thought we were on a search and observe patrol."

Brannon tapped the chart with his dividers, touching the port of Balikpapan. "The Dutch, to be precise, the Royal Shell Petroleum Company, built a big oil refinery here, back in eighteen ninety-nine. The whole area is full of oil—they say it's almost pure stuff. The people who were running the refinery tried to sabotage it when the Japs moved in, that would be last January, but they didn't do much of a job of sabotage. The Japs have got the refinery in operation. Japan lives on oil, you know. This is one of their biggest sources of supply.

"Which means that they are going to protect it, protect the oil tankers that leave here for Japan. I think we're going to find as many destroyers in that harbor as there are tankers. I've tried to talk to the Old Man about the possibility of tanker convoys under strong escort but he just ignores me. He used to be willing to talk about everything with me. Now he only tells me what he has to tell me. He's changed a lot since the ship was put in commission."

"He's got more reasons than most of us to change," Rhodes said. "He's lost more than any of us."

"His wife? Yes, that's a reason, Chief. But that's behind him now. The ship comes first. This patrol isn't going to be any picnic. The Japanese are getting damned good at anti-submarine warfare and they're going to get a lot better!"

"How would we know how good they are?" Rhodes said. His eyes were veiled, his face without expression.

"Chief," Brannon said slowly, "you and every other Chief of the Boat hold a position found only in submarines. You aren't one of the officers and you aren't really one of the crew. You sort of float in between both. So I'm going to tell you something for your ears alone, understand?

"We lost the *Perch* a little while back, in March. She survived a number of attacks before they got her and her Captain got off several messages before the Japs got the ship. From what he said the Japanese anti-submarine attacks were extremely well coordinated, they have sonar equipment much better than we ever realized and they used it with great skill. He tried every evasive maneuver he had been taught and none of it worked! He said in one message that they were so sure of him that they played with him like a cat with a mouse!

"We've lost seven submarines this year and the war isn't nine months old! I try to talk to the Old Man about evasive tactics and things like that but he doesn't seem to want to talk. I'd just like to know what's got into him, why he's changed."

"We notice it," Chief Rhodes said. "He used to be an easy Skipper, easy to live with. Hard if you didn't know your job but easy if you did. Now he's easy one day, hard the next. He doesn't stop and shoot the shit with the crew like he used to do. They notice things like that. Some of the people wonder if the lousy luck we had the first patrol has made him afraid, nervous."

"He's not afraid, Chief. Not that! If anything I'm afraid that he's not afraid at all! But I guess we've all changed a little. If you're going aft will you ask the baker to give me a cup of hot coffee and a couple of doughnuts?" He watched Rhodes' broad back move toward the After Battery Compartment. *The rest of us might change, he thought to himself, but the Chief of the Boat won't change. He'll always be what he always has been, a solid rock of a man, an invaluable link between the Wardroom and the crew, governing the enlisted men with a shrewd practical psychology backed with the unspoken threat of sudden physical violence if his orders were not obeyed to the letter.* He turned to his chart and went back to work.

"Coffee's coming up," Rhodes said to him a few minutes later. "No doughnuts this morning, sweet rolls. The baker will split a couple and fix 'em with butter for you."

"That canned butter!" Brannon made a face.

"Soaks in real quick, doesn't taste too bad," Rhodes said with a chuckle. He went forward through the Forward Battery Compartment where the officers and chief petty officers slept and into the Forward Torpedo Room. "Ginch" Ginty, the *Mako's* leading torpedoman, was sprawled in a folding canvas chair in front of the shiny brass doors of the six torpedo tubes. He stood up as he saw Rhodes approaching, balancing his massive weight on his toes.

"Old Man get the word on the exploders, Chief?"

"The Exec. told him. They must have talked a lot about it. The Exec. is worried that if we turn any fish in to the Base at Pearl we'll all get a General Court for modifying the exploders. The Old Man says not to worry, he's going to shoot all the fish!"

"Hot damn!" Ginty said. "Sounds good!" He sat down in the canvas chair.

"It won't sound so good if those exploders don't work," Rhodes said.

"They got to work!" Ginty rumbled. "Once these babies are armed, once this warhead hits anything with four pounds of impact force, that exploder is gonna work! You're gonna hear the biggest fucking noise you ever heard!" He reached up and patted the dull bronze 600-pound warhead that loomed over him. "This baby will make the biggest noise in the world if the Old Man can find anything to shoot it at and if he can hit it!"

"He isn't a bad shot," Rhodes said. "He made some nice approaches on those targets on the first patrol. And we got hits with those two fish that were set for two feet. He said he saw the fish hit the side of the ship and then bounce up in the air and fall away without exploding."

"He says he saw that," Ginty snorted. "Wasn't no one but him lookin' through the periscope!"

"Lieutenant Cohen was on the sound gear," Rhodes said. "He said he tracked the fish right into the target."

"Him!" Ginty said derisively. "What the fuck does he know? Fucking Reserve feather merchant! He ain't a sailor! What was he in civilian life, some sort of preacher?"

"He was studying to be a Rabbi," Rhodes answered.

"Rabbi? That's a Jew preacher, ain't it? So what does he know about torpedoes and submarines? You know what that silly fuck told me one day? He said he could hear shrimp on the sound gear! How the hell can you hear shrimp? They can't swim! What do they do, talk to him in Jew talk?"

"They click their tails when they move along the bottom," Rhodes said. His voice sharpened a trifle. "And lay off using that word 'Jew.' It isn't polite. People can be sensitive about things like that."

"I've got a sensitive ass," Ginty growled. "And I'd like to get off my ass and open these outer doors and shoot these babies!"

"I think you're going to get your wish," Rhodes said slowly. "In fact, I'd bet money on it. Just keep your fingers crossed that the exploders work!"

CHAPTER 2

The blast of the diving klaxon sent the *Mako* sliding down under the sea before the first light of the false dawn. Captain Hinman stood in the Conning Tower, waiting until the diving officer had leveled the ship off at 63 feet. Then he cautiously raised the periscope and began a methodical search of the horizon. As he finished, Mike Brannon's voice came up to him through the hatch.

"Crew is at Battle Stations, sir. Torpedo tube doors are closed. Repeat closed. We should be at the approach to the harbor entrance in twenty minutes. Sunrise should be in twenty-four minutes. When the headland on our starboard hand bears zero five zero, sir, we'll have to make a one-hundred-and-eighty-degree turn to port and proceed on the reverse course. We should have time to run in, run out and run in again before the sun gets too high to blind anyone looking for our periscope."

"Very well," Captain Hinman said.

The *Mako* slid silently through the water. As the ship neared the mouth of the harbor, Captain Hinman, searching the area to his stern, flinched at the blaze of the rising sun in the lens of the periscope.

"The sun is up now, Control. Bring me up another ten feet. Slowly! I don't want to broach!" He nodded at Chief Yeoman John Maxwell who stood in the after end of the Conning Tower with a notebook and pencil ready.

"Stand by, John. Take down everything I say." He swung the periscope through another complete turn, examining the sea and the sky. Then he steadied the lens on the harbor. Maxwell saw the muscles of Hinman's shoulders bunch under his thin khaki shirt.

"I see one . . . three . . . six, seven . . . nine . . . eleven oil tankers in the harbor!" Hinman's voice was crisp. "Five of those ships are in the center of the harbor. I can't tell from this distance and angle whether they are moored or anchored. Estimated tonnage of those five ships ranges from five to eight thousand tons.

"There are two ships at docks at the far end of the harbor. These are much larger ships, look to be twice the size of those in the middle of the harbor. The five tankers in the middle of the harbor appear to be fully loaded.

"There are four destroyers underway in the harbor! One of the destroyers is very large, estimate it to be a *Fubuki* destroyer leader." He pulled the periscope around. "Headland now bears zero five zero, Control. Commence your turn to port." He swung the periscope back to the harbor.

"The four destroyers have formed up and are now standing this way, coming toward the harbor mouth! The *Fubuki* is in the lead!" He began to turn the periscope to the right as the *Mako* began to turn left.

"I'll stay at this depth for two more minutes," he said to the Control Room. "When I give you the word take me back down to sixty-three feet. Here we go again, Chief. I see four ships deep in the harbor, this is in addition to the others recorded. These ships are either anchored or moored. All appear to be some sort of freighters, I cannot estimate tonnages from here. There are several warships, destroyers or destroyer leaders moored in a nest. I count six destroyers in that nest.

"The Japanese destroyers are now nearing the mouth of the harbor. Range to the lead destroyer is four zero zero zero yards! Open the outer doors on all torpedo tubes! Take me down to sixty-five feet! Fast!" He slammed the handles on the search periscope into the up position and jammed his thumb against the button that lowered the periscope.

"Left fifteen degrees rudder!" He thumbed the control button to raise the attack periscope, a thin-necked tube with a small viewing lens that left very little wake at slow speeds.

"Sound reports screws bearing two one zero, sir," Brannon reported.

"Very well," Hinman said. He handed the periscope control to the quartermaster. "Up slowly, I'll ride her up." He crouched down on the deck and as the periscope rose out of its well he snapped the handles down and clamped his face against the rubber eyepiece and rode the periscope upward. The quartermaster watched him carefully, his thumb on the button that would stop the upward travel of the periscope. Hinman saw the solid green water in the lens break into foam and daylight.

"Stop!" Hinman snapped.

"Lead destroyer now bearing zero zero zero! Range is two five zero zero! Helm amidships! Meet her head right there! By God, I don't think they know we're here!" He watched the big *Fubuki*, its high knife-like bow cleaving the water as it passed directly in front of *Mako*, followed by the three smaller ships.

"They're going so fast they can't hear anything on their sound gear," Hinman said. "Take a fathometer reading, Mike. I want to know how much water we've got under our keel over here."

He heard the muted "ping" of the fathometer and then Mike Brannon's voice came up through the hatch.

"Forty feet under the keel, sir. Repeat. Four zero feet." Hinman shuddered. The *Mako* was in water far too shallow to do any evasive maneuvering. He looked at the line of destroyers again. The *Fubuki* was now well out of the harbor and picking up speed. He saw a burst of bright color at the *Fubuki's* foremast yardarm as the ship began a turn to the left, heading north. Similar bursts of color showed at the foremasts of the other three destroyers as they obeyed the turn signal.

As the destroyers pulled away, the *Mako* slid toward the harbor.

"We'll go right into the harbor mouth," Hinman called down to the Control Room. "We'll make a turn to starboard to come out, we know there's plenty of water in the channel. John, stand by with your pencil. I'll make another count of the ships." He ran up the search periscope with its big viewing lens. His ship count was correct. He gave orders to reverse course and looked to the north. He could see the faint outlines of the destroyers, still heading northward.

"Close Torpedo Room outer doors," he called down to the Control Room. "Mr. Simms, turn the dive over to the Chief of the Watch and come up here and take the deck. Close torpedo tube outer doors. Crew can stand easy on Battle Stations. Cooks can serve coffee now, breakfast later when I give the word. Maintain quiet about the decks. I'll see Mr. Brannon in the Wardroom in five minutes with his charts. Smoking lamp is lighted."

Captain Hinman sipped at a cup of black coffee as he studied the chart Brannon had laid out on the Wardroom table. Brannon spooned sugar into his coffee cup and poured canned milk into the cup.

"I want to set up a patrol course along the coast from the harbor north," Hinman said. "As long as those tin cans are out of sight to the north we can risk fathometer readings as we go. We might need that information later." He put his thick thumb on the chart. "I'd like to patrol from the harbor to about here, about ten miles up the coast and back again."

"What do you think they'll do?" Brannon's eyes were innocent as he sipped his coffee.

"I saw five tankers in there loaded to their Plimosol marks," Hinman said. "And a big *Fubuki* and three other tin cans came out of the harbor and went north. What do you think?"

"I'd say the tin cans are making an anti-submarine sweep, a search," Brannon said. "That's what I'd do if I was getting ready to put a convoy out to sea. I'd search the area first."

Hinman nodded, his face expressionless. "What else?"

"Well, if they don't find anything and I don't think they will because there's not another submarine of ours within five hundred miles of here, they're all well north of us, I'd say the tin cans will come back and escort some tankers out of the harbor."

"When? Before or after dark?"

"After dark." Brannon warmed to the questions he was being asked. "If I were on that *Fubuki* I'd come back with my other cans and make another sweep around the harbor mouth and then lead out my convoy, form them up and start north. I'd stay close to the land mass so the ship's outlines couldn't be picked up against the mountains. There's good water, deep water all the way in to the beach according to this chart we have. That would be the safest thing for them to do, don't you think?"

"I'm asking you what you think," Hinman said. He stood up and stretched hugely.

"He'd be safe from observation from the sea," Brannon said slowly. "But what he wouldn't know is that we are in between his ships and the beach!" He looked up at Captain Hinman.

"Exactly!" Hinman said. "I'm going to get some sleep. Wake me if the periscope watch sees anything at all. Secure Battle Stations. Serve breakfast. Maintain quiet about the decks." He left the Wardroom. Brannon watched him go. He hadn't said anything about his battle plan. Or had he? Brannon sighed and looked at the chart.

CHAPTER 3

Mako surfaced after full dark, the water streaming from her superstructure and deck in a silver cascade. Her big diesel engines began hammering out a battery charge as she wallowed on a course close in to the land mass of Borneo. Captain Hinman had been awakened twice during the late afternoon, first with a report that the *Fubuki* and the other three destroyers had returned and the second time to hear that the four destroyers were conducting an antisubmarine search to the east and south of the harbor.

The *Mako* had been on the surface for three hours when the stern lookout cleared his throat.

"Running lights bearing one seven zero, Bridge! I've got a white masthead light and a red port running light in sight! Moving from our port to starboard."

"Running lights?" Captain Hinman snapped from his place on the cigaret deck. "Running lights? You sure?"

"Yes sir, Captain," the lookout called down. "Now I can see another set of running lights behind the first one. There's two ships back there!"

"Who's up there on stern lookout?" Hinman asked.

"Grabnas, sir," the lookout answered. Hinman's mind flicked over the roster of his crew. Grabnas, Andrew, Seaman First Class. Enlisted in Florida. Worked on his uncle's shrimp trawler from the time he was a child, a born seaman. He reached upward and grabbed a railing and hauled himself up beside Grabnas. He focused his binoculars and saw the running lights.

"Third ship standing out behind the other two, sir," Grabnas said. "Now there's someone sending blinker signals, sir."

"Very good," Hinman said. He dropped down to the cigaret deck. "Bridge, ask Mr. Brannon to come up here."

Hinman pointed astern at the lights, visible now from the cigaret deck.

"Mike, get the Plot going. Use the search 'scope to get your bearings. I'm going to stay on the surface for a while."

"Do you want Battle Stations, Captain?"

"I'll tell you when I want Battle Stations," Hinman said. "Get the Plot team going right now!"

"Ships are making a left turn, Captain," Grabnas called.

"Make your reports to the Officer of the Deck, not to me!" Captain Hinman grated. He heard Brannon leave and focused his glasses on the lights astern. The convoy was probably three ships. He hoped they were oil tankers, some of those he had seen in the harbor that appeared to be loaded. Now the problem that had to be solved was how best could he attack the convoy, granting that the *Fubuki* and the other three destroyers would be escorting the ships?

He stood at the after rail of the cigaret deck, his square hands gripping the rail. One convoy formation, he reasoned, would be to form up the three ships in a single line. He rejected that idea. Three ships in a line would be too difficult to guard with four escorts. No, the more logical formation would be two of the ships abreast of each other, a thousand yards apart. The third ship astern another thousand yards. The big *Fubuki* with its superior speed could range out ahead of the convoy to search for enemy submarines.

Where would the *Fubuki* commander position his other three destroyers? He reasoned out the problem; one destroyer would have to be kept astern of the convoy. There was no danger from the land side so the other two destroyers could be put on the sea side of the convoy. He put his glasses to his eyes and studied the lights of the ships. They had all turned left and were approaching *Mako*. He looked upward and saw the broad viewing lens of the search periscope turning slowly. Mike Brannon's voice came up through the bridge hatch, asking for permission to come to the Bridge.

"We've got a formation on the convoy, sir," Brannon said to Hinman. "It looks like there are two ships in line and one astern. We've lost sight of the *Fubuki*. Last time I saw it the ship was out ahead of the first two ships. They're tankers from the look of them, best as I can see. We have one destroyer aft of the convoy. We assume the other two destroyers are on the sea side of the convoy."

"That's what I figured they would do," Hinman said. "As the Executive Officer, second in command, what should our next move be?"

"I've worked out a problem, sir," Brannon said. His voice was eager. "We can stay on this course until the convoy passes. Then we can cross the convoy's track astern and swing out beyond them and make flank speed, pull off an end-around and get ahead of them and submerge and make a night periscope attack, take them as they come to us! We can do that even if they increase speed to ten knots. The convoy speed now is seven knots, sir."

"You're wrong!" Hinman said bluntly. "Once that *Fubuki* skipper has made a couple of sweeps up ahead he's going to have that convoy making every turn in its screws! That's what I'd do if I were sitting in that *Fubuki* skipper's bridge chair and thank God I'm not! Try working out your problem if the convoy makes fourteen knots. We'd never get position ahead of them!"

Brannon stood, silent.

"Go back down to Plot," Hinman said. "Give me an intercept course and speed to close to six hundred yards on the tanker that's closest to us. Send the crew to Battle Stations. I'm going to attack on the surface! The first target will be the tanker closest to us. Second target the tanker astern. Third target will be the tanker outboard of us. If we live that long!"

He heard the Battle Stations' alarm gong ringing and the soft rush of feet below him. Brannon's voice was tinny over the bridge speaker, reporting that all hands were at Battle Stations. Hinman moved to the bridge speaker and took a deep breath.

"This is the Captain," he said slowly. "We have three oil tankers up here that are carrying oil to Japan. They are escorted by four destroyers.

"We are going to attack on the surface, go right in among them! That is something no American submarine has ever done, so far as I know. The Germans do it all the time in the Atlantic and we're as good as the damned Germans!

"I expect the Japanese destroyer captains to respond to our attack. I expect the response to be very heavy. We are going to need every bit of skill we have to drive this attack home and then make our escape. Now let's go get 'em!" He heard the sound of cheering coming from below and he smiled grimly to himself and then turned as Mike Brannon's voice came through the speaker.

"Course to the first target is zero three zero. Repeat. Zero three zero. Speed required to close to six hundred yards is fifteen repeat fifteen knots, Bridge."

"Very well," Captain Hinman said. "Come right to zero three zero. Make turns for fifteen knots. Mr. Brannon, turn the Plot over to Mr. Grilley and come to the bridge." He turned to the Officer of the Deck.

"Mr. Simms," his voice was loud enough to be heard by all three lookouts above the bridge. "I want each lookout to keep his eyes in his sector only. No matter what happens no lookout is to turn his eyes away from his own sector! There are four destroyers out there and I will not be surprised by one of them coming up on us because a lookout was not doing his duty!" He waited until the OOD had relayed his orders.

"Very well, Mr. Simms. You can go below and stand by to take the dive if we have to dunk. I'll take the deck."

He leaned his elbows on the bridge rail and studied the dark bulk of the enemy convoy through his binoculars. No doubt of it, these were tankers and heavily loaded. He heard Mike Brannon come up the hatch.

"Making turns for fifteen knots, Captain," Brannon said. His voice held an undertone of excitement.

"Very well," Captain Hinman said. "Take the cigaret deck, Mike. Cover my stern. If you see anything, any danger, any target back there my orders are that you set up with the After TBT and shoot from the after tubes." He bent down to the bridge speaker.

"Stand by to open tube doors fore and aft," he said. "I'll slow down before I give the order so you people in the Forward Room won't break your back on those Y-wrenches! Set depth on all torpedoes at four feet. Repeat. Four feet!"

Mako rushed onward through the night toward a point on the black water where her course and that of the closest oil tanker would cross. Captain Hinman stood quietly, his mind sorting out the factors of the battle that was about to begin.

The torpedoes had to run 425 yards before the tiny propeller in each warhead would arm the exploder for action. If he began firing at his first target at 600 yards he could shoot two fish at that target and then swing right and shoot two more at the tanker trailing behind. If he got hits on both ships he could increase speed and head between the two ships for a set-up on the third ship.

What would the enemy destroyers be doing while all that was going on? He tried to put himself in the place of the other ship captains. The *Fubuki*, once alerted by hits on the tankers or by radio, would come rushing back to its charges. But that would take some time. The two destroyers on the far side of the convoy were another matter. Their captains would face a problem: should they interpose themselves between the attacking submarine and their charges? It would be a difficult decision to make and the two destroyer captains could be expected to delay a few minutes until they had made a decision. He needed those few minutes.

"Depth set four feet all torpedoes," the bridge speaker said.

"Very well," Hinman said. He went back to his problem. The captain of the destroyer guarding the stern of the convoy faced no problems at all. He would attack as soon as he saw the *Mako*. That would be Mike's problem if he were still occupied with the oil tankers. The speaker rasped.

"You will have a firing solution in five minutes, sir, allowing for time to slow down and open the tube outer doors."

"Very well," Hinman said. "Control Room: All stop on all engines. Open tube outer doors both rooms. Resume speed as soon as the doors in the Forward Room are open. Give me a countdown from fifteen seconds to firing solution."

He stood, his elbows braced on the bridge rail, his binoculars at his eyes, studying the first target. The deck under him shuddered slightly as the *Mako* resumed speed, her bow wave crisp and clean in the starlight.

"All tube doors open, Bridge. Torpedo depth set four feet!"

"Very well." Captain Hinman marveled; it was a wonder some lynx-eyed lookout on one of the Jap ships hadn't seen *Mako*'s bow wave by now. He felt that somehow he was detached, a spectator in a drama that he had dreamed. Lieut. Don Grilley's voice came up the hatch.

"Fifteen seconds to a shooting solution, sir."

"Very well." Hinman stood, legs braced against the *Mako*'s plunging movement, his eyes glued to his binoculars.

"All hands! Keep a sharp lookout! Here we go!"

"Ten seconds!" the metallic voice in the speaker said. "Nine . . . eight . . . seven . . . six . . . five . . . four . . . three . . . two . . . one . . . "

"*Fire one!*"

Captain Hinman's voice was a sharp bark.

"Right five degrees rudder!" He felt the thumping shock in his legs as the 3,000-pound torpedo hurtled out of Number One tube, driven by a giant fist of compressed air, its steam engines screaming into life as it passed through the torpedo tube. He counted to himself methodically.

"*Fire two!*

"Right fifteen degrees rudder! More speed, Control, give me more speed! Stand by . . . stand by. . . .

"*Fire three! Give me more speed, God damn it!*

"*Fire four!*"

A booming roar echoed over the ocean as a torpedo slammed home into the waist of the first tanker. A giant sheet of flame erupted and towered high into the dark night as the second torpedo blew the stern of the tanker apart with a smashing roar.

"Two hits on the first target!" Hinman screamed into the bridge microphone. "Meet your helm right there, damn it! Give me ten degrees left rudder!" His voice was drowned out in another booming roar as the second tanker exploded in fire.

"Hit on the second target!" Hinman yelled. He heard a voice above him screaming.

"Destroyer astern coming this way!" The stern lookout's voice was a thin wail above the noise of the exploding oil tankers. "Son of a bitch has got us bore-sighted! Comin' fast as hell!"

The captain of the Japanese destroyer guarding the sea astern of the convoy was on his ship's bridge, waiting for the order from the convoy commander in the *Fubuki* up ahead to increase convoy speed to 15 knots. He gasped in disbelief as he heard and saw the first tanker erupt in a gout of flame and then he saw the submarine, low down in the water, turning. He saw the wakes of the torpedoes streaming toward the second tanker and screamed in rage as the second ship exploded with a great roar. He howled orders for emergency speed and slammed his fist into the alarm button to alert the depth charge crews on the squat fantail of his slim, deadly ship. To lose two of his tankers to such an attack! His ship's bow reared upward and then came down as the ship's engines roared into full speed. He had the American submarine boxed between the two burning tankers. If the submarine tried to dive he would be over him before he could escape and his depth charges would shatter the submarine. If the submarine commander chose to stay on the surface he would ram, slice the submarine in two with his bow.

A lookout yelled a wordless warning and he saw the bubbling wake of a torpedo racing across his bow. He hesitated a long moment, deciding if he should change course. The lookout cried out again, agony in his voice, and the destroyer captain saw a lengthening finger of bubbles pointing at his ship's side, reaching for him.

Mike Brannon saw the wake of the first torpedo he fired pass ahead of the Japanese destroyer. He saw the wake of the second torpedo heading straight for the side of the destroyer's bow. Then the wake ended at the ship's side and for a long second there was nothing. Then with a shattering roar the entire bow of the Japanese destroyer disintegrated in a massive explosion that sheared off the ship back to its bridge. The destroyer's engines, still turning the ship's screws at maximum speed, drove the stricken ship under the surface of the sea. Brannon turned away, conscious that his stomach was suddenly roiling. He winced and realized that the second tanker, afire from bow to stern, was close by on the starboard side of *Mako.* He could feel the furnace blast of the fire's heat on his hands and face. Above him the lookouts were trying vainly to shield their faces from the scorching blast of heat.

"For God's sake, Captain!" Brannon yelled. "We'll burn up!" Hinman didn't reply and Brannon ran forward to the bridge to repeat his warning and then he stopped dead, a cold tremor shaking him. Captain Hinman stood, crouched in the bridge, staring at him, his face set in a ghastly grin, his eyes glittering in the red glare of the burning ship.

"How much water have we got under us, Mister?"

"Water?" Brannon's voice faltered.

"Water, damn you! I want to dive this ship! I can't outrun that bastard out there!" Hinman's arm swept out to one side and Brannon's eyes followed it and saw the *Fubuki* in the distance, its bow throwing up a great sheet of water as it raced toward the burning ships. He heard the scream of a shell overhead and a crumping explosion as the ship beyond them took the shell in its burning superstructure.

"Two hundred feet under the keel, Bridge. Repeat. Two zero zero feet under the keel." Chief Rhodes' voice over the bridge speaker was calm.

"Clear the bridge!" Hinman shouted. As the lookouts slammed past him on their way below decks he turned to look at the oncoming *Fubuki.* The other ship's lookouts had picked up *Mako's* outline against the burning tankers. The shell fire proved that. He hit the button of the diving alarm twice with his hand and dropped through the hatch, twisting to one side as the quartermaster lunged upward and grabbed the hatch lanyard and slammed the hatch closed.

The *Mako* knifed downward, driven by her speed and the hard dive angle on the bow and stern planes. Captain Hinman stood in the Conning Tower, watching the depth gauge.

"Twenty-degree down angle until we pass one hundred feet!" he snapped. "Level off at one five zero feet! Do it smartly! I don't want to hit bottom! Left full rudder!"

The *Mako* rolled like an aircraft in a shallow bank and Hinman grabbed at the bridge ladder for support. He clung there, watching the helmsman's gyro repeater.

"Rudder amidships," he ordered. *Mako* eased upright and Mike Brannon came up the steps to the Conning Tower and stood on the ladder, his face above the hatch.

"Give me a course back to where we started the attack," Captain Hinman ordered. "He'll think we'll try to clear the area. There's not enough water here to get away from him if he finds us. Make turns for dead slow. Pass the word for silent running. I don't want to hear a sound! Shift to manual power on bow and stern planes and the rudder. Manual power on the sound heads. I want continual reports from sound, Mr. Cohen." He stared down at Mike Brannon's face.

"They'll know that *Mako* was here!" he said.

CHAPTER 4

The Control Room telephone talker bobbed his head at Mike Brannon, who held a finger to his lips to caution the talker to keep his voice low.

"Sound reports hearing sounds like a cigar box breaking up, like it was being stepped on," the talker said. "That's what Mr. Cohen says."

"That's one of our targets breaking up as it sinks." Captain Hinman stepped from the Conning Tower ladder and walked over to the chart table on top of the gyro compass. He studied the attack plot Brannon had drawn in on the maneuvering board. His stubby forefinger traced *Mako*'s course from the start of the attack to the deadly insertion into the tanker convoy. He looked at Brannon.

"Now the guessing game begins," Captain Hinman said softly. "He guesses what we'll do, we guess what he'll do." He looked at Mike Brannon.

"My guess is that he doesn't know if there's one submarine or two that hit his convoy. Or three. If I were the *Fubuki* captain I'd figure there were at least two submarines. If I figured that," he paused and rubbed his chin and then looked down at the chart, "if I figured that, I'd be more interested in getting my other tanker out of here in a hurry, before another attack. But if he guesses there's only one submarine then he'll begin a search and if he finds us he'll call in at least one of the other two destroyers." He bent lower and looked at the depth figures on the chart. "We'd have to run for deeper water, to the east. So we'll do the opposite. Mike, get us back on a course to where we started the attack run. Let's see what happens. Mr. Simms, one hundred fifty feet. Make turns for two knots. Pass the word absolute silence about the decks."

The silence within *Mako* was eerie. All the ventilation fans had been turned off. Men moved very quietly and softly when they moved. The heat began to build within the ship. Mike Brannon mopped his plump face as he saw a drop of sweat fall on to his chart.

"Sir!" the Control Room talker said. "Mr. Cohen reports two sets of screws bearing one two zero and one two four. Both sets of screws seem to be moving away from us slowly."

"They're searching, the other two destroyers," Hinman said. "Searching out to the east!"

"Another set of screws, twin screws, very heavy sound!" the talker said. "Bearing two five zero. Big ship. Coming very fast and picking up speed! Mr. Cohen says the ship is closing on us, sir!"

In the After Torpedo Room Billy-Joe "Spook" Hernandez, Torpedoman First Class, narrowed his large brown eyes as the telephone talker in the After Room repeated the conversations in the Control Room.

"Son of a bitch has heard us!" Hernandez said. "Nineteen years in this fucking Navy, twelve years in submarines and now I'm gonna get depth charged for the first time!" He moved suddenly and snatched one of the big Y-wrenches used to open the torpedo tube outer doors from an empty lower bunk. He handed it to an engine room oiler who was lying in an upper bunk.

"Make love to this son of a bitch, hug it, don't let it hit nothin' and make a noise if that Jap bastard drops charges on us! Listen to that son of a bitch come!"

The sound of the *Fubuki*'s twin screws was drumming at the *Mako*'s thin hull as the destroyer neared. Captain Hinman gripped the edge of the chart table in his hands, his eyes turning upward.

"He knows we're here or he doesn't," he said in a low voice. "And we're going to find out damned soon!"

The sound of the destroyer's screws increased until it was a deafening roar and then began to recede.

"Mr. Cohen says the destroyer did not drop any charges!" the telephone talker said suddenly.

"How in the hell would he know in all that racket?" Hinman muttered. "But if he did drop we'd know it by now." He turned to the chart and the plotting board.

"He must figure there's more than one of us here," Hinman said to Brannon. "He's going to gather up his one sheep he's got left and get it the hell out of here with one of his other tin cans, I'd guess. Then he'll come back and try to find us. So let's go back to where we came from. He shouldn't guess we'd do that.

"Work out the course and give it to Mr. Simms." He moved to one side so Brannnon could work at the small chart table. Hinman and Brannon turned as the telephone talker cleared his throat.

"Mr. Cohen reports that the ship that went over us has slowed and there's a lot of pinging bearing one seven zero." Hinman nodded.

"Mr. Cohen says one ship is pinging and that he has three sets of screws on a course zero one five relative, and they're moving away from us."

"He's formed up with his tanker and one of his tin cans and left one can to search for us," Hinman said. He grinned suddenly. "We guessed right!"

Brannon nodded. "That Nate Cohen is one hell of a man on the sound gear, Captain."

"I don't have to be told the capabilities of my officers, Mike," Captain Hinman's voice was low. He turned and went through the water-tight door to the Wardroom.

The *Mako* crept silently through the sea, blind at 150 feet but able to hear. In the Forward Torpedo Room sweating men worked in the stifling, close heat to turn the two big sound heads that projected beneath *Mako*'s hull by hand.

"Son of a bitch doesn't care if we all get a hernia," Ginty grunted to Dusty Rhodes. "Fucking Kike officer on them earphones ain't heard shit for an hour. Why the fuck doesn't the Old Man go back to hydraulic power?"

"He thinks you need the exercise," Rhodes said. "Stand clear and let me have a turn at that back-breaker. Take five."

"Fucking Jap could hear me puffing for air if he'd listen," Ginty grunted and slumped against a torpedo rack. "You wait, when the Old Man does give the order to belay this heavin' around and go back to hydraulic power he's gonna want the fucking tubes reloaded and I'll bet a case of beer that he's gonna want that done without making any noise! How the fuck do you reload four fish up here without making no noise?"

"You do it quietly," Rhodes grunted.

Another two hours crept by with the team of Lieut. Nathan Cohen, USNR, and Billy Stratton, Radioman Second Class, USN, listening to the sounds picked up by the slowly turning sound heads and finding nothing of interest to report. Cohen looked around at a touch on his shoulder.

"Still getting nothing, Mr. Cohen?"

"Nothing of interest, Captain. There's a lot of shrimp on the bottom but they're not causing us any trouble. I heard a whale a while ago, blowing on the surface. That might be a sign that the surface is clear of ships. Whales are generally pretty shy." Hinman nodded and turned away. He went over to the chart table and looked at the ship's track Brannon had drawn in. He looked at his watch.

"It's been three hours and five minutes since we had any sound of the other ships. Let's go back to hydraulic power, Mr. Simms. Pass the word to stand easy at Battle Stations but maintain silence about the decks. Galley can serve coffee to each compartment. I'll give you the word on breakfast a little later. I want a report from Sound every five minutes. Mike, bring your charts into the Wardroom."

Lieut. Peter Simms issued the orders he had been given and turned to the Torpedo and Gunnery Officer, Lieut. Don Grilley.

"That's one hell of a man, that Captain!"

"Depends on your definition of a man," Grilley said softly. "He's efficient. He knows his job. But there are times when he turns as cold as a dry hole in an oil field. Hard man to figure out. If that makes him a hell of a naval officer I won't argue. I'm just an unemployed geologist."

"And a damned Reservist, a feather merchant!" Simms said. He was balanced on the balls of his feet, his fists clenched at his sides. Grilley took in his aggressive stance and grinned.

"I'll say one thing for the Old Man," he said, his own smile hardening. "We gave him good fish and exploders that worked and he's one hell of a good shot!" He turned his back on Simms and took a cup of coffee offered to him by one of the watch standers.

Mike Brannon spread his charts out on the Wardroom table and smiled his thanks at Tommy Thompson, the Officers' Cook, who had put a cup of coffee in front of him. He spooned sugar into the coffee and poured canned milk into it until the liquid turned a creamy yellow.

"We'll be back at our submerged patrol line along the coast in two hours and ten minutes, Captain," Brannon said. Hinman nodded and reached for the sound-powered telephone on the bulkhead.

"This is the Captain speaking," he said softly to the talkers manning the telephones. "I want to see the Chief of the Boat in the Wardroom."

Dusty Rhodes pulled aside the green baize curtain that served as a door to the Wardroom and stepped into the Wardroom and stood at attention.

"At ease, Chief," Hinman said. "How long will it take to reload the tubes in both rooms? I want it done with no noise."

Rhodes thought a moment, his eyes half-closed.

"Twenty minutes, sir. Give or take a couple of minutes."

"Can we do both rooms at once or would you rather do one at a time with you in charge of each operation?"

"Both at once, sir. Spook is a good man back aft. If I tell him no noise he won't make any noise."

"Ginty?"

"Ginty is touchy but not the way Hernandez is. If I go up forward and heave around Ginty will think he's in charge but with me there he won't holler and stomp and yell at all hands."

Hinman nodded and reached for the telephone.

"Control Room. This is the Captain. Tell Mr. Simms that we're going to reload four tubes forward and two aft. When he's made his weight compensations ask Mr. Simms to tell the Chief of the Boat to start the reload." He turned to Rhodes.

"Control Room will give you the word when to start. Do it as quickly and as quietly as possible."

Eighteen minutes later Rhodes knocked softly on the bulkhead of the Wardroom, pushed aside the curtain and stepped in. He was panting and his shirt was black with sweat.

"Reload completed, sir. All torpedo tubes ready for firing. Gyro spindles engaged. Depth set four feet all fish. Speed setting is high and speed spindles disengaged. Request permission to shift the outboard fish in the Forward Room to the reload position and to stack the empty torpedo racks outboard when we can, sir. We can't do that without making some noise."

"I'll give you the word on that later, Chief." Hinman sat back in his chair. "How does the crew feel?"

"Pretty happy, sir. The lookouts who were topside during the action have been telling all about it ever since we began standing easy on Battle Stations. It's not like the first patrol, sir. Crew feels pretty cocky."

"Tell them to get over that!" Hinman said. "We were damned lucky we didn't get depth-charged. Next time we might not be lucky."

"Yes, sir," Rhodes said. He backed out of the Wardroom and went aft to the Crew's Mess in the After Battery Compartment and drew a cup of coffee. Ginty was standing near the coffee urn.

"What'd the Old Man say about the fucking reload, Chief? Ain't any ship in the fucking submarine Navy can reload four fish forward and two aft in eighteen minutes without making one fuckin' bit of noise! What did he say about the way those exploders worked?" He stood, balancing his massive body on the balls of his feet, his scarred face set in a grin, ready to accept the plaudits that Rhodes would pass on to him from the Captain, ready to shrug off the praise of the crew members sitting with their coffee cups at the mess tables.

"He didn't say anything," Rhodes said, sipping at his cup.

"Bastard!" Ginty rumbled. "The fucker is too busy figurin' out what kind a medal he'll get! That son of a bitch has sure changed a lot since we put this shit-kickin' ship in commission!"

"So have you," Rhodes said. "First time I ever saw you put fish in the tubes you didn't wind up so hoarse you couldn't talk!"

"Shit!" Ginty said. His eyes flicked around the crowded compartment. "Man don't have to yell when he's got a reload crew trained like I train 'em and when he's got the Chief of the Boat pushin' his flat ass off against a fish!" He bent his head and ducked through the water-tight door, grinning to himself as he heard a gust of laughter sweep around the mess compartment. He padded forward to his torpedo room, scowling at the green curtain at the Wardroom door as he passed it.

Captain Hinman drained his coffee cup and looked at his watch.

"I want to go up and have a look through the periscope," he said. "Mike, I want you to take the dive. I want sixty-five feet. Not one inch higher."

Brannon drew a deep breath. "Skipper, here we go, my big Irish nose and me. We're standing easy at Battle Stations and Pete Simms is the Battle Station Diving Officer. I'll stand by him when we go up but I don't want to take over his Battle Station, sir, not unless you insist on it."

Captain Hinman studied the troubled face of his Executive Officer. When he spoke his voice was flat, level.

"Mr. Brannon, I am the Captain. I know what you're thinking about, why you spoke up. I'd suggest that if you are practicing for the time when you get your own command—if I so recommend—I suggest you do your practicing somewhere else!"

Brannon dropped his eyes.

"Aye, aye, sir. To sixty-five feet. Not one inch higher!"

Captain Hinman nodded and left the Wardroom.

CHAPTER 5

*M*ako surfaced in the first full dark of the night and wallowed sluggishly on a course southward down the coast of Borneo, her bull nose pointed in the direction of the harbor in Balikpapan. Lieut. Nathan Cohen leaned his elbows on the teak rail of the bridge and stared through his binoculars at the mountainous bulk of the island.

"I never noticed before," he said to the quartermaster on watch. "At night. The mountain over there looks as if it's only about five hundred yards away! I'd swear we were going to run aground if I didn't know better!"

"Yes, sir," the quartermaster said. "But the chart shows that we're almost three miles off the beach. But it does look awful close, yes sir."

"Those little spots of light on the beach," Cohen said. "They must be fires, probably cooking fires. I wonder what kind of people they are? What food are they cooking?" He heard Captain Hinman's footsteps as he moved from the cigaret deck into the bridge and stood beside him.

"I find it strange, Captain; there are people over there around those fires who have no knowledge of our presence here, our mission. People who probably don't even know there's a war going on and who don't care at all about who wins or loses."

"I know, Nate," Hinman said quietly. "I stand up here at night and I wonder about the same things. It's a very strange world. Those people around those little fires probably have their own enemies, fight their own wars, live and die and we don't know anything about that, either.

"I have to go below and write up a contact report and the action report for the Staff at Pearl. I'll call you to encode when I'm ready. Keep a sharp lookout." He went down the hatch and Cohen turned and began to study the horizon through his glasses. An hour went by and he jumped as the bridge speaker rasped tinnily.

"Bridge. Executive Officer requests permission to come up."

"Permission granted, sir," Cohen answered. Mike Brannon hauled himself up through the hatch and took a deep breath of the night air.

"Skipper wants you in the Wardroom, Nate. I'll take the deck. You don't have to hurry; stop and get some coffee when you're through if you want."

"Yes, sir, thank you," Cohen said. "We're on course one seven five, speed . . . but you know all that, you're the navigator." He turned to go below but Brannon's hand stopped him.

"Always go through the whole routine, Nate," Brannon said gently. "Course, engines on propulsion or battery charge, state of the battery charge, what fuel oil tanks are on the line, state of the diving trim, conditions of the ship, any changes of course in the night order book, the whole thing."

Cohen felt the hot rush of blood to his face and hoped Brannon wouldn't notice in the dark. He obediently rattled off the ritual demanded of all officers who turn over the OOD watch to another officer and went below to the Wardroom.

"Sit down, Nate," Captain Hinman said. He shoved two pieces of paper across the felt-topped table.

"Two messages. The first is a report of all the shipping we saw in the harbor at Balikpapan. Send that message in the usual code for reporting on shipping.

"I want the second message sent in plain language. I want every submarine skipper on station who hears us to know what we did and exactly how we did it!"

Cohen studied the second message.

> While observing ships in harbor at Balikpapan from a submerged position in the harbor mouth *Mako* saw a *Fubuki*-class destroyer leader accompanied by three destroyers leave harbor and begin submarine search to the north of the harbor. *Mako* finished observations and took up a patrol station on a course close to the island of Borneo north of the harbor.
>
> At twenty-three hundred hours *Mako* saw a three-ship oil tanker convoy leave harbor and proceed on a northerly course escorted by three destroyers. The *Fubuki* ranged ahead of the convoy.
>
> *Mako* took position to the west of the convoy and launched a night surface torpedo attack, closing to six hundred yards before opening fire with the forward torpedo tubes. Fired four torpedoes from the forward tubes at two tankers. Two hits on first ship. One hit on second ship. Both targets exploded and burned fiercely. Fired two torpedoes from stern tubes at a destroyer and got one hit. Torpedo blew entire bow off destroyer, which sank immediately.
>
> Commanding Officer, U.S.S. *Mako* formally advises Staff that Mark VI exploders were modified at his express orders to deactivate magnetic feature of exploders and to insure that exploder ring would unseat at four-pound impact. All torpedos were set to run at four-foot depth in a calm sea. These actions, while contrary to published directives, were deemed essential and necessary to the war effort in view of disastrous experience with Mark VI exploders on *Mako*'s first war patrol. Commanding Officer states it is his belief that the aggressive attack on the surface at night confused the enemy and resulted in no

repeat no retaliatory action. *Mako* is now on station as per patrol orders. If another opportunity presents itself for aggressive action against the enemy within the patrol area *Mako* requests permission to so attack.

Lieut. Cohen looked up from the message. "Sir, you want this sent in plain English? I mean, many of the enemy read English, Sir."

"Mr. Cohen," Captain Hinman said, "the enemy knows precisely what ships it lost. It knows how the attack was made. The enemy knows by now that we have had trouble with our torpedoes, too many enemy ships have been hit by torpedoes that didn't explode. So what do we have to hide from them? Now they'll think we have our torpedo problem licked and the knowledge that we made that attack alone will probably shake them up and make them re-evaluate their defense measures. It should make them uncertain of what they are doing now and that will help us." He took a sip from his coffee cup, eyeing the lean, swarthy man sitting across the table.

"I have other reasons, personal reasons, for sending this second message in plain language," he continued.

"I want the other submarine captains on station to know how we made this attack. I want that damned hidebound Staff at Pearl to know they know! And I want to bring this exploder problem out in the open where the Staff at Pearl can't hide it any more!"

"I don't quite understand, sir," Cohen's face was troubled.

"I keep forgetting you're a Reserve, that you don't know all the background on the torpedo exploders," Hinman said. "You do know we had a lot of trouble the first patrol. Hell, nothing but trouble!

"Well, basically, the problem is this. The torpedo exploders have a magnetic detecting device built into them. The detector is supposed to pick up the disturbance in the Earth's magnetic field that occurs when a metal-hulled ship is moving through the water. When the disturbance is picked up the exploder fires the explosive charge in the warhead. The firing of the warhead can be delayed so that the torpedo, again theoretically, is under the target ship's hull when the warhead goes off.

"This should be the perfect weapon for a submarine. Water cannot be compressed to any measurable degree—you should remember that from your physics courses in college. So if you set the torpedo to run at a depth that will take it beneath the hull of the target and the torpedo warhead explodes under that hull then the entire explosive force of the warhead would divert up through the air-filled hull of the ship and break its back. Theoretically, only one torpedo should be needed for each target ship. Our orders say we should fire only one torpedo at a ship unless it is a very large ship or a major warship.

"You know that on our first patrol we fired at ships and you heard the torpedoes running right through the bearings of the target ships." Cohen nodded.

"Then I set the depth of the torpedoes at two feet so the fish would hit the ship. That's the old-fashioned way of firing a torpedo, fire it to hit the ship and explode. And the torpedoes didn't explode! The damned exploders are defective! They won't work! Chief Rhodes and Ginty disconnected the magnetic circuits in the exploders and did some minor modifying to the contact part of the exploder and they work!" He sat back in his chair.

"But why doesn't the Staff at Pearl order the exploders fixed, modified, so they will work?" Cohen's face was puzzled.

"Because they won't believe their perfect weapon isn't perfect!" Hinman snapped. "They tell us that we're not hitting our targets! Now, by God, they'll know who's wrong!

"And there's one other reason I want that message sent in plain language. I want those skippers who get it to know that if you want to win this war you've got to be aggressive, to attack the enemy, not run from him!" He squeezed his hard hands around his coffee cup.

"Nate, we've got submarine skippers out here who are just plain afraid to attack Japanese ships if there's an escort around! The tactics book they wrote before the war says that a submarine shouldn't attack if there are two or more enemy escorts nearby. That's all some of our peacetime submarine captains need to know! The tactics book says that all torpedo attacks should be made from a submerged position, even at night! Hell, the Germans have been shooting our convoys to ribbons in the Atlantic, attacking in wolf packs on the surface, running right in among the convoy ships!

"Some of these older commanders who have their sights set on four gold stripes and then an Admiral's billet won't deviate one inch from that book. They sight a convoy at night and go through the motions of trying to get far ahead enough of the convoy to submerge and God knows, in most cases it can't be done! The convoys are faster than the submarines! They run away from them! Which suits some of our cowardly lions very well!

"Well, by God, they gave me a defective weapon and I made it effective! They gave me pussy-footing tactics and I changed them! We're out here to kill Japs, to win a war! By Heaven, that's what I'm going to do!" He relaxed suddenly.

"I'm sorry, Lieutenant. I shouldn't flare up at you. You're not Navy, you're a Reserve. And your people, no offense meant, Mr. Cohen, your people don't know much about war."

Cohen stood up, the two messages in his hand.

"With all due respect, Captain, war is war. The Jew knows about war.

"Masada, sir, seventy-three A.D. Nine hundred and sixty Jews, half of them women and children, stood off the famed Tenth Legion of the Roman Army. The Jews were outnumbered by at least twelve to one. Yet they fought for a very long time and when defeat was inevitable the surviving Jewish soldiers killed their women and children and then each man was killed by another until there was only one Jew left. He fell on his sword! They chose death and honor rather than slavery!"

Captain Hinman's nostrils flared, his face white. He drew a long breath.

"I stand rebuked, Mr. Cohen! I should have known better. I apologize, sir."

"I intended no rebuke, sir, and I cannot accept an apology for something that was not offensive." He picked up the curtain at the door and left the Wardroom. Captain Hinman stared for a long time at the green curtain.

Copies of Captain Hinman's two messages were laid in front of each place at a long polished table in the submarine Staff headquarters in Pearl Harbor. The Staff members filed in and stacked their uniform caps on a small table and then moved to the coffee sideboard and drew cups of coffee and took their places at the table. There was a dead silence as each member of the Staff read the two messages.

"Well?" Capt. John F. Severn's harsh voice rasped down the table. "Well? Anyone got anything to say? That damned practical joker has gone too far this time! If this is one of his jokes I will personally run him out of this Navy! You know him better than any of us, Rudd, he was your Executive Officer. Is this one of his jokes?"

Comdr. Robert Rudd raised his eyes from the messages and looked at Captain Severn.

"No, sir. I don't think this is any joke. I've heard through the grapevine that he hasn't been in a joking mood since Marie bought it at Hickam. I admit he used to be a happy-go-lucky man but I hear that isn't so these days."

"I don't believe it," Captain Severn snapped. "Once a clown always a clown! I should never have endorsed your recommendation to give him command!"

"He'd earned my endorsement, sir, and yours," Rudd said stubbornly. "He's an efficient, loyal officer."

A slim, dapper Commander sitting down near the end of the table smiled wolfishly.

"Since he was your Exec. I presume you taught him to be efficient and loyal, Bob. Did you also teach him to disobey Captain Severn's orders?"

"Go looking for your Brownie points in some other barnyard, Andrews," Rudd growled. "I don't need your comments!"

A frosty smile touched Captain Severn's lips. He enjoyed seeing his staff quarrel among themselves. He believed that anger brought out a man's hidden weaknesses and that he could take advantage of those weaknesses. He rapped on the table with a bony knuckle and winced as an arthritic pain shot through the finger.

"Andrews is right," he said flatly. "Hinman has disobeyed my orders, disobeyed every order he could! He attacked a convoy guarded by four destroyers! He attacked on the surface at night! He tampered with the exploders!" His words were dropping like stones into a pond.

"We've lost too many submarines too early in this war! We'll lose more now that this idiot has broadcast his disobedience to the entire Fleet!" He raised his shoulders slightly to ease the tightness he felt in his chest.

"Commander Rudd, order the *Mako* to return to Pearl at once! Notify all submarines in *Mako*'s path to stand well clear and let her go through. I want Hinman back here!"

"Splendid idea!" The voice from the far end of the table belonged to Lieut. Comdr. Ben Butler, USNR. Butler was new to the Staff. A Reserve, he had volunteered for service and left his editor's chair at a Chicago newspaper. Unsure of where to place a slightly paunchy, irascible newspaper editor, a personnel specialist in Washington had suddenly had what he thought to be a brilliant idea. His job classification manual indicated that there was a vague relationship between newspaper employees and public relations. The Navy badly needed public relations after the disaster at Pearl Harbor. He assigned Butler to the Submarine Staff, Pacific Command, where Captain Severn suffered his presence as part of the price a professional Navy man had to pay to fight a war.

"Splendid idea!" Butler repeated. "The country needs a Navy hero; we haven't had any since Pearl Harbor. And now we have a man who charged right into the middle of an enemy fleet, sank ships right and left and got a Japanese warship as well!

"What a story! Every newspaper in the country will banner it on the front page! Think what a lift it will give all those people who work in the factories making war materials! Brilliant idea, Captain!"

Captain Severn's face went blank as he marshaled his thoughts. He put his hands in his lap and began to massage his arthritic knuckle. He looked down the table at Butler.

"Go on, Butler. Tell me why you think Captain Hinman is a hero. And what it means."

"I think it's quite simple, sir. Do we have another submarine captain who took his submarine, on the surface as I read this message, took his ship right in among the enemy and killed them right and left and got away scot-free?"

"Using the jawbone of an ass?" Comdr. Andrews said softly.

"No." Butler grinned broadly. "Using the torpedoes he was intelligent enough to modify so they would work! I don't know

Captain Hinman, sir, but I understand he is not a Samson in size so the jawbone of an ass with which Samson slew a thousand Philistines is hardly apropos. But a David with his sling and his pebbles, in this case torpedoes, that is fitting! Americans will take their heroes any size at all, sir. And I submit, as a newspaper editor of long experience, that America needs heroes!" He smiled broadly.

Captain Severn cleared his throat. "Mr. Butler, there are things you don't understand. You are not a Navy man."

"I know that, sir," Butler replied. "But there are some things that I do understand, things that perhaps with the press of your duties you have not had time to study.

"I know how the average American responds to news. I know what excites his interest, what rouses his disapproval. We have a hero. We can use him. I suggest, sir, that Captain Hinman could be sent on a tour around the country and sell more War Bonds than any movie star. And we need money as well as heroes. I am sure that's what you had in mind, sir."

Captain Severn nodded. The ex-newspaper editor had him boxed in. The man cared nothing about how the Navy had to be governed. The man knew little or nothing about the necessity for strict discipline. If he brought Captain Hinman in and court-martialed him, as he had every intention of doing, and this Reservist with his talk of heroes should tell the story to his newspaper friends—Captain Severn shuddered inwardly. He could see his chances of wearing the broad gold sleeve stripe of an Admiral disappearing. He cleared his throat loudly and pulled a handkerchief from his sleeve and wiped his lips.

"We still face a problem, gentlemen," he said smoothly. "Captain Hinman did disobey orders. But without doubt he did also conduct himself and maneuver his ship in a most heroic manner. We cannot afford to ignore that fact. This is a war, not a tactical exercise.

"However, we cannot afford to relax discipline, we cannot open the door for other submarine captains who may not be as skilled as Captain Hinman," his voice dropped a tone, "or as lucky, to depart from orders that have been most carefully thought out before they were issued.

"I am fully aware, as Commander Butler has noted, that the

nation desperately needs a hero. I am vigilant in the effort to provide a Navy hero, although as a career officer I must say that I resist the thought that civilians need to know everything we are doing to defend their liberty."

He looked down the table. Commander Rudd was looking away from him, trying to suppress a smile. He'd have to put Rudd in his place and soon. The man obviously approved of what Hinman had done. Andrews was scowling. Well, he knew Andrews was on his side. He could be useful even if he did kiss-ass too openly. Butler was sitting, impassive as a Buddha. The best thing he could do about Butler was to get rid of him as swiftly as possible. God only knows what the man wrote to his newspaper friends. Most officers who censored letters never looked at a fellow officer's mail as a courtesy. He reached for his handkerchief and cleared his throat, hawking into the white cloth. He studied the blob of sputum. Clear and white, white as the cloth. No sign of blood or heavy phlegm. The humidity of the Islands irritated his lungs.

"Very well, gentlemen. Mr. Rudd, take care of the order to Hinman to proceed here at once. Andrews, please notify the exploder experts on the Base of Captain Hinman's actions, with my direct order that what you tell them must not be repeated to anyone else.

"Butler, since this is your area of, ah, expertise, you will arrange for *Mako*'s reception in Pearl. The welcome will be restrained. We are fighting men, not idolators. You will also make the arrangements for Captain Hinman to embark on a tour to sell War Bonds. Hinman will be available for that detached duty forty-eight hours after *Mako*'s arrival. Rudd will cut his orders. Anything else?"

"One item, not small, sir," Commander Rudd said. "*Mako* will need a new skipper."

"I have someone in mind," Captain Severn said. "Comdr. Arvin Mealey. He's a disciplinarian and without doubt the *Mako* needs some old-fashioned Navy discipline."

"He's awfully close to the top of the list for Captain, sir," Rudd protested. "Not more than four or five, I think."

"All the better," Captain Severn smiled. "One or two good patrols should cinch it for him. His father, Admiral Mealey, he's retired now, was my skipper when I was a youngster. Very strict man, old Admiral Mealey. He made a man of me! There's good blood in the Mealey line, good blood.

"While we're at it we'll give *Mako* a new Executive Officer. I'll leave that to you, Rudd. Pick a man who will appreciate Commander Mealey's devotion to rules and regulations. Check with me before you cut any orders." He rose as a sign of dismissal and the Staff rose a second later and retrieved hats and put their coffee cups on the sideboard. Outside of the Staff headquarters building Rudd fell into step beside Ben Butler.

"Nice thinking, Ben," Rudd said. "Damned quick thinking!"

"I figured that white-headed old rascal was going to crucify this Captain Hinman, whoever he is," Butler said. "But I didn't stretch anything, Bob. We do need a hero, a real honest-to-God hero! Americans have always been suckers for heroes. Tell me something, did this Hinman do such an awful thing?"

"He broke every rule in the book!" Rudd said with a slow smile. "And the book was written by Captain Severn!

"I had Art Hinman as my Exec. on my last command here at Pearl. Hell of a good man. Great sense of humor. He saw fun and games in everything. Go to any length to play a practical joke. But a hell of a fine officer, the kind of man who could lead a crew to hell and back with all hands laughing all the way. I fought like hell to have him recommended for command. Severn, who hates Hinman's guts, finally gave in and sent him to new construction, just to get him out of his hair. That was a couple of years ago.

"I almost pissed my pants when you turned Severn's rudder around against him! But I'll give old Iron-Ass credit, he's cute. He could see he was looking right down the muzzle of a loaded gun! And you'd better watch it, my friend. He'll find some way of getting rid of you and then who in the hell would I have to talk to?"

"Maybe he'll send me on the bond tour with Hinman," Butler said. "There's a cooking editor on my newspaper, hell of a good-looking woman. I never could get into her pants when I was her editor. Maybe if I go back in uniform with a hero in my hip pocket she'll give."

"If you have that sort of problem there's always the Navy nurses," Rudd said.

"Let's have a cup of coffee and talk about that," Butler said. Rudd shook his head.

"Later. Right now I have to write a dispatch to Hinman telling him to come home and I've got to make it sound like it isn't a reprimand and at the same time make it read so that all the other skippers out there who will read the message really get the message—which is don't cross Captain Severn unless you sink a whole damned convoy!"

"Have fun," Butler said.

Lieut. Cohen finished decoding the message addressed to Captain Hinman, U.S.S. *Mako* from Staff, SubPac and stared at the words. He shook his head and folded the paper carefully and put it in his shirt pocket and went in search of Mike Brannon. He found him in his tiny stateroom, wiping a smear of shaving cream from his chin. He held out the message.

Brannon's eyes narrowed as he read the words. "Damn it! He never should have told them what he did!"

"It means trouble for him, doesn't it?" Cohen asked

"I don't know, I think so," Brannon said. "Old Severn, that's Captain Severn, Chief of Staff, Submarines, Pacific Fleet, Nate, he's got to be pulling his white hair out! The Old Man broke all the rules that Severn laid down for combat. But there's something funny here. You can read this message two ways. They could be saying 'Come home and let's sit down and find out how you did this so we can tell others how to do it' or they could be saying 'Come home and get your ass reamed out!'

"I don't know, I just don't know but I think it's the latter, they're gonna ream him out! And maybe me as well!"

"Should I give it to him or do you want to do that?"

"You'll have to give it to him," Brannon said. "He'd have your ass in shreds if he knew you showed it to me. Put it in an envelope and carry it up to the bridge. There's enough moon up there tonight to read by. And then stay out of his way for an hour or so. If he gets the idea they're bringing us home so they can ream him out let him take it˙ out on me. That's what Executive Officers are for, Nate, to take the shit the Captain hands out. Remember that when you get to be an Executive Officer." He put on a clean shirt and went into the Wardroom and poured himself a cup of coffee and waited.

Captain Hinman came in and filled a coffee cup and laid the message in front of Brannon. Brannon read it and looked at Captain Hinman.

"Do you want to lay out the course, sir?"

"Well, first I'd like to see a little enthusiasm, Mike! It's no fun being ordered back to port with eighteen fish still aboard but I think we've done something for the cause. We've broken the dam, Mike! We modified the exploders and they worked! We attacked on the surface and it worked! Now they won't have any choice but to write a new book of tactics, that's the way I read it, don't you? Show by doing, that's the Navy way!"

"I guess so," Brannon said slowly. "We sure as hell showed them," he looked down at the message slip. "Departure route to Pearl is Seven George, Four X-Ray Zebra. I better get on that right away, sir." He left the Wardroom and headed for the Control Room and his charts. Hinman watched the green curtain swing back into place after Brannon had passed through it.

He knows, he thought to himself. *We're being called home with eighteen fish aboard for only one reason, to be made an example of for disobeying orders. Well, let them do their damnedest! If I never fired another torpedo at an enemy ship I've made a down payment on evening the score for Marie's death.* He sat at the Wardroom table, thinking.

This would be the third time since the war started that he had returned to Pearl Harbor and for the third time there would be no long, lean, wonderful woman waiting for him. No one would ever wait for him again. He was alone, now.

But I remember, he said to himself, *I remember the other times when she was waiting for me after we'd been apart.*

CHAPTER 6

He remembered the last time they had met after a long separation. He had spent that morning cleaning the sparse quarters the Navy had assigned him at the New London, Conn., Submarine Base when he had reported there to take command of the submarine that was to be called the U.S.S. Mako. Then he had showered and shaved and put on his best dress blue uniform and went out and bought two bottles of champagne and a big bouquet of flowers. He put the champagne in the refrigerator to chill and dragged the wobbly-legged table in the living room of the quarters to a position where Marie would see it as soon as she entered the room. He put the flowers on the table, took a final look around to make sure everything was ready and then he had gone to the train station to wait for his wife. When the passengers from New York came streaming into the station he stood on tip-toe, straining to see Marie's head above the crowd. He saw her, far down the platform and swiftly rehearsed his opening remarks.

"Going somewhere, baby?" he asked as he fell into step beside her.

"What do you have in mind, sailor?" she said.

"A drink or two, something to eat, show you my tattoo."

"Sounds exciting," she said. "But I'm expensive."

"Who cares? Money doesn't mean anything to a sailor when he's chasing a pretty girl."

She reached out and patted him on the head.

"You're a little short for me, aren't you?"

"I'll stand on a bucket or, better yet, I'll put the bucket over your head and hang by the handle," he said and they both broke up, howling with laughter, clutching each other. The train's passengers streamed by them, some frowning at the sight of a Naval officer and a woman behaving like kids in a public place.

"I want to show you my ship," he said shyly as they walked out of the train station. His words held a quiet pride that she was quick to detect.

"I want to see your ship," she said. "Let's do that first."

"First before what?" he asked as he opened the door of the car he had borrowed from the Naval Base Motor Pool.

"You know first before what!" she said. "It's been almost eight months since I've seen you! Whaddya mean? You got a girl or something like that here?"

"Had one," he said as he shifted the car into gear and began to drive away from the train station. "I kicked her out this morning. Little blonde with a big, big bosom. It was time she got out. She left hair in the wash basin all the time." He fumbled for her hand, found it and squeezed it gently.

She stood beside him on the dock, looking at the Boat. The submarine's topside was a clutter of electrical cables and welder's hoses that ran everywhere in a crazy-quilt spider's web. From somewhere deep within the hull the muted clatter of a riveter's gun punctuated the warm June air. Marie Hinman looked at the ship with a critical eye.

"I can see why you like her," she said. "She's long and skinny and ugly, just like me."

He slid his arm around her waist. "She's long and she's lean, yes, but she's beautiful, just like you."

"Take me home, sailor," she said softly.

She made lunch after admiring the flowers and encouraged him to talk about the ship as she waited for the coffee pot to boil.

"We're almost at full strength in the crew," he said. "The Wardroom is pretty damned good, we've got one guy coming from the Submarine School and another who'll join us in Pearl when we get back there. All of the Chiefs and the senior petty officers have been aboard for weeks and the crew is all here except for a few firemen for the engine rooms and one or two lower-rated people in the torpedo gangs and the radio gang.

"The routine can start tomorrow, now that the Captain's lady is on board. I've talked to the Chief at the Officer's Club about holding a small buffet for the officers and their ladies. I'd like to do that next week if you will."

She nodded. "No problem. How's Mike Brannon? Gloria wanted me to write to her, tell her how he looks, how he is."

"He's a little thinner," Hinman smiled. "Old Mike's had his tail worked off! But he's fine. Misses Gloria and the little girl. Shame that she didn't come with you from Pearl."

"She wanted to come," Marie said, "but the little girl picked up some sort of a cold or something and the doctor at the hospital said it wouldn't be a good idea. It's a long, long way from Pearl and those trains aren't the best thing for anyone to ride, let me tell you. Who are the rest of the officers?"

"No one you'd know," he said. "They gave me a mix of Regulars and Reserves. Mike is the Executive Officer, you know that. The First Lieutenant and Gunnery Officer is a guy named Donald Grilley, a Lieutenant. He's a Reserve. Geologist in civilian life, he worked for some big oil company out West. Doesn't say much but nothing seems to get by him. Very sharp. Gets along with almost everyone."

"Married?" Maria asked.

"Girl named Bernice. Tall, very pretty, slim. Green eyes and black hair, an Irish type."

"You don't miss much, do you?" she grinned.

"I've missed you," he said. "I've missed what I should be getting right now instead of sitting here talking."

"Can't make love with coffee yet to drink and dirty dishes in the sink," she said. "Is this Irish beauty a mother?"

"No. They've moved around the country a lot, searching for oil. You'll like Bernice. She's solid.

"Let's see, that takes care of that one. Pete, Peter Simms is the Engineering Officer. He's a Regular. Played football at the Academy. He's all Navy, a driver. Came off a battleship but we'll take some of his starch out when we begin the shakedown cruise. He's married, her name is Mary. Very nice woman, a little heavy. They've got a little girl about four years old, almost as old as Mike and Gloria's daughter."

"You're not too sure about this Simms, are you?" she said.

He raised his eyebrows. "You do sense things, don't you? I'll have to watch that, letting my feelings show when I talk about someone. But you're right, I'm not too sure about him. He talks a good fight, you know what I mean? And he's had some family trouble since he and his wife got here. I understand that his wife isn't the best housekeeper in the world and Pete gets on her all the time about that. I haven't done anything about it because I knew you were coming. Your extra duties start with Mary Simms. Get her to shape up a little more. I don't want Pete to be distracted.

"Pete Simms' assistant is a Regular, a Lieutenant Junior Grade named Bob Edge. He's another football player from the Academy. He'll have the electrical gang as well. He's single but I don't know how long that's going to last. Two or three girls around here are after him.

"That's it, so far. I'm getting a man from the Sub School tomorrow or next day. They say he's the best man they ever saw on sound gear, got ears that can hear a fish changing its mind. I'm going to give him the Radio and Sonar stuff and the Commissary. His name is Nathan Cohen, he's a Reserve J.G."

"Jewish?" she asked, her voice rising slightly.

"Obviously," he said.

"That's odd," she said. "We've never had any Jews in the submarine service, have we?"

"Not that I know of. Damned few of them in the Navy. I've only known of one who got command and there was a hell of a stink when that happened even though his ship was only a minesweeper. Man named Hyman Rickover. But I'll cross that bridge when I come to it. All I know right now is that Cohen is some sort of a whiz on the sound gear and that he was a Rabbinical student.

"The other officer we're getting is a guy named Paul Botts. I think I knew him years ago when I was in R-Boats. He was a Chief then and he made Warrant and just recently got himself bumped up to Ensign. I think he must have about twenty-two years in."

"That makes him pretty old, doesn't it?" she asked.

"I would think in his early forties," Hinman said. "But that might be all for the best. He could be a steadying influence on the younger people in the Wardroom."

She poured the coffee. "Who's your Chief of the Boat?"

"Lady Luck kissed me not once but about four times," he said, thanking her with his eyes for the coffee.

"I got Dusty Rhodes as the Chief of the Boat. You should remember him, he was the Chief of the Boat when I was Exec. under Bob Rudd in Pearl."

"I do!" she said, clapping her hands. "He's that big man, very quiet. Married to that sweet little Island girl. They have two boys if I remember. She's a beautiful little thing! I saw her about three weeks ago in the Commissary at Pearl."

He nodded. "That's him. The other Chiefs are aces. I've got John Barber in the Engine Rooms and he knows as much about a diesel engine as the man who invented it. His wife and Dusty's wife are close friends from what I hear.

"J.J. Maxwell is the Chief Yeoman. You wouldn't know him. He's been doing duty here at New London on O-Boats. Used to be a Marine and then switched to the Navy. The Chief Electrician is Hendershot. Everybody calls him Hindu. You might remember seeing him a few years back when we were in Panama. Good-looking man! From Kentucky. Regular lady-killer.

"The rest of the crew is a mix of Regulars and Reserves. Most of the leading petty officers are Regular Navy, all qualified submarine men. Most of the Reserves have never been to sea. But once we're commissioned and operating we'll make sailors out of them or kill them."

"When is Commissioning Day?"

"That was going to be a surprise," he said with a slow grin. "But I might as well tell you right now.

"On August the fifteenth in this year of Our Lord, Nineteen

Hundred and Forty-One, Marie Hinman will break a bottle of champagne across the bow of that submarine she looked at a couple of hours ago and christen it the United States Ship *Mako.*"

"This isn't one of your jokes, is it?" she said. "Do you mean that the Navy Department is going to let the wife of a Lieutenant Commander christen a ship, not let the wife of a Senator or a Governor do it?"

"You're the daughter of a respected Admiral," he said. "No, it's not a joke. You will do the honors. But if I can work it, I'll switch the bottle of champagne for a bottle of sea water and we'll come back here and have an orgy."

"I'm in favor of that!" she said.

"You'd better be," he said, "because the day after that you start across country and go on to Pearl Harbor in charge of the officers' wives and families. I won't see you again until we reach Pearl."

She turned from the sink where she was wiping the dishes. "You mean I came all the way here from Pearl Harbor and I've got to leave in two months?"

"Yup," he said. "Don't blame me, the orders came from on high. Finish the dishes and get your skinny rear end into bed!"

"Always the romantic sailor!" she made a face at him and went into the bedroom. He waited, grinning.

The screech that came out of the bedroom was followed by a naked Marie holding a long rubber snake.

"You bastard!" she hissed. "I almost had a heart attack!"

He doubled over in the chair with laughter and she was on him, throwing him from the chair to the floor, her long legs clamping around him in a scissors grip. He howled with glee and squirmed upward until he could put his mouth against one of her small breasts. She stiffened and gasped and then she spread herself for him, pulling his head upward, searching for his mouth with hers, undoing his clothing, drawing him to her and into her.

"More coffee, Captain?" He looked up and saw Thomas Thompson, Officers' Cook, standing in the door of the Wardroom.

"No thank you," he said. "I must have been day-dreaming."

The tall, powerfully built black man looked at him shrewdly.

"My Grandma used to say day-dreaming was a gift of God," he said in his deep voice. "But it don't do you any good to dream about the past, according to her. You got to dream about the future."

"Is it that easy to see?" Hinman said.

"For me it is. I been with you a long time, sir. Grandma used to say you could remember the past but don't think on it. Ain't nothin' back there but hurt. You don't think it's hurt but it is, it leaves scars you can't cover up."

CHAPTER 7

The U.S.S. *Mako* slid through the oily waters of Pearl Harbor in the first full flush of morning, passing the torpedoed, burned hulks of Battleship Row to port. The off-duty crew members, dressed in clean dungarees and white hats, were standing at ease in two long rows on the after deck, their eyes taking in the feverish activity of the Pearl Harbor Navy Yard to starboard. Captain Hinman stood on the starboard side of *Mako*'s small bridge with Mike Brannon, who held a folded chart of the harbor. Brannon studied the course line he had drawn on the chart as the quartermaster sang out the bearings from a pelorus mounted on the bridge rail.

Down in the Maneuvering Room, just forward of the After Torpedo Room, Chief Electrician's Mate Robert E. "Hindu" Hendershot sat at the big electrical control console beside one of his electrical gang, ready to go into action at the ring of the annunciators ordering him to change the rpms of the propellor shafts for one or both screws or to throw the massive electrical motors that turned the propellor shafts into full reverse. He lounged on a padded bench, one sandaled bare foot propped negligently against the shiny steel edge of the control console.

"Bridge talker says he'll give us the word when we make the turn into the Southeast Loch," the telephone talker said to Hendershot. "Mr. Simms is standing by in the Control Room."

"Standing by for what?" Hendershot said in his soft Kentucky drawl. He waggled a foot at the ten control levers that stuck up out of the console and the score of dials above it. "Fucking battleship sailor knows the book but he don't know what it's like to be down here playin' on this piano when the Old Man starts calling the square dance for docking. If we don't make any mistakes he won't come back here and tell us so, but if we fuck up one ring of those bells he's gonna be back here hollerin' his fool head off." He pushed a curl of black hair from his white forehead. His dark blue eyes, fringed with luxuriant long lashes that were the envy of every girl he went out with, took on a dreamy look.

"Wonder if that Lola is still dealin' beer off the arm at the Blackstone?" he said. He nudged the electrician beside him on the bench. "Now there is a broad, that Lola! She gives the best blow job you ever had, turn you inside out in about three minutes!"

On the bridge Mike Brannon studied his chart. "We can come right into the Southeast Loch in about one minute, Captain." Hinman nodded, his eyes searching the harbor. He gave the order for the course change and the *Mako* turned slowly to starboard to head up the Southeast Loch toward the Submarine Base. As they neared the long concrete pier where they were to tie up, Brannon nudged Hinman's arm.

"Look at the crowd on that pier!" He fumbled for the pair of binoculars that hung from his neck but Hinman's hand stopped him.

"Don't let them see you looking at them with the glasses," he said in a low voice. "There's always a crowd for a hanging!"

On *Mako*'s deck Dusty Rhodes checked his line-handlers. A submarine on war patrol carries no mooring lines, anchor or anchor chain. Mooring lines are stored in slatted lockers beneath the deck in several different locations and if a depth charge should rip those deck lockers open the hundreds of fathoms of four-inch manila line could foul the propellors. Depth charges could also cause the 105 fathoms of 1-inch steel anchor chain to rattle in its metal locker under the forward deck and give away the position of the submarine or worse, could dislodge the 2,200-pound anchor from its billboard and cause it to drop, dragging out the anchor chain and virtually immobilizing the submarine as it tried to maneuver submerged.

"Don't try to catch the monkey fist when they throw over the heaving lines," Rhodes cautioned a young seaman. "The monkey fist on the end of the heavin' line is full of lead, it'll break your hands. Let it drop, haul in the eye of the mooring line and get it on your cleat. Don't panic." His sharp eyes studied the pier. "That's only old Admiral Nimitz standing there waiting for us!"

The *Mako* turned into the docking area, moving slowly, and then a huge boil of water erupted at her stern as Captain Hinman ordered both screws to back at full speed. A steady stream of orders to the helmsman and the Maneuvering Room came out of Hinman's tight lips as he judged the way of his ship, the distance to the solid concrete at the end of the pier, the distance to the side of the pier where he was to dock his ship. His voice rose suddenly.

"All stop! Take the mooring lines and double up fore and aft!"

The line handlers on the dock whipped their heaving lines across the *Mako*'s deck as the long, lean submarine shuddered to a dead stop alongside the pier. Rhodes, standing on the forward deck, saw Admiral Nimitz nod his head in approval of Captain Hinman's perfect docking. Rhodes turned to face the Bridge.

"All mooring lines are doubled up, sir. Request permission to take the brow from the dock?"

"Permission granted," Captain Hinman said and as the portable gangway rumbled down from the dock to *Mako*'s deck Hinman walked aft to the *Mako*'s cigaret deck and swung himself nimbly down to the main deck. He stood at the foot of the gangway as Rhodes supervised the securing of the brow lines. Admiral Nimitz put one foot on the gangway and paused.

"Permission to come aboard, Captain?"

"Welcome aboard, Admiral," Hinman said. Admiral Nimitz went down the gangway, pausing to salute the flag and the quarterdeck. He held out his hand and took Hinman's square fist and pumped it.

"Well done, Captain! Fine patrol!" He looked up at the side of *Mako*'s Conning Tower where three small flags had been painted, two of them Japanese merchant shipping flags, white with a red ball in the center, the other the Rising Sun warship flag of the Japanese Navy.

"Fine patrol!" the Admiral repeated. "Damned fine shooting!" He turned and nodded toward the pier and a stream of officers began to move down the gangway to *Mako*'s deck.

"I'll be seeing you tomorrow, Captain," the Admiral said. "If you'll excuse me I see an old friend and the Chief of Staff wants to talk to you."

Captain Severn came down the gangway with his staff at his heels. He nodded curtly at Hinman and stood to one side as his staff, led by Commander Bob Rudd, lined up to shake hands with Hinman. Chief Rhodes moved into the group and saluted Hinman.

"Request permission to release the crew from quarters and to take mail and fresh fruit aboard, sir," he said.

"Permission granted," Hinman said. He turned to Captain Severn.

"My crew will be ready for transportation to the Royal Hawaiian Hotel at your convenience, sir. My officers and Chief Petty Officers are at the disposal of the Relief Crew Officers for consultation on repairs requested, sir."

"Transport to the hotel will be provided at twelve hundred hours," Captain Severn said. "Uniform of the day is clean undress whites, white hats and shined shoes. Arrangements have been made to feed the crew its noon meal at the hotel. I want the reports of materiel performance and damage in the Wardroom in ten minutes for the Relief Crew Officers and Chiefs." Hinman turned to Mike Brannon.

"Mr. Brannon, I want a clean sweep down fore and aft. Tell the Chief of the Boat to have the crew topside at eleven hundred hours and forty-five minutes in clean undress whites and white hats. With shined shoes. Division Officers and Chiefs will have their damage and repair reports in the Wardroom in five minutes." He followed Captain Severn as the older officer walked to the gangway. Severn turned, his mouth set in a grimace, his eyes flinty. Hinman followed Severn's eyes and saw Admiral Nimitiz in deep conversation with Chief Dusty Rhodes.

"The Chief of the Boat served with the Admiral, sir," he volunteered. "They're old friends."

"Admirals and Chiefs of Staff have no friends, Captain," Severn snapped. "When the Admiral leaves the ship you and your Executive Officer will report at once to my office. It's only a short walk from here." He turned and left the ship, followed by his Staff officers. Hinman waited patiently until Admiral Nimitz and his aide walked up to the gangway. The Admiral looked at Hinman.

"Results count in war, Captain. Never forget that. I don't." He shook hands again and went up the gangway. Hinman went in search of Mike Brannon.

A Chief Yeoman was waiting at the door of Captain Severn's office.

"Sir," he said to Captain Hinman, "Captain Severn would like to see you alone, first. Mr. Brannon is to wait out here with me." Hinman nodded and went into the office, removing his hat and tucking it under his left arm. He walked with measured stride to the desk where Captain Severn was sitting and came to a halt.

"You should not be misled by Admiral Nimitz's cordiality," Severn began. "The Admiral is very aware of what he calls public relations." He stopped and drew a deep breath and Hinman saw there were beads of perspiration on the pale forehead of the man sitting back of the desk.

"You deliberately disobeyed my orders!" Severn's words came out like a whiplash. "You not only disobeyed my orders, you had the audacity to broadcast your disobedience to the entire Fleet! Who do you think you are, sir!"

Hinman stood silent, his cold eyes staring at the ashen face of the man in front of him.

"You will answer when addressed, sir!" Severn's voice was virbrant with the emotion he was concealing.

"With all due respect, sir, I was sent to sea with a weapon which my past experience convinced me was defective."

"Who gave you the authority to sit in judgment on any weapon? Who gave you the authority to follow your own inclinations? Who gave you the authority to broadcast your actions, your damned disobedience, sir, to the entire Fleet, to the enemy?" Captain Severn's bony forefinger began to tap the top of his desk. The faint noise made by the tip of his fingernail hitting the wood of the desk sounded to Captain Hinman like the slow beat of a distant drum, a drum that was heralding his march to the scaffold of disgrace.

"I offer no excuses, sir," Hinman said. "I thought I was being constructive, that if I achieved positive results my actions would clear the way for what every submarine commanding officer knows is a necessary modification of the Mark Six exploder mechanism, sir. If my disobedience failed to get results I was, and am, prepared to take the consequences."

Severn stood up, the muscles on the sides of his lean jaws working convulsively. He walked past Hinman to his office door.

"Chief, bring Mr. Brannon in. Stand by to record my comments when you are given the word." He walked back to his desk and sat down. The Chief Yeoman seated himself at a small desk over on the side of the office and uncapped his pen and opened a notebook.

"Captain," Severn began, "Admiral Nimitz and his staff will pay another visit to your ship at twelve hundred hours to award submarine combat pins to your officers and crew. You will be in dress white uniform without sword, as will your officers." He turned to the Chief Yeoman.

"You will record my orders as of now:

"Acting as Chief of Staff, Submarine Command, Pearl Harbor, I hereby notify you, Lieut. Comdr. Arthur M. Hinman, United States Navy, that as of thirteen hundred hours on this date you are relieved of command of the U.S.S. *Mako* for reason of direct disobedience of orders!" He turned his bleak face toward Mike Brannon.

"As Chief of Staff, Submarine Command, Pearl Harbor, I hereby notify you, Lieut. Comdr. Michael P. Brannon, United States Navy, that you are officially relieved of all duties aboard the U.S.S. *Mako* as of thirteen hundred hours this date for reason of failure to officially protest your Commanding Officer's direct disobedience of published orders.

"You will both report to Commander Rudd's office at once for further assignment. That is all."

Hinman's lips thinned against his teeth and his body tensed and then he felt Brannon's heavy arm pressing against him. He closed his eyes for a few seconds and then opened them, staring past Captain Severn's head at the air conditioner in the room's window.

"Permission to leave, sir," he said in a thick voice.

"Granted!" The harsh planes of Severn's face began to work. "Leave! Get out of my sight, damn you!"

Commander Rudd's office was empty of its normal complement of a dozen hard-working officers and yeomen when Hinman and Brannon entered. Rudd jumped to his feet and closed the door to the corridor. He got clean cups from a cupboard and poured coffee.

"Sit down, relax, damn it!" Rudd lounged back in his chair, rubbing his chin. "Old Iron Ass must have chewed you up pretty good! Both of you looked like you'd been hit with a five-inch shell when you walked in my door!" He raised his coffee cup in a mock salute.

"I figured he'd do something like that. He's been eating himself up inside ever since you sent your patrol action report and he realized that every skipper in the Fleet was laughing at him! You had a good chewing out coming, Art. Damn it all, I taught you better than that!"

Hinman sat rigid in his chair, holding his coffee cup in both hands, his face set.

"Oh, come on!" Rudd said. "I'm not mad at you, for Christ's sake! Relax, man! It isn't as bad as you think it is!"

"What isn't as bad as I think it is?" Hinman said. He could feel the moisture gathering in the corners of his eyes and he blinked rapidly. "Losing my ship isn't bad? What could be worse? Getting shot at dawn?"

"I think old Iron Ass entertained that idea," Rudd said with a broad smile. "If you'd been at that Staff meeting where we all read your contact and action report I think he'd of hung you to the nearest yardarm if he could have found one and if he couldn't he would have ordered up a firing squad!

"The only thing that stopped him was a new guy we had on the staff, came aboard a couple of months ago. A Reserve they sent to us to do public relations, whatever the hell that is. The dude's name is Ben Butler and he used to be the editor of a big newspaper in Chicago.

"This dude Butler spiked old Iron Ass' guns like I never saw anyone's guns get spiked before! He didn't leave old Iron Ass sea room to turn around in! And he did it so damned smoothly!" He leaned back in his chair and described the Staff meeting at which Captain Severn had ordered *Mako* home. As he talked he noticed that Hinman was beginning to relax, to sip at his coffee. When he had finished he grinned at Hinman.

"So that's the deal and it isn't so bad, actually."

"Well," Hinman said slowly, "I certainly owe this man Butler my thanks and I want to thank him personally. But it's still nothing to be happy about, Bob. I've lost my ship! And with that letter in my service jacket my career is ruined! I'll never get command again! And what's worse, I've ruined Mike's career!"

"Don't blow your damned ballast tanks so soon!" Rudd growled. "Item one: I've got a Chief Yeoman in this office who is the best damned man you ever saw at losing things like the letters that Captain Severn writes! We've had to do it two or three times. My God, do you think I'm going to let that iron-assed old bastard ruin the career of a man who's only fault was that he fought the enemy? Bullshit! How do you think I could handle Mike's transfer if that damned letter was in his record?"

"Mike's transfer?" Hinman's eyebrows went upward.

"To new construction, Portsmouth," Rudd said. He opened his desk drawer and took out a thick envelope.

"Here you are, Captain Brannon. You take over the U.S.S. *Eelfish*. She goes in commission in eight weeks. You'll be short of shakedown cruise time, so work your ass off when you get there because we need every damned submarine we can get our hands on. The damned Jap is getting very good at sinking our ships."

He stood up back of his desk and stuck out his big hand. "Shake hands, Mike. Accept my congratulations, you deserve them. Anyone goes to sea under someone I trained deserves to be patted on the back! I only wish I could cut some orders for myself and take out a boat but

Nimitz says I'm too senior and that he needs me around." Rudd turned to Hinman.

"Damn it, Art. Could I cut orders for Mike to take over a new boat if that shitty letter was in his service jacket? The letter is going to be taken out of both your jackets, don't worry about it. Come up into the fresh air and start breathing again!" He turned to Mike Brannon.

"You remember Riley Morrison? He was a class or two ahead of you, I think. Riley had the *Eelfish*, new construction. He had a heart attack ten days ago, maybe it was two weeks, I forget. He's going to be all right but he won't be going to sea again for a long time. So you get the *Eelfish*."

Brannon's face was working strangely as he tried to keep the tears from spurting out of his eyes.

"I thank you, Bob, jeez! I mean, what can I say? It's going to be great. . . ." His voice trailed off and his eyes took on a stricken look.

"I know what you're thinking," Rudd boomed. "You aren't leaving tomorrow! I don't want Gloria banging me on the head with a shovel! You've got about eleven or twelve days before you have to leave." He turned back to Hinman.

"You, old friend, ain't got that much time. We're getting you out of here in forty-eight hours, as per Captain Severn's order!"

"I don't mind leaving in a day or two," Hinman said. "I'll be glad to get away from Captain Severn. But I don't know if I like the idea of going on this tour, Bob. I could make a damned fool of myself."

"You listen to me, Art," Rudd leaned both arms on his desk, his beefy face stern.

"I was going to let Ben Butler tell you this himself but I guess I've got to do it now.

"Butler's been pulling strings. He's got so much influence in Washington that it scares me! Your first stop on this bond tour is at the White House. FDR is going to shake your hand in front of the newsreel cameras and call you a damned hero—which you and I know you ain't, you're just a helluva good submariner—but nobody else knows that so you'll be a hero on every newsreel in every theater in the country and overseas."

"President Roosevelt?" Hinman's voice was shaky.

"The Man," Rudd said. "The way Butler figures it is this: If FDR puts his arm around you and pats you on the back can Captain Severn block you from another command? Figure it out, old Severn wants to be an Admiral so much that he wouldn't dare!

"That's one angle. I've got another. Butler says that when you get to the White House, FDR will want to sit down and talk to you privately. Right then is when you can drop a bug in his ear about the defective exploders and torpedoes. You get the picture?"

"It's politics," Hinman shook his shoulders. "In the end it all comes down to politics and I don't like politics! But I see your point, Bob. It could do some good. If that man in Washington pushes a button then things should get done."

"It finally gets through your thick head," Rudd said. He turned to Brannon. "Butler's got a little thing cooked up for you, too. You'll be interviewed after you get to Portsmouth. He'll brief you on that but from what he's told me your line is going to be that you'll hope that by the time you take the *Eelfish* to sea on a war patrol all the little things that go wrong in a war will be cleared up. There's been leaks about bad torpedoes and that sort of thing so we don't want to let too much get out. Butler will talk to you about that." He walked around his desk and put his arm around Hinman's shoulders.

"Damn it, Art, I'm proud of the way you carried out that attack on that convoy! It reminded me of the old days when we'd sit in the Wardroom and talk about tactics and how a submarine should be used. You used to agree with me in those days, follow my judgment. Do that now. Take it easy on this damned bond tour, it's only for a few weeks. Ride with the sea. Don't make any waves." He walked the two men toward the door of his office and into the corridor and to the front door of the building.

"After Nimitz gives out the medals this noon." He stopped, his grin spreading all over his face.

"Old Iron Ass didn't say anything about medals, did he? I knew the son of a pup wouldn't! Well, Nimitz is giving you a Navy Cross, Art, and he's giving Mike a Silver Star! We can't have a hero without a fucking medal, you know! FDR will repeat the medal-giving on camera, as Butler says." He laughed out loud.

"Art, you've got a lot to learn about how things are done on shore. You've been at sea too damned long. Where was I? Yeah. When Nimitz is all through I'll have a car and a driver at your gangway. I want you and Mike to come to lunch with me. Butler will be there."

"I want to thank Butler," Hinman said slowly, "but there's something else I want to do as soon as I can."

"I know," Rudd's booming voice went soft. "Lunch won't take long and the car and driver will be waiting. Now get your asses out of here, you've got about an hour before Nimitz comes aboard and if I know you, Art, it will take that long for you to find your white shoes!" He watched the two men go down the steps and enter the rear seat of the car waiting for them. He crooked a finger at the car's driver and the man came up the steps to him.

"Take Captain Hinman and Commander Brannon to the *Mako*," he growled. "Stand by there until the Admiral leaves. Then bring both of them to the O-Club. Get your chow while they eat and then stand by. And don't forget this: When Captain Hinman gets out of the car at the cemetery you get out and take a walk! You understand?" The driver saluted and trotted down the steps. Commander Rudd watched the car pull away and went back into his office and his paper work.

CHAPTER 8

Chief John Barber climbed out of the Engine Room hatch on the after deck and picked his way forward through crew members who were sitting and squatting on deck, reading their mail and chewing at apples and oranges that had been brought aboard. He saw Dusty Rhodes standing up near the bow and walked up to him.

"Saw you talking with Nimitz," Barber said. "He say anything about the patrol, what you did to the exploders?"

"No," Rhodes said. "He asked about June and the boys. Told me to be sure to tell her to call his office or his wife if they need anything, any help." He took a sip from the coffee cup he was holding and offered it to Barber, who turned it so he could drink from the other side of the cup.

"That all he said?" Barber asked.

"He did ask me if I'd go back to sea with Captain Hinman," Rhodes said slowly. "Told me I didn't have to answer that question if I didn't want to, said he was just trying to get some information from an old shipmate."

Barber eyed Rhodes. "And?"

"I told him I'd go to sea with the Skipper as quick as I'd go to sea with him. He said that was all he wanted to know. I kind of think he wanted to hear that." Rhodes looked up the pier and saw a bow-legged Chief Warrant Officer rolling down the pier.

"Well, here it comes," he said to Barber. "That's Gimpy Haines, the Chief Warrant in charge of the exploder shop on the Base. I had him as a Chief of the Boat once, a long time ago. Hard son of a bitch but usually pretty straight. He's probably heard we did something to those exploders and he wants to get the story from me before his people start unloading fish."

"See you later," Barber said.

Haines boarded the *Mako* and walked up the deck to Rhodes, who stuck out his hand and greeted him.

"Heard you had a pretty good patrol," Haines said.

"Pretty good," Rhodes answered. "The shop gave us good fish. No trouble with them at all. The six we fired all ran perfectly. Fired two at a tanker and got two hits. The ship exploded. Fired two at another tanker and got one hit. That ship blew up. Fired two down the throat at a DE and got one hit. Blew the bow of the DE. Sorry that your people have got to take eighteen fish back. If we'd stayed out there the Old Man would have fired the whole load."

"And we never would have known what you did to those damned exploders, would we?" Haines smiled crookedly.

"I wouldn't say that. The Old Man wrote it all up in his patrol report. He asked me to make a special report on what I did and that's in my report on the torpedoes."

"You got what, close to twenty years in now?" Haines looked away from Rhodes.

"Nineteen last month," Rhodes said.

"Hell of a chance to take, disobeying a BuOrd directive," Haines said. "Whole nineteen years could go down the slop chute."

"I acted on orders from the Captain."

"Makes two of you don't give a shit about your careers," Haines rasped. "Or was there more than two of you in this?"

"Ginty, the First Class in charge of the Forward Room, helped me work on the exploders," Rhodes said. "He's a damned good man. The Old Man asked us what we thought was wrong with the exploders and we both said we didn't know. So he ordered us to try and find out. We found out what was wrong and we fixed it."

"This man Ginty around?"

Rhodes looked down the deck and saw Ginty standing near the Conning Tower, eating an apple. He beckoned and Ginty came padding up to the two men.

"Mr. Haines, Ginch Ginty, S-Boat sailor, Asiatic Fleet before he came to *Mako*. Ginty, this is Chief Warrant Haines, the man in charge of the exploder shop on the Base."

Ginty nodded. Haines returned the nod.

"Mind telling me what you did to the exploders?" Haines asked. "I'd like to know what kind of mess I've got when we pull those eighteen fish."

"No mess," Rhodes said. "We deactivated the magnetic circuits of the exploders. Didn't cut any wires, just disconnected the circuits to and from the capacitor and taped the leads. Then we did a modification to the exploder ring." He took a deep breath.

"Let me get something straight, Mr Haines. Are we talking here unofficially? I mean, are we talking man to man like we used to when you were my Chief of the Boat and I ran your torpedo room for you?"

"Unofficial all the way," Hines grunted. "What goes in my ear don't come out my mouth. I just want the straight dope before all those hot-shots start fucking around. You know they flew some people all the way out from Newport Torpedo Station when they heard what you people had done? Once those experts begin talking and farting around I won't be able to find out nothing so I want to know now."

"That's good enough for me," Rhodes said. "All we did was to deactivate the magnetic circuits, like I told you. When we had the first exploder out on deck, we'd taken the fulminate of mercury cartridge out of it, we thought we'd see if the exploder ring would unseat if we rapped the edge of the exploder housing with a rawhide maul."

"Fucking exploder ring wouldn't unseat when you took a full swing at the exploder with that maul!" Ginty rumbled. "Whoever

designed that Goddamn thing ought to have their head examined!
Too much spring tension in the ring to unseat so we relieved some of
the tension. Fucked around with it, little by little, until we had it so
it would unseat if you gave it a good rap.

"There's another thing you people ought to be worrying about. All
these fish got those oversized warheads on 'em. That's gotta make the
fish run deeper than they're set to run. We told the Old Man about
this and he figured we're right so he set the fish we fired to run at four
feet and we had targets that drew pretty good, maybe fifteen feet or
more."

Haines nodded, his seamed face thoughtful. "We've been talking
about depth settings at the shop. I just can't believe that every skipper
out there is a bad shot. The Chief in charge of the After Body Shop
says he's willing to bet a case of beer that the fish are running a lot
deeper than they're set to run."

"Why in the hell don't you take a net and go out on the far side of
the harbor and fire a fish with an exercise head on it and find out?"
Rhodes said.

"We'd like to do that," Haines said. "But to do that I've got to
have a submarine to fire from. Captain Severn says there's nothing
wrong with the torpedoes, that they're running at the depth set. He
used to be at Newport, you know, he's one of the old Gun Club boys.
He thinks the torpedoes are perfect and the fault is all with the
skippers. I'm not so sure. What I'm waiting for is for one of the boats
to come in with a malfunctioning torpedo tube. Then I'll fire a
torpedo out of the tube when it's fixed and we'll find out." He stared
at Rhodes and Ginty.

"We aren't fighting you people, you know. The Chief in the
After Body Shop has got the net all ready, had it made at the Sail
Locker and he's got it stowed away. Soon as we can get the chance
we're gonna find out about how deep those fish run."

"While you're waitin' for that why don't you put an exploder in
an old exercise head and have a crane drop the son of a bitch nose
down on the dock?" Ginty rasped. "I won't bet you any case of cheap
beer, I'll bet a case of Schenley's that the fucking exploder ring won't
upset when you drop that fucker twenty feet!"

Haines nodded his head slowly. "You might have something there, sailor. I might do just that. Otherwise, it doesn't look too bad to me."

"What do you mean?" Rhodes said, his voice flat.

"You should know how the Navy operates by now, Chief," Haines had a wry grin on his face. "There's two ways to do everything. The right way and the Navy way. I've got orders to put those exploders you changed back the way they were. If you've only done what you said then it won't be too much of a job."

"God Almighty!" Rhodes snorted. "If you do that they won't work!"

"I know that. You know that. But those are the orders I got from Captain Severn. See you around. I hope." He turned and left.

"Jeeesus!" Ginty breathed. "This fucking Navy Yard Navy! You goin' to the hotel with us, Chief? We're gonna throw a beer party this afternoon like you never saw!"

"You don't want me at your party," Rhodes said. "I'll drop by the hotel in a couple of days and buy you a brew. But thanks for asking me."

The awards ceremony on Mako's salt-stained, slotted black wooden deck was brief. Admiral Nimitz pinned the Navy Cross on Captain Hinman's high-necked white dress tunic and shook his hand. He moved to the line of officers and pinned a Silver Star on Mike Brannon's chest and shook hands with each officer. One of the Admiral's aides read a letter of commendation for Mako's patrol run, a copy of which would be put in each crew member's service record with a letter authorizing Mako's crewmen to wear the silver Submarine Combat Pin, the insignia of successful war patrol. Then Admiral Nimitz moved slowly down the double line of sailors, shaking hands with each man, talking briefly to those he knew. As he left the ship two Navy Yard buses parked at the land end of the pier clanked into gear and began to move slowly down the dock. Mako's crew, shouting and laughing, crowded aboard the buses and rolled off to two weeks of "R & R," rest and recreation in the Royal Hawaiian Hotel on Waikiki Beach. Rhodes and Barber picked up their small duffel bags of shaving gear and began walking to the end of the pier where their wives had been waiting for the past hour.

The table in the Officers' Club where Captain Hinman and Mike Brannon sat while they waited for Commander Rudd and Ben Butler was conspicuous for its isolation. Word had flashed around the Submarine Base that Hinman and Brannon were being relieved for disobedience of orders. The officers entering the O-Club for lunch veered away from Captain Hinman's table, taking tables as far away from Hinman and Brannon as they could find. There was a small stir in the room when Commander Rudd and Lieut. Comdr. Ben Butler entered the O-Club and went directly to Hinman's table and sat down. After the introductions had been completed and coffee poured Captain Hinman went directly to the heart of the matter.

"Will you be going with me on this bond-selling tour?" he asked Ben Butler.

"Only as far as Washington," Butler said. "I'll be with you through the meeting with the President and the first press conference and then I have to come back here. I wanted to go the whole route but Admiral Nimitz decided I should get back here as soon as possible to help out Captain Severn." He smiled. "Captain Severn doesn't think I should come back at all or that he needs my help." A waiter appeared and they ordered lunch.

"You people who spend your lives at sea may not have paid much attention to the news," Butler continued. "You've got women in the Navy now. They call them WAVES, Women Accepted for Voluntary Emergency Service. The first classes of officers and enlisted women graduated a few weeks ago.

"A woman I know in Chicago, she works in public relations for a big advertising agency, got all full of patriotism and enlisted. They made her a Lieutenant, Junior Grade. She wrote me about her enlistment and her rank and when this thing began to shape up I figured she'd be just the person you needed on this tour so I asked a couple of guys in Washington to arrange it and they did. She'll meet us in Washington."

"Why this one particular woman?" Hinman asked.

"Let me put it this way, Captain," Butler said. "There are some things I assume you don't know about this war that I do know, as a newspaper editor." He stopped and drew a little circle with his forefinger on the table cloth.

"You're a Naval officer, sir, the Captain of a submarine. How much do you know about the press? Not much, I'd guess and there's no reason why you should. What you have to know is that a pretty fair section of the press, quite a few newspaper publishers, hate this war! They're against President Roosevelt and they're against what they call 'Roosevelt's War.' "

"My God!" Hinman snapped. "This isn't 'Roosevelt's War' or whatever you called it! We were attacked! Look at that harbor out there! We were attacked, we didn't declare war on anyone!"

"I know that," Butler said patiently. "You know that. But the people who are against this war blame the Japanese attack on President Roosevelt's decision to give help to England in the war against Hitler. Those same people didn't want us to give any destroyers or food or munitions or anything else to England.

"What I'm saying is that not all the reporters who will be interviewing you will be friendly. Some of them will be out to trap you, to make you look foolish or what's worse, dangerous!" He sat back in his chair, his eyes on Hinman.

"Captain, you put me aboard your ship and I confess I would not know what to do. I admit that. Yet I'm a Lieutenant Commander. I would guess that I outrank most of your officers. But I'm not a Naval Officer, not at all. What I am is a damned good newspaper editor, a civilian, a Reservist doing what I can in this war.

"If I were working for a publisher who was against this war, if I were against this war and I assure you that I am not, but if I were I could sit down to interview you and when I got through I'd have enough—taken out of context I admit—I'd have enough to make you look like a bastard in print!"

He smiled softly. "Unless you knew what my real feelings were, where I stood. Then I wouldn't stand much of a chance, would I? You'd be careful.

"That's why I want Joan Richards to be with you on this tour since I can't go. Joan's been around newspapers and reporters for years. She is a very smart broad. I mean smart! She knows the political leanings of every major publisher in this country and by the time we get rolling she'll have a book on most of the others. All you'll have to do is listen to her and I'd advise that you listen damned closely because she's just as much an expert in her field as you are in yours. And she's a hell of a good-looking woman, if that's of any interest to you."

"That's of no interest to me," Hinman said. "I'll accept your statements that there are people in our nation who are against the war. I've heard a few things about that. It makes me sick at the stomach but if that's the way it is then that's the way it is.

"I'd like to say one thing, though, and I don't want to hurt your feelings, Mr. Butler, because I appreciate what you have done for me so far. I still think that it might have been better if this business of the exploders had gone to a court-martial. Then it would have been out in the open and I, for one, wouldn't be messed up in politics and newspaper reporters and things like that."

"You're nuts!" Rudd said, leaning over the table top. "You go in front of a court-martial and who are you talking to? To a bunch of old fogies who think the same as Severn does! The Navy is never wrong, you know that! This is the best way. We save your ass and I think we should because in my mind you did the right thing and we get the word to old FDR that the war is being fucked up!"

"All right," Hinman said, his mouth setting in a thin line. "Now indulge me a little more. Mr. Butler, how in the hell is it that you have so much influence? Setting things up so that I meet with the President of the United States! Presidents talk to Admirals, not two and a half stripers!

"How can you, sitting here in Pearl, arrange things so that you get a WAVE officer or whatever you call her assigned to go with me on this tour? The last time I tried to get a man I wanted for my own crew it took months of work! Yet you do this in a week or so!"

"Captain," Butler said slowly, "never forget one thing. All

politicians are the same. That is, their first worry is to get re-elected. After they have done that then they think, sometimes they think, about doing what they promised the voters they'd do.

"The President is a politician, one of the best. To get re-elected or even to get his programs through the Congress he has to have the support of the people. The easiest way to get that support is to first get the approval and support of the major newspapers, the support of their editors and editorial writers. That's basic.

"I'm the editor of a major newspaper, one of the largest in the country. Before I got that job I was the head of my newspaper's Washington bureau. I met FDR then and I liked him. He's a hell-raiser. So am I. He liked me."

"Why?" Hinman asked.

"I used to ask myself that same question," Butler said. "And I came to the conclusion that he liked me because I used to attack him every once in a while. I wrote a column in those days that was widely syndicated. If I thought FDR was wrong I'd say so. I'd tear his ass off every once in a while and he loved it. He's a cynic, you know, about politics. He knew I was a cynic and he sort of liked it because I didn't kiss his ass.

"You work in Washington long enough for a big enough paper, you write a column that pokes a finger in people's eyes and you get well known. Senators and Representatives come around and talk to you. The bureaucrats—and they're the people who really run this country if you don't know that—the bureaucrats feed you little bits of information. What happens is that in time you find yourself holding a lot of IOUs from a lot of people. All I did in this case was to call in two or three small IOUs, Captain. No big deal."

He paused and tapped the tablecloth gently with his finger.

"What it boils down to, Captain, is that when I called in a couple of little IOUs I did it as Ben Butler, who is going to be the editor of that newspaper when this war is over." He leaned back in his chair. "I did it without ever meeting you because Bob, here, said you were worth any effort I could make. Now that I've met you I'm glad I did it."

"You're putting me in a tough spot," Hinman said. "I want you to know I appreciate what you've done."

"You can show it by listening to Joan Richards," Butler said. He smiled. "She sure as hell doesn't look like a man but she thinks like one."

Hinman stood up. "I'll be at your office tomorrow for the flight to the mainland." He turned to Commander Rudd. "Bob, my deepest appreciation for all you've done for me. If it's all right with you I'd like to borrow your car and driver now. Mike, can I drop you off at home on my way?"

"If you don't Gloria will beat on you," Brannon said. "A pleasure meeting you, Mr. Butler. If you get back here before I leave here I want you to come out to the house for dinner, meet my wife and daughter."

Butler watched the two men walk out of the O-Club. He turned to Rudd.

"Those are two very nice gents," he said.

"Hinman is tough," Rudd said. "You can see that. But don't be fooled by Mike Brannon. That Irishman may look easy and soft but he's a fighter. When he takes over the *Eelfish* he's going to be another Art Hinman and in this war that ain't bad."

CHAPTER 9

The two women waiting at the end of the pier for Dusty Rhodes and John Barber were a study in contrasts. June Rhodes was tiny, barely five feet tall with a slim, girlish figure. She was one of the Island people of mixed racial strains that so often produced women of exquisite beauty. In her veins ran the blood of the old Polynesians, of Japanese, Chinese, Hawaiians and white missionaries. The slight slant of her large, dark eyes gave a piquancy to the pale copper tones of her skin. Her hair was jet black, thick and luxuriant and hung to her waist, caught at the back of her neck in a simple clasp.

June Kanakaia met Dusty Rhodes when he was a young sailor and she was seventeen. She had accepted his grave courtship with a naive trust that had awed him and which he had never violated. Gordon, Jr., was born a year after their marriage. Alan two years later. In Dusty Rhodes' view June was the ideal Navy wife. She kept a spotless house, never complained of not having enough money and helped her husband study for his promotional examinations. She reared their children with a firm discipline that brooked no disobedience but was tempered by the love that flowed from her as naturally as the rising of the sun each day. She accepted the long separations from her husband when she had to be both mother and father with a stoic resignation, living for the day when Rhodes would have put in his twenty years of service and could take a job in the Pearl Harbor Navy Yard and be home every night.

Dottie Barber was tall, blonde, buxom and as outgoing as June Rhodes was reserved. A Los Angeles secretary, she had saved her money until she could afford a third-class ticket on one of the Lurline cruise ships that traveled between the West Coast and Hawaii. She met John Barber in a department store in Hawaii. He was buying a spool of white cotton thread and she had giggled uncontrollably when the sales girl sold Barber a darning egg and tried to explain its use.

Barber had tipped his white hat back on his head, eyed her and said that if she knew so much about how to darn socks maybe she could tell him about it over a cup of coffee. She admitted to being an expert, that she had darned her father's socks for years. The cup of coffee had extended into a quiet dinner and ten days later she wrote home for her clothes and personal possessions, cashed in her return ticket and used the money to finance a week-long honeymoon.

The two women, as unlike as night and day, had been close friends for years. When Rhodes and Barber won the right to wear the Chief Petty Officer's billed cap on the same day, June and Dottie had hosted a celebration for the promotions with as much pride and joy as if the elevation to the rarified atmosphere of a Chief Petty Officer in the prewar, peacetime Navy was theirs—as in a real sense it was.

"The reception committee is waiting," Rhodes said to Barber as they walked up the pier.

"Yeah. One good thing about being married is there's always someone there to say hello when you come in to port."

"Didn't know you had any trouble in that line when you were single," Rhodes said.

"Been so long I forgot about it," Barber said. The two men reached the end of the pier and Rhodes bent and gravely kissed June on her mouth. She hugged his arm and they both turned at Dottie Barber's cry.

"Hoo hah! Lemme show you how to welcome a sailor!" She threw her arms around Barber's neck, knocking his cap to the ground, ind hugged him fiercely while she was kissing him. The embrace went on and on until finally Dottie stepped back, smoothing her skirt.

"There, you sex maniac! Let that hold you until we get home! June, I'll call you tomorrow about noon if I'm able."

"No, you drive," Rhodes said. He walked around the front of their shiny 1938 Ford and got into the passenger's seat.

"The boys busy?"

"They're finishing up the housecleaning and setting the table for lunch," June said. She sat up very straight on the thick pillow she used so she could see over the steering wheel. "When we heard, day before yesterday, that *Mako* was on the way in Gordy and Alan took over. They washed and waxed the car, cleaned the yard and then started on the house."

"What brought all that on? Usually they have trouble with hanging up their clothes."

June smiled, her white teeth gleaming in her copper-hued face. "Gordy has found out about sex and women. He told me that I shouldn't be all tired out when you got home!"

"My God!" Rhodes muttered. "At fourteen? I was raised on a farm and I knew about breeding cows and pigs when I was ten but I never connected it with men and women until I was at least, oh, sixteen, maybe later."

"All you people from Minnesota are backward," she said. "I think he's known about it for a long time. This is his way of letting me know that he knows. When you leave on the next war patrol I'll start the sex education for both of them."

"You think you ought to do that? It's kind of, well, it's a delicate subject."

"The old Polynesian fathers taught their daughters about sex by deflowering them in front of the tribe," she said in a prim tone. "The girls learned by doing. The boys learned by watching. After that they could practice with each other as much as they wanted to. I don't intend to do that with my sons but I'd rather tell them what's what and have them get it straight than let them pile up a lot of bunk from other kids."

He nodded. "Other than that, how's everything?"

"We're all fine," she answered. "I made the last payment on the radio. The car needs a new fan belt. Gordy wanted to put it on but I told him to wait until you got home so you could see what a good mechanic he is." She looked at him and grinned. "Not such a long patrol this time, shorter than the first one."

"Thirty-five days is long enough," he said. "Took us fourteen days to get on station. We spent a week there and then got called home. Is Dottie okay, their girl all right?"

"They're fine," she answered. "We followed the same sort of routine we had when you were both on the East Coast putting the *Mako* in commission and all during the first war patrol. We called each other every day, got together every couple of days or so. Gloria Brannon came over to the house every Sunday after church. Except the last two Sundays."

"Was something wrong?"

"Well, you know how it is. You're the Chief of the Boat so if any of the wives of the crew or their girl friends have a problem they come to me if you're out at sea. Captain Hinman's wife is dead now," she shuddered slightly, "so she isn't here to give any help to the officers' wives. Gloria Brannon has to do that and she just isn't very good at it. She's too sweet to deal with the problems other people have."

"What problems?" he said softly.

She drove for a few moments without speaking and then she pulled over and parked the car by a curb. She turned to him and her words came out in a rush.

"Mary Simms is sleeping with a civilian, a Civil Service engineer they sent out here to work on the sunken battleships!"

"Who knows, who else beside you and Gloria Brannon?"

"Who doesn't? According to what I've heard every officer's wife on the Base knows about it. He's been living at Mary's house. He moved out two days ago when we heard you were coming in."

Rhodes' big right fist clenched and he began to beat his fist against his knee.

"He's been living in Simms' house? In his damned house? With their little girl there?"

"No," June answered. "The little girl wasn't there. She was staying at Gloria's house. The Brannons' little girl is about the same age. They played together."

"What the hell is wrong with Mary Simms?" Rhodes grunted.

"The right question is what is wrong with her husband," June said. "From what I hear your Mr. Simms is an all-out bastard. He's all-Navy. Clean sweep down fore and aft twice a day. When the ship is in port he holds quarters in the front room before he leaves for the ship each day and issues his orders for the day to his wife and daughter. Then he inspects when he comes home to make sure his orders were carried out! Shape up or ship out! Dottie said that if John ever tried anything like that she'd raise a lump on his head as big as a watermelon!"

"You didn't get involved, did you?"

"Oh, no! I've been married to you for fifteen years, remember? I know the Navy! Enlisted men do not fraternize with the officers. Enlisted men's wives say 'yes, ma'am, to officers' wives and they lower their eyes when they meet the Captain's wife in public."

"Now wait a minute! Marie Hinman wasn't like that!"

"No, she wasn't," she agreed. "Marie Hinman, may God give her soul rest and love, was a wonderful woman. She liked everyone. She spoke to everyone and it didn't matter if it was some deck hand's girl friend or the Admiral's wife. Gloria is every bit as nice but she hasn't got the steel in her that Marie Hinman had. She doesn't know how to cope with what she calls 'marital infidelity' but I call it screwing all hands!"

"You're talking dirty, woman!" His big hand touched her thigh gently as she put the car in gear. She looked at him and smiled.

"I'm a vulgar woman and I'm raunchy and I haven't had a man, not even a civilian, in thirty-six days and I'm going to kill you tonight! She tried hard to make her soft voice growl.

"You gonna let the boys watch, old Polynesian?" He caught her back-handed slap at him and laughed.

"I shouldn't be kidding about those things," she said as she wheeled the car into their street. "I didn't know if I should tell you or not. I'm glad I did."

"I'm glad you did, too," he stared through the windshield and then slammed his knee with his fist.

"Shit!" he snapped.

"Watch your language, sailor, we're almost home."

"Well, damn it, we're losing the Old Man and Mike Brannon and that means that Pete Simms will probably be the Executive Officer next war patrol. If his marriage is breaking up, if it affects him, it could be bad. An Exec. who hasn't got his whole mind on his job could lose the ship!"

"Captain Hinman and Mike Brannon both leaving?" She slowed the car slightly. "Honey, we heard things, little things, the last week or two. What happened out there?"

"Later," he said. "There's the boys on the lawn. My God, look how Alan has grown this last month!"

Dottie Barber rolled over in bed late that night and reached for a cigaret.

"Pappy John," she said, exhaling a long plume of smoke toward the ceiling. "Pappy John, you are still the best man who ever started a rusty engine and made it purr like a kitten! Now rest easy and get your strength back and let me tell you about your engineering officer."

When she had finished John Barber reached up and rubbed his balding head.

"Goddamn it!" he muttered. "That son of a bitch Simms is bad enough now. If he finds out about this he's gonna be hell on wheels with the throttle stuck wide open."

"He'll find out," she said. She lit a cigaret for him. "Everyone on the Base seems to know about it."

"What sort of a guy is it she's been shackin' up with? You ever see him?"

"He was pointed out to me when I went to the Commissary on

the Base one day," she said. "Nice-looking man, little bit chubby, just like Mary is. I heard he's married, has a wife and four kids on the East Coast."

"She's got to be out of her skull!" Barber said. He ground out the cigaret in an ashtray Dottie was holding on her bare stomach. "I could understand her shacking up if Simms was dead, lost at sea or something. But she shouldn't be screwing all hands just because we're out at sea for a few weeks!"

"She's not screwing all hands," Dottie said sweetly. "Just one little civilian. And from what I hear she's just as lonely when the ship is in port as when you're gone!"

"How would you know that?"

"Marylin, the mixed-blood who lives at the end of the street, the one who's married to that Yard machinist? You know him. Well, Marylin babysits for officers when they have a party and does house-cleaning for some of them. Marylin says that Mary Simms always calls her when Pete Simms is due home from sea to help her clean the house. Your nice Mr. Simms walks in, pulls on white gloves and walks around feeling over the tops of the doors and inside cupboards, looking for dust. He must think he's an Admiral on inspection tour!"

"I know," Barber growled. "The son of a bitch came off a battleship. He pulled that sort of shit when we were shaking down the *Mako*. One day one of my firemen put a bucket of dirty oil at the bottom of the ladder that goes down to the auxiliary diesel and then he unscrewed the light bulb.

"Simms went down the ladder in his white gloves and put his foot in the bucket! You'd a thought a main engine had blown up! Got his white gloves all dirty trying to get his shoe and sock off. Came back to the engine rooms later and told me to put all hands to scrubbing the bilges with their toothbrushes!"

"My God!" she said. "How'd you get out of that one?"

"That's what you got a Chief of the Boat for," he said. "I went to Dusty and he got Mr. Simms straightened out. Does Dusty know about this, you think?"

"June knows about it so I guess that he'll know," she said. "But Mr. Simms is as much your problem as Dusty's, isn't he?"

"In a way," he said. "The Chief of the Boat is the only Chief with enough weight to go to the Old Man and tell him one of his officers is carrying too much right rudder. Stop that, will you! I'm too old for that stuff!"

"Oh no you're not!" she giggled.

"I am so!" he said. "You're a crazy woman!"

"You're not too old!" she giggled. "I've got a handful already!"

Mike Brannon waited until just before noon before telephoning Lieut. Don Grilley's house. Bernice Grilley answered.

"Don's in the shower and I'm stirring up a mess of real Oklahoma-style flapjacks and there's some great pork sausage my Daddy sent me a few days ago and y'all bring Gloria and little Glory over and have some lunch." She listened to Brannon's remonstrations for a moment.

"Too late, friend. While you were talkin' I poured in some more flour and if y'all don't come over I'll have a lot of wasted flapjacks. Now come on, right away, y'hear?"

She greeted the Brannons at the door and led the way to the dining room, a tall, slim woman whose self-assured manner had been developed through several years of making a home for herself and her geologist husband in the out-of-the-way places of the United States.

"Last batch of the first bunch is on the griddle," she said as she went into the kitchen. "Don, old buddy, start dishing up will you, while I turn these 'jacks?"

They ate hugely, Gloria Brannon protesting that she really shouldn't take a third helping, and then Bernice Grilley put little Glory Brannon in the front room with a big coloring book and a box of crayons. She brought a big pot of coffee out to the kitchen.

"You wanted to talk to me?" Don Grilley said. He lit a cigaret and touched his wife's hand in thanks as she poured coffee.

"Well, it's not my responsibility now," Mike Brannon said. "I'm officially detached." His round face was troubled. "But I'm concerned about this thing, what it could do at the *Mako*."

"You're talking about the Simms mess?" Grilley said.

Brannon nodded his head. "Mess is the right word."

"We've seen that sort of thing in the oil camps," Bernice Grilley said. She reached over and got one of her husband's cigarets.

"A man leaves his wife alone too much. Sometimes she goes wrong because she's just too lonely. Sometimes she welcomes the absence so she can cat around."

"What did you do about things like that?" Mike asked.

"Nothing," Grilley answered. "Not anyone's business. I wonder sometimes why the Navy makes it their business when something like this happens. The Navy is government and government shouldn't be sticking its nose into private affairs."

"Oh, you're wrong!" Brannon said. "When you're out at sea, especially in a submarine, and a man is all upset because of something like this he could lose the ship, sink it!"

"You can get killed working on an oil rig just as easily," Grilley said. "But it doesn't happen that often. But that's none of my business, the Simms thing I mean. All I want is for this war to end so I can go back to being a civilian." He noticed that Mike Brannon's face had begun to set in what the Wardroom called "The Executive Officer's 'Now Hear This!' expression."

"Don't get me wrong, Mike. I've learned a lot from some of the people I've met. You, for one. If all the officers in the Navy were like you and the Skipper I'd consider putting in to be a Regular. It's the Pete Simmses that bother me." He turned to his wife.

"Tell Mike and Gloria what Simms did when we invited him and Mary over after our first patrol run. We asked them over to have a Mexican-style dinner," he explained to Mike.

"Well, he came in and then he began touching things, tables, over the doors, things like that. And he told me I wasn't a very good housekeeper. He said that as long as I was in the Navy that I should run, what did he call it, Don?"

"A taut ship," Grilley said with a grin. "Now tell them what you said!"

"I told him to gather up all the dust he could find, pat it into a little pile and then stuff it—you know where!

"He looked at me as if I'd hit him in the face! Then he told me that an officer's lady didn't talk like an enlisted man's riffraff. I told him that I certainly wasn't an officer's lady by choice and that the sooner Don was back to being a civilian, the better I'd like it."

"It must be very hard for two adult people to jump into Navy life with both feet like you've had to," Brannon said slowly. "I mean, those of us who are Regulars have been at it since we left high school. The Academy, all that. Usually we marry a Service brat and she knows what it's all about. Or we marry a young girl who's adaptable and the older wives help her out.

"Gloria wasn't a Service brat but her father was a quarterman in the Brooklyn Navy Yard, a leading shipfitter. She knew all about the long separations, the lousy quarters they give to junior officers.

"You should have seen the shack we lived in when we were sent to Panama! Roaches big enough to carry off a bag of groceries, if we'd ever had enough money to buy a whole bag of groceries. The roof leaked in the rainy season and they wouldn't fix it then because they couldn't work in the rain. When the dry season came they couldn't fix it because they didn't know where it leaked!"

"What's Mary Simms' background?" Bernice asked.

"Civilian," Gloria Brannon said. "She met Pete when she was working in some Senator's office in Washington. He was attached to the color guard or something like that. He was a football player at the Academy, you know, big man on campus sort of thing. Very good looking, as he is now. She was much slimmer then, she's let herself go a little since they had the baby.

"She told me once, when they were commissioning *Mako*, that he made her do thirty minutes of calisthenics every morning when they got up. Then he'd take his shower and she'd fix breakfast because he wanted his breakfast as soon as he was dressed. And then he'd chew her out for not being showered and cleaned up! He said she shouldn't sit at an officer's table in a robe and hair curlers!"

"Nice man," Grilley said. "You had a little trouble with him at New London, didn't you?"

"Just a little," Mike said slowly. "He started getting on Nate Cohen, needling him because Nate's Jewish. I stopped it."

"Simms is a fool," Grilley said. "Cohen is ten times as smart as Simms is ever going to be. Did you know he was studying for the Rabbinate, Mike?"

"Yes. The Skipper told me he saw it in his service jacket. I wondered," Brannon's face was solemn. "I never served with a Jew before, never even knew a Jew for that matter. I thought they had to eat special foods off special plates, things like that."

"If they observe dietary laws, they do," Grilley said. "But I think Nate would have asked for a dispensation because of service in a submarine in wartime."

"You got along very well with Cohen?" Brannon was speaking slowly, picking his words.

"Yes," Grilley said. "I had some Jewish professors in school. I admired them as men and for their learning." He was conscious as he spoke of a subtle change in the room. The same sort of change that came about whenever Nathan Cohen walked into the *Mako*'s Wardroom was here in this slightly shabby room in this seedy house that the Navy had appropriated for Officer's Quarters. There were only a few Jews in the prewar Navy. The Jew was unknown. Therefore he was dangerous. Grilley changed the subject abruptly.

"I think there's something you ought to know, Mike. We, all of us in the Wardroom and I'm sure that everyone in the crew—we're going to miss you. You were one hell of a fine Executive Officer. I know you're going to make a hell of a good Skipper."

Brannon blushed, the solid red flush mounting swiftly from his open shirt collar to his black hair. His bright blue eyes squeezed shut for a moment and then opened.

"Well, Don, that wasn't necessary. I'm going to miss *Mako*, all of you." He spread his hands, almost helplessly.

"You know, when you Reserves started coming in with us we resented you. Yes, we did! Called you shoe salesmen and ribbon clerks. You got ranks that some of us worked years and years to get. I think you can understand how we felt. We'd been doing our work for years, ever since high school and in you came and got braid some of us couldn't get. And I, for one, want to go on record as saying that most of you people are damned smart!"

"It cuts both ways," Grilley said softly. "Most of us who came into the Navy had a pretty low opinion of Regular Navy officers. We thought you were parasites, you'd been getting free hospital care, free dental care, a free education and that sort of thing and we'd been on the outside, fighting to get through school in the Depression years.

And most of us have found out that most of you are damned good men, damned good.

"I found out that it isn't much different in here than it is outside in many ways. You have a system. In the oil fields you learn very quickly to lean on the chief rigger. He's the man who knows everything. Here you lean on the Chief of the Boat. He knows everything."

"Let's end this mutual admiration society," Bernice Grilley said, "before you wind up crying on each other's shoulders. When do you have to leave, Gloria?"

"We've got about another eleven days," Mike Brannon said. "We get to go together, privilege of command. But we'll be together for only a few weeks, and then *Eelfish* will go to sea. Gloria is going to stay in the States, with her folks."

"I don't like that part," Gloria said. "I won't be here to see Mike bring his ship in at the end of his first war patrol."

"I don't think you'd see that anyway," Mike said. "Bob Rudd told us at lunch yesterday that Nimitz is thinking of sending most of the new submarines to Australia. Down there we'll be closer to the islands the Japs have captured and closer to their supply ships."

"Do you know anything about this new Captain we're getting?" Grilley asked.

"I know Capt. Arvin Mealey," Brannon said. "His father was an Admiral. I served under him in R-Boats in Panama."

"What's he like?" Grilley asked, his voice as casual as he could make it. He could feel the atmosphere in the room change. Reservists didn't ask leading questions about Regular Navy officers.

"He's a strict Commanding Officer," Brannon said slowly. "He lives by the Book, by the rules and regulations of the Navy. If you know the Book, if you live by it, you'll get along with him just fine. If you don't, well, I've seen some who didn't . They had a lot of trouble. I got along with him pretty well."

"How about the man who's taking your place?"

"I don't know him," Brannon said. "He's a Reserve, I was told, an engineer from M.I.T. You didn't go there, did you?"

"No," Grilley smiled. "Oklahoma. A Reserve as the Exec.? Pete Simms will have a fit! He thinks he's going to be the new Executive Officer of the *Mako!*"

"I think he should be," Brannon said slowly. "I don't know of any other Fleet Boat with a Reserve for an Exec. I don't know how Captain Mealey will like that. He may not like it at all!" He rose and Gloria went into the front room to get little Glory.

"You people take good care of *Mako*," Brannon said as he reached the front door. He walked throught the door quickly so Grilley wouldn't see the tears filling his eyes. Once he was away from the house and in the shadow of a tree he turned.

"You keep a sharp lookout when you've got the deck, Don. You'll see the *Eelfish* one of these days!"

CHAPTER 10

The Royal Hawaiian Hotel on Waikiki Beach was the R & R center for submarine crews in from a war patrol. The men were given two weeks to unwind from the rigors of a war patrol while repair crews at the Submarine Base, called "relief crews," repaired and repainted their ship. The hotel's spacious grounds were large enough for those men who, after weeks of living shoulder-to-shoulder with others, wanted nothing more than solitude and quiet. The comfortable rooms were a welcome contrast to the steel-framed bunks and the confining curve of the ship's hull. The sunshine and high blue sky were savored by men who in the course of a long war patrol often never saw even the night sky.

As *Mako's* crew came piling out of the buses they were met by a grim-faced Chief Boatswain's Mate and his crew of Masters at Arms, the hotel police force.

"Pile your gear on the starboard side of the lobby," the Chief barked. "My people will stand watch over it while you eat. When you're through with chow fall in by your gear."

The Chief Bos'n's Mate lined them up after they had eaten. His seamed face split in a small smile as he told them to stand at ease.

"I don't want any of you people to get the wrong idea," the Chief began. "We're not here to make trouble for you unless you insist on it. There ain't too many rules you have to obey. But there are some rules and here they are.

"You'll keep your rooms shipshape. No laundry will be hung from the room balcony railings. You'll wear uniform of the day at all times outside of your rooms unless you're going to the beach to go swimming. No drinking in the rooms. You got three bars on the first deck, do your drinking there.

"No broads are allowed on the grounds or in the hotel. And if any of you people want to fight," his tough face broke into a wide smile, "I got two Fleet champions in my detail. They'll give you all the fight you want, inside the ring or out.

"Honolulu is under martial law. That means nobody except security personnel is allowed on the streets between sundown and sunrise. That goes for all civilians, too. I mean you can't go out on the streets after sundown! You go wandering out of this hotel after dark and some trigger-happy Army fuck-off is liable to shoot you dead!" He took a deep breath.

"Now because all of you people are war heroes you get some special privileges.

"There's some whorehouses downtown. The cab drivers know where they are. They open at zero eight hundred for ordinary sailors who ain't heroes. You people can get in the whorehouses at zero seven hundred. To do that you have to get a special pass from the desk that lets you out of the gate at sunrise. You'll find cabs coming to the gate right after that. Now lemme give you some advice about them whorehouses.

"First place, they're on the second deck in one block of town. On the first deck there's a big grocery store. You'll find a lineup of women doin' their shopping. Be on your best behavior when you go through that line. Don't make no cracks! Them women know what's topside in that building.

"When you get topside you're going to be the first people of the day. You don't have to take no wet decks. But those places are so busy you only get three minutes with a girl. If you can't get it off in three minutes they give you a rain check and you can go back another day for half price.

"Another thing: The Army polices the whorehouses. They got MPs in there with clubs. Most of those fuck-offs are Reserves, cops from the South. They like to break heads. So don't start any trouble in the whorehouses.

"One last thing: Don't get any ideas you can make it with the women around town. Those broads got the pick of the crop. They's about a thousand men here for every woman and they don't have to pick crazy submarine sailors.

"We want you to have a good time while you're here. You get drunk we'll put you to bed if you don't make no trouble. You get sick someone will clean up after you. Now line up at the desk over there, Chiefs first, and get your rooms. You'll find chow schedules and laundry lists in your rooms. That's all. Dismiss."

"Those bastards tell you rest and recreation," Ginty growled to one of his torpedomen as he found his sea bag in the pile near the wall. "First thing they do they hit you in the ass with a Chief Master at Arms who looks like he'd have fun biting a sick bulldog in the ass! Soon's you get your gear in your room you get your ass in gear and make the arrangements for the beer party. Go to that fuckin' Chief and find out the drill and take care of things. Check with me later."

By five that afternoon—seventeen hundred hours in Navy parlance—the *Mako* beer party was rolling in high gear. The amateur drinkers had long since staggered off to their rooms. The Masters at Arms kept their distance from the party, moving in only when a *Mako* crew member decided it would be fun to go in the sea for a swim. The Masters at Arms were gentle but very firm. No swimming unless in the uniform of the day for swimming, regulation trunks.

The hard-core drinkers had gathered in a circle around Ginty, who presided at the beer keg tap. A kitchen worker from the hotel appeared with a big box of sandwiches and Ginty rewarded him with a beer. Spook Hernandez turned to Ginty as he handed out the food.

"Beer's all right as a belly wash," he grumbled, "I need something better. Gimme the key to the alky locker in your Forward Room, Ginch. I got time to grab a cab back to the Base, get a five gallon can of alky and get back here before sundown. We can stow the alky in my room, big-deal the galley out of some grapefruit juice and have us a real submarine party, like the old days."

Ginty shook his massive head. "Nope. Ain't givin' you no key to no alky locker. I do that and Dusty Rhodes finds out he's gonna land on me like a fuckin' ton of bricks!"

"What the hell you afraid of Rhodes for? "Hernandez demanded. "You're bigger'n him. Fuckin' Chief of the Boat got no business interferin' with the troops on leave. Gimme the key!"

"Two things you gotta get straight, Spook," Ginty said. "First thing is I ain't afraid of Dusty Rhodes. I just got good sense which you ain't got. The man was Fleet heavyweight champ for three years. I served with a dude in the Asiatic Fleet fought him. Got knocked out inna first round! Old Dusty got him a string of about twenty KOs in the first round!

"Second thing is that I ain't givin' you no key to the alky locker so forget it and have another beer."

"You're a fucking shithead," Hernandez said, "a real shithead! Don't never come back to my After Room to borrow a tool because you dropped one in the bilges and you're too lazy to dig it out! Just don't come aft of the fucking Maneuvering Room, you hear?" He turned and began weaving his way through the sand toward the hotel.

"Fuckin' Spics can't drink," Ginty pronounced. He drew a stein of beer and rubbed his head. "Got to get me a haircut tomorrow. Anyone seen old Hindu Hendershot? Bastard was here a while ago."

John Maxwell, the Chief Yeoman, held out his empty stein. "Gimme a refill, Ginch. Hindu went lookin' for that second class of his who wants to change his rate to radioman."

"What's he want with a fuckin' Reserve?" Ginty grunted. He filled Maxwell's stein and handed it back to him. "Shit, that Reserve, that Billy Strong, he had two beers and left!"

"Chief Hendershot, in his wisdom, has decided that Billy Strong has disgraced his electrical gang by wanting out," Maxwell drawled. "So he's gone to the guy's room. He hopes the room is high enough up in the hotel that when he throws Billy Strong off the balcony he'll bounce at least one floor high!"

"You better go find Hindu and change his mind," Ginty said.

"Hindu's good people. He shouldn't get fucked up over a Reserve."

Maxwell smiled happily, the beer foam covering his thick black mustache. "You're a First Class Petty Officer last time I looked at your service record, old Ginch. First Class can't give orders to a Chief, you know that."

Ginty lowered his head and stared at Maxwell. "I don't want no trouble with you, Chief. But a Chief tells another Chief not to do something, savvy? First Class don't go tellin' a Chief not to throw a silly fuckin' Reserve offa no balcony. Chief's gotta do something like that. Another thing, you're nothin' but a fucking ex-Marine joined the Navy because the chow was better. So go find Hindu and do your thing."

Maxwell rose and flexed his wide, muscular shoulders.

"I had a Gunnery Sergeant when I was in the Corps was just like you, Ginty. He was so ugly that when he farted you couldn't tell which end it came out of!" He whooped with joy and dodged the empty beer stein Ginty threw at him. He was still laughing as he went up through the white sand to the hotel.

Breakfast hours in the Royal Hawaiian were generous by Navy standards. The dining room served coffee and doughnuts from 0530 to 0700 for early risers and for those who wanted to get into town to be first in line at the crowded brothels. Regular breakfasts were served from seven until mid-morning. Each table was stocked with pitchers of ice-cold milk and tomato juice for those who had imbibed too well the evening before. Ginty left his room shortly after eight and padded down the hall. He passed an open door and heard Hindu Hendershot's Kentucky twang singing. He went into the room. It was empty.

"You in here, Chief?" he bellowed. "I can hear you moanin' but where the fuck are you?"

"In the head," Hendershot's voice floated out of the bathroom into the room.

Ginty walked into the big bathroom and saw Hendershot, stark naked, walking up and down in a bathtub that was a third full of soapy water.

"What in the fuck you doin'?"

"Washing my clothes," Hendershot said happily. "Walkin' up

and down on 'em is easier than bendin' over and doin' it by hand. Makes my head ache to bend over the tub. Where you goin'?"

"Breakfast," Ginty said. "Gonna eat this hotel right out of hot cakes and sausages. Get dressed and let the clothes soak. Come on and eat."

A duty Master at Arms hailed the two men as they walked across the lobby.

"You *Mako* people, Chief?"

Hendershot nodded.

"There's a notice going up on the bulletin board right soon," the MAA said. "All you people got to be in uniform of the day at fourteen hundred. They're gonna take you back to your ship."

Ginty pushed forward, his big face hard. "Whaddya mean, take us back! We only got here yesterday!"

"It's only for an hour or two," the MAA said. "You're getting a new Skipper. It's a change of command thing." He turned to Hendershot.

"Would you pass the word, Chief? Much obliged if you would. Lotta people don't know we got a bulletin board."

Ginty was starting on his third stack of hotcakes when Johnny Paul, his Second Class Torpedoman, came up to the table, pulled out a chair and sat down.

"Who asked you to sit down?" Ginty growled.

"Ginch, a terrible thing happened!" Paul said.

"What'd you do, piss the bed?"

"It's Hernandez. You know, the First Class got the After Room?"

"I know who Hernandez is and where he works," Ginty said. He speared a wedge of hotcake and pushed in into his mouth and chewed, his eyes on Paul.

"I don't have to have his name, rate, serial number and blood type. What about Spook?"

"He's blind!" Paul said in a low voice.

"You crazy?" Ginty said. "He was drinkin' beer with us on the beach yesterday afternoon."

"They heard him screaming!" Paul said.

"You are the worst bastard I ever saw to tell anyone anything!" Ginty said. "Will you the fuck get it out?"

"The below-decks watch in the relief crew on the *Mako* heard Spook screaming!" Paul looked around the dining room and then he bent over the table and dropped his voice to just above a whisper.

"Guy I know came out here to tell me. Spook and Barney Saunders, the quartermaster, went aboard the ship yesterday afternoon, late. The below-decks watch said they went up in the Conning Tower and closed the hatch to the Control Room. He said they had a bottle looked like it was gin with them.

"After a while the below-decks watch heard a funny noise in the Conning Tower and then he heard someone screaming and he opened the hatch and went up. Spook was on his hands and knees by the helm pukin' and screamin' and in between pukin' and screamin' he was yellin' that he was blind. And that ain't the worst part!"

"What's worse?" Hendershot said quietly.

"Barney Saunders is over the other end of the Conning Tower, aft by the periscopes, and he's sittin' on deck and he'd put the muzzle of a forty-five in his mouth and blowed his brains all over the overhead!"

Ginty reached out a huge hand and clamped it around Johnny Paul's arm. "Don't you spread this scuttlebutt around, sailor! You do and I'll personally break all your arms and legs! The shit that you people talk about! Worse than a bunch of fucking old women!"

"This ain't scuttlebutt, Ginch!" Paul began to massage his arm where Ginty's hand had grabbed him. "The guy who came here to tell me is my cousin, he's a Pharmacist's Mate at the hospital at Aiea. That's where they took Barney and Spook, to Aiea. My cousin said Barney is awful dead and Spook is blind from drinkin' wood alcohol!"

"Shit!" Ginty said as he got to his feet. "Hindu, see you can get hold of Dusty. His old lady's phone number ought to be in the book. I'll try to raise Grilley, he's a good head and we ain't got Mike Brannon now. He'd sure as hell know what to do."

Hendershot fell into step beside Ginty as the big man's legs ate up the distance across the hotel lobby.

"Where the hell did they get the wood alcohol?"

"Who the fuck knows?" Ginty growled. "Hernandez wanted me to give him the key to the alky locker in my Room. Anybody but a Spic I mighta said okay, that torpedo alky is a hundred and eighty proof, good stuff for drinkin'. I told him to suck ass, he wasn't gettin' no key to no alky locker from me. He went off with a sour puss. Bastard musta got Saunders and gone back to the Base and found some wood alky somewheres and didn't test it. Fuckin' wood alky will turn you crazy! What a mess this is going to be with the new Old Man coming aboard this afternoon!"

"You know Captain Mealey?" Hendershot said as he opened a telephone book.

"No," Ginty grunted.

"You'll know him this afternoon," Hendershot said as he ran his finger down the line of R listings in the telephone book. "I had him on an R-boat in Panama. Captain Mealey doesn't drink, he doesn't smoke, he doesn't swear and he don't like sailors that do any of those things!"

CHAPTER 11

The buses rolled to a stop at the land end of the pier where *Mako* was docked. The crew got out, sullen and silent. They were prepared to dislike their new Commanding Officer; to be taken away from the hotel, even for an hour or two, was an insult. Captain Severn's Chief Yeoman found Dusty Rhodes and asked him to line up the crew. Rhodes formed the grumbling sailors into two ranks and took his position at the right hand end of the first rank, two paces apart from Chief Barber. Lieutenant Grilley walked over from the small group of *Mako's* officers.

"I suggested to Commander Rudd that it might be better to hold this here, as far away from *Mako* as we could get and yet within sight of her," he said quietly. "Naval Intelligence has the ship sealed off while they investigate. Probably won't be over until sometime tomorrow." Rhodes nodded.

The crew stood quietly at ease in ranks. Occasionally there would be a subdued ripple of whispers as an officer hurried aboard *Mako* or left the ship. Word of what had happened in *Mako's* Conning

Tower had flashed all over the hotel that morning and Johnny Paul, mindful of Ginty's murderous rages and his awesome strength, had hurried to Ginty's room to tell him that everyone was talking about the tragedy and that he wasn't the source. Ginty was shaving and as he rinsed his face he stared at Paul. The younger man backed away.

"I know the word's gettin' around," Ginty said through a towel he was using to dry his face. "Fucking yeoman on the Base is spreadin' the word. Just keep your own nose clean."

Captain Severn's Chief Yeoman coughed discreetly and nodded his head at Dusty Rhodes as two staff cars pulled up. Rhodes stepped out a pace and faced left.

"Dress right!" he rasped. He waited a moment as the two ranks shuffled into a straight line.

"Front!" He watched carefully and as he saw four gold stripes on the shoulder boards of Captain Severn come into view he drew a deep breath.

"Tennn-Shunn!" He turned and stepped back into line.

Captain Severn walked over and stood in front of *Mako*'s small group of officers, drawn up rigidly in a line. Two other officers, one a three-stripe Commander, the other a two-and-a-half–stripe Lieutenant Commander, got out of the cars and walked over. The Lieutenant Commander took up a position to one side. The Commander walked up to Captain Severn and saluted smartly. Captain Severn returned the salute and motioned the Commander to stand to one side. He pulled a handkerchief out of his sleeve and coughed and hawked into the white cloth, looked at it and returned the handkerchief to his sleeve.

"I have a few words to say," he began in a nasal drone.

"We are here to observe a tradition that is as old as our Navy. All of our ship captains have gone through this ceremony we participate in today—the change of command of a warship of the United States Navy, the designation of a Captain to command a warship.

"Command is a very heavy responsibility in time of peace," he went on, his cold eyes sweeping over *Mako*'s officers and men. "In time of war it is a crushing responsibility!

"We who serve in submarines know we are the nation's only

effective weapon at this time. Until the Navy is able to regroup it is the submarines which must defend our nation.

"It is the submarines which must show the enemy what it means to stage a sneak attack on Pearl Harbor!" His voice rose.

"The submarine force is showing the enemy its teeth! It will do that with even greater force and resolution in the months to come. We are going to make the Jap wish he had never heard of Pearl Harbor!" His voice was shaking now.

"By the Grace of our Christian God Almighty in Heaven we shall win this war in His name!" He turned toward his yeoman to take the envelope the yeoman was holding and Rhodes caught a glimpse of Nate Cohen's lean profile. Cohen had a slight smile on his face. Captain Severn held out the envelope to the Commander who had been standing back of him during his talk.

"These are your orders, sir. Please read them aloud to your command."

The Commander, a tall, slim man with a thick, sun-bleached white mustache, saluted and walked over and stood in front of *Mako's* officers. He ran a thumb under the flap of the envelope and the heavy red wax seal made a dry cracking sound as it broke. He took out a sheet of paper and began to read, the traditional recitation of the orders assigning an officer to command of a warship. When he had finished he faced Captain Severn and in a loud, clear voice said:

"Sir, I, Arvin R. Mealey, Commander, United States Navy, do hereby acknowledge receipt of orders to take command of U.S.S. *Mako* and to discharge my duties as that ship's Commanding Officer to the best of my ability, so help me God."

He snapped off a smart salute that was returned by Captain Severn, who stepped forward, his hand outstretched.

"Congratulations, Captain! Strike the enemy hard and often! My yeoman will be in touch with you later, I want to have you and your lady to dinner with me at my quarters this evening." He turned and walked rapidly toward his car. Captain Mealey turned to face his crew. He eyed them for a long moment, his face set and stern.

"At ease," he said. "I have very little to say to you. I do not make speeches. I will tell you this.

"This is not my first command. I know what I want done on a ship I command. I know how to get it done.

"There is a body of rules of conduct called Navy Regulations. You may call it by another name, the Book. I live by it. You will live by it. If you do, we will get along fine. If you do not, you will be in trouble. I have no time, no desire, to play nursemaid to sailors who cannot or will not obey orders. I will see all the officers aboard *Mako* tomorrow morning at zero nine hundred. I will see all the Chief Petty Officers at ten hundred hours. Dismiss!" He turned and walked away, toward the other staff car.

The Lieutenant Commander who had arrived with Captain Mealey and Captain Severn was still standing where he had first positioned himself, at one side. He walked toward *Mako*'s officers and Don Grilley stepped out to meet him.

"Sir?" Grilley said.

"I'm Joe Sirocco," the Lieutenant Commander said. "I've been ordered aboard *Mako* as the Executive Officer."

There was a dead silence in the small group of *Mako*'s officers. Back of the officers those crew members who had not begun to walk toward the buses turned and stood quietly, listening. Lieut. Peter Simms spoke, his voice harsh.

"Did you say you were the new Executive Officer? By whose orders, sir, and when did you get your orders?" Simms' eyes were hot, studying the other man's face. Sirocco met his angry stare with a slow smile.

"Why, by order of Captain Severn, the Chief of Staff, sir. I received the orders from Commander Rudd, yesterday."

"What class are you?" Simms demanded.

"I don't follow you, Mister," Sirocco said.

"What year did you graduate from the Academy, damn it! Do you follow that, Mister?"

"Oh," Sirocco said, "the Academy. I didn't graduate from the Academy. I graduated from M.I.T. I'm a Reserve officer."

"A *Reserve*!" Simms' voice was strangled. "I'm going to find out about this!" He wheeled and walked away, his back stiff, heading for the Staff Headquarters building.

"Mr. Simms is a little upset, sir," Don Grilley said in a low voice to Sirocco. "I apologize for him. I think he had expected to be assigned as the Executive Officer."

"So I was told yesterday," Sirocco said.

"Oh? By whom, if I may ask, sir."

"You may," Sirocco said with a grin. "The Chief of Staff made a point of saying that Mr. Simms had his sights set on the job."

"I'm forgetting my manners," Grilley said. "I'm Don Grilley, I take care of Torpedo and Gunnery stuff. I'm a Reserve. Pete Simms is the Engineering Officer and Bob Edge, here, is his assistant. This is Nate Cohen, the best damned Sonar Officer in the whole fleet and a joy to talk with off-watch, and this is Paul Botts, our old man in the Wardroom, Paul's a mustang." Grilley looked around and beckoned to Dusty Rhodes.

"This is Lieutenant Commander Sirocco, Chief. Mr. Sirocco, Chief Torpedoman Rhodes, called Dusty by his friends, the Chief of the Boat."

The two men eyed each other. Sirocco had perhaps an inch on Rhodes' own six feet one and weighed a good twenty pounds more than Rhodes. Sirocco put out his hand and Rhodes took it.

"I've heard good things about you, Chief," Sirocco said. "I asked Commander Rudd about the Chief of the Boat yesterday and he talked for twenty minutes about you. I hope you'll give me the benefit of your knowledge and experience when I draw up the Watch Quarter and Station Bills and in all other matters?"

"I'll do my best, sir," Rhodes said. "Welcome aboard."

"One other thing," Sirocco said. "I'd like to come out to the hotel and meet the other Chiefs and the leading petty officers. At your convenience, of course. If you would do so, please get in touch with me through Commander Rudd's office."

"I will do that, sir," Rhodes said. Grilley turned to Joe Sirocco.

"We were all going out to my house for coffee and doughnuts, sir. My wife makes the best doughnuts you ever broke a molar on. I'd be honored if you'd join us?"

"I'd like that," Sirocco said.

"It's a shame we can't go aboard *Mako*," Bob Edge said. "She's a great ship! But the word is that we can't go aboard until sometime tomorrow."

"I was aboard last night," Sirocco said slowly. "With Captain Mealey and the Chief of Staff." *Mako's* officers bunched around Sirocco, their eyes questioning.

"Was it messy?" Edge asked.

"Very," Sirocco said. "Inside the Conning Tower and later, in Captain Severn's office."

Rhodes caught up with Barber and Hendershot as they were getting into Barber's car.

"Can you give me a lift home, John?" Rhodes said. "June drove me here but she had to get back to the house right away."

"You hear how Simms spit out that word 'Reserve' when the new Exec. said he was a feather merchant?" Barber said as he started his car. "That man Simms is about to pop his relief valves! He could be a problem for me, for you, for the new Exec. and the Captain this next patrol."

"He's already a problem," Rhodes said. "What I'm going to tell you goes no farther than you two. Reason June had to go home is that Mary Simms called her last night from a drug store and June drove over and got her. She was crying when June got her to our house. Simms slapped her around pretty hard, I guess. June was up all night."

"He break anything on her?" Barber said. "Mark her up any?"

"Not where any can see it," Rhodes answered. "June said both her breasts are bruised and she's got some black and blue marks on her stomach and ribs."

"He must of found out she was puttin' out to that civilian," Barber grunted. He slowed for a sailor weaving down the street.

"I don't know," Rhodes said. "June told me she asked her that pointblank and Mary Simms said that all he, all Simms said when he was slapping her around was that she was a lousy housekeeper. I don't know if he knows about the civilian or not. I don't think so."

"He knows," Hendershot growled. "He's gotta know. He's done the same thing too many times himself when he was single and after he got married. He's a tom cat, always been."

"He even tried to make the radioman's wife, what's her name? Yeah. Samantha. Samantha Aaron. Hell of a pretty girl. He tried it when we were on the East Coast; it was just before we went to sea."

"Why didn't you tell me if you knew that?" Rhodes asked.

"No need to, Dusty. You had a lot on your mind then and old Aaron handled it real good. He didn't need any help. One of my electricians was down in the engine room flats checking out the light circuits and he heard Aaron take on Simms right above him, in the Engine Room.

"My guy said Aaron was very polite. Said he figured that Mr. Simms had mistaken his wife for one of the town girls. Said he could forgive that kind of mistake and the language Simms had used because his religion taught him to forgive honest mistakes. Simms tried to bluster it out but my guy said Aaron cut him off short and said he was glad it was a mistake because if his wife had been dishonored he would have had to kill the man who dishonored her! From what my guy said Simms was doing a shuffle on those deck plates, almost shitting in his pants!

"That Aaron could do what he said, too. He's big enough to pull a gang plow through a rocky field. I don't like being around those religious types when they get their dander up! I want to be on the other side of a thick brick wall and when they bust through the wall I want to have a machine gun handy!

"No, I'd say that Simms knows that someone else been plowin' in his field. He knows the routine. You said he didn't hit her where it would show? That sort of proves it. That man's got a mean streak in him a yard wide."

Rhodes was whistling a tuneless tune. He stopped and took a deep breath.

"If he's got that eating at him and if he's eating his guts out over not being the new Exec. it could mean a lot of trouble this patrol. And if the Chief of Staff made the assignment of this dude Sirocco then it means that the Chief of Staff was taking a dig at Simms. He ain't going to be easy to live with." He paused, "Either of you people know anything about this Sirocco?"

"When I heard he was the new Number Two I called a Chief I

know was on the *Gudgeon* first two war patrols," Barber said. "This Sirocco was sent to *Gudgeon* before the war as a sort of Reserve super-cargo. He made two runs on *Gudgeon*, good runs, too.

"This Chief, Masters is his name, I had him when he was a first class, good dude; he said that Sirocco is one helluva smart dude. Very easygoing until you fuck up and then it's Katy-bar-the-door! Sirocco's a big old boy, isn't he? Bigger'n you are, Dusty. Got a face looks like it came through a cement mixer!"

"You people want to have coffee at my place?" Rhodes asked.

"Not if Mary Simms is there," Barber said. "I'll drive Hindu out to the hotel and then I'm goin' home. What the hell you gonna do with Mary Simms, Dusty?"

"Me? Nothing. That's June's department. She's got her own ways. She sat down last night in the room where she put Mary to sleep, she fed her some warm milk with something in it to make her go to sleep. She sat down on the floor and began to meditate. She says she talks to the old gods of her fathers. I woke up about four and got up and looked for her and she was still sitting there on the floor in the room. Her lips were moving but I couldn't hear what she was saying so I got the hell out and went back to bed. She'll handle the thing her own way."

"Sounds spooky," Hendershot said.

"I used to think it was spooky but I don't any more," Rhodes said. "I've seen her come up with the right answers to all sorts of problems I didn't know how to tackle." He peered through the windshield.

"There's young Gordy. Better stop, John. I'll get out here." He got out of the car and walked toward his older son.

"Mom says to tell you that she put your dungarees and tennis shoes in the car," the boy said. "I got the bat and the mitts and a baseball and we're supposed to go over to the playground. Alan is in the car. You can change clothes in the head at the playground. Mom gave me the car keys. Can I drive the car here, where you are, Dad? I'll be careful."

Rhodes nodded. "You may. Remember to let the engine warm up a little before you put it in gear." The boy started to race away and then stopped and came back.

"I almost forgot. Mom says chow is at eighteen hundred and we should be home in time to take a shower. Mrs. Simms will be gone by then, sir."

"Orders received and acknowledged," Rhodes said gravely.

CHAPTER 12

The meeting between *Mako*'s officers and Captain Mealey was brief. Captain Mealey and Lieut. Comdr. Sirocco appeared at precisely 0900. The new Captain took his seat at the head of the Wardroom table and Joe Sirocco squeezed his bulk into place on the padded seat outboard of the table. A mess steward from the O-Club on the Base appeared with a box of cups and saucers and a big pot of coffee and served it.

Five minutes into the meeting it was apparent to *Mako*'s officers that Captain Mealey had read every word of Captain Hinman's patrol run reports on *Mako*'s first two patrols and had, as well, read every word of each officer's service jacket. He began by asking each officer to summarize his naval and civilian experience and then he began asking questions about each man's own department. The questions were pointed and at times savage as Captain Mealey probed for information. When he had talked to each officer he stared at them, his lips thin under his white mustache.

"I will repeat once again what I said yesterday when I assumed command of this vessel.

"I live by the Book, by the rules and regulations of the U.S. Navy. You will live by it. If you do not I will have you detached and recommend that you never again be transferred to sea duty." He touched the right side of his white mustache with his forefinger and a thin smile came to his lips.

"I know that such a threat means little to a Reservist who is doing his duty to his nation by serving. It means everything to a Regular whose entire career can be blighted. But for those of you who are Reserves I want to assure you that the Navy has some God-awful duty stations, and if you fail to do your duty on *Mako* you may well find yourself tending weather instruments on the northern slopes of Alaska!

"There is one more thing I want to say. It will be the only time this matter is discussed after this moment.

"I do not sit in judgment on Captain Hinman. I know him. I knew his late wife. I respect her memory. I respect Captain Hinman. I will brook no comparisons, favorable or insidious, about how Captain Hinman handled *Mako* or her crew and how I will handle my responsibilities. I was given command of this submarine to seek out the enemy and sink him and by God—mine and yours, Mr. Cohen—I am going to do that!

"I would like to see Mr. Cohen for a very few moments. Thank all of you for coming by."

Captain Mealey looked at Nate Cohen. He touched his white mustache tentatively.

"Mr. Cohen, I want to make several things clear to you, sir.

"One thing is that I have a deep respect for all religions, no matter what their ideology or their method of worship.

"Another is that you have served with distinction on two war patrols. You have the right to ask for a more responsible assignment than Commissary Officer and Radio and Sound Officer. In the case of this ship that would mean that I would have to ask for your transfer so you can be given a more responsible assignment. I hope you do not make that request. I am selfish, Mr. Cohen. I want the best officers and men I can get and your abilities as a Sonar Officer seem to be outstanding." He leaned back in his chair and stared at Nathan Cohen.

"I do not intend to ask for a transfer, Captain," Cohen said slowly. "I am not an experienced man at sea but I like this ship, I like the men aboard. If you wish me to stay aboard I will be very happy to do so."

"Thank you," Captain Mealey said. Cohen got up and went out of the Wardroom and stopped in the passageway as Pete Simms came up to the green curtain and rapped softly. He went into the Wardroom in response to Captain Mealey's order.

"Sir," Simms said, "I have a personal request."

"I'll hear it," Mealey said.

"As you know, I am responsible for the engineering plant. I'd like to have permission to stay aboard for the rest of the overhaul period, live aboard, sir, so I can oversee the repairs and other work we requested."

"I understand you're married, live ashore with your wife and daughter, is that right?" Mealey's face was impassive.

"Yes, sir."

"Request denied," Captain Mealey said. "Please ask the Chief Petty Officers to come in as you leave."

"I am impressed," Captain Mealey said after the Chiefs had taken seats at the Wardroom table. "I am very impressed by the extraordinary condition of the machinery of this ship. You have had no breakdowns, your repair list was very small, the ship is very clean." He brushed the right side of his mustache with his finger.

"I expected that Chief Hendershot's department would be in excellent shape; we served together once before. I am most impressed with the engine rooms, Chief Barber."

"They gave us good material, sir," Barber said. "We made sure it was installed right and we take care of it. Hendershot and I work together pretty closely on our gear, so much of it is an overlap. We do all the repairs we can ourselves. I'd rather do the repair work that way, then I know it's done right."

Mealey nodded and looked at John Maxwell, the Chief Yeoman.

"Your office records are excellent, Chief. Unusual in a ship of this sort. I note, also, that you served in the Marine Corps for what, eight years?"

"Yes, sir," Maxwell said.

"You were decorated for gallantry in action in Haiti?"

"Yes, sir," Maxwell said.

"Why did you leave the Corps? You had a good record."

"I got tired of field rations, Gunnery Sergeants and getting shot at in peacetime, Captain. After I got paid off at the end of my second hitch I made a liberty with a Chief Yeoman who worked in the recruiting office in Washington. D.C., sir. He talked me into shipping into the Navy. I'm not sorry. I like the Navy. I like my work. I like this ship."

Mealey nodded. "I have one more thing to say. I run a tight ship. I expect my Chief Petty Officers to keep the ship taut, to make it unnecessary for me to step in.

"I will back you to the hilt in front of your men until you show me you are not worth such support. If that time comes and I do not expect it to come at all on this ship, but if it does, I will put you ashore. Thank you for giving up a morning of your rest period. I'd like to see Chief Rhodes alone for a few moments. If one of you has given him a ride here or if you have driven over with him, it will take only a few minutes." He waited for the three Chiefs to file out and then turned to Dusty Rhodes.

"I saw you box in the ring a number of times when we were both a bit younger, Chief. Is that how you maintain discipline on the *Mako,* with your fists?"

"No, sir," Rhodes' voice was level.

"How, then?"

"By doing as I was taught to do by Chiefs of the Boat I respected, sir. You and the Executive Officer give me your policy, your orders. I carry them out. The crew carries them out. If I can't handle a man, if I decide I can't handle him, sir, then I'll come to the Executive Officer and ask for his transfer. Or mine."

Captain Mealey nodded briefly, his face impassive. His finger crept up and touched his mustache.

"I've read the patrol report on what you did to the torpedoes, Chief. Can you add anything to that report?"

"No, sir. Captain Hinman told the exact truth, exactly what Ginty and I did to the exploders."

"This man Arnold Ginty," Mealey said. "I understand that he's what some people might call a character, that he has a huge blue eye tattooed on the top of his head! Is that true?"

"Yes, sir. When he reported aboard from an S-Boat in the Asiatic Fleet, that was pre-commissioning, sir, I ordered him to let his hair grow. He let his hair grow but Ginty hasn't got a very thick head of hair and sometimes, if he's sitting down and someone is standing over him they can see the tattoo through the hair."

"He got that tattoo on the Asiatic Station?"

"Yes, sir, but I'd like to say this. Ginty is one of the best torpedomen I've ever seen, sir. He runs a torpedo room as I think you want it run. A lot of people live in that Forward Room, as you know, sir. You won't ever find a piece of clothing adrift, a scrap of paper on the deck or a speck in the washbowl. He takes care of the torpedoes the same way. I don't know of a better man for the job. I think he should be judged on his ability, not on some foolishness he did years ago in Shanghai."

"Hong Kong," Captain Mealey said softly. He looked away and then back at Rhodes.

"Mrs. Simms," he said, very softly. "Is she still at your house, Chief?"

"No, sir. My wife took her home yesterday afternoon."

"Is she marked up in any way, marked so she can't appear in public?"

"I can't answer that, sir. I can say that her face is not marked. My wife said there are some bruises on her body," Rhodes' strong face was working, his eyes troubled.

"With all due respect, sir, this is something I have no business talking about!"

"Mary Simms is the wife of a Naval officer," Captain Mealey said quietly. "An officer under my command. She turned to the wife of an enlisted man for help in a marital crisis. There must have been a reason for her doing that rather than turning to another officer's wife. You must know that reason, Chief. My point is that you do know about this business, as you call it. I want to know what you know if you will tell me."

Rhodes sat silent for a moment. "Sir," he began, "there is a reason for Mrs. Simms' turning to my wife. Captain Hinman's wife is dead. If she were alive I know Mrs. Simms would have gone to Marie Hinman. Mr. Brannon is detached. June, my wife, is well known for her ability to solve problems for the enlisted men's wives and their girl friends. It's something she is very good at. I'm sure if Mr. Brannon had been aboard that Mrs. Simms would have gone to Mrs. Brannon."

"Mary Simms did need help, then?" Joe Sirocco spoke for the first time.

"I have no personal knowledge of Mrs. Simms' affairs, Mr. Sirocco, again, with respect, sir. If someone puts their confidence in my wife she doesn't violate that confidence, not even to me." Rhodes' voice was stubborn, his face set in grim lines. "I'm sure that some of the officers aboard would be a better source of information, sir."

"That may be true, Chief," Sirocco's voice was matter-of-fact, his heavy face almost devoid of expression. "But Mrs. Simms did not seek out an officer's wife, she turned to your wife. Which, I think, is admirable. It must be wonderful to know someone to whom you can turn when in trouble.

"My point is that we, as the Executive Officer of this ship and as the Chief of the Boat, might have a problem with Mr. Simms. If Mr. Simms is a troubled man, it could mean some problems for Chief Barber and his Black Gang, it could mean some problems for you as the Chief of the Boat. Do you see my point?"

"I do, sir. If the time comes when I feel that I have to talk about Mr. Simms or any other officer, sir, I'll come to you. I have no sign at this time that there is any problem with Mr. Simms and Chief Barber or Chief Hendershot or anyone else aboard."

"Thank you, Chief," Captain Mealey said. "One more thing, if you will.

"You disobeyed a direct BuOrd regulation when you modified those Mark Six exploders. Captain Hinman, who always has been an excellent shot with torpedoes, had astounding success with his torpedoes. It is my information that those exploders you turned in have been returned to their original condition, that the exploders we are getting for our torpedoes will be in the same condition. Is that your information?"

"Yes, sir, it is. Chief Warrant Haines of the exploder shop already told me that he had been ordered to do that."

"That means they won't work?"

"I would say that, sir."

"We have to make them work properly, Chief," Captain Mealey said. "Do I make myself clear?"

"Yes, sir. They can be made to work."

"That's all, Chief. Thank you. Thank you very much!"

After Chief Rhodes left Mealey looked at Sirocco.

"He's close-mouthed and very damned correct, Joe. I like that. He should be an officer; he handles himself better than most of the recent Academy graduates."

"I've heard he's one hell of a good man," Sirocco said. "I heard the same thing about Barber. We threw Rhodes a couple of wicked curves but he didn't bite once, just let them go by. What I'd like is to meet that man's wife. She must be an extraordinary woman, don't you think?"

"I asked Bob Rudd about her," Mealey said. "Bob said she's some sort of a mystic. She's of Island stock, very beautiful as so many of those women are. He also told me that Admiral Nimitz and his wife are very fond of Mrs. Rhodes." He stood up and stretched and smoothed his mustache.

"Not that that should make a difference—but it does."

Walking up the pier toward where John Barber was waiting Rhodes thought about the two officers and the interview. He couldn't figure out Joe Sirocco; he'd always had trouble figuring out civilians—they thought differently than Navy people.

Captain Mealey was no problem. He'd served with officers who lived by the Book before. You followed the Book and everything went fine. He wondered what Mealey's weaknesses were. He'd have to ask Hendershot about him—Hindu had served under him. He recalled Mealey's habit of touching the right side of his mustache. Once, when the Captain's finger had touched the hairs a little harder than usual, Rhodes had thought he detected a scar there. Did he have a harelip? No, the Navy wouldn't take a man into the Academy with a deformity like that.

Maybe the Captain's habit of constantly touching his mustache was vanity. The fit of his uniform, the knife-edge creases in the heavily starched khaki were a sign of a man with a great deal of pride in his appearance.

Then there was the obvious rapport between Captain Mealey, an Academy graduate known for his toughness, and Joe Sirocco, who was a Reserve. Why did they get along so well? Sirocco's role in questioning without interference from Mealey had startled Rhodes. He raised a hand as he saw Barber wheel his car toward him.

There was another thing he'd better check on; it was obvious that Captain Mealey had access to a lot of information. He knew too much about Pete and Mary Simms, too much for a new Captain to know about. He knew too much about June Rhodes.

CHAPTER 13

"The Secretary of War, that's Henry Stimson, decided the Army should share in some of the glory," Ben Butler said as he and Hinman walked toward a car that flew a two-star General's flag from its fender. "Stimson said that once the Navy got you here to Los Angeles, the Army would fly you on the tour. They're giving you a Dakota, they also call it a DC-3, for the tour. It's fixed up for a General to fly and work in, got bunks, an office, a little kitchen, the works."

"Things move too fast, Ben," Hinman said. "I don't even know which cities I'm going to go to, how long this whole thing is going to last. Do you?"

"Nope," Butler said cheerfully. "I only thought of the idea. I know you'll be going to Washington because we see The Man there. I know you're going to New York and Chicago and back here to the West Coast to L.A. and 'Frisco and some aircraft factories. But the President's people worked out the rest of the schedule."

"I suppose they'd know where the best places to sell war bonds would be," Hinman said thoughtfully.

"They know that and they also know where the President needs to pick up some votes when he runs again in two years, if he does and I'm sure he will. That man Willkie scared him, you know, two years ago. Willkie got a bigger popular vote than FDR did. The Old Man has been mending fences ever since." He returned the salute of an Army Sergeant who was standing at the rear door of the car.

"Your luggage is being collected, sir," the Sergeant said. "As soon as the Corporal gets it here I'll take you to your aircraft. They're waiting for you."

"It comes down to politics, doesn't it," Hinman said.

"You say that word like it was something dirty," Ben Butler said. "You shouldn't. Politics isn't a dirty word, it isn't a dirty profession. Some of the people who practice it are bastards, I'll admit that. Maybe most of them. You have to remember one axiom, 'Politics is the art of the possible.' In the military service you can order a man to do something he doesn't want to do and he has to do it or be punished. Can't do that in many places in civilian life. Hard to do it at all in government. So you politic, you do what is possible. FDR is a politician. He had to see this tour as a chance for him to shore up some weak areas in his vote-getting powers. Don't let it worry you. Now here's what I got when we arrived, the instructions that were waiting for me.

"You'll see the President tomorrow morning at the White House and have a private talk with him. Then he'll hold a full dress press conference and introduce you to the newsreel cameras, the radio networks, the newspaper reporters and the rest of the world. Don't get upset if one or two reporters take some heavy shots at the Old Man. He may be your Commander-in-Chief and mine but to reporters he's just a politician who won the biggest race. He knows how to handle those people, you don't. So while we're on the plane I'll give you some pointers.

"Lieut. Joan Richards, the WAVE, will meet us after the press conference. I sent her copies of the speeches I wrote for you and she'll probably have nasty things to say about the way I write."

"You wrote speeches for me? When?"

"When you were on your way back to Pearl," Butler said. "I

wrote ten speeches. Bob Rudd went over each one and corrected the technical mistakes I made about submarines. I made quite a few of those," he grinned.

"All of the speeches say the same thing, basically. Some are tailored for wealthy business groups, some for Veterans' organizations, that sort of thing.

"We'll be in Washington tomorrow and after that's over I leave you. Joan will go with you to New York and you'll get the key to the city or some other damn fool thing and make two speeches there and hold press conferences. Then you go to Chicago and the Mayor is going to roll out the red carpet. Motorcade from the airport, parade up State Street and two speeches there with press conferences afterward. You'll be staying in the Palmer House. I think it's got the best food in the city. I don't know the rest of the itinerary; Joan will have that. All I know is that you wind up talking to workers in aircraft factories."

"What the hell does a submariner say to people who make aircraft?" Hinman grumbled.

"You inspire them," Butler said, smiling. "You tell them that if they turn out good planes for the war in the air you'll do your part by winning the war underseas."

"Oh, bullshit!" Hinman said.

"Agreed," Butler said. "But that's what the people want to hear, what they need to hear. It may turn your stomach but I know that it will make a lot of people happy and it will raise money. Wars run on money just as much as they do on oil, maybe more so."

The Dakota's crew met Hinman and Butler as they walked to the steep little stairs that had been let down from the side of the plane. A young Army Air Force Captain with a smudge of new mustache on his upper lip stepped forward.

"I'm Captain Fredericks, sir. This is First Lieutenant Daniels, my co-pilot, and Master Sergeant Broker, our engineer. We're honored to have you aboard, sir." He grinned, showing a little-boy gap between his two upper front teeth.

"You'll forgive me, sir, but you look awfully young to be the C.O. of a big submarine."

"You look too young to fly this aircraft," Hinman replied.

"Tricks to all trades, I guess," Captain Fredericks said cheerfully. "As soon as your luggage is aboard we'll leave. We'll be making two fueling stops on the way to Washington. Our ETA is zero eight hundred tomorrow, sir."

Walking up the sidewalk toward the White House steps Butler tugged gently at Hinman's sleeve.

"Don't look, don't stare at his legs," he whispered. "Just keep looking at his face."

"What are you talking about?" Hinman said.

"The President is crippled. I guess a lot of people don't know that. He had polio when he was thirty-nine, about twenty years ago. The reporters never mention it, the photographers never take pictures of his legs or his wheel chair."

A Navy Lieutenant with a gold aiguillette draped from his shoulder met them at the door of the White House and escorted them down a long hall past the grand staircase and to the President's office. As they walked down the hall of the old building, Hinman could feel the aura of power that seemed to be everywhere. He marched into the President's office and stood at attention in front of a massive desk that had a small American flag on one corner and the Commander-in-Chief's flag on the other.

The face of the man sitting in back of the desk was familiar, he had seen it scores of times in newsreels, magazines and newspapers. The massive head looked larger in real life than it did in the pictures and the heavy shoulders beneath the fabric of the blue suit bulged the cloth. The President's eyes were clear behind his rimless glasses and his cigaret holder was cocked at a rakish angle in his wide mouth. He stretched a hand across the desk and Hinman, responding to Butler's nudge, stretched his own hand across the desk and was surprised at the iron grip of the older man's fingers.

"Welcome, gentlemen," the President said in his sonorous, rolling tones. Ben Butler smiled. The Old Man was giving them the full treatment, using the measured cadences he used in press conferences and in his fireside chats on radio.

"I am particularly pleased to meet you, Captain Hinman. As for

Ben, well, one cherishes old and honored adversaries." He waved a big hand spotted with the brown marks of advancing age at two chairs that stood against a wall. He propelled his wheel chair from behind his desk and rolled to a stop in front of the chairs. A sudden upward jerk of the cigaret holder clamped in his mouth brought his Naval aide to his side.

"Coffee for all of us, if you will, sir." He swiveled the chair slightly to face Hinman. "Now, Captain, tell me about this running sea battle you waged against the Japanese destroyers and the oil tankers they were guarding. From what Ben wrote me it appears that you used your submarine in a most unorthodox manner." The massive head lifted and Hinman saw that the President's eyes were not focused on him but on something very far away.

"I was an Assistant Secretary of the Navy, you know." The President's voice was soft. "In 'Thirteen, Nineteen-Thirteen under President Wilson. Before this." His big right hand gently touched one of his withered thighs. He straightened in his chair and his eyes focused on Captain Hinman.

"Tell me, Captain, about your action in your own words. I understand ship-handling terminology." He listened intently as Hinman spoke and when he had finished he leaned back in his wheel chair, his clear eyes studying Hinman.

"It is an axiom, Captain," the President said, "it is an axiom that generals always fight the war they find themselves in with the tactics of the last war they fought. The French Maginot Line is a perfect example of World War One thinking. The French generals assumed the Germans would attack frontally. They did not, they outflanked the Maginot Line and left it, a monument to outdated strategy!" He paused and eyed Hinman.

"Would you say, sir, that our Admirals have built a Maginot Line of sorts in their orders to submarine commanders on how to fight this war?"

Hinman felt rather than saw Butler's sudden tension. "I cannot say that, sir," he said. "I can say that none of us, high command or submarine commander, has ever fought a submarine war. My reasoning, sir, is that you have to feel your way, to find tactics that will work. Then you analyze those tactics and use what is good. When I was an Executive Officer in peacetime I had a Captain who thought that way. After we had gone through a battle exercise we'd sit down and try to figure out how we could have done it better.

"One of the things we always talked about was the feasibility of a night surface attack. We were never allowed to use that tactic then, we are forbidden to use it now."

"So you took it upon yourself to disobey orders?"

"I did, sir." Hinman realized that he was making an effort to face the magnetic eyes of President Roosevelt, to resist the feeling of immense power that radiated from the man in the wheel chair.

"By Heaven, I'm glad you did!" The President's meaty hand slapped the arm of his chair. "Not only did you sink ships, you have also upset some of the old fogies who run our Navy!" He reached for his coffee cup and eyed Hinman from over its rim.

"Do you know about the Graf Spee, Captain?"

"The German pocket battleship, sir? I know her Captain was ordered to scuttle his ship rather than take her out to sea to fight a superior British force."

"Would you have obeyed those orders if you had been her commanding officer?" The President's voice was very soft.

"No, sir! I would have gone to sea to fight!"

The President smiled. "Winston told me he would have shot any British Captain who scuttled his ship rather than face the enemy!" The big head canted to one side, the cigaret holder jutting out like the bowsprit of an old sailing man-of-war. "I cannot officially condone your disobedience of orders, Captain, but I can say this to you sir: My mind goes back in history to Commodore Perry at the Battle of Lake Erie, one hundred years before I became an Assistant Secretary of the Navy. Perry sent a message, 'We have met the enemy and they are ours!' That message cheered a beleaguered young nation. In a smaller way the story of your ship action did the same thing. After Pearl Harbor, the loss of the Philippines, we needed something to prove that we are a nation of seafarers, that the enemy can be beaten with determination and courage.

"That's why I agreed to Ben's plan to have you make a tour to not only sell War Bonds but also to let the people who build our weapons see you, to see a man who took his ship among the enemy and destroyed that enemy! Now there is one more item before we finish; Ben wrote a long letter outlining some things he said were of great concern to you, and to other submarine captains."

"Well, sir," Hinman said hesitantly, "one thing is personal; I'd like to go back to sea in command of a submarine.

"What concerns me, all of us, most, is the failure of the Mark Six exploder. Theoretically, this is an ideal weapon. It needs a lot more work, there's a flaw in the design. If the people who designed the exploder would admit that, we'd have a superior weapon." He paused.

"The last thing is, well, delicate. I think that too many of our submarine commanders are too senior in rank."

"Too old?" the President said softly.

"Maybe, sir. I think they're too cautious. I think that we should be using our submarines as offensive weapons, not defensive ships. Until the surface battle fleet is rebuilt the submarines are all we have." He sat back, his face stiff. He'd said it, brought up the deficiencies of age to a man far older than any submarine commander.

"Point number one," the President said calmly. "You can be sure of a submarine command when the bond tour is finished." He looked at his aide. "Make a note of that, sir.

"Point number two. I will let it be known that I am distressed at the nonperformance of the exploder mechanisms. That will make a lot of people uneasy and I am sure the problem will be solved.

"Point three. You are out of order to suggest to your Commander-in-Chief that the wrong men command submarines!" The big face softened and there was a glint in the President's eyes.

"There are many benefits that come with age, sir, as you will someday learn. But I acknowledge that in some areas we need the élan, the arrogance of youth. Your younger men will come to command soon enough; we have a vast program of new submarines to be built." He turned to Butler.

"You have, I trust, instructed the Captain on how a press conference is conducted in the White House?"

"Yes, sir," Butler said. "We will stand behind you and laugh at all your jokes." Butler's face was bland. The President cocked his head to one side, his eyes merry.

"You talk as if you were still a Washington columnist and you were getting ready to criticize me for running for another term."

"Well you are going to do that, aren't you?" Butler said.

"Of course I am!" President Roosevelt's laugh boomed out in the office. "Of course I am! Now let's show our friend to the people who call themselves the Gentlemen of the Fourth Estate."

Captain Hinman barely remembered the details of the chaotic press conference. He was conscious of the big crowd of reporters, of the cluster of large microphones, the intensity of the lights that had been put in place for the newsreel cameramen. He recalled the President's sonorous voice describing the details of *Mako*'s attack on the Japanese oil tankers and destroyers and how proud that he, the President of the United States, was to be able to introduce Captain Hinman to the people of the United States and the world. He remembered best the foolish questions that had been yelled at him.

"What did you think about, Captain, as you steered your small submarine into the enemy battle fleet?"

"Did you see a lot of dead Japs floating in the water?"

"Did you shake your fist and curse the enemy, Captain?"

"Did your crew cheer when they fired the torpedoes at the enemy ships, Captain?"

"What did it feel like, Captain Hinman, to have killed thousands of the enemy?"

He had answered the questions as briefly as he could, gently correcting the idea that he had sailed into the middle of a "battle fleet." He had pointed out that merchant ships and oil tankers carried very small crews and that *Mako*'s action was a tiny piece in a giant jigsaw puzzle and that a submarine captain in battle is far too busy to think about cursing the enemy or shaking his fist, those things were done only in movies.

He recalled the dead silence that had fallen over the crowd when he had said the Japanese Navy was tough, efficient and a deadly fighting force. Then he heard a sardonic voice from the crowd of reporters.

"Is what you are saying, Captain, is that we shouldn't be in this war, that the enemy is too powerful for us? Is what you are saying is that we were sucked into this war by our leaders who are more interested in saving Britain's neck than in taking care of our own people?"

"No," he said carefully, "I am not saying that or anything like that. What I am saying is that I do not underestimate the enemy. The Japanese Navy is formidable. It can be beaten. It will be beaten. But I give my opponent the same respect as I think Joe Louis gives his opponents when he steps in the prize-fighting ring. I do not take the enemy lightly. I respect him. I do not fear him." There had been a spatter of applause at that and then a voice saying, "Thank you, Mr. President," and it was over.

Later, sitting in a hotel suite in downtown Washington, Hinman pulled the knot of his tie downward and undid the top button of his shirt. He reached for a sandwich and a cup of coffee.

"My God, Ben," he said, "I can't take this every day!"

"I don't know why not," Butler said. "You did pretty well."

"Those questions are stupid, Ben! Do I shake my fist at the enemy and curse him! Did I see dead Japs in the water! What the hell do they think a submarine captain does in battle?"

"That's the point, Captain. They don't know what a submarine captain does at any time! I know some questions are stupid. Some reporters are stupid. But sometimes the stupid questions aren't stupid at all, they're designed to make you angry, to get you to say something you don't want to say!

"I think you handled it very well. A little rough around the edges here and there but Joan will smooth those out for you. She ought to be here in a few minutes. We'll go out to dinner after we're through here; she was in the back of the room at the press conference, you know, so she could watch you at work. Before I forget it, you remember that guy who asked you if you thought we were in the war wrongly?"

Hinman nodded.

"You fielded that very well. I liked the reference to Joe Louis. Good copy for the reporters. The guy who asked you that question, incidentally, works for a publisher who thinks that Adolf Hitler's anti-Semitic stand is the best thing that could happen to the world! He'd a lot rather see us on Hitler's side than fighting the Germans.

You're going to get more of this as you go around; not everyone likes this war, as I've told you."

"I don't like the war," Hinman said. "I don't know how anyone could like a war if they've been in it. But the whole Congress of the United States voted to go into this war after the attack on Pearl Harbor!"

"You're wrong," Butler said. "The vote for a declaration of war against Japan was not unanimous in the Congress. One very honest, decent lady from Minnesota, Representative Jeanette Rankin, voted no on the declaration of war.

"And don't forget this: The America First Committee did its best to defeat FDR in the election two years ago, in Nineteen-Forty. They believed that FDR was dragging the United States into the war in Europe by helping England. They almost did beat him, Willkie got a bigger popular vote than FDR did, which of course meant nothing but it scared FDR. Hell, Charles Lindbergh was one of the most effective speakers against the war for the America Firsters!

"There's quite a lot of sentiment against the war and you'll run into it on this tour. Give reasonable answers to unreasonable questions. Never lose your temper. And remember this little slogan my favorite uncle used to use all the time. 'Never get into a pissin' contest with a skunk.' "

Hinman shook his head. "You ought to give seminars at Pearl, Ben. Tell some of our officers what people think about the war. I didn't know some of those things you've told me. Maybe it would help some Academy officers understand our draftees and Reservists. God knows we don't understand them now."

"You can't cram too much education down a naval officer's throat," Butler said cheerfully. "I told Captain Severn once, at a staff meeting, that in thirteenth-century India, according to Marco Polo's diaries, a sailor was not allowed to testify in any legal matter or even to be a guarantor of anything because at that time it was believed that a man who went to sea was a man in despair!"

"I'll bet Captain Severn loved that!" Hinman said.

"He asked me what Fleet this Marco whoever-he-was had commanded and what did that have to do with winning the war against Japan? I had to admit, not much. Hasn't got anything to do with our situation either except I thought it would amuse you. Just don't forget you're going to run into some bastards but Joan Richards will be able to brief you on most of them. I think that's her timid knock on the door," he got out of his chair as the room door rattled under a second firm knock.

Hinman got to his feet, buttoning his shirt collar and cinching up his tie as Lieut. (jg) Joan Richards, WAVES, entered the room. He looked away politely as Joan kissed Ben Butler solidly and affectionately.

"Ben, you old bastard! You outrank me!" She turned to Captain Hinman. "Editors of newspapers always pull rank on people who work in public relations and he's done that to me for years and now he's got two-and-a-half stripes to my one-and-a-half and he's done it again! You're Capt. Arthur Hinman and I'm glad to meet you."

Hinman looked at Joan Richards. The WAVES uniform, designed in haste for the women who volunteered for service in the Navy, tried but didn't hide the fact that Joan Richards was a woman. His eyes went from her small feet, encased in black uniform shoes, up past her slim legs and her flaring hips that nipped in to a small waist and then the deep bosom and above it a pert face with deep blue eyes and blue-black, curly hair. *The woman vibrates,* he thought to himself, *she makes the whole room vibrate!*

"Sit down, sit down," Butler said. "Have a cup of coffee. There's a couple of sandwiches left; we didn't get a lunch. We'll go out for dinner later. How the hell are you, Joan?"

"Full of fascinating information," she said. She sat down and poured herself a cup of coffee. "The Navy is a funny place, Ben. They put us in a barracks that had been built for men. It had urinals in the toilets, those waist-high things? So one of the girls filled the urinals with dirt and planted some flowers in them. When the Captain came around on his first inspection he almost had a heart attack! He didn't know what to stay so he just stomped out so mad he could spit!" She grinned, her dark blue eyes dancing in merriment.

"And I'm absolutely up to the minute on venereal disease! They gave us lectures with motion pictures. Very graphic. Showed close-up pictures of how a man can tell if he's got the clap. You should have heard some of the girls moan! I think they would have liked to date the man who was the model even if he did have the dirty old VD! Look at Captain Hinman! He's blushing!"

"I am not!" he spluttered. "It's hot in here!"

"Indeed it is," she said, and took off her uniform jacket. The white fabric of her severely cut shirtwaist strained and threatened to burst as she turned and flung the jacket on the couch and Hinman felt a tightening in his groin.

"Don't mind me, Captain," she said. "I've been talking to editors like Ben here for so long I've forgotten how to talk like a lady, not that I ever was one. Is there any more coffee?"

"A ship's captain, Joan," Butler said, filling her cup, "usually reads the service record of a new person who comes aboard his ship to acquaint himself with the person's abilities, marital status, age, things like that. Captain Hinman is now your boss so why don't you fill him in on your background?"

"Fine," she said. She pulled a package of cigarets out of her black Navy purse and lit one.

"Joan Esther Richards. Age, thirty-four years. Height, five-feet-two inches. Weight, one hundred twenty-five pounds. Condition of health, perfect. Father was Irish, mother Spanish. Temperament, said by some to be explosive. I think I'm rather sweet, myself.

"Marital status, divorced. No children. Married when I was twenty-one to a boy of twenty-three who was still a boy of twenty-three two years later. He showed no signs of growing into a man. I had become a woman, an adult. So I divorced him. No romantic interests at this time.

"Professional background: I went into advertising at the age of twenty-one as a secretary. Worked my way up to assistant copy writer, to copy writer, to assistant account executive, the first woman in my agency to hold that position and finally to head of public relations for the agency. Joined the Navy because most of the men in my agency were asking for special deferments to keep from being drafted. So far I'm not sorry. What else, Ben?"

"You left out that you're honest, capable, hard-nosed and very humble," Butler said. "But not bad to look at, not bad."

"Ben wanted me to marry him, years ago," she said, turning to Hinman. "I refused. He's just too damned bright to talk to at breakfast every morning. You don't have to return the courtesy of telling me about yourself, Captain. I nosed around in the Navy Department the other day. I think I like you."

"So far I think I like you," Hinman said. "But I have to say that gallantry is not my strong suit."

"Good. Phoniness isn't something I admire," she said. "Now should we get down to work?" She opened a briefcase she had brought with her and took out a large ring notebook.

"Your itinerary is on the front page, sir. The advance work has been done on all the stops up to and through Houston. I can do the rest of it while we're on the first half of the tour. The schedule of appearances and speeches follows the itinerary. With very few exceptions I can tell you in advance who the bastards are. Ben has told me all about what he wants done in that area.

"I've gone over the speeches you wrote, Ben. There's a couple of things I want to change in the speeches aimed directly at the women's groups he'll be talking to but we can talk about that." She gave the book to Captain Hinman, who leafed through it.

"It seems to me to be something like a circus," he said slowly. "You provide the elephant and I ride on it and smile and wave my hand and make a speech whenever you press my button."

"It isn't a circus," Joan said. "There is no elephant and no one is going to make you say anything you think is wrong. You are scheduled to make twenty-five speeches, sir. I could book you into a hundred and twenty-five without half trying! The people want to see you. They want to hear you. You have to understand that! All I'm here for is to try to make sure you don't put your foot in your mouth and fall on your ass!"

Hinman looked at her, his hard face beginning to break into a smile.

"I believe you can do that, Lieutenant. I do believe you can do that. Now what do you want me to do now, next?"

"Read that first speech," she said crisply. "There isn't one person in a hundred who knows how to read a speech to a live audience. Ben has done a marvelous job with these talks so get up on your feet, sir, and show me how you read. Let me give you one tip, if you don't mind. An audience is made up of individual people so when you stand up there in front of a sea of faces remember that and talk to someone in the second row for a few minutes and then go back a few rows, maybe shift over to the other side of the group and talk to someone there. Keep doing that every few minutes. It makes it easier for you and it establishes a rapport with the people who are out there listening to you."

"This isn't going to be as easy as I thought it would be, Ben," Hinman said. He held the notebook in his two hands, balancing his weight on the balls of his feet.

"It's easy now," Butler said. "Wait until you goof in public and afterward our sweet-tempered angel here gets you alone where no one else can see or here and reads you off like a longshoreman and then throws her earrings at you. She's famous for that."

"The Navy won't let us wear earrings, Ben dear. I'll throw my shoes at him!"

"As long as it isn't your lingerie," Butler said.

"That's a bad idea? Look, Ben, our submarine captain is blushing again!"

CHAPTER 14

Mako eased slowly away from the pier, her screws making a bubbling swirl in the oily water of the Loch. Chief John Barber stuck his head up out of the After Engine Room hatch and waved at his wife and daughter on the pier and then his head disappeared and the heavy black hatch cover came down, its hand wheel whirling as Barber secured the hatch for sea.

Spook Hernandez stood apart from the families of *Mako*'s crew who had been invited to watch the ship leave on its third war patrol. The blindness brought on by the wood alcohol had passed after four days of hospital treatment. On his right sleeve he wore the insignia of a Second Class Torpedoman. The court-martial Captain Mealey had called for had reduced him one grade in rank, fined him three months' pay and, acting on Captain Mealey's harsh demand, had disqualified him for all further submarine service. The reduction in rating didn't bother Hernandez greatly, he had been broken in rank before and won it back. The disqualification for submarine duty was what made his bile rise in his throat. It meant that he now could serve only on destroyers, a ship he hated, or work in a torpedo shop at a Naval Base.

"Fucking near twenty years in the Boats down the drain, you white-mustached son of a bitch!" he muttered to himself as he watched Captain Mealey ease the big submarine away from the pier and turned the ship for its passage down the Southeast Loch and through the harbor. "I hope the fucking Jap sinks you!" He turned away and walked by June Rhodes and her two sons, who were watching *Mako* leave.

Chief Rhodes walked to the after deck of the Mako as the ship completed its turn and raised his hand to his family. Then he went about his duties, checking each deck hatch to make sure it was secured, leaning his weight on the handles of the ammunition lockers that were built into the Conning Tower, checking the two squat 5.25 deck guns to make sure their barrels were tightly secured in the stands. Both guns were built of stainless steel so no clumsy breech and muzzle covers were needed. Satisfied, he asked for permission to leave the deck and go below. He climbed up on the cigaret deck and went below to begin his rounds of checking everything below decks. When he had finished he drew a cup of coffee from the urn in the Crew's Mess and sat down at a mess table beside John Barber.

"How's Simms?" Rhodes asked in a low voice.

"He's like he always is," Barber said. "I don't see any changes. I didn't like the bastard before, I don't like him now. Like to drove me crazy last three days with do this and do that and do it yesterday. Dottie tells me he wasn't at home last eleven, twelve days of the rest period. Where was he, aboard?"

"At the BOQ," Rhodes said. "Nate Cohen told me that when we went to the ship to meet Captain Mealey, after the other officers had left Simms asked for permission to live aboard, to supervise the overhaul. The Old Man asked him if his family was here on the Base or in town and when he said yes the Old Man cut him off at the knees, told him no. I guess he checked in at the BOQ that day."

"One of these days Hendershot is going to brain that simple bastard," Barber said morosely. "If I don't do it first! He treats us as if we don't know anything. Hell, Hendershot has forgot more about a submarine than Simms will ever know! That ol' Kentucky boy is gettin' hot as hell under the collar. He's gonna read off Simms one of these days and we both know the Old Man won't stand for that."

Rhodes nodded. "I'll speak to Hindu. You hear where we're going on this patrol? I asked Grilley but he said only the Old Man and the Exec. know but that he thinks the Old Man will give the officers the word after we get clear of the net at the harbor entrance. Hinman used to tell us before we got away from the pier."

"Nope," Barber said. "I don't know. I don't worry about stuff like that. Wherever we go I ain't gonna see it from those engine rooms. All I worry about when we start a run is will the damned torpedoes work right."

"The fish will run good," Rhodes said. "Ginty and the new guy in the After Room, DeLucia, and I went up to the Torpedo Shop and did the finals on each fish ourselves. And the Old Man has given me the word to modify the exploders again."

"No shit!" Barber said. "He told you that?"

Rhodes nodded and sipped his coffee.

"He told me he wants to be there to help Ginty and me when we modify the exploders," he said. "From what he said he knows a little something about torpedoes and exploder mechanisms."

"He knows engines," Barber said. "He came back to the engine room when I was fine-tuning the fuel injectors and he sure as hell knew what questions to ask and I sure as hell knew I'd better give him straight answers. I like to go to sea with a man like that."

"So do I," Rhodes answered. "Most of the crew isn't too happy. Cutting off liberty the last three days for all but the married guys didn't sit too well. They figure he's a hard-ass."

"Don't make a shit to me what they think," Barber said. "All I want is for him to get me home safe. Getting so it's harder and harder to go off and leave Dottie and the kid. Must be a sign that I'm gettin' old or something."

The destroyer that had led *Mako* through the harbor net and out to sea whooped its whistle three times and turned away and *Mako*'s crew settled down to the boring routine of running down the long sea miles to the patrol area. Captain Mealey sent Joe Sirocco to the bridge to take over the deck and summoned the officers to the Wardroom.

"Joe has read our patrol orders," he said. "I want you to know where we're going this trip." He touched the right side of his white mustache with his finger.

"We've got a good patrol area, one that should give us a lot of targets. It's south of Luzon, on the shipping lanes out of the harbor at Manila. We'll run on the surface as long as we can on the way out. I am going to hold drills, a lot of emergency drills on the way out. This crew and all of you have to be letter-perfect in everything. We'll hold deck gun firing drills beginning the day after tomorrow. Chief Rhodes fixed up some small kegs with flags on them for targets."

"Are you going to attack on the surface with the deck guns, Captain?" Lieutenant Simms was grinning. "Hell, I'd like to pick a boarding party from the crew, sir. We could board and destroy the way the old Navy did it!"

Captain Mealey stared at his Engineering Officer. "If I contemplate boarding an enemy ship, Mr. Simms, I will pick the men to board." He stood up. "You have my permission to tell our patrol area to your people."

Lieutenant Grilley found Chief Rhodes and sent him to the Forward Torpedo Room to tell the people up there where *Mako* was going and went aft to talk to the people in the After Room himself. He met Rhodes in the Crew's Mess.

"Sounds like a good area, Chief. People up forward happy?"

"Reasonably, sir. They're still hot about no liberty the last three days but they'll get over that. Ginty is worried about if the Japs have closed the bars in Manila."

Lieutenant Simms yelled his information about the patrol area to the men on watch in each Engine Room and then went back to the Maneuvering Room to give the word to Chief Hendershot and his people. When he had finished he stood, leaning negligently against the door of the head. Chief Hendershot was sitting on the padded bench in front of the control console.

"The Old Man is thinking about forming a boarding party to take smaller ships, stuff too small to waste a torpedo on," he said with a grin. "He wants me to lead the boarding party, take the prize at cutlass point!"

"Didn't know we had any of those aboard," Hendershot said. "I think we got six old bayonets around. Could use them I guess. They won't fit the rifles but we could carry 'em."

"Officers have swords," Simms said. "I've got mine with me. It was my graduation gift from the Academy; my father paid over two hundred dollars for it. Beautiful piece of steel—you can shave with it."

"Kinda hard to do that in that small stateroom you people live in, isn't it?" Hendershot's mouth was smiling but his eyes were wary.

"Your sense of humor went out of style in the Depression, Chief," Simms said. "What we should do with this submarine is to take out the tubes in the After Room and the rest of the gear back there and cut the hull so it could be opened up like a clamshell. Then we could keep a PT boat back there, flood down, launch the PT boat and really raise hell with the enemy! Excuse me, I've got to use the head." He opened the door to the tiny toilet and backed in and closed the door. He came out in a few minutes and went forward. Hendershot went over and opened the door to the head and turned back, his face dark with anger.

"You!" he said to one of his gang. "Get a bucket and a brush and clean that fucking toilet bowl. That bastard's got a revolving nozzle for an asshole! Sprays the whole damned bowl! Fucker has got a head of his own in the Forward Room and a guy to clean it. Why in the hell does he have to use our head?"

He asked the same question of Dusty Rhodes as the two men sat in the Chief's Quarters, next to the Captain's stateroom, his voice low but vibrating with anger.

"I don't know of any regulations says he has to use the head in the Forward Room," Rhodes said slowly. "The man on watch at the torpedo tubes in the Forward Room can use the Officers' head up there if he has to piss and there's no one to relieve him. About all I can do is to tell you to grin and bear it. Maybe he won't do it again."

"Shit!" Hendershot rasped. "He did it every fucking day on both the other patrol runs! He'd come back there and shoot the shit with the guy on watch at the board and then he'd go in our head and spray that damned bowl with his crap! I don't like cleanin' heads, neither do you. We've both cleaned enough of them in our time. I'm gonna think of something."

"Think twice when you do," Rhodes said crisply. "You know this Old Man, you served with him. Don't put your head in the meat grinder. He's nobody to fuck with, this Old Man."

"Oh, shit, I know him," Hendershot said. "He's always been a hard rock. But he's tougher now than he used to be. Used to be he'd hit you with the Book if you fucked up but he didn't use to disqualify anyone like he did Spook. That was a hell of a belt for getting drunk. It was enough the silly bastard got the shit scared out of him, blind for four days."

"It was where he got drunk," Rhodes said. "He got drunk aboard and Barney killed himself on that drunk. The Old Man could have given him a General instead of a Summary Court."

"It was still a hell of a belt," Hendershot insisted. "I didn't hear about anyone trying to help Spook out at the trial."

"Grilley tried, he tried real hard," Rhodes said. "Nate Cohen volunteered to give testimony about Spook's character and they heard him and said thank you."

Hendershot looked at Rhodes. "You know that; you must have been there."

"I was," Rhodes said. "Captain asked me to give my opinion of Spook's ability. I gave him a good send-off, said I'd go back to sea with him any time."

"Old Man asked you to do that? Well, that was fair. But that's the way he is, hard son of a bitch, but pretty square. He was that way when I was with him in Panama. Another thing you better know about this dude. He knows the gear aboard. Knows my stuff fuckin' near as good as I do. I've been with hard-asses before who didn't know nothin'! Acted hard to cover up. This dude acts hard because that's the way he is, hard."

It took Hendershot two days to perfect his plan and when he was ready to carry it out he turned to the man who was on watch with him at the control console.

"Go up forward and draw me a cup of coffee, black. Take ten minutes before you come back. I got some things to do I don't want you to know about. What you don't know about you don't have to lie about." The man nodded and left and Hendershot busied himself in the small head.

The head in the Maneuvering Room was built into the after port corner of the compartment. The head floor was covered with a thick layer of linoleum and the bow of the toilet itself was made of bronze so it wouldn't shatter under a depth charge attack. A small metal foot rest was fastened to the deck in front of the bronze bowl. The entire head was so small that to use it a man had to back in, sit down and then close and latch the Monel metal door.

Lieutenant Simms appeared the next day on schedule. He talked in grandiose terms about his plan to turn the After Torpedo Room into a PT boat berth. Hendershot, lounging on the padded bench in front of the control console, nodded.

"Been thinkin' on that idea, Mr. Simms. Sounded crazy to me at first but now it doesn't sound so crazy. Like you say, all we'd have to do is flood down a little aft, open the clam shell with hydraulic power and the PT boat could get under way."

"I can see myself at the helm, roaring into a Jap harbor!" Simms said, his eyes glittering. "Four torpedoes in the deck tubes, all set to go! Machine guns manned! We could be among the ships in the harbor like a wolf in a herd of sheep!"

"Sure as hell would scare the Japs shitless," Hendershot said. "Scare me shitless, too, waitin' here for you to get back!"

"I'd get back!" Simms said, arching his broad chest. "When I played fullback at the Academy, I was all-conference, did you know that? When I played football and we had to have two yards the little quarterback we had would look at me in the huddle and say 'Pete, I don't know how you're going to do it but we need those two yards. You call the play.' And I'd get the two yards! Every time! When I set my mind to do something I always do it! Excuse me, I'll use the head."

He backed into the head and closed the door. Hendershot cocked his head toward the closed door. He heard the steady drum of urine into the bowl and he reached down and closed a small knife switch that lay back of the padded locker on which he sat.

A wild scream burst from the head and the door burst outward. Lieutenant Simms, screaming, fell out of the head, both his hands clutching at his genitals.

Hendershot poked his head through the watertight door to the After Torpedo Room.

"Two men! In here! Now!" he yelled and stepped back as two burly torpedomen came through the door.

"Pick Mr. Simms up and get him forward to the Crew's Mess,"

Hendershot ordered. "You!" He turned to the man on watch with him. "Call the auxiliaryman in the Control Room and tell him to get Doc in the Crew's Mess in a hurry."

The two torpedomen grabbed Lieutenant Simms, who was curled into a fetal position on the deck, alternately screaming and moaning. They carried him forward through the two engine rooms and into the Crew's Mess and laid him on a mess table where he curled up tighter and screamed. The Pharmacist's Mate, roused from sleep, rubbed his eyes and looked at him.

"What in the hell is wrong with him, anybody know?"

"Don't know," one of the torpedomen said, trying hard to hide a grin. "All I know is I heard a God-awful scream and then Hendershot yelled for two men to carry him up here. The man is heavy, you know? He didn't say nothin', just yelled a lot."

Johnny Johnson, Ship's Cook First Class, came out of his galley and looked at the officer lying on the mess table.

"If that guy has got the clap or some other good disease get him off'n that table, Doc. People got to eat there in an hour."

"I don't think he's got the clap," Doc Whitten said.

"Then why's he holdin' his cock and balls for?" Johnson asked. "He's probly got a stricture or somethin', can't piss. I had that once on the Asiatic Station. Like to killed me."

"Couple you guys straighten him out and hold his hands so I can see what the fuck is going on," Doc Whitten said. "How come his shorts and skivvies is down around his ankles?"

"He was in the head back aft," one of the torpedomen volunteered. "Takin' a crap, I guess."

"Look at that!" one of the spectators said. "His little old cock is swellin' up and it's turnin' blue! Look at his nuts! Fuckers're gonna be big enough to play basketball with they keep goin' like this!"

Dusty Rhodes' deep growl scattered the people standing around the mess table. Doc Whitten turned to Chief Rhodes.

"Don't ask me what happened, Chief. The guy on watch dragged me out of my bunk and when I got in here they'd laid Lieutenant Simms on the table. He was all curled up in a ball, yelling like hell."

"You wait and see, the man's got the clap, got hisself a stricture, can't piss," the cook said. "Happened once to me on an S-Boat."

"Shut up, Cookie," Rhodes snapped. "Let me sort this thing out. Who brought Mr. Simms up here and why?"

"Me and him," one of the After Room torpedomen said. "We was cleanin' the Bos'n's locker when Chief Hendershot yelled for two men. We went in the Maneuverin' Room and Mr. Simms, here, was laying on the deck all curled up in a little ball and yellin' like hell. Hendershot, the Chief I mean, he told us to bring him up here. Door on the head's busted off, I think!"

"You know what's wrong with him, Doc?" Rhodes asked.

"If I was back in Wyoming where I'd like to be, I'd say he got crotch-kicked by a horse but they ain't any horses aboard. Son of a gun is sure turning blue, isn't he? Look at his nuts! Pretty near as big as tennis balls already!"

"Well, what the hell are you going to do?" Rhodes said. "At least do something for the man to ease his pain!"

"He's probly got the clap," Johnson said dolefully. "Got hisself a stricture, can't piss."

"Oh, shut up, Cookie! Get back in your damned galley!" Rhodes voice was harsh.

"Well Jesus Christ, Chief!" Johnson muttered as he went toward his tiny galley. "Don't have to bite a man's head off for tryin' to help!"

"Give him a shot of something," Rhodes said to Whitten. "Something to stop his pain. The Old Man's gonna be in here in another five minutes he keeps yelling."

Ginty walked into the compartment and looked at Simms.

"Hot damn!" he said in his deep growl. "Hope it ain't anything minor, Doc."

"Shut up, Ginch," Rhodes snapped. "Make yourself useful. Take his legs and help carry him up to his bunk. You ready, Doc?" Whitten nodded and withdrew the needle from Simms' shoulder.

"He'll stop kickin' in a second or two. Gave him enough to keep him under a couple, three hours. When we get him in his bunk I'll pack some ice bags on him, see if that helps."

Captain Mealey and Joe Sirocco listened to what Chief Rhodes told them without comment and then went aft to the Maneuvering

Room. Sirocco looked with interest at the door of the head, which was badly dented outward at about the center of the door and hanging by one hinge. Captain Mealey turned to Hendershot.

"You were on watch, Chief?"

"Yes, sir."

"Can you tell me what happened?"

"Well, sir, Mr. Simms was back here, he comes back here almost every day to talk about his plans for a PT boat in the After Room, sir, and he was talking like he always does."

"PT boat in the After Room?" Captain Mealey's voice went up a notch.

"Yes, sir, his plans. Mr. Simms said we should split the hull in the After Room like a clamshell and take out the tubes and the bunks and the other gear and put a PT boat back there. Then we could get outside a harbor and he could take the PT boat in the harbor with his cutlass and sink ships. He said submarines aren't aggressive enough, sir. I thought it was something you-all were talking about in the Wardroom, sir. That's why I didn't say anything to anyone else, I thought maybe he shouldn't have been talking about it, sir."

"Go on, Chief. What happened to Mr. Simms."

"He was talking about that like he always does back here and then he had to use the head, he said. He went in and closed the door. In about a minute, maybe, we heard him scream and he came bustin' right out through the door. Broke the latch and put a dent in the door and tore off the bottom hinge but we can fix all that, no sweat.

"He was yelling when he came out through the door and he landed in a heap there on the deck where Mr. Sirocco is, his shorts and his skivvies down around his ankles and he was all curled up in a ball, holdin' himself, sir. He landed on the deck on his head and face, I think, but it sure didn't stop him from yellin'! I got two men out of the After Room to carry him up forward and I had the other man on watch call the Control Room and get the Doc for him."

"You don't have any idea what's wrong with Mr. Simms, Chief?"

Hendershot's large, dark blue eyes were as innocent as those of an Apprentice Seaman on his first day in Boot Camp.

"No, sir. He closed the door to the head. I don't know what he was doing to himself in there, sir, he might have hurt himself. I don't know. All I know is he screamed and busted right out through the door!"

"Very well, Chief. Have you inspected the head?"

"Yes, sir. Everything in there is normal. It's just the head, the one we all use every day."

Captain Mealey turned to Joe Sirocco who had been kneeling in the door to the head, examining the interior.

"How does it look to you, Joe?"

"As the Chief said, sir. Normal. Nothing out of order."

Captain Mealey nodded and the two men went forward to the Wardroom and looked in Lieutenant Simms' small stateroom that he shared with Bob Edge. The black-haired officer was lying in the lower bunk, his eyes closed, breathing slowly and heavily. Two ice bags wrapped in towels were jammed up between his legs. Joe Sirocco gently lifted the ice bags away and Mealey's breath went in with a gasp.

"My God!" Mealey said. "It does look like Doc said, as if he'd been kicked by a horse. The whole area is black and blue! Put the ice bags back, Joe. I'll take his watch until he's recovered. You'd better sit down quietly with the Chief of the Boat and find out what you can. I don't think you'll find out anything but you might get a clue or two as to what went wrong back there if you handle him right."

Mako had reached that part of the Pacific where she had to submerge all day to escape detection before Lieutenant Simms was able to resume his regular duties. The crew noticed that while he walked normally, although he went through the water-tight doors with their 18-inch high combings with more care than he had in the past, he never went aft of the Forward Engine Rooms. Early one morning, two days after Lieutenant Simms had been put back on the watch list, Joe Sirocco climbed to the cigaret deck with his sextant and watch and his notebooks to go through the morning ritual of star sights so he could plot *Mako*'s position on the trackless reaches of the ocean.

"I'll hold your gear, Joe," Don Grilley said. "Skipper wants to see you on the cigaret deck."

A strong breeze was whipping across *Mako*'s deck and Captain Mealey put his lips close to Sirocco's ear.

"Have you figured out what happened and why it happened?"

"I know why it happened, sir, and I think I know how. I think we'd better talk about it in the Wardroom or your stateroom, after we dive." Mealey nodded and Sirocco retrieved his sextant from Grilley and took his morning star sights.

"What happened?" Mealey said as he cradled a cup of coffee between his hands in the deserted Wardroom.

"First, sir, if you will, why," Sirocco said. "Simms was in the habit of going back to the Maneuvering Room every afternoon to shoot the breeze with the electricians. Every time he went back there he used their head. I don't think anyone back there would object to his using the head in an emergency but he did it every day, been doing it every day all through the first two patrol runs. The men who live back there, the ones who clean the head, Chief Rhodes makes all hands clean heads in turn and he takes his turn, you know, the men got angry at Mr. Simms."

"Isn't that unreasonable?"

"Perhaps, but understandable, Captain."

"What did they do to him?"

"I don't know, sir. I have no proof they did anything to him. But I've figured out how it could happen. All I have is a theory and I couldn't pin it on anyone at all."

"Let me hear it, Joe. If Hendershot was back of it there wouldn't be any proof. I had him on an R-Boat in Panama. The best electrician in the whole submarine force and a very clever man."

"Well, sir, the bowl of the toilet back there is bronze. It sits on a thick rubber gasket. There's that little foot rest made of metal that is anchored to the deck in front of the bowl. The seat on the bowl is made of wood.

"If you ran electricity, a wire, to the toilet bowl and then you ran another line to the foot rest and to the ground, if you had the hot line going to the toilet bowl and the ground line going to the foot rest and if that circuit were to be completed . . ."

"I can see the pitcure," Mealey said. "If he sat down on the toilet and began to urinate the stream of urine would complete the circuit. My God! Two hundred and twenty volts going up that stream would be like the kick of a mule!"

"That's one way it could be done, sir. There is no evidence at all that it was done that way and there's no way of finding out, sir. If it was done that way the wires would have been ripped out while they were carrying Pete up to the Crew's Mess."

Captain Mealey caressed the right side of his mustache with a finger. "If there were no amperage in the jolt it wouldn't damage him too much, would it? I mean, would just the jolt perhaps make him sterile or impotent?"

"I wouldn't know that, sir," Sirocco said. "There was no sign of a burn anywhere in the area around his crotch, just the swelling and the black-and-blue color. And the bump on his head, that was a beauty! The latch on that door was designed to hold the door closed during a depth charge attack. We'll have to run him into the hospital when we got back to port, sir. He's told Doc that he has no trouble urinating and that he had, ah, erections in the morning when he awakened, sir." Mealey nodded and turned as he heard a gentle tap on the bulkhead. Lieutenant Cohen pulled the curtain to one side and stepped in and laid a message flimsy in front of Mealey.

"This came in just before we dove, sir," Cohen said. "I just finished decoding it, sir."

"Thank you, Nate," Mealey said. He read the message and his lips smiled under the mustache.

"Get your charts, Joe! I want to know, right away, how far we are from Truk Atoll!"

"I can give you a rough idea now," Sirocco said as he struggled out from behind the Wardroom table. "Truk is almost abeam to port, about four hundred miles or less."

"Tell Grilley to turn the dive over to the Chief of the Watch and get the officers in here, please," Mealey said. He waited until all the officers were crowded around the small Wardroom table.

"We have been diverted from our assigned patrol area," Captain Mealey said slowly.

"The intelligence people in Washington say a Japanese battleship of the *Kongo* class is enroute from Japan to Truk Atoll. We are directed to intercept her and attack! The report says the battleship will enter Truk Atoll via the Northeast Entrance of that area and suggests, and Pearl Harbor concurs, that this will be the most advantageous point of intercept. Joe, how far are we from the point of intercept?"

"Give me a minute," Joe Sirocco said. He made a final thin pencil line on the chart and pushed the parallel rulers to one side and picked up a pair of dividers and began to prick off the distance.

"I make it three hundred and seventy miles from Truk," he said. "If we can run say nine hours at night and make eighteen knots good and we should be able to do that, the bottom is still clean, and make good three knots during the time we're submerged, we should be in position by the time we're ready to surface, a little less than, oh, thirty-six hours from now, sir. That's about twelve hours before the ETA of the battleship, according to the message. We'd spend the night on station, waiting for the target to appear, the message says the target will arrive at the Northeast Entrance at dawn, local time about zero five forty.

"Or we could slow down a little on the way and arrive there just ahead of the target if you didn't want to spend the night off Truk."

"The question of air patrol from Truk has to be considered," Mealey said slowly. "But I'd rather risk the air patrol than take the chance that the battleship would arrive on time. They might be ahead of their ETA and what the hell sort of an excuse do you make if you get there after the horse has got safely into the barn?" He looked at the circle of officers.

"We'll make all possible haste, get there as soon as we can. If he's early we'll be waiting for him. If he's late we'll be waiting for him."

"Is he proceeding alone or does he have an escort?" Grilley asked.

"He'll have medium to long distance air patrol out of Truk, I'd guess," Mealey said. "The intelligence report says there are twelve destroyers with the battleship. Six of those destroyers are going to relieve six other destroyers now stationed at Truk."

"Twelve destroyers for an escort, six more tin cans in Truk and we're going to attack at the entrance?" Simms said. "My God, we'll never have a chance to even get in a shot let alone get away!"

"Spoken like an experienced PT-boat commander," Mealey said dryly. "I don't want the content of this message told to the crew. I'll decide when to do that.

"Mr. Grilley, I want every torpedo aboard to be fully routined, including those in the tubes. That must be done at once. Mr. Simms, any and all repairs, large or small, that must be done in your department are to be taken care of at once. Mr. Cohen, I want the baker to have plenty of doughnuts and sweet rolls baked the night we spend on station. If we go to the attack and if he's got twelve destroyers with him we may be under a long, long time with no chance to cook meals. Doughnuts and sweet rolls will have to suffice. Deck officers will double up on watch while we run submerged. Periscope will be manned continually, one hour on and one hour off. Joe, you make up that watch list. I want both torpedo rooms to double the watch, two men on watch. The same for the sonar watch, man it continually while submerged. Get everything that has to be done in your respective departments done in the next twenty-four hours. After that it's going to be a game of dice and if we're lucky we'll have the first roll. That's all, gentlemen. Joe, I'll help you work out the course."

An hour later Sirocco pushed aside the chart and paused, listening to the clank of a chainfall in the Forward Torpedo Room and Ginty's muttered cursing.

"Captain," he said softly, "I think you'll have to give the crew the word on our destination and target pretty soon, don't you?"

"I'd rather not for a while," Mealey said. "Sailors are always sailors, there'll be more talk than work." Ginty's heavy voice came through the water-tight door that led to the Forward Torpedo Room.

"Don't bellyache at me, shithead! Just get your fuckin' back into haulin' on that chainfall! The Old Man wants fish routined so we routine fish. Don't ask me why. I don't know. All's I know is that this is a bunch of shit!"

"I see your point," Mealey said. He reached for the telephone handset on the bulkhead and turned the switch to the circuit that would be heard in all compartments.

"Now hear this," he said slowly. "This is the Captain.

"We have been given a special assignment. That is why all of you have to do extra work today.

"We are on our way to Truk Atoll, in the Carolines. Truk is held by the Japanese. It is a major naval base and air base. We expect to be there in less than thirty-six hours.

"Naval intelligence has told us that a Japanese battleship will arrive at Truk within twelve hours or so after our arrival.

"We are going to attack the battleship!" He paused to let his words sink in.

"The battleship will have air cover from Truk and it will be escorted by twelve destroyers. In order for our attack to be successful, every torpedo must run perfectly, every piece of machinery must function perfectly, every man must do his job not only perfectly but superbly.

"No other American submarine has ever had a crack at a battleship! We are going to get that chance and when we get the chance we are going to sink the battleship!

"That is all. Carry on with the ship's work."

Ginty looked around his torpedo room and wiped a stream of sweat from his broad chest.

"A wagon and aircraft and twelve destroyers! Shit! We're on a fuckin' suicide mission!"

"How do you get through twelve destroyers and attack a battleship?" Johnny Paul asked.

"How? I guess you dive under the fuckin' tin cans and come up and shoot everything you got out of both ends and then you ask for a transfer to shore duty! How the fuck do I know how to get through twelve destroyers, shithead? That's the Old Man's job. That's why he's the Old Man and not me!"

Hendershot stuck his head through the opening of the water-tight door to the After Room and called to Mike DeLucia, the Torpedoman First Class who had replaced Spook Hernandez.

"You think you and the Exec. had some action on those two patrols on the *Gudgeon,* wait until this cold-eyed son of a bitch we've got here takes us in on this tea party!"

"We might learn something," DeLucia said. "Hard-asses like him sometimes ain't so hard when the chips are down. If he's got a soft middle we've still got Sirocco. Now there's one gent who's all guts!"

"I wouldn't worry about the Old Man," Hendershot said. "He's got that look in his fucking eye. He'd kick the Devil in the balls and then sell him an ice pack!"

CHAPTER 15

The press conference in the Palmer House Hotel ballroom in Chicago had been wearing. The highly competitive reporters from the four Chicago newspapers, the wire services and the radio stations had bombarded Captain Hinman with questions. Most of them he fielded easily, a veteran now of Washington and three press conferences in New York.

Joan Richards had warned Hinman about a reporter from the *Chicago Tribune* and had described the man so he'd know him if he spoke up. The *Tribune* was violently anti-Roosevelt while at the same time it was fervently pro-war. Colonel McCormick, the newspaper's owner, had for years trumpeted that he had won World War I because of his promotion of the machine gun as a weapon.

The *Tribune*'s reporter let the other reporters ask Captain Hinman the usual questions before he bulled his way to the front row of reporters confronting Captain Hinman.

"Captain," he said in a loud voice, "all of us admire your ability as a submarine commander and your courage. But I wonder, my editors wonder, sir, is this all there is to you? Do you ever think about being a pawn in Roosevelt's war? Do you ever think about anything except what you see as your duty?"

"I wasn't aware that this was 'President Roosevelt's war,' as you call it, sir." Hinman was speaking slowly, carefully. "It is common knowledge that the United States was attacked at Pearl Harbor by the Empire of Japan. No provocation had been offered to warrant such an attack. Over two thousand Americans died in that sneak attack. We are responding to that infamous attack. We are fighting, I think, for our own lives, our freedom, the freedom of all nations."

"All of us sorrow for those who were killed in that attack, Captain, and I won't argue here with you whether there was a provocation or not. I think there was. I imagine yours is a vendetta, isn't it? Your wife was killed in that attack, wasn't she? I offer you my deepest sympathy, sir.

"But answer my question: do you and all those like you in the military forces ever think about why you are fighting Roosevelt's war?"

"I think about the war, yes." Hinman was fighting to keep his anger under control. The remark about Marie's death had been uncalled for. "I think about it a great deal. I imagine that the more than twenty members of your own editorial staff think about it in much the same way all of us think about it. I am right, am I not, more than twenty of your newspaper's reporters and editors are now in military service?"

"Your adviser should do her homework, Captain," the reporter nodded toward Joan Richards, who was standing to one side of Captain Hinman. "If she had she'd have told you that almost all of our people who are in uniform are there because they were drafted. That's not offering their services. The others are war correspondents. They're doing their job to make sure the American people know what you, ah, professional fighting men are doing."

"I give honor to those who are drafted, Mister," Hinman said evenly. "The concept of the military draft is not to shanghai men into the military service, it is to insure that we have adequate numbers of trained men to defend our liberty. I honor war correspondents as well. They go into battle situations without any weapons. The American press has, I think, always distinguished itself in finding ways to report the truth, to report honestly to the American public and the world."

"That's a very pretty speech, Captain. I hope your lady aide didn't write it out for you. But if you honor war correspondents so much why don't you allow them to go to sea with your submarines? How do we know you sank two Japanese oil tankers and a destroyer if no unbiased reporter was there to see it?" The reporter's tone was bantering but underneath the apparent humor Hinman detected the bitterness in the man.

"I would welcome a reporter aboard my ship, sir," Hinman said. "But I must point this out to you: A submarine is a small, very sophisticated fighting ship. Every man aboard must be not only a specialist in his own rating, he must also be familiar with everyone else's specialty. That demands a high level of intelligence. If, sir, you are qualified in that latter respect, please volunteer!"

The gust of laughter that swept the ballroom ended the *Tribune* reporter's questioning and as the other reporters took up the questioning Hinman relaxed. When it was over Joan Richards poured him a cup of coffee in his hotel suite.

"He sucked you in!" she said accusingly. "I warned you about that brass-plated bastard and he nailed you and you fell for it!"

"What the hell else could I do?" Hinman snapped.

"I'll tell you what you could have done! You didn't have to get in that crack about his intelligence! All you had to do was explain why people on submarines have to know a lot more than the average sailor and then ask him, ask him, Captain, to help you find a war correspondent who could qualify to make war patrols on your submarine!

"You've got to try to get these bastards on your side, sir! You've got to be all sweet reason and helping-hand-Mary. For God's sake, don't let your balls rule your head!"

"There are times, Lieutenant," Hinman said gravely, "when you sound like a torpedoman working on a fish that won't run right. You have the damndest vocabulary I ever heard in a woman!"

"The only reason for language is to communicate, Captain, to let others know what you want, what you think, to let them know precisely what you want and what you think." She poured coffee for herself and refilled Hinman's cup.

"That applies to everything, right down to boy-girl things. I'd much rather have a man I liked and whom I knew liked me come right out and ask me to go to bed with him than to have him fool around and just hope that I was getting the message!"

"I didn't know that ladies talked like you do in this year of Our Lord, Nineteen and Forty-Two," Hinman said with a small grin. "It's traditional, isn't it, that a certain amount of courtship adds spice? Would you do away with all the small courtesies, the fun of the courtship?"

She shook her head and her crisp black curls danced. "No, Captain, but have you ever thought that a girl can get weary waiting for the stupid jerk to sweep her off her feet and into bed? Sure, a courtship can be fun. It can also be damned boring!

"Times are changing! You saw those women working in the shipyard in Brooklyn the other day. They call them 'Rosie the Riveter.' Those women are doing men's work and in many cases they're doing it a lot better than men did! Women are building tanks, they're making ammunition and they're even building your submarines.

"Life in this year of Our Lord Nineteen and Forty-Two, as you so quaintly put it, is changing. Do you think that those women are going to go back to being a person without a voice in things once this war is over?

"That change is going to apply to everything, all across the board. Back in the eighteenth century a woman who liked sex was called a 'bawd.' Men made that a bad word because they were afraid of a woman who liked sex. When this war is over women are going to demand that they be treated as equals and that applies from sex to everything you can think of! Our sex has earned the right to be free, to be liberated!"

"Would you call yourself a free woman, Lieutenant?"

"I never considered myself anything but that. I divorced a man I loved because he not only refused to grow up, he refused to allow me to grow up, to admit that I was every bit as much a person as he was.

"Now I'm going to say something else to you because you didn't flinch when that bastard from the *Tribune* brought it up. From what I heard in Washington you had a great marriage. From what little I know of you this past week I can't believe that you would deny your wife the chance to be her own person."

"I'd rather not talk about that," he said.

"Sooner or later, sir, sooner or later you're going to have to talk about it with someone you like and respect and who respects and likes you. Until you do you aren't going to be a whole man."

He looked at her solemnly. The doctor in Pearl Harbor had told him the same thing, in almost the same words. He nodded his head briefly.

"Let's get back to business, shall we? What about the speech this noon?"

"Standard Club," she said briskly. "The Standard Club is a very exclusive Jewish organization. Mostly Jews of German descent or extraction. Very wealthy people for the most part. Very patriotic people. You had a Jew on your ship, it's mentioned in the speech. Someone is going to want to know how important he was to you, to the ship, to the attack you made."

"Every man on a submarine is important," Hinman said. "We don't carry any unimportant people."

"I've heard you say that before but even if this guy is a *schlemiel* give him as much credit as you can. These are very proud people, very proud."

"I don't think he was what you said he was, whatever that means," he said. "In fact, Lieutenant Cohen was vital to our safety. He was on the sound gear. We were too deep to use the periscope and it was his ears, his judgment, that I depended on for the positions of the enemy ships. He's got ears like, well, I don't know, a bat, an owl."

"That's all you have to say, in just that way," she said. "If you stumble around trying to find words, fine.

"The parade is at two this afternoon. You'll be riding in the lead car with the Mayor. He's a politician. All he'll be thinking about is how many more votes he's going to get because he's with you. Don't let him bore you. He's harmless."

"You're a little hard on politicians," Hinman said. "I've noticed that before."

"My father, bless his unreconstructed Republican soul, taught me to look at all politicians with a deep sense of distrust until they proved they were worthy of trust. I've never found one worthy of my trust."

"Not even the President?"

"Not even him. You wanted to get back to business. This evening there's a dinner here in the Palmer House. That's speech number seven in the book. I've changed a few things in it. I've noticed that you tend to stumble a little bit when you run into two or three very short words in a row. So I've eliminated those booby traps. You'd better read it. And where I've put a red check mark in the margin—get a little more belligerent there."

"That's sort of phony," Hinman protested.

"No it isn't," she said flatly. "You're here to let the people know this war can be won if they help out by buying war bonds and they are certainly doing that! You're breaking all the records in that department in the short time we've been on tour. Me, I'm here to make sure no underhanded son of a bitch trips you up and makes you look bad. I'm trying to do that."

"You're an amazing woman, Lieutenant Richards," Hinman said.

"I know that. And if you tell me that if I were a man you'd like to have me on your ship I'll burst into tears and run out of the room!" A grin spread across her full lips. "And if you don't stop calling me 'Lieutenant' and 'Miss Richards' when we're alone I'm going to ask for a transfer! I know you have to do that in public but when we're working alone, two people working at a job, let's have some of that famous camaraderie you're always talking about in the submarine force."

"Very well, Lieutenant junior grade Joan Richards," he said. Then he smiled. "Joan, kick your damned shoes off and come over here and sit beside me on this sofa and show me where you've changed this speech. I thought I was saying the words pretty well."

"Why should I kick off my shoes?"

"So you won't throw them at me if I don't like your changes."

"You're leaving me without anything to throw," she said, her eyes dancing. "I might have to throw my brassiere at you if you get snotty. and if that hits you, you'll know you've been hit!"

"You're talking to a sailor, Miss Joan, a submarine sailor and most submarine sailors are more sailor than other sailors."

"That's another thing you're going to have to face," she said. Her smile was suddenly gentle. "Some woman is going to be very lucky when you come to grips with that problem and overcome it. Let's get to work."

CHAPTER 16

The coral atoll that is called Truk is a drowned mountain range ringed with coral reefs. The reef encloses more than 1,300 square miles of ocean and is dotted with more than 30 small islets and a dozen large islands, ancient tree-studded mountain peaks, some of which soar 1,500 feet into the air.

There are only four main passages through the coral reefs into the waters of the atoll, dangerous passages swept by fierce tides and strong currents.

Once under German control Truk and the Caroline Islands, a part of the South Pacific's Micronesian Island belt, had passed to Japan after World War I. Japan, always frantically concerned about its own safety, had recognized the strategic importance of Micronesia. The islands sprawled across thousands of miles of the Pacific Ocean and bisected the sea lanes between the United States, the Philippines, China and Japan. Japan had heavily fortified the major islands in Micronesia and none was more heavily fortified than the atoll called Truk.

All four main passages through the reef were guarded by coastal guns. The Northeast Passage, most commonly used by Japan's naval ships, was the closest passage to the island of Dublon where the main town was located and which also held a major seaplane base, a submarine base, massive storage facilities for ammunition and torpedoes and repair facilities for ships and aircraft. The Northeast Passage was also close to Eten Island with its air strip of more than 4,000 feet where light and medium bombers were stationed.

Mako moved into position off the Northeast Entrance to Truk after full dark to wait for the arrival the next morning of the battleship and its destroyer escorts. Captain Mealey had ordered a cruising depth of 250 feet all the previous day, aware that a patrolling aircraft might detect the dark bulk of *Mako* in the clear water if he ran for extended periods at periscope depth. Four times during the day Captain Mealey had ordered the *Mako* to 65 feet where he made a quick sweep around the horizon with the periscope and then *Mako* had been sent down into the depths.

The atmosphere within *Mako* was calm. The crew went about its duties with no more apparent concern than if *Mako* were on a practice cruise. Underneath, however, the tension ran high. The appearance of outward calm was deliberate. It was a common belief in submarines that no matter how frightened a man might be he should not give any evidence of that fright lest it trigger an outburst from another man equally frightened.

Ginch Ginty had muted his bull-like roar to a low rumble in the Forward Room when he worked on the torpedoes prior to the arrival at Truk. As he finished each torpedo he had carefully painted a message on each warhead with white paint. "Herohito Special" was his favorite. When Johnny Paul pointed out that he had misspelled "Hirohito" Ginty had glared at Paul and rumbled:

"This son of a bitch hits that 'wagon ain't no one gonna know if it was spelled wrong, shithead!"

John Aaron, Radioman Second Class, USNR, read his Bible daily, underlining each verse as he read it with a thin red pencil line. It was a habit of Aaron's; when he had read through the Bible, underlining in red, he went through the Book again, this time underlining each verse in blue pencil. Then he sent the Book to his wife Samantha and bought another Bible. He had been kidded about his habit when it was first discovered but his farm-developed chest and shoulders and the steady glare of his clear, guileless blue eyes discouraged the kidding and now his habit was not only accepted, it was welcomed by *Mako*'s crew.

John Barber prowled his engine rooms, searching for evidence of a pending failure of equipment, growling because he could find nothing. Occasionally Lieutenant Simms would go as far aft as the Forward Engine Room to talk with Barber. Hendershot, whenever he saw Lieutenant Simms, would smile warmly at him and Simms would turn away.

In the Wardroom, Officers' Country as it is known all over the Navy, Captain Mealey spent hours in consultation with Joe Sirocco. Sirocco had joined the U.S.S. *Gudgeon* months before the attack on Pearl Harbor and in those months *Gudgeon* had compiled an enviable record in firing practice torpedoes. The *Gudgeon*'s team of Captain Elton Watters, "Joe" Grenfell and Lieut. Robert Edson "Dusty" Dornin, *Gudgeon*'s fire-control officer, had "sunk" thirty out of thirty-two target ships they had fired at, a record that no one had ever come close to matching. Yet, in *Gudgeon*'s first approach against an enemy ship that same team of torpedo firing experts missed their target despite what Captain Grenfell later said had been a virtual text-book problem.

Captain Mealey had never fired a torpedo at an enemy ship and he wanted to know why Joe Grenfell and Dusty Dornin had missed. Joe Sirocco, a trained mechanical engineer with a retentive mind, had been aboard *Gudgeon* during the pre-war torpedo firing record and during *Gudgeon*'s first two war patrols. Sirocco tried to explain why the difficulties in hitting an enemy ship existed in terms that wouldn't offend Captain Mealey's stiff-necked Academy pride, why the Navy's peacetime training for submarine torpedo firing had been so wastefully inefficient.

The difficulty, as Sirocco saw it, was rather simple. Basically, seven factors had to be determined to work out the mathematical formula necessary to hit a target ship with a torpedo. The firing ship's course and speed were known, as was the speed the torpedo would travel. The course of the target ship, its distance from the submarine at the moment of firing, and at the moment the torpedo arrived, and the distance the torpedo would have to run were not known and had to be determined.

The distance of the target ship is not difficult to determine if sufficient time for periscope observation is available. An instrument in the periscope called a stadimeter gives that distance if the height of the target ship's masts is known. The course of the target ship can be determined by the "angle on the bow (or stern)" that the target ship presents to the officer manning the periscope. The angle on the bow or stern is purely a judgment factor made by the periscope officer. If the target changes its course, if it zig-zags or if it varies its speed from time to time then these factors must also be considered and worked into the torpedo problem.

The difficulty, as Sirocco saw it, was that the Navy had used its own destroyers for submarine targets. The submarines fired torpedoes equipped with "exercise" warheads, dummy warheads that were filled with water that was blown out of the head when the torpedo run was completed so the torpedo would float, head upward. A smoke pot in the exercise head aided in the recovery of the torpedo.

Submarine officers knew the height of the destroyer masts to the inch so estimating range was simple. They knew the outline of the destroyers so well that estimating the target ship's course by its angle on the bow or stern was routine.

There was no information on the height of Japanese masts on merchant vessels. Japanese warships periodically lowered or raised the overall height of their masts to confuse a submarine captain. The unfamiliar silhouettes of Japanese ships, the often oddly shaped bow and stern lines of those ships were also confusing and often made the determination of the vital angle on the bow or stern a matter of wild guesswork.

To further complicate the difficulty it was widely believed that in firing an "angle shot," a shot in which the torpedo is fired out of the torpedo tube and then changes course, by means of a pre-set gyroscope within the torpedo, that if the torpedo was fired in the direction of the Earth's spin, i.e., to the west from a ship facing roughly north or south, the torpedo would skid farther in making its turn than if it were fired in the opposite direction.

"As I see it, sir," Sirocco summed up his arguments the afternoon before the Japanese battleship was due to arrive at Truk. "As I see it, making an approach on a friendly destroyer in peacetime and doing the same thing out here on an unfamiliar target is two different kettles of fish."

"Granted," Mealey said. "If Joe Grenfell and Dusty Dornin had trouble then all of us who aren't as good as that pair at firing torpedoes are going to have a great deal of trouble. The way it looks to me is if the target is valuable enough you go in to point-blank range, eight hundred yards or less! Preferably from a place abeam of the target so we don't get confused by the angle on the bow of a type of ship we've never seen before." He reached for his coffee cup and took a swallow.

"According to the intelligence report the battleship and its escorts should show up before dawn tomorrow, just before dawn. We should be able to get a fix on them with the periscope before we dive and then we can track them on sonar. We'll go deep, two hundred and fifty feet and hug the reef. There's a shelf there on the chart that shows about four hundred feet of water and then it drops off to over a thousand fathoms. If we stay on top of the shelf until we're ready to commit ourselves they shouldn't be able to pick us up on sonar.

"When we've got the problem down pat with sonar bearings we'll come up, confirm the problem factors and start shooting!"

Sirocco rubbed his craggy face with a big hand. "Armor plating," he said. "That battleship is armor plated way below its water line. Our exploders are modified for contact hits. You'll have to set them to run deep, hit her below the plating."

"Armor plating usually goes down twenty feet below the water line," Mealey said. "I'll set the torpedoes for twenty-two feet. If they're running deeper than the depth set as everyone complains they do, we should nail her down near her keel. The book says she draws thirty-five feet."

"Our book's old," Sirocco said.

"The battleship isn't new. No matter how they've modernized her she'll draw the same amount of water or more. When I start the sonar plot, the preliminary plot, I want you and Grilley to work on that at the gyro table in the Control Room where we can talk to each other. I'm going to have Edge and Botts with me in the Conning

Tower. Edge can handle the TDC. He's bright and quick. Botts can handle the periscope motors and read off the bearings to Edge. That's about all the old man is good for. I'm thinking seriously of recommending he be given shore duty after this run."

"The destroyer escorts, sir. How do you think they'll deploy the twelve destroyers?"

"I've tried to put myself in the place of the commander of that destroyer squadron," Mealey said slowly. "I served as Executive Officer on a destroyer once. I've tried to think as he would think. If I were in his shoes I'd put at least two, probably four destroyers out ahead of the battleship to make close in and distant sweeps, to clear out any submarine that might be lying in wait. I'd put two more ships aft for the same purpose. I think I'd put the remaining ships on either side of the battleship. But who the hell ever heard of using twelve destroyers to escort one battleship!"

"Let me continue to be the Devil's Advocate, sir," Sirocco said. "What happens to that sort of destroyer formation when the battleship nears the Northeast Entrance? We don't know anything at all about that entrance but there's bound to be some strong currents running through the reef, maybe even a strong tide. We don't have tide tables, either. How will the destroyer commander use his ships? Will those ships out front sweeping go into the atoll itself?"

"I don't think so," Mealey said. "There's no danger inside. The danger, if there is any and there is—we're here—the danger will be outside. So I think his destroyers in the van will peel off the circle until the Big Boy is well inside. Then they'll go in to the anchorage.

"That's when I intend to go under the destroyer screen, when they're maneuvering and getting out of the way of the Big Boy so her Captain can take her in through the reef. There'll be enough screws pounding away that they won't be able to hear us."

"Aircraft?"

"There will be air cover from that big airfield on that one island," Mealey said. "But our own peacetime experience has shown us that fliers don't usually pick up a periscope. And the Japs have weak eyes, we know that."

"One last point, if you don't mind," Sirocco said.

"I don't mind, I welcome it, Joe."

"If they're on time we should pick them up when they're an hour or more away from attack point. If he has destroyers out in the van, sweeping, what will we be doing during that time?"

"The chart shows a shelf along the sea side of the reef," Mealey said. "You pointed it out to me yesterday. The water there is what— four, five hundred feet deep? It falls off down the side of that submerged mountain to a thousand or more fathoms. I intend to slide along at two hundred and fifty feet so the aircraft patrols can't pick up our shadow, on top of that shelf. When we move in to the attack we'll bore right in, come up to periscope depth, verify the sonar plot and begin shooting!

"I intend to begin shooting at eight hundred yards. That's point-blank range! As point-blank as you can get. We're here, a good ten to twelve hours ahead of the ETA the intelligence report gave us. If it shows up on time, it if isn't already inside the atoll, there is simply no way I can explain a failure to get into position and shoot. My whole Naval career is riding on this one action! If I miss this opportunity I'll be commanding a desk in some recruiting station for the rest of my career." He got up and went through the door and into the Control Room.

Sirocco turned to Don Grilley, who had been sitting at the far end of the Wardroom table during the discussion.

"It's a matter of priorities, Don," Sirocco said in a half-whisper. "The importance of the target is relative to the factor it plays in your promotion. How are the torpedoes?"

"As good as we can make them," Grilley said. "Rhodes wore a path from the Forward Room to the After Room when they were routining them. All the air flasks are topped off to three thousand pounds to the square inch and the rudder throws have been adjusted to a gnat's ass, to quote one Ginch Ginty. The gyroscopes were taken out, spun with air and oiled and put back in. Rhodes and Ginty did that job themselves."

"They use sperm oil to lubricate the gyros, don't they?"

Grilley nodded. "It has no acid to corrode anything. Put it in with a hypodermic needle. I'm sure we'll get a hot, straight normal run out of each fish. If we fire at eight hundred yards and the wake of the torpedo shows up two hundred yards aft of where the fish is, how long does that give the target ship to get out of the way? Torpedo runs at forty-five knots."

Sirocco fiddled with his slide rule. "A little over twenty-one seconds. Not enough time to get a ship out of the way. If he gets in close and makes good periscope observations, he's going to get hits. It's what happens after he unloads all the tubes that concerns me."

"Maybe he's thinking that if he sinks a battleship, a post-humous Congressional of Honor Medal will be worth it!" Grilley said with a sad smile.

"Doesn't help us feather merchants," Sirocco said. He stood up and stretched, the muscles in his heavy shoulders cracking. "I'd better get to work and figure out a course along that reef. What I'd like to do is get some sleep."

"Who wouldn't?" Grilley answered.

Captain Mealey climbed into the Conning Tower where Pete Simms was standing by the periscope.

"Full dark came down an hour ago, sir," Simms said. "We'll need five hours and thirty minutes for a full battery charge."

"Very well," Mealey said. "We'll go up in a few minutes. I want to check something with Joe." He went down the ladder to the Control Room and saw Aaron with his Bible in his hand.

"I hope you're reading that, son," Mealey said. "Pray for our success tomorrow morning."

"I'll do that, sir," Aaron said. "But I think there's something you should know about prayers, sir."

"What?" Captain Mealey said sharply.

" 'No' is also an answer, sir, to a prayer for help."

Mealey nodded shortly and consulted with Sirocco briefly at the chart table and then went back up to the Conning Tower.

"Sixty-five feet, Control," he ordered. *Mako* crept upward in the dark sea until her periscope broke water. Mealey made two full sweeps with the periscope and then snapped the handles closed.

"Stand by to surface!" he ordered. "Let's go up. Surface! Surface! Surface!"

Mako shuddered as compressed air blasted into her ballast tanks and she rose, buoyant, her periscope shears breaking the skin of the water, and then the Conning Tower burst through the surface, the sea water streaming in silvery cascades down the camouflaged sides. *Mako* wallowed on the surface and with a giant snort the four main diesel exhaust stacks cleared the residual water from the outboard exhaust lines and then the engines settled down into a steady rumble, one engine on propulsion and the other three charging the two giant storage batteries that powered *Mako* submerged. Overhead a thick cloud pattern hid the stars. The starboard lookout raised his binoculars and sang out.

"Lights! White lights bearing zero eight zero, Bridge! Very small white lights."

Standing on the cigaret deck Captain Mealey raised his binoculars and studied the lights. Shoreside lights, he concluded, shoreside lights on one of the islands within the atoll. The starboard lookout cleared his throat.

"I see surf, Bridge, looks like a reef bearing all along the starboard side. Can't tell how far away it is."

Mealey nodded to himself. The reef should be a mile to starboard. Sirocco's navigation was excellent for a Reservist, he reflected. The man was extremely capable. Mealey thought a moment; not only was Sirocco capable but he apparently had very powerful friends. His assignment to *Mako* had come directly from Washington. It was unheard of to put a Reserve aboard a submarine as an Executive Officer. He wondered, as he had wondered many times before, if Sirocco was Naval Intelligence put aboard to find out about the defective Mark Six exploders. It was possible; Commander Rudd had mentioned that Captain Hinman was going to tell the President about the exploder problem.

"Permission to come topside and dump trash and garbage?" Mealey heard the voice of the mess cook and walked to the Bridge.

"Permission denied!" he snapped. "Stow the trash and garbage in the freezer locker until further orders."

Standing at the bottom of the ladder that led to the Conning Tower, Andy "Grabby" Grabnas, Seaman First and a mess cook, shrugged his shoulders. Behind him there were eight burlap bags of garbage, each sewn tightly closed, each with a heavy stone in the bottom of the bag that had been taken from a stock of stones carried expressly to weight down the garbage bags so they would sink.

"Should have known better, Grabby," Chief Rhodes said with a grin. "Captain isn't going to dump garbage this close to an enemy base."

"That wagon won't show up," Grabnas said. "You think I believe that stuff? I worked on my uncle's shrimp boat down in the Florida Keys and he was the best seaman I ever saw and he couldn't tell you within two days when he'd get us into port." He went aft, his shoulders sagging under the weight of two bags of garbage.

At three in the morning Joe Sirocco drew a cup of strong black coffee and wolfed down two fresh doughnuts, then went to the Conning Tower and reported that he was standing by to make periscope observations to search for the target. Captain Mealey, standing on the cigaret deck, nodded approvingly as he saw the long, wide lens of the search periscope turn first toward Truk Atoll and make a long search there before turning to look toward the open sea.

An hour went by with negative reports at five-minute intervals from Sirocco. Another half hour went by with the same negative report, no masts visible. Standing on the cigaret deck Captain Mealey could see a horizon that was four and a half miles distant. The searching lens of the periscope above him could reach out to a horizon a little more than eight miles away. Given the fact that the masts of the lead destroyers would be at least as high above the sea as the periscope lens, the tops of those masts should come into view when the destroyers were still sixteen miles distant, their superstructures and hulls below the horizon. It was not likely that any lookout on the destroyers would pick up *Mako*. The positioning worked out by Sirocco put *Mako* in a line between the approaching flotilla and the dark bulk of the large island of Truk.

Captain Mealey fidgeted on the cigaret deck. In a half hour the first light of the false dawn would begin to show and he'd have to submerge to escape detection by the morning air patrols. He gripped the twin barrels of the 20-mm machine gun on the cigaret deck and ground his teeth together in frustration. Joe Sirocco's voice floated up through the hatch from the Conning Tower.

"Bridge! Here they come!"

Mealey pushed by the OOD and paused at the hatch. "I want the lookouts to strain their eyeballs until they pop a blood vessel! I won't be surprised by some aircraft out early or a damned patrol boat nosing along the reef!" He dropped down the hatch to the Conning Tower. Sirocco stepped away from the periscope.

"Bearing three two two, sir," he said. Mealey put his eye to the rubber eyepiece and stared at the distant horizon. It was bare. He moved the periscope minutely from side to side and then he saw them.

Far away, barely visible against the still dark sky he saw two tiny, hair-thin sticks, the upper masts of the leading destroyers. He clung to the periscope handles, centering the periscope's cross-hairs on the faint lines. He watched, fascinated by the sight of the thin masts and then suddenly he realized that the thin lines were thickening, growing more distinct.

"Mark!" he snapped and Sirocco noted the periscope bearing. Mealey swung the periscope in a full circle to search the horizon and the sky and then came back to the bearing where he had seen the two masts.

"Damn it!" he said. "The horizon's getting light and they're getting close! The bastards are an hour late! We'll never be able to get a fix on them before we dive!"

"Bridge, sah!" The deep rolling voice of Thomas Thompson, the Officers' Cook and a superb night lookout came down the hatch.

"Bridge! I have two small dots on the horizon bearing three two five, sah!"

"Bridge!" The starboard lookout's voice was a yell. "Aircraft! Bearing zero nine zero, taking off and circling!"

"Down periscope!" Mealey said, snapping the periscope handles up against the barrel of the periscope as Sirocco jammed a broad thumb against the button that lowered the periscope. Mealey took two long steps to the ladder to the Control Room and turned his face toward the bridge hatch.

"Dive! Dive! Dive!" he yelled.

Sirocco heard Pete Simms yell "Clear the bridge!" and then the lookouts were thudding down into the Conning Tower, taking one practiced step backward and turning and plummeting down into the Control Room. Simms slid down the ladder to the Conning Tower deck, edging to one side to let the quartermaster reach up past him and grab the toggle that hung from a short length of bronze cable fastened to the inside of the bridge hatch. The quartermaster heaved downward on the toggle and as the hatch slammed shut and latched Simms reached up and spun the locking wheel tight. *Mako's* bow buoyancy tank sighed noisily as its vent valves opened and all seven main ballast tanks burped mightily and *Mako* slid under the sea.

"Two hundred and fifty feet!" Mealey said to Simms as he landed on the Control Room deck. "Make it fast! We've only got four hundred feet of water so don't hit our ass on the rocks!"

As *Mako* leveled off at 250 feet Mealey punched the Battle Stations alarm button. The clanging of the gong sent *Mako's* crewmen racing through the ship to their battle stations. When all the compartments had reported all Battle Stations manned, Mealey picked up the telephone and turned a switch that would let him talk to all compartments by loudspeaker.

"This is the Captain," he said.

"The enemy destroyer line is in sight. Somewhere astern of the destroyer line there is a big battleship.

"The battleship is our primary target.

"This morning we are going to make submarine history. No other American submarine has had a shot at a battleship. No other submarine, to my knowledge, has ever successfully broken through an escort of twelve destroyers helped out by aircraft.

"We are going to make that penetration!

"We are going to hit and sink that battleship!

"Now hear this: I want complete silence about the decks. The success of our attack depends entirely on surprise, on our ability to slip under the destroyers and attack.

"Set depths on all torpedoes at twenty-two, repeat two two, feet.

"I intend to fire all tubes forward and then swing ship and fire all tubes aft.

"As soon as possible begin a reload forward of tubes one, two, three and four. Set depth on the reload torpedoes at two, repeat two feet.

"As soon as possible aft begin a reload of tubes seven and eight. Set depth on reload torpedoes at two repeat two feet.

"Reload of torpedo tubes fore and aft will begin as soon as

possible without direct orders from me. Once we shoot down this battleship we're going to have to fight our way out of here against the destroyers.

"Rig ship for depth charge attack!"

Ginty grunted as he knelt down on the deck between the two vertical banks of torpedo tubes and set the depth at twenty-two feet on the torpedoes in tubes five and six. He snapped out the depth-setting spindles and yelled at his telephone talker.

"Tell 'em depth set at twenty-two feet all fish and spindles disengaged!" He got to his feet and walked back into the torpedo room and began to lay out the block and tackle, called the "Tagle," used to pull the reload torpedoes into the tubes.

"You fuckers in this here reload crew," he growled. "Don't panic when you see water pourin' in from the inner doors when they open. I ain't gonna wait until them tubes is dry enough to sleep in before I open the inner doors! Soon's as I can manhandle that fucking inner door it's gonna open and when it does you get the safety strap off'n the fucking fish and start pullin' the bastard into the tube!"

Lieut. Nathan Cohen sat in front of his sonar dials, his ears covered by the big muff-like earphones, and listened to the distant sounds of ship's propellers. He sat loosely on a stool, his eyes closed, opening them only to note the bearings on the dials, which he reported in a soft voice to Joe Sirocco. Captain Mealey watched as Sirocco plotted in the bearings on a tracking chart. Mealey turned to Lieutenant Simms.

"We've got maybe an hour before they get here. You'd better review your compensation figures. Once I start shooting and they start reloading fore and aft you're going to have to be sharp as hell, Mister!" Captain Mealey's voice was cold, impersonal.

"You broach me or dip the periscope so I can't see and you'll think the end of the world has come and it will have, for you!" Simms nodded and managed a sickly smile as he took a small notebook out of his shirt pocket and began to study the rows of figures he had written down earlier.

Sirocco glanced at Simms and felt a sudden pang of sorrow for the man. Simms was an able Diving Officer but the assignment he was facing called for a sensitive feel for the ship and a mind that could coolly handle a dozen or more intricate mathematical calculations simultaneously, interpret them and then give the necessary orders.

Adjusting the trim, or balance of a submerged submarine is an intricate exercise in mathematics at any time. Determining the amount of negative buoyancy that will be just sufficient to allow the submarine to cruise at a desirable depth can be figured, can be figured so closely that a single man walking from either end to the center of the ship will cause the ship to slowly sink downward.

A submerged submarine can be compared to balancing a yardstick on the edge of a razor blade after putting dozens of tiny weights of varying sizes along the length of the yardstick. Move one weight a fraction of an inch or remove a weight and the yardstick is out of balance and will tip one way or the other. When Captain Mealey began shooting at the battleship each torpedo that was fired would represent the loss of 3,000 pounds. The water that would pour into the open torpedo tube would not be as heavy as the torpedo and when the outer door to the tube was closed that water would be blown to a Water 'Round Torpedo (WRT) tank that was aft of the torpedo tubes. Each torpedo that was reloaded represented a different problem: the shifting of 3,000 pounds 30 feet farther forward than where it had been resting on its rack. The problems that would be raised as a torpedo was fired every 6 seconds from the forward and then the after tubes was enough to drive a diving officer mad. To solve the problems the Diving Officer had to first calculate all the weight changes and write them down and then, as was usual, adjust his calculations to the speed of the Captain's firing. It required, as well, a perfect performance from the machinist mate who manned the trim manifold which, with a trim pump, controlled the water pumped from or flooded into the forward and after trim tanks, two auxiliary ballast tanks, negative and safety tanks. Vic Abbruzio, a Boston Italian who had ten years on submarines, stood at the trim manifold, balanced on the balls of his feet, ready for the challenge he faced. He looked at Lieutenant Simms' wan face and grinned, his white teeth flashing in the dense black beard that covered his lower face. He made a thumbs-up motion and Pete Simms managed a weak smile.

In the Forward Torpedo Room Ginty walked over to the port side where a small brass Buddha was fastened above a bank of gauges. He rubbed the brass belly of the Buddha with a spatulate thumb.

"Give us your luck, little Chiney man," he said softly.

Lieutenant Cohen's voice was soft but in the dead silence of the Control Room it carried to everyone's ears.

"I have several sets of high-speed screws, Plot. These are screws that criss-cross each other's bearings from two four zero to two nine zero. Somewhere in the background of those high-speed screws I have a very heavy multiple screw beat, probably four screws, that I cannot get a fix on as yet." He paused for a moment.

"If I am permitted an educated guess I would say, estimating the decibel levels, that the range to the high-speed screws has been cut roughly in half, Plot, cut in half since we dove."

"Mr. Cohen," Captain Mealey's voice was low, "the screws closest to us, those are high-speed screws? Doing what?"

"Coming closer," Cohen said. "There appear to be four sets of those screws, sir. They criss-cross. There are some other screw noises in the background, they appear to be single screws but I can't get any fixes on them as yet."

"Do you think they're making too much noise to hear us?"

"I would think so, Captain. The high-speed screws are revving up pretty strongly. I know that no one on those ships can hear anything at all over sonar. There is a chance, I'd do it if I was on the other side, that they've got one or two ships going very slowly and trying to listen to whatever they can hear above the sound of their own ship's noises."

"Let's hope they don't think of that," Captain Mealey said. "Can you give me any estimate of the rate of closing?"

Cohen looked at a stop-watch that hung from a cord around his neck.

"I'd say the high-speed screws will pass ahead of us in eighteen to twenty minutes if they continue as they have been for the last hour, sir."

Captain Mealey nodded at Sirocco and Grilley who were standing at the chart table over the gyro compass with their maneuvering boards and pencils. He climbed into the Conning Tower.

Mako waited.

CHAPTER 17

Lieutenant Nathan Cohen's lean body was slumped on his stool in front of his sonar dials. His long, hairy legs stuck out at right angles from his rumpled khaki shorts. His eyes were half-closed as he listened to the clutter of sounds coming from the two rotating JP sound heads below *Mako's* keel. Joe Sirocco came over to him and Cohen pushed one earphone up on his temple.

"I'm going to start the preliminary plot," Sirocco said. "Can you give me any identification of the ships up there for the plot? So I know which ship is which?"

"I've got more ships up there than I've heard ever before at one time," Cohen said. "The target ship is easy to pick up. It has a definite, slow beat. Four screws. He's been on the same course since I picked him up. Doesn't change course, doesn't change speed.

"There are four other ships between his sound and our position. These are fast ships, twin-screw, very fast propellors. One of them has a nicked blade or a bent blade, he's got a funny sound.

"There are some other ships out there but I can't tell how many.

Single-screw stuff making about the same speed as the target. I've heard three or four of those, maybe more."

"The ships running between the target and our position are the van," Sirocco said. "The Skipper figured they'd be there. They're sweeping, looking for submarines. The other ships must be the rest of the escort. How about giving me some names for the ships?"

"I wouldn't want to try that with each ship," Cohen said slowly. "I could get fooled too easily. The main target is easy to identify, we could give him a name. Why not just give a name to the other groups, the four ships running fast and the other ones?"

"Fine," Sirocco said. "What do you want to call the target?"

"Call it 'Aleph,' that's the first letter in the Hebrew alphabet. It means 'ox.' "

"That's 'Alpha' in Greek, isn't it?" Sirocco asked. Cohen nodded, smiling.

"Okay," Sirocco said. "Give me a name for the van, for those ships running ahead of the target, the fast-screw ships."

"They remind me of a folding door someone is opening and closing all the time," Cohen said. "In Hebrew 'Delt' means folding door. In Greek that's 'Delta,' okay?

"The others, well I don't know. Let's stick to the Middle East since we started there. Call them the camels. 'Gamel' in Hebrew, 'Gamma' in Greek. How about the aircraft the Captain said would be overhead? If I pick them up on the sound heads you want me to give them a name?" His lean face was solemn but his brown eyes were twinkling merrily.

"Nate, you're a character!" Sirocco said. He got up from his squatting position and heard his knee joints creak. "I'm getting too old for this sort of thing."

He walked over to the gyro table where Don Grilley had laid out the plotting charts. Grilley had spent hours drawing in the details of the atoll, the Northeast Entrance and the water depths shown on the chart on sheets of transparent paper. Then he had affixed each sheet of transparent paper to a plotting sheet so that by flipping the transparent sheet over the plot the position of the target, its escorts and *Mako* in relation to the reef could be seen at once.

In the Conning Tower Captain Mealey turned to Lieut. Bob

Edge, who was at his station at the TDC, the Torpedo Data Computer.

"Pass the Is-Was down to the Executive Officer," Mealey said. "I don't want to clutter up the TDC with the preliminary sonar plots." Edge nodded and took the celluloid "banjo" from a knob where it hung by a loop of cord. Before the development of the TDC the Is-Was had been the only fire control tool a submarine captain had at his disposal to work out the complicated mathematical problem in order to fire a torpedo at a target. Edge bent down and dangled the Is-Was by its cord and Sirocco took it and hung it around his neck.

"Let's begin the preliminary shooting plot, Joe," Captain Mealey called down from the Conning Tower. "Let me have your first plot as soon as you have it."

Cohen nodded at Sirocco and watched his dials and made notes and then he began to feed a steady stream of information to Sirocco and Grilley, who worked rapidly over a plotting sheet. Sirocco reached for the Is-Was and began to work out the problem on the plotting sheet. He looked upward at the Conning Tower hatch.

"We have the target steady on a course of two three zero, sir. That jibes with the course we assumed it would take to make its entrance to the atoll.

"Our planned point of intercept is eight hundred yards from the target's course into the mouth of the atoll with an intersect angle of ninety degrees.

"We have been on our intercept course to that point for some time, now. We should be at our shooting point in thirty-seven minutes, assuming a torpedo run of eight hundred yards, sir.

"If we assume the target was one mile astern of his van when we sighted the masts of the van, that is, the target was seventeen miles distant when we dove and that he was making fifteen knots, as the intelligence report said he would probably make, the target should be at the point of intercept in thirty-seven minutes, sir. With all due respect, sir, our timing is too tight. We have no allowance for planing up for a periscope observation, no allowance if the target decides to change course or speed. Mr. Cohen says we have a good fix on the target so you wouldn't have to waste any time if you went up for a look, sir." The hint in his words was just a trifle stronger than it should have been and the people in the Control Room and Conning Tower recognized that Sirocco was telling Captain Mealey what to do. Don Grilley raised his head from the plot and looked at Sirocco, his eyes widening, and then he bent his head to the plotting sheets.

"Very well, Mr. Sirocco," Mealey's voice was edged. "I plan to make two observations before we begin to shoot. Mr. Cohen, give me a bearing on the battleship." Asking Cohen for the bearing rather than asking Sirocco to get it from Cohen was an implied rebuke to Sirocco, and the people listening recognized that, too. Cohen let his head drop on his chest, concentrating on sorting out the clutter of sounds filling his earphones. He spoke softly into the telephone microphone he had hung around his neck.

"Main target, designated as Alpha, bears three three seven, sir. Repeat: three three seven."

"Make turns for four knots," Captain Mealey called. The helmsman moved his annunciators and Mealey heard the click of the response from the Maneuvering Room as Hendershot moved his pointer to match up with the order.

"Making turns for four knots," the helmsman said.

"Very well," Mealey said. "Bring me up to sixty-five feet, Control. I will take no more than seven seconds for this look. Begin planing back down to two hundred fifty feet after I've been up for seven seconds."

"Six five feet, sir," Simms said from his post in the Control Room. "Return to two five zero feet seven seconds after we reach six five feet, aye, aye, sir."

At 65 feet *Mako*'s periscope would be 18 inches out of the water. From that height the horizon would be only a little more than a mile and a quarter away. But the battleship, with its lofty superstructure and towering masts, would be visible from a distance of more than 10 miles.

If the target had been traveling at the speed the intelligence report said it would travel; if *Mako* was not detected as it rose to make the periscope observation; if Captain Mealey could get an accurate range on the target and get the "angle on the bow" so the target's course could be determined as a check on the sonar bearings; if *Mako* could get back down to 250 feet, then Captain Mealey and Joe Sirocco would have a set of accurate data on which to base the solution of the torpedo problem.

The telephone talkers passed the word in whispers throughout the ship that the Captain was going up to take a look and there was a dead silence in *Mako* as the ship planed upward through the water. This was the first of what could be a number of crucial moments. If a patrolling aircraft saw *Mako*'s long, dark shadow beneath the surface of the clear water, if the white feather of the periscope's wake attracted the eye of a lookout on a destroyer, the long run to get into position would be wasted and *Mako* would be the target of a dozen destroyers and no one knew how many aircraft as the target, the battleship, alerted, sped for the safety of Truk Atoll.

"Make turns for two knots," Captain Mealey said as the depth gauge showed 110 feet. "I'm going to raise the scope at eighty-five feet, Control, watch your angle when I do." Raising the periscope would create a drag that would tend to tip *Mako*'s bow upward more than desired.

Mealey squatted down by the periscope well and raised his left palm upward as a signal to Paul Botts to raise the periscope. Botts pushed the button that raised the periscope and stopped it as the periscope handles cleared the deck. Mealey snapped the handles outward and rotated the periscope until the lenses were in line with the last bearing given by Cohen.

"Seven zero feet and holding a half-degree up bubble," Simms reported from the Control Room.

"Very well," Mealey said. "Up periscope!" He clung to the handles, his face pressed against the heavy rubber eyepiece, his forehead tight against the rubber bumper above the eyepiece, clinging to the periscope handles as it rose upward.

"Six eight feet! six seven feet!" Simms chanted. "Six five feet, sir, and holding!"

"Mark!" Mealey snapped.

"Bearing—three three eight!" Botts sang out. Captain Mealey was rotating the range finder knob below the right handle of the periscope.

"Range! One three zero zero zero yards! Angle on the bow one five starboard! Down 'scope! Take me down, Control! Fast! Aircraft on our starboard beam! Two destroyers bearing zero two five! *Hard Dive! Hard Dive!*"

"Six seconds!" Grilley said, looking up from the stop-watch that hung around his neck on a cord. "That is one damned fast periscope observation!"

"You're not kidding," Sirocco grunted. He plotted the position of the target and fiddled with the Is-Was.

"Everything is on the nose, Captain," he reported. "The target has to run twelve thousand yards to the point of intercept. The target will reach that point in twenty-five minutes!"

"Two five zero feet, Captain," Simms interrupted. "Making turns for four knots, sir."

"Give me your recommended speeds, Joe," Mealey asked.

"We will be at the shooting point in fifteen minutes at this speed, sir," Sirocco answered. "We'll have too much time to stooge around. Recommend we run at four knots for eight minutes and then slow to two knots. We should be able to come up at our shooting range of eight hundred yards at that point."

"Very well," Captain Mealey said. He turned to Edge.

"Work that out on the TDC." Sirocco heard the order and his craggy face flushed slightly.

"Reduce speed to two knots at seven minutes and fifty-five seconds from the time of observation," Mealey ordered. Grilley looked at Sirocco and grinned. The difference of five seconds was meaningless but it was a continuing rebuke to Sirocco's suggestion to the Commanding Officer that he go up for a look.

"Mr. Cohen," Mealey's voice was crisp. "Try to keep one ear on the target. Advise me at once if he changes his speed or course and continue to give me all you have on the other ships."

"The ships out ahead of the target are doing what they have been doing, sir," Cohen said. "Running back and forth across the target's course. The decibel level is rising steadily, they're getting closer to us. Main target's screws are steady."

Sirocco took a plotting sheet and climbed half way up the Conning Tower ladder, resting his broad back against the rim of the hatch. Mealey turned and squatted to look at the plot.

"Captain," Sirocco said, "if the ships sweeping ahead of the target peel off and go back toward the target's stern to sweep there they should be passing over us when we are less than three minutes from our shooting point."

"We'll go up then," Mealey said. His forefinger traced the track on the plotting sheet. "They'll be making so much noise they won't be able to hear us coming up or hear the outer tube doors being opened." He touched the plotting sheet again.

"I don't think any of the four destroyers out front will go into the atoll. This is the sticky part of the voyage for them. I think they'll all peel off and circle backward, that's what I'd order if I were in command of them." Sirocco looked at the stop-watch that hung around his neck.

"Suggest we reduce speed to two knots, sir. We're within a thousand yards of our shooting point. We have fourteen minutes to go before we shoot!"

"Make turns for two knots," Captain Mealey said.

"Two sets of twin screws, one behind the other and coming this way!" Cohen's voice floated up through the hatch. "This seems to be consistent with the previous maneuvering but now they're a lot closer to us!"

In the Forward Torpedo Room Ginty cocked his head suddenly and listened.

"Ship movin' fast out there on the port bow," he said slowly. "Got to be one of the tin cans guardin' the wagon. Son of a bitch ain't too far away, either! Listen, they's another one!" He moved down the length of the room, his restless hands plucking at the block and tackle that would be used to haul the reload torpedoes into the tubes.

"If those bastards pick us up and start droppin' shit on us don't grab at the fuckin' fish!" he growled at a young sailor from the Engine Rooms who had been picked for the reload crew because he was as strong as a horse. "You got to grab somethin'," Ginty continued, "grab your cock!"

"You think we'll get depth charged, Ginch?"

"Fucking ay!" Ginty snorted. "That Old Man back there in the Connin' Tower ain't got no blood in his veins! He's fulla ice water! Ain't no skipper in this whole fuckin' Navy got the guts to make an approach like this, bust right underneath twelve tin cans! When he sticks that fuckin' 'scope up he's gonna start shootin' at that fuckin' wagon and them destroyer captains is gonna go nuts and they'll hit us with more shit than you ever heard!"

As the enemy's screws thudded louder and louder Cohen began to draw his skinny legs together and to sit straight up on his stool. Sirocco noticed that Cohen's knees were now almost touching and he wondered if the change in Cohen's position was unconscious, that as danger grew nearer the move to close his legs had been a defensive reflex to protect his genital area. Sirocco shook himself, he had more to think about than wondering about Cohen's legs. He bent over his plot. Cohen was sending him a stream of bearings now and Sirocco and Grilley plotted rapidly.

"Give me the time to shooting, Plot," Mealey's voice seemed detached, without emotion. He stood in the Conning Tower, looking at Bob Edge and Paul Botts and seeing neither man. In his mind's eye he was seeing the deployment of the ships above and ahead of him, sorting them out from the profusion of bearings that Cohen was feeding to the Plotting party. He was preparing himself for the critical moments that are the acid test of a submarine commander in war, the ability to make accurate judgments of critical distances, speeds and angles. The Executive Officer with his Is-Was and the officer on the TDC would work out the firing problem but it was the information he fed to them as he looked through the periscope that would determine a successful attack or a failure. It was his judgment of the maneuvers the destroyer captains would go through that would determine if *Mako* carried out the full attack and got away or whether *Mako* went down, a victim of the destroyers' attacks.

"Four minutes, Captain," Sirocco said. "We can begin to come to periscope depth in one minute if the escort ships leave."

"Very well," Mealey said. "I'm going to shoot all six tubes forward as he goes by us and then swing ship and give him the after tubes."

"He's just over six hundred feet long, sir." Sirocco said. "At fifteen knots he'll pass the first firing point in about twenty-five seconds, sir."

"Understood," Captain Mealey said. He cocked his head upward as the thunder of ship's screws overhead filled *Mako*'s hull with sound, shaking the ship.

"Three ships have turned this way and are coming over us," Cohen's voice was cracking slightly. "Target ship is steady on course, no change in speed, sir."

Mealey touched the right side of his mustache with his forefinger. He had hoped only two ships would turn toward *Mako*, leaving the other two destroyers of the van on the far side of the target and temporarily out of the fight.

"Sixty-five feet," he ordered. "We'll open the torpedo tube outer doors at one hundred feet! Torpedo Officer to the After Room. Chief of the Boat to the Forward Room!"

Sirocco looked at the depth gauge in front of the bow planesman. It read 175 feet, the long black needle moving. The needle passed 150 feet and then 120, 110.

"Open outer doors on all torpedo tubes!" Captain Mealey ordered, his voice crisp. He looked down into the Control Room from his squatting position beside the periscope well.

In the Forward Torpedo Room, which had no depth gauge, Ginty had been watching a gauge that showed the water pressure outside of *Mako*'s hull. As the needle of that gauge crept downward Ginty placed the socket of a big Y-wrench over a stud on the end of a shaft that would turn a worm gear and open the outer torpedo tube door and slide back the hull shutter for Number One tube. He nodded at Johnny Paul, who put his own Y-wrench in position on the stud beside Number Two tube.

The pressure needle touched 44.4 pounds and Ginty heaved mightily on the Y-wrench as the telephone talker cried, "Open all outer torpedo tube doors!" Ginty's broad back seemed to widen as he spun the wrench viciously, felt the door come up against the stops and then he whipped the wrench off and started on the tube below Number One, the Number Three tube. He finished opening that door and dropped down into the bilge in front of Number Five tube and wrestled the big wrench around in a flashing circle. The reload crew listened in awe to Ginty's mighty gasps for air in the humid heat of the Torpedo Room. Ginty felt Number Five door come up against the stop and glanced upward. Paul was still working on his second outer door, to Number Four tube.

"Shit!" Ginty grunted. He slammed his wrench onto the stud on the bottom tube of Paul's bank, Number Six.

"Watcha fuckin' legs," he snapped as he spun the last tube door open.

"Tell 'em, fuckhead!" he gasped at the telephone talker. As the talker reported, Ginty hoisted himself up to the deck, his big chest heaving as he fought for air, hearing the talker finish his report with "Green board. Forward, Bridge!"

"After Room?" Ginty gasped.

"Reporting now, we beat 'em!"

"Fuckin' ay we beat 'em! Six tubes to four and we beat 'em!" He took up a position between the two vertical banks of torpedo tubes, his meaty hand resting lightly on the brass metal guard over the manual firing key of Number One tube.

"Eighty feet!" the telephone talkers whispered. "The periscope's going up!"

As the periscope rose out of its well Captain Mealey grabbed the handles and rode it upward until he was standing, crouched slightly, staring through the lens as it cut through the water below the surface.

"Watch your depth!" he snapped. "Lens is breaking water! Bring me up to sixty-five feet!" Sirocco heard Captain Mealey's breath go out in a mighty whoosh.

"Mark!" Mealey snapped.

"Bearing—three five zero!" Botts said to Edge, who cranked the information in to the TDC.

"Range . . ." Mealey's fingers found the range knob. "Range to the target is seven zero zero! Angle on the bow is zero nine zero!"

"You can begin shooting in ten seconds, sir," Edge said.

"My God!" Captain Mealey's voice held a note of awe. "He fills the whole field of vision! There are men on the foc'sle, anchor detail, I think!"

"Stand by, Forward!" Sirocco said quietly into his telephone.

Two thousand feet above the water the pilot of a VAL dive bomber banked his aircraft slightly to get a better look at the battleship. His eyes widened as he saw the dark shape of *Mako* ahead of him. He tipped his plane over in a shallow dive and then he saw the tiny feather of white foam midway down the dark shape and identified it for what it was, the periscope of a submarine. He yelled into his throat microphone and tipped his VAL over in a nearly vertical dive, centering the cross hairs on the plastic windshield on the tiny feather of foam beneath him.

CHAPTER 18

"*Fire one!*" Captain Mealey barked.

Ensign Botts pressed the firing key in the Conning Tower and repeated Mealey's order into the telephone that hung around his neck. Ginty jammed two thick fingers down on the manual firing key a split second after the impulse firing air roared into the flooded torpedo tube at 600 pounds pressure to the square inch, kicking the torpedo forward, tripping the torpedo's firing latch and starting the torpedo's steam engine into screaming life.

"Number One fired electrically!" Ginty bellowed at his telephone talker. "Standing by Number Two!" He reached up and back with a long arm and yanked open the poppet valve lever for Number One tube. The sea water rushing into the empty torpedo tube pushed the impulse firing air backward and down through the poppet valve vent line into the bilge, thus avoiding any telltale bubble of air outside the ship that could betray its position.

"*Fire two!*" Captain Mealey was counting to himself, allowing six seconds between each shot.

"My God, he's a big one!" Mealey said. "Stand by Three!"

"Number Two fired electrically!" Ginty yelled and moved out from between the torpedo tubes as Johnny Paul ducked in to take his place. A frenzied ballet of strength, agility and cooperation had begun in the Forward Torpedo Room.

Once a torpedo has been fired and the firing air has been gulped back into the ship through the poppet valves, those valves must be closed and the outer tube door closed. Then a series of drain valves must be opened, air pressure put on the tube and the sea water that filled the torpedo tube after firing blown down into a special holding tank called the WRT, the Water 'Round Torpedo tank. Then the air has to be shut off, the valves closed, the tube vented of all pressure and the inner door opened so that the torpedo tube can be reloaded. The torpedo is pulled into the tube with a block and tackle (the "tagle") positioned precisely in the tube, the inner door closed and locked and if the torpedo is to be made ready for firing again valves must be opened, air pressure put on the WRT tank and the tube vented and water blown up around the torpedo and the impulse air tank which fires the torpedo out of the tube charged. After which the outer door must be opened and the gyro spindle engaged through the side of the torpedo tube into the torpedo.

To do all of this precisely and swiftly requires long and arduous training. To do it under battle conditions, to fire all six torpedo tubes and start a reload before the last tube has been fired requires a degree of cooperation, exquisite timing and enormous physical strength from a group of men that is seldom seen anywhere outside of the submarine service.

"Number Three fired electrically!" Johnny Paul yelled.

The VAL dive bomber's two bombs, released a fraction of a second too late, missed *Mako*'s periscope and landed just above the Forward Torpedo Room with a booming crash, driving Ginty to his knees and throwing the reload crew around the room like rag dolls. Ginty hauled himself upright, his big hand reaching for the poppet valve lever of Number Three tube.

Dusty Rhodes had wrestled the inner door open on Number One tube. He turned to yell at the reload crew.

"Unstrap that fish and get it moving, you bastards!"

"We're being depth charged!" a man yelled. He turned and

started for the closed water-tight door at the end of the Torpedo Room. Rhodes was on him in three long strides, catching the man's shoulders in his powerful hands, his mouth close to the man's ear.

"Don't panic!" he half-whispered. "It's all right! A little noise! The Old Man's still shooting! He's depending on us! Just keep your eyes open, your ears open, watch me, listen to me!" He released the man and spun back to his position, noticing that Ginty was closing the outer door to Number Two tube with one hand, spinning the big Y-wrench as if it were a toy. The torpedo was sliding into the Number One tube and as its screws passed the set of rollers on a heavy stand in back of the tube, Rhodes raised his hand to stop the reload crew heaving on the tagle. He took the tagle off the torpedo.

"Lay out that tagle for Number Two," Rhodes barked. He turned and put his big hands carefully on the exhaust pipe of the torpedo, braced his back against the rollers and pushed the torpedo the rest of the way into the tube with sheer strength, moving it gently until he felt it come up against the stop bolt. He grabbed the brass propeller safety guard from the torpedo and stuck it in his pocket and closed the inner door. Automatically, he reached over and adjusted the tail bumper stop in the center of the inner door. Moving swiftly and surely, he blew water up around the torpedo from the WRT tank, closed the valves, vented off the tube, charged the impulse tank and opened the outer door and made way for Ginty, who was closing the outer door on Number Three.

"Engage the gyro on Number One!" Rhodes barked at Johnny Paul.

"*Fire four!*" Captain Mealey's voice was vibrant with emotion. The target was visible again, the huge sheet of water thrown up by the exploding bombs had subsided. He saw two aircraft above the battleship, streaking toward him. He counted down slowly. *Mako* and Captain Mealey were committed. The firing would go on, one torpedo every six seconds until all the torpedoes had been fired or the target had sunk.

"First two fish running hot, straight and normal!" Cohen's voice sang out. "Can't hear Number Three running. Number Four is running hot, straight and normal!"

"*A hit!*" Mealey yelled. "Just abaft his bow! There's another hit! Farther aft! There's smoke over his bow!"

"*Fire five!* . . .

"*Fire six!* . . . There's another hit! Lots of smoke over his bow!

"*All back emergency!*

"*Right full rudder!*

"*Give me all you've got, maneuvering!*"

Mealey felt the *Mako* shudder under his feet as Chief Hendershot in the Maneuvering Room threw all the voltage and amperage in *Mako*'s two huge storage batteries across the buses of the electric propulsion motors, adjusting the immense, surging power with a delicate touch so as not to blow out the circuit breakers and leave *Mako* helpless, without propulsion. *Mako* began to go astern, gathering way, her bow swinging widely to port. A second VAL sighted on the periscope, stooped and shot downward. The two bombs missed well to the right side of *Mako*'s swinging bow.

"*All stop!*

"*All ahead full!*

"*All ahead full! Stand by to shoot aft!*" Mealey twisted the periscope around.

"Another hit! Right under her bridge! Here we go, Plot!"

"Mark!" Botts read the azimuth ring bearing and Edge cranked the bearing into the TDC.

"Range . . . six zero zero! Meet your helm right there! Meet it, damn it! Don't take me off course!

"Angle on the bow . . . one four zero starboard!" He looked at the battleship, hearing the gears in the TDC whir.

"We've got a solution, sir," Edge said.

"*Fire seven!*" Mealey counted down from six to one.

"*Fire eight!*"

The precision ballet began in the After Torpedo Room with Mike DeLucia as the ballet master and Lieut. Don Grilley assisting.

"*Fire nine!*

"*Fire ten!* Another hit! Under his after turrets! Lots of smoke from his bow! Now there are flames shooting way above his bow! There's a big explosion, lots of flame! Another hit! Amidships! Six hits! Six hits!" He swung the periscope around, chanting the bearings of the ships racing toward him.

"Range to the nearest destroyer . . . three zero zero zero yards . . . I'm going to have to shoot at this one!"

"Torpedo Tubes One and Two reloaded forward," Sirocco's voice held a note of repressed excitement. "Outer doors open, gyro spindles engaged, depth set two feet. Number Seven aft is ready, outer door open, gyro spindle engaged, depth set two feet. Number Eight will be ready in five seconds, sir! You've got One and Two forward and Seven and Eight aft!"

"Very well," Captain Mealey said. He steadied on the onrushing destroyer.

"Zero gyro angle! He's coming too fast for a plot! Right down his throat! . . . Stand by . . . *Fire one!*" He paused. "Close tube outer doors! Flood negative! Take me down! Fast, Control, damn it, fast! Left full rudder! Down periscope! Stand by for depth charge attack!"

The torpedo burst out of the Number One tube and flashed toward the destroyer that was rushing at *Mako*. It roared down the destroyer's port side, missing by 10 yards, leaving behind a trail of bubbles that reduced the lookout on the destroyer's port side to gibbering fright. The destroyer's captain, recognizing the lookout's stammering shriek for what it was, pressed the buzzer to alert the depth charge crews at the destroyer's stern and at the two Y-guns that would hurl charges far out to each side. He picked up his VHF microphone.

"*Eagle*'s Feather One to *Eagle*," he said calmly. "We have the enemy in sight and have commenced an attack run. Enemy fired one torpedo, missing down our port side." He nodded to his gunnery officer and the two Y-guns boomed and the depth charges began to roll off the squat stern of the destroyer.

"Drop is made, sir," the gunnery officer reported. "Depth charge exploders were set for one hundred feet." The destroyer captain nodded. Back of his ship there was a low rumble and the ocean began to erupt in great gouts of water.

On the bridge of the *Fubuki* destroyer leader designated as *Eagle*, Fleet Captain Akihito Hideki of the Imperial Japanese Navy, lately the commander of the Japanese Navy's Advanced School for

Anti-Submarine Warfare, rubbed his small gray goatee. Captain Hideki was a small man, physically, with delicate bones and a scholarly manner. That manner and his standing as the ranking expert in the Japanese Navy's anti-submarine warfare department had led to his nickname, the "Professor."

He rubbed his goatee again and then smoothed it and turned to the *Eagle*'s commander.

"Please tell all the Small Birds to deploy in a half circle from here to here. . . . " His narrow forefinger traced a line on the chart that lay on the table beside the *Eagle* Captain's position at the starboard wing of the bridge.

"Small Birds are to form a sonar listening line and report to us. *Eagle*'s Feathers One and Three form up port and starboard of *Eagle*'s Feather Two. Ask our friends in the Air Force on the atoll to please put some observation planes in the air at once. The water is very clear. They should be able to see the submarine down as far as two hundred feet."

"The battleship, sir?" *Eagle*'s Captain's face was stricken. The safety of the battleship had been the responsibility of the destroyer squadron and he was second in command only to the Professor.

"We can do nothing for her now," the Professor said calmly. He steadied his binoculars and looked at the burning ship.

"She still has some way on her. I presume her commander is trying to beach her on the reef. The fires appear to be out of control."

A junior officer approached, saluting smartly.

"Your message sent and acknowledged, sir." The Professor nodded and looked down at the chart. Then he raised his head and looked at the battleship, flames soaring high above its forward turret area.

"A skilled, daring attack!" he said slowly. "Does the battleship commander know how many torpedoes were fired at him? How many hits he took?"

"He reported seeing the wakes of nine torpedoes, sir. He took seven hits, all down near the keel. The second torpedo set fire to his ammunition storage for the forward turrets, sir." The junior officer was standing at ramrod attention, his moon face impassive.

"Lucky shooting!" *Eagle*'s commander said.

"No!" the Professor said. He touched the chart with his

forefinger. "*Eagle*'s Feather One attacked here. The submarine got under us undetected and closed to point-blank range! That is not luck! That is skill and daring! Seven hits out of nine torpedoes is remarkable shooting! And getting his hits below the armor plating! We'd better make a note to inform Intelligence that the Americans have apparently solved their torpedo problems." He looked at the chart again.

"He fired nine at the battleship and saved one if he were attacked. He fired that one at *Eagle*'s Feather Two and missed. So now his fangs are drawn! He can't risk a reload, reloading torpedoes is a noisy and slow business." He rubbed his hands together and the skin made a dry, rasping sound.

"You know, I'd like to meet with this man below us, talk to him! But that is impossible because we are going to kill him! So we must now put ourselves in his place, think as he will think." He turned to *Eagle*'s Captain.

"When I had you as a student you were very good at putting yourself in the place of a commander of a Japanese submarine. Now let me see how you will put yourself in the place of an American submarine commander! What will he do, do you think?"

The destroyer Captain looked at the plot drawn in on the chart by one of the junior officers.

"If I were he? I'd head straight for the target!" he said calmly. "He'd like us to believe that he might go into the atoll itself but he knows we won't believe that. It would be too easy to put the cork in that bottle and keep him inside. But he should head for the battleship. Before he gets there he will turn to starboard and head down the reef. We would have trouble following him with sonar if he did that, the reef would interfere."

"I agree with you up to there," the Professor said. "But if he follows the reef line he is restricted; he can only go in two directions, forward and to his starboard. He knows by now that we have a number of ships after him. We could wall him off if he went along the reef."

"But he might make his turn in that direction, follow the reef for a short distance to fool us and then make his move to go to the open sea, hope to find a layer out there and lose us."

"I think that is what he will do, Isoruko," the Professor used his former student's given name easily. "There are no layers in this area where we are now but there are some farther out."

"You anticipated an attack close to the entrance?" The destroyer Captain's eyes widened slightly.

"No, I did not," the Professor said. "I anticipated an attack, one always does that. But the logical place for the attack would have been farther out to sea and with more than one submarine. I ordered the layer check so I could know conditions."

"Contact!" the radio operator on the bridge sang out. "*Eagle's* Feather Two reports it has the target on sonar and is pinging. Bearing three five five, sir. Target is at two five zero feet and moving slowly."

The Professor bent over the chart. "He's on a course to the target! He is doing what you had anticipated he would do! As I anticipated he would do! Which means that he is intelligent!

"Order *Eagle's* Feather Two to maintain the contact. *Eagle's* Feather One and Three will form up behind and to each side of the sonar ship. I suggest that we take position astern and see what this fellow does."

Captain Mealey looked down at the plot Joe Sirocco had drawn of the attack, noting the positions of the enemy ships.

"We're going to have to make a turn very soon," he said. "What's that son of a bitch thinking about up there, what are all those sons of bitches thinking about?" He touched his white mustache gently. He put his finger on the chart.

"We have several courses of action. We could run for the entrance and go inside and he won't believe we'd do that because we won't, it would be suicide.

"We could turn to starboard and run down the edge of the reef but if we did that we'd be restricted, no maneuverability. But we could do that and make the bastard think that's what we're going to do and then turn to sea.

"The problem is that we have no chance for deception. He's got us on sonar and he's going to know what we're up to as soon as we start anything. So we'll keep it simple, we'll come left and go out to sea, or try to do that." He looked at Nate Cohen.

"Do you have anything on the battleship?"

"The target is still under way," Cohen said. "He's going very slowly, I can only hear one screw. He bears zero zero five."

"We crippled the son of a bitch," Mealey growled. "Why the hell doesn't he sink with six fish hitting him?"

"He might be sinking now," Sirocco said. "He's close to the reef, getting closer each bearing. He might be taking a lot of water and trying to get his bow up on the reef before he sinks."

"Two ships bearing one zero six and two zero zero and making slow turns," Cohen said.

"They're waiting for us to make our move," Mealey said. He studied the plot closely.

"Okay, let's start the performance, gentlemen. Left full rudder and steady on course zero zero zero. Make turns for two knots. I'm not going to waste the battery any more than I have to."

"Another set of screws crossing astern, sir," Cohen said. The sound of the searching ship's sonar beam hitting *Mako* was making a ringing sound throughout the ship. In the Forward Torpedo Room Ginty looked at Rhodes.

"Bastard has got us nailed! Why in fuck don't he start droppin' his shit?"

"He will," Rhodes said. He went down the room touching each member of the reload crew and the room's torpedomen lightly on the shoulders or arms.

"Let's keep it very quiet, fellows. Very quiet! It's going to get awful noisy in a little while!"

"Four hundred feet," Captain Mealey said to Pete Simms. He turned to Sirocco. "We'll let him get a half dozen good pings on us, enough to show him that his triangulation indicates we're down deeper than before. That will mean he'll have to reset his depth charger exploders and that will give us some time."

"Steady on course zero zero zero, sir," the helmsman said.

"Very well," Captain Mealey said. "As soon as he starts his run—let me know, Nate, when he does that—as soon as he does we'll go down to six hundred feet. Throw the bastard off!"

On the bridge of the destroyer designated as *Eagle* the radio operator sang out.

"*Eagle's* Feather Two reports target is on course zero zero zero and is now at four zero zero feet, sir."

"To all captains," the destroyer's Captain snapped. "Reset depth charge exploders for five hundred feet!"

The professor smiled to himself as he walked a few steps away from the younger officer. His face was glowing, this submarine captain was an expert! Few if any of his own Navy's submarine captains had shown as much imagination as this American down below when they were acting as targets for his anti-submarine warfare school destroyers. A worthy opponent, this man down below him, a worthy opponent for a man recognized as knowing more about killing a submarine than any other Naval officer in the world!

"The target is steady on his course and depth, sir," the destroyer's Captain said. "Would you do me the honor of taking command of this depth charge run?"

"No," the Professor said. "You are doing very well, sir. I leave that honor to you." He stood at the bridge wing as *Eagle* took position to begin the first depth charge attack.

In *Mako's* Control Room all eyes were on Nate Cohen's lean back. Cohen raised his head lightly and Sirocco tensed, ready to pencil in the bearing he knew Cohen was about to give.

"Very slow twin screws bearing one eight zero, sir," Cohen said. "That's the ship that has been pinging on us. One ship bearing one six five, one ship bearing one nine zero. One set of twin screws has circled those three ships and is coming to a bearing, now he's steady on one eight zero and he's picking up speed! This is an attack run, sir!"

Captain Mealey picked up a telephone and pressed the talk button.

"This is the Captain speaking. All telephone talkers pass this word. The dance is about to begin. All men not needed to man stations get into bunks and stay there. Report any damage to the Control Room at once." He turned to Nate Cohen.

"He's coming fast, now, Captain. He's committed!"

"Six hundred feet!" Mealey said to Simms. The Engineering Officer's eyes widened in protest. *Mako* was built to operate at a maximum depth of 400 feet with a 50 percent safety factor. Six hundred feet was her theoretical maximum depth, one to be risked only if circumstances made the depth unavoidable. He turned to the men on the bow and stern planes.

"Five degree down bubble. Six hundred feet."

"Here he comes!" Mike DeLucia said to Lieut. Don Grilley in the After Torpedo Room. The sound of the destroyer's screws began to fill *Mako*'s hull as the ship up above raced down *Mako*'s invisible wake.

In the Control Room Captain Mealey unconsciously rose to the balls of his feet and stood, quietly, beside the gyro table. As the sound of the destroyer's screws built to a roar within *Mako*'s gull he said,

"Right full rudder! All ahead flank! He can't hear us now, he's making too much noise! How's the depth?"

"Five hundred and fifty feet, sir." Simms reported, his voice rising in an effort to be heard over the sound that was filling *Mako*'s hull.

"He's dropped charges!" Cohen yelled. "Two other sets of screws back there are picking up speed, sir!"

Cohen half-turned on his stool to see if Captain Mealey had heard him and the first depth charges exploded with a gigantic roar that hurled *Mako* sideways and downward. Cohen was thrown from his stool. Sirocco, who was standing at the chart table gripping its edge with both hands, felt himself lifted and then flung bodily into Captain Mealey, who crumpled under Sirocco's weight and went sliding across the deck into the legs of the machinest mate who was stationed at the high pressure air manifold, bringing that man down in a heap. The lights went out, leaving only the feeble glow of the emergency lanterns. The helmsman, who had been thrown backward into Lieutenant Simms, picked himself up and got back to the helm.

"No power!" he said. "We've lost power to the helm, sir!"

"Shift to manual power on the bow and stern planes and the helm," Mealey croaked from the other side of the Control Room where he was trying to untangle himself from the machinist's mate. Cohen, flat on his back, but still wearing his earphones, rolled over.

"Two more sets of screws coming fast, sir! This is an attack run!" He got to his knees and reached for his stool and then thought better of it and sat on the deck, his stool cradled between his legs, his eyes on his dials.

"Left full rudder!" Mealey snapped as he got to his feet. "Come back to zero zero zero!"

"Both ships have dropped charges, sir!" Cohen said.

Mako bucked and rolled under the impact of a dozen or more depth charges dropped by *Eagle*'s Feathers One and Three. A spray of water jetted across the Forward Engine Room and Chief John Barber scrambled to the fitting with a wrench in his hand and brought the stream down to a trickle.

"Damage reports!" Captain Mealey snapped. Sirocco spoke softly into his telephone set.

"Nothing major, Captain. Electrical power is being restored, circuit breakers jumped out for the lights and auxiliary systems. Some minor leaks, nothing serious. Few bruises and bumps but no broken bones."

"Very well," Captain Mealey said. "What do you hear, Nate?"

"Hard to hear anything right at the moment because of all the disturbance from the depth charges, sir," Cohen said. "That's why he isn't pinging on us. But he'll be back in a minute."

Mealey touched Dick Smalley, the Gunner's Mate who was manning the bow planes, on the shoulder.

"Our depth charge exploder mechanisms have a limit of what, four hundred feet, Gunner?"

"Yessir," Smalley said. "But the book says if you screw the spring down to more than three seventy-five you might rupture the diaphragm and get a dud. Chief I know on a tin can told me that they had orders never to set charges for deeper than three fifty, sir and that they had failures even then."

"Let's hope their depth charges have the same limitation," Mealey said, "but from the sound of that last barrage they seem to be deeper than that. If we can stay below his depth charges we can get out of here with nothing worse than a bad shaking up!"

The destroyer designated as *Eagle* swung back in a long curve, heading for the place where the bulk of the depth charges had been dropped.

"All lookouts keep their eyes open," the destroyer Captain said. "Look for an oil slick, debris of any kind or large air bubbles."

"I hope with you," the Professor said softly to the younger man. "But I don't think we got him! A beautiful attack! But I am sure this man down there is a thinker. It is easy only in the classroom, eh? Do we still have contact with him?"

The radio operator overheard the question and answered without being asked.

"*Eagle*'s Feather Two has resumed sonar search, sir." A junior officer trotted on to the bridge with a message flimsy in his hand, saluted and handed over the message and then retreated.

"This is an intercepted message, sir," the destroyer's Captain said to the Professor. "The Captain of the battleship is reporting to the command at Truk that he has grounded his ship on the reef. Fires are still out of control. A list of casualties will follow later. At present he is estimating three hundred or more dead."

"If this were an American movie we'd all be going through the ceremony of *Hara-kari*," the Professor said with a small smile. "And then who would be left to catch this man underneath our keels, eh?"

"The ceremony is an honorable one!" The destroyer's Captain spoke in stiff, formal tones.

"Oh, I grant you that!" the Professor said "But so wasteful when there is so much work to be done. *Arte purire sua,* the old Romans were fond of saying. 'One perishes by one's own cunning.' This is a cunning fox we fight. We must help him perish by his own cunning!"

"Contact!" the radio operator's voice was loud. "*Eagle*'s Feather Two has contact with the enemy, sir!" The destroyer's Captain looked at his superior officer.

"Again, sir, would you like the honor of conducting this attack?"

"And again, no thank you. But I appreciate your courtesy."

"Sir, this man below us is clever! I would feel better if you were in charge."

"Very well," the Professor said. "We will enjoy a joint effort, the two of us pitted against the one man below. I have one suggestion; we know that he turns to one side or the other as soon as one ship begins its high speed run to drop charges. Then he comes back to his original course to foil the other two who are attacking and staying well outside the first ship's run.

"*Eagle's* Feather Two has done all the sonar work so far and her commander must be impatient. So I suggest that you issue him orders to make a delayed attack up the middle of the attack plot and see if we can catch this fellow after he sneaks back on his original course, eh?"

The younger man nodded, a small grin touching his lips. The Professor was a tricky man, he had sent many a destroyer commander almost weeping in rage and frustration to his quarters at his anti-submarine school. He issued the necessary orders in a harsh, chopped voice and the destroyers under his command began to form up for the attack. As his own ship heeled in a tight turn and took position he nodded at the signal officer and a bright flag at the foremast yardarm snapped open as its binding cord was pulled and *Eagle* moved to the attack, its screws biting the water, the depth charge crews standing ready. The second assault on *Mako* was under way.

The first attack had done little real damage to the submarine. The electricians had quickly replaced the few light bulbs that had broken. The cork insulation that had rained down in the first burst of charges and the broken glass from gauge faces had been tidied up.

Ginty was swearing softly in the Forward Room as he massaged a purpling bruise on his massive thigh, suffered when he had been thrown from his feet against the face of one of the torpedo tubes. Dusty Rhodes wore a large bump on his forehead from hitting a torpedo tube rack. Johnny Paul, his face white, managed a smile.

"God! I'm glad that's over!"

"Shit!" Ginty rumbled. "This is on'y the beginnin'! They's twelve fucking tin cans up there and that means they got a lotta depth charges!" He looked at the small clock near the torpedo tube doors.

"It's only zero nine hundred, means we got about nine, ten hours of daylight up there! Them fuckers got plenty of time to throw everything they got at us and time to run more charges out from that base they got inside the reef!"

In the After Torpedo Room Mike DeLucia looked at Grilley.

"It ain't fun, sir!"

Grilley nodded and squinted at a pressure gauge on the board next to the tubes. He did the mathematics in his head; 310 pounds of sea pressure divided by 44.4 pounds for each 100 feet. He blinked his eyes in surprise: 700 feet?

"My God," he said in a wondering tone. "We're at seven hundred feet!" In a bunk up near the overhead on the port side a man began to sob uncontrollably. Grilley moved to the bunk and stood on tiptoe so his head was just above the bunk rail. He saw the man's contorted face, the tears staining his cheeks.

"We're gonna die!" the man sobbed, spittle spraying from his bitten, bloody lips.

Grilley felt suddenly helpless. He reached out hesitantly and put his hand on the man's shoulder and felt his body shaking violently. He patted the bare shoulder.

"You're not going to die, none of us is going to die! Look at that pressure gauge over there! We're down at seven hundred feet! Depth charges can't hurt us down that deep, they just make a lot of noise! The Captain knows what he's doing. It's going to be noisy for a few more hours but we'll be all right!"

The man's head turned toward him and Grilley saw the naked fear in the man's eyes. The man's mouth opened and then shut and Grilley saw his teeth clamp together on his lower lip and bite in and a fresh stream of blood ran down the man's chin. He patted the shaking shoulder again.

"Now get yourself under control, fella! We're going to need you for another reload in a little while, okay?"

He turned away, a sick feeling in his stomach. How did you deal with that kind of terrible fear? DeLucia saw the indecision on Grilley's face and, with the wisdom of years of submarine service, spoke up.

"You heard the Lieutenant! We're under any depth charges that go off so they ain't gonna do any harm! The Old Man knows what he's doing! Got right under twelve Jap destroyers and punched that Jap battleship fulla holes, didn't he? So he knows what he's doin'! All you guys button your fucking lips and listen to me. And to the Lieutenant. All we got to do is wait it out!"

"That's what I don't like," one of the reload crew said. "While we're waitin' the Jap is figurin' things out. Japs are good at figurin' things out, Mike, real good! They'll figure what we're doin' and they'll stay after us!"

"They can figure all they want but they won't know," Grilley said. "Now let's knock off the talking and noise."

In the Control Room Captain Mealey was studying Sirocco's plotting board. He reached for an eraser hanging from the edge of the gyro table by a cord and erased a long pencil mark left by the pencil Sirocco was holding when he was thrown across the gyro table.

"We've got five ships on the plot, Joe. Where are the other eight destroyers?"

"I lost contact with Gamma, the single-screw ships we had earlier, Captain," Cohen said. "All I have now is the Delta group, four fast ships with twin screws, the ones who have been attacking." He rattled off four sets of bearings and Sirocco plotted them in on his chart.

"They're sitting up there waiting to see what we're going to do," Captain Mealey said. "Aaron, what do you have on that bathythermograph?"

The bathythermograph, a crude instrument, measured the temperature of the water and the submarine's depth in a line scrawled by a tiny stylus on a piece of smoked paper. Some years earlier oceanographers had discovered that there were random areas in the oceans that were saltier than the surrounding waters. The saltier areas were colder by a few degrees than the water around them and dense enough to cause a sonar beam to deflect, or bounce off them and continue without bouncing back to the transmitting ship's receiver. The effect was that the searching ship would believe its sonar beam had hit nothing and therefore there was no ship in the area.

If a submarine could locate one of those saltier areas, or "layers" as they were called, and could stay under it, the chances of being detected by searching ships was very small. The hunters could not hear the submarine. Nor could the submarine hear the hunters but that drawback was acceptable to a submarine under attack.

"All isothermal, sir," Aaron said. "No layers."

A ringing *ping!* hit the ship and then another and another.

"Here they come!" Cohen said. "One, two, no, three ships coming very fast!"

The growing thunder of the destroyers moving to the attack shook *Mako*'s hull. Within *Mako* the crew could hear the sharp "*crack!*" of the depth charge exploder mechanisms going off and then the massive, shattering, thundering explosions began, shaking *Mako* like a rat in the teeth of a terrier. Lights shattered and cork insulation rained down, gauge glasses shattered, the glass shards scattering across the deck. Ginty shook his head, as a prize fighter will when he is badly hurt, his teeth clamping tightly together as he fought the terrible impulse to scream aloud. Dusty Rhodes reached for a towel on a bunk and fought his way aft, clutching at the torpedo skids, grabbing at handholds to keep his feet as *Mako* bucked and shook under the violent attack. He reached an after bunk and used the towel to stanch the flow of blood from the face of a vacant-eyed man who had been thrown upward out of the bunk he was lying into the springs of the bunk above him. Rhodes wiped the blood from the man's face and slapped him lightly on the cheek, slapped him again very lightly and the man's eyes came into focus.

"You're not hurt, just a couple of scratches," he said. "Trouble with you, sailor, is you haven't got any lead in your ass! You went flying right up in the air when those charges went off!"

The man managed a wry grin. "Last time we had reload drill you told me to get the lead outa my ass, Chief! Now you're saying I got it outa my ass and they's why I went flyin' up inna air!" Rhodes looked at him narrowly, knowing that the line between jocularity and a screaming loss of control was very narrow. He punched the man on the shoulder lightly.

"Won't ever tell you that you've got lead in your ass again," he said solemnly. He went back forward to where Ginty stood.

"Keep an eye on him," he said to Ginty, "he's near the edge."

"Makes three I got to watch," Ginty growled. "That kid, the seaman we took aboard last time in, up there in the top bunk. He's passed out and he's shit himself if you ain't smelled it yet! And this fuck head wearin' the telephones is like an old lady, so fuckin' scared I don't think he can talk!"

"I can so!" the man said, his chin chattering up and down. "I can do my fuckin' job!"

"Do it then and stop slobberin' spit all over the fuckin' telephone mouthpiece!" Ginty said.

Captain Mealey studied the faces of the depth gauges in front of the bow and stern planesmen. The long black needles read 690 feet.

"Seven hundred feet," he said in a low voice. "Keep us at seven hundred feet!" He turned to Sirocco.

"I'm going to stay this deep, she seems to be taking it, and go right out of here! I think we can take anything they throw at us. God knows it couldn't be any worse than that last attack!" He looked over at the bathythermograph.

"Maybe if we can keep going we can find a layer."

"Here they come again!" Cohen said.

CHAPTER **19**

"Send *Eagle's* Feather Two up the enemy's track, please," the Professor's voice was gentle but underneath the soft tones there was the assurance of command. "I want to know, exactly, how deep the enemy is running." He took off his billed cap and rubbed his bald head and then smoothed the ruff of gray hair that fringed his head. He waited, his face serene.

"*Eagle* Feather Two reports enemy is steady on a course of zero zero zero, sir and he is at depth seven hundred feet, seven zero zero feet, sir," the radio operator on *Eagle's* bridge said.

"Seven hundred!" the professor's eyebrows went upward a fraction of an inch. "We set our charges too shallowly!"

"Our experience, sir, has been that American submarines do not operate below four hundred feet sir," the destroyer captain's face was stricken. "That is why I ordered the depth charges set at five hundred feet."

"All life is an experience, one new experience after another," the Professor said kindly. "So now we have learned something. The submarine is relatively safe from attacks at seven hundred feet. We can do him no structural damage of any consequence. If he makes a mistake, comes up from that depth for any reason, then we can get him but," he paused. "Will you please call your gunnery officer to the bridge, Isoruku?" He used the younger man's given name deliberately, to soften the rebuff he had just given.

The Gunnery Officer, a young Lieutenant, hastily buttoned his uniform jacket and set his hat straight on his head as he went toward the ladder that led to the bridge.

Why does he want to see me? he said to himself. One depth charge did not explode, that fool of a gunner forgot to pull out the safety key, but that old man couldn't know that, he couldn't count each explosion in the middle of an attack. Or could he? He walked out on the bridge and stood rigidly at attention.

"Oh, stand at ease, sir," the Professor said. "I have a technical question to ask you. What is the very deepest, the absolute maximum you can set our depth charges to explode?"

The Lieutenant let his breath out slowly and carefully, he didn't want his apprehension to show.

"With the new exploder mechanisms, sir, seven hundred feet. But the instruction manuals all say that six hundred and seventy-five feet is the maximum for consistent performance. When the tension spring is screwed up to seven hundred feet the pressure on the diaphragm is excessive and there is a danger of diaphragm failure. That would mean no explosion, sir."

"But you rechecked each diaphragm on my orders, did you not? And you replaced all diaphragms that were not seated properly or appeared to be old or defective?"

"Yes, sir. All the ships in the squadron did this."

"So we have good diaphragms which means we have a certain explosion of the depth charge at six hundred and seventy-five feet but an uncertain explosion at seven hundred feet?"

The Lieutenant saw the trap yawning at his feet. "I would say that, sir, if we could be sure of every diaphragm. Even some of the replacements we unpacked had cracks in them."

"I won't hold you personally responsible for what some civilian has manufactured, young man," the Professor smiled gently. "Tell me if I am correct if I say this: If all the diaphragms in the exploders are properly made, if they are all carefully seated, if we use care in exerting maximum spring pressure against the diaphragms then we could expect performance at seven hundred feet? The reason I ask is that the enemy submarine is now cruising at that depth."

"At seven hundred feet?" the gunnery officer's eyes opened in surprise.

"Precisely," the Professsor said. "Now please answer my questions."

"We found over twenty percent of the diaphragms in the depth charges to be defective sir. Those were replaced." The friendly air of the small man with the four circles of salt-stained gold on his rumpled jacket sleeve emboldened the young Lieutenant.

"I would say that we have a better than eight-to-one chance that all our depth charges will function at seven hundred feet, sir!"

"Good!" the Professor said. "I am always happy to see young officers who are sure of themselves, even at eight-to-one odds! Set all depth charges on the racks at seven hundred feet. Do not change the settings on the Y-gun charges. If he decides to come up a little shallower I don't want to waste time re-setting charges." He turned to the destroyer's Captain.

"Please order the other ships to follow suit." He waited until the order had been given and then walked over to the chart table and studied the plot.

"His strategy is obvious, don't you think, Isoruku?" the Professor's thin finger touched the chart. "See, here; he heads for the open sea. He hopes to find salt layers out there so he can hide under them and evade us or at worst, he will try to string out his defensive tactics until after dark when we will have a problem in maneuvering for closely coordinated attacks.

"He won't expect our depth charges to harm him at his present depth because his own Navy's depth charges are useless below four hundred feet, as ours used to be until we modified them."

"We have about eight hours of daylight left," the destroyer's Captain said. "If we press him, make him evade at high speed, he will use up his storage batteries and that will force him to the surface." He rubbed his chin. "We might even be able to smash him at seven hundred feet!"

"If we make perfect attacks," the Professor said. "But the perfect attack can only be made when the target acts as he is supposed to act and this is not a man down there who will do the obvious. He is a fox!" His finger traced a line on the chart.

"When he reaches this point please send a message to Small Birds to deploy thus," his finger made a curve on the chart. "When we have them deployed we will begin dropping charges from the Small Birds to turn him. I mean to drive him in a circle, like the American cowboy movies show cattle being driven! If we can keep him in this area where there are no salt layers we will have him!

"It is going to be a long day. Please lay out the plots and issue the orders to the Small Birds. And if you will, sir, ask the galley to send some food and hot drink to the crew. They have been on station for many hours and face many more hours of work."

"For you as well, sir?"

"After the men have eaten we will eat," the Professor said.

Mako crept doggedly along the course Joe Sirocco had laid out on the chart. The steady ringing of the noise of the pinging from the destroyer had become a major irritant. Men flinched as the sonar tone rang through the ship. Captain Mealey, taking advantage of the lull in the depth charge attacks, had ordered the galley to serve hot coffee and doughnuts and sweet rolls. As soon as each compartment had been served the water-tight doors were closed behind the mess cook and dogged down tight. Joe Sirocco munched a doughnut and sipped at a cup of coffee and looked at Aaron, who shook his blond head.

"All isothermal, sir. No layers yet."

Mealey sipped at his boiling hot coffee. "Got to be some layers somewhere, damn it!" he growled. "I don't want to string this thing out until way after dark, we'll be out of battery before midnight!"

"Here he comes, sir!" Cohen said suddenly. "Three ships, all on an attack run! All three coming at once!"

The telephone talkers in each compartment relayed Cohen's words and those men who had got out of bunks to drink their coffee climbed back in, gripping the side rails of the bunks with both hands. Ginty braced himself between the torpedo tubes and stared at Dusty Rhodes, who was standing in the center of the Torpedo Room, his hands holding on to a torpedo skid.

The sound of the destroyer's screws began to echo through *Mako*'s hull and then the three ships passed overhead, the thunder of their screws reverberating throughout the submarine's hull.

"Brace yourselves!" Rhodes said in a low voice.

The thunderous explosions of more than thirty depth charges going off in a rolling attack shook *Mako* heavily. In the Control Room Sirocco saw the ladder that led to the Conning Tower bulge outward as *Mako*'s hull squeezed inward under the shock of the heavy explosions.

"Damage reports!" Captain Mealey snapped and Sirocco spoke softly into his telephone. Then he held up his thumb and forefinger, making a small circle with the fingers.

"Nothing serious, Captain. Some minor leaks, some bruises and bumps. No bones broken. Chief Barber reports that the welds around the exhaust lines have shattered and he's taking some water in the engine rooms but nothing serious."

"Very well," Mealey said.

The next attack came with the three enemy destroyers running in a line. *Mako* reeled under the depth charges of the first ship and then bucked and staggered as the next two ships rained down depth charges. There was no longer any cork insulation to shatter and fall down. Those few lights that had survived the previous attacks were now shattered. *Mako*'s crew went about the job of checking for leaks and damage in the dim lights of the emergency battle lanterns. The lack of bright lights added an eerie atmosphere to the fetid smell of fear that pervaded the *Mako*'s hull.

The attacks came without pause as the hours wore on. Time after time Cohen reported that one or two or all three destroyers were moving to the attack. Time after time *Mako*'s crew shivered under the crashing thunder of the explosions. At mid-afternoon there was a sudden halt in the attacks and the mess cooks hurried to each compartment with fresh coffee and the last of the doughnuts.

"What do you think they're doing up there?" Sirocco asked.

"They're probably emptying out their depth charges lockers for some more attacks," Mealey grunted. He wiped his dripping face with a towel he had hung around his neck.

The atmosphere in *Mako* was now oppressive. The air conditioning and all ventilation had been shut down since the attack on the battleship. The temperature stood at 110 degrees with 100 percent humidity. The long hours submerged, the heavy work of reloading torpedoes with men straining and hauling and using huge quantities of oxygen had depleted the oxygen level of the air to the point where a match that was struck would fizzle and then go out.

Mako crept through the sea at two knots, depth 700 feet. Just past 1500 hours, three in the afternoon in land time, Cohen raised his dripping face.

"Screws bearing zero one five and three five zero, sir. Single screw ships, sir." His eyes widened suddenly.

"They're dropping charges out ahead of us! They're quite a way out in front and they're depth charging!"

The distant thunder of the depth charges could be heard in *Mako*. Captain Mealey looked down at the chart.

"Single screw ships," he said to Sirocco. "Those are the rest of the escort, the ships Cohen lost earlier today. What the hell are they doing dropping charges way out ahead?" He rocked back on his heels, his face grim.

"Is that son of a bitch up there trying to fence me in? Is he trying to make me turn? I'll bet that's what he's up to! The bastard!" He turned to Cohen.

"Give me bearings on the ships that have been attacking us, Nate. If you can, give me an estimated range."

Cohen nodded his head. His deep-sunk eyes stared at the Control Room, not seeing the sweating, straining men on the bow and stern planes, not seeing Lieut. Pete Simms clinging to the Conning Tower ladder, gasping for air. Cohen's whole being was concentrated on the welter of sounds in his earphones.

"The ship that has been pinging on us and is still pinging bears one seven zero, sir. There are three others up there, all bearing from one seven zero or two one zero sir, moving slowly. I don't know about range, I don't know how good my ears are after all this noise but from the decibel level I'd say under two thousand yards, sir." He stopped, listening.

"Here they come, sir!"

The three destroyers moved to the attack once more, running

just fast enough to get away from the depth charges rolling off their sterns. *Mako* shook and shuddered under the impact of the roaring explosions, its hull twisting in the torque of the explosive force of the depth charges. Ginty, braced solidly between the torpedo tubes in the Forward Room, watched a stream of sweat running down his chest fly off in a spray of drops as the depth charges shook the ship.

"How about that?" he said. "That son of a bitch is gonna save me using my sweat rag!"

The attacking now was continual. One ship would make a run and then wheel out to one side as its sailors wrestled depth charges into position for the next run as the ship fell in behind the other attacking ships moving to the attack. The thunder of the explosions was continual, *Mako*'s only respite coming when the searching destroyer's sonar was unable to find *Mako* in the explosive-wracked water. With the first *"ping!"* of re-established contact the attack would begin again.

Captain Mealey was braced, legs spread, hands gripping the edges of the gyro table, his eyes studying the plot sheet. A steady drip of perspiration fell from his chin into a crumpled towel Sirocco had placed on the gyro table. Periodically, Aaron would change the smoked card in the bathythermograph. As he did so Mealey's eyes would look at the stylus as it traced its even curve. Then, seeing no evidence of a salt layer, Mealey's head would drop down and his eyes would return to the plot.

At 1700 hours, three full hours from dark, Captain Mealey raised his head.

"I think I've had enough of this!" he said coldly. "By now he expects us to be the patsy, to take everything he hands out without hitting back! Well, I'm going to hit back!" He clutched the gyro table as a half-dozen depth charges shook *Mako,* the ship's steel hull creaking and groaning in the turmoil.

"Right after those bastards make the next run I'm going up to periscope depth and get one of them! Give me the phone!"

"Now hear this, you telephone talkers. This is the Captain speaking.

"We've been taking it on the chin long enough! In three hours it will be dark. In three hours we might not have any battery left. So right after this next attack we're going up to periscope depth and we're going to sink one of those bastards who've been hitting us! And then we'll come back down to this depth and continue our escape. I want all hands alert! We'll open outer tube doors at one hundred feet! Everyone sharpen up!" He stopped as Cohen turned his head toward him.

"Here they come again, sir, all of them!"

"Here they come!" Mealey said into the telephone. "And then we'll send one of them to hell!"

The attack was a murderous barrage of depth charges that tossed *Mako* from one side to the other. As the explosions roared through the ship Mealey grabbed the Conning Tower ladder.

"Blow Negative!

"Bring me to periscope depth! Plot, give me the picture, give me bearings!" He climbed into the Conning Tower where Bob Edge and Botts had been for hours, suffering the horrendous noise of the depth charges which made the Conning Tower vibrate and ring like the inside of a drum.

"Get on the TDC!" Mealey snapped. "Stand by the periscope!"

Mako planed upward, rolling violently in the after wash of the explosions. In the Forward and After Torpedo rooms weary men wrestled the tube outer doors open and the talkers reported that tubes Two and Three, Seven and Eight were ready. Sirocco repeated the information to the Conning Tower.

"Up periscope!" Mealey snapped as the depth gauge showed 75 feet. "Give me sixty-five feet!"

He swung the periscope around, blinking as the lens broke water.

"Mark!"

"Bearing one eight zero!" Botts rapped out and Edge set the bearing into the TDC.

Mealey's hand found the range knob and spun it.

"Range to the target one zero zero zero! Angle on the bow is zero nine zero port! Oh, I've got you, you bastard! Stand by aft! Stand by Seven!"

"*Fire seven!*

"*Right full rudder . . . flood negative . . . close the outer tube*

*doors . . . my god this bastard's coming right after us! Take me down! Hard
dive! Hard dive!"*

"Torpedo is running hot, straight and normal!" Cohen yelled.
"Screws bearing one five zero speeding up and coming fast!"

The starboard bridge wing lookout on *Eagle* saw *Mako's* periscope break water and his screaming warning brought the Professor
and *Eagle's* Captain rushing to the bridge wing. They both saw the
long finger of bubbles reaching toward *Eagle's* Feather Two.

"*Eagle's* Feather Two turn hard right!" The destroyer Captain's
voice was a scream and the bridge radioman hesitated slightly before
relaying the order.

"Set depth charges at one hundred feet!" the Professor said to
the bridge talker, an older man and poised. "Quickly!" On *Eagle's*
fantail two gunners began to frantically reduce the tension on the
diaphragm springs of the two depth charges at the end of the release
rack.

Eagle was under the full drive of her engines, turning to where
Mako's periscope had shown briefly. A shattering roar filled the air
and the Professor saw a huge gout of water rise beside *Eagle's* Feather
Two and then as the water subsided he saw the ship, broken in two,
its bow rising high, the dull red anti-fouling paint showing in the
clear air, its stern twisted off to one side and then the bow began to
slide downward.

"Don't lose him!" the Professor said softly and the destroyer's
Captain nodded grimly, his lips set. *Eagle* raced toward where *Mako*
had shown. The Captain raised his hand and then brought it down in
a sharp chopping motion. On *Eagle's* stern the gunners pulled back on
their release levers and two big depth charges set to explode at 100
feet rolled off the stern.

The booming roar of *Mako's* torpedo hitting the enemy ship
shook *Mako* and Joe Sirocco clicked his stop-watch and looked at it.

"That was a hit!" He yelled up at the Conning Tower. He spun
and looked at the depth gauge needle as the roar of an enemy ship's
screws filled *Mako*. The needle showed 110 feet, moving steadily.

As the roar of the *Fubuki's* screws filled the ship the crew looked
at each other with naked fear in their eyes, turning instinctively

toward the telephone talker to find out what was being said in the Control Room.

"Sound says he's dropped!" the talkers said. The crew waited, some lying tensely in bunks, others braced defiantly, holding on to torpedo racks and rails in the engine rooms. They waited.

The two depth charges exploded as *Mako* passed 125 feet. The noise, the racking shock of the two explosions, were greater than anything *Mako* had experienced before.

"Agggh!" Ginty cried as his grip on the handle of Number One torpedo tube door was broken and he was thrown violently to the deck. Farther back in the compartment the man who had kidded with Dusty Rhodes about not having enough lead in his ass began to scream, a long ululating sound that went higher and higher in pitch until it seemed impossible that the human throat could make such a sound. Rhodes, spitting out the fragments of two broken teeth, fought his way down *Mako*'s bucking deck to the bunk and yanked the man out of the bunk and on to his feet.

The sailor's face was blank, his eyes closed, his mouth wide open, his wailing scream exploding into the torpedo room. Rhodes carefully jabbed the man's chin with his left hand, closing the man's mouth and then crossed the right in a short, chopping blow. The man spun sideways into the arms of one of the reload crew.

"Stow the son of a bitch in a bunk and if he yells again smother him with a towel!" Rhodes growled.

"Damage report! Control wants a damage report, Chief!" The talker's voice was trembling.

"No leaks that I can see," Rhodes snapped. "Report just that! Tell 'em I'll give them a full report in one minute!"

Mako twisted downward, seeking the safety of the depths. Sirocco turned his face toward the Conning Tower hatch.

"Mr. Grilley reports that After Trim tank may be ruptured," he said. "The grease fittings on the bulkhead back between the tubes have blown out. DeLucia is plugging them now."

"Very well," Mealey said. "Mr. Simms, take note of that; you may have to compensate with a flooded After Trim." He dropped down the ladder to the Control Room.

"Seven hundred feet," he said to Simms. "Get back on course zero zero zero. Now we'll see what that bastard will do!"

In the After Torpedo Room DeLucia had dragged a bright orange canvas sack filled with tapered wooden plugs of varying sizes to the torpedo tubes. He stood to one side, gauging the course of the two streams of water that were jetting into the room. Then he edged in between the banks of the torpedo tubes with his bag, a short-handled sledge tucked under one arm.

"We're at four hundred feet and going down," Grilley warned, his eyes on the pressure gauge. "Don't get a hand in front of those streams of water! At this depth that water will cut like a knife!" DeLucia nodded and squatted under the two streams of water. He pulled a tapered oak plug from the bag.

Carefully, moving very slowly, he moved the point of the plug up the bulkhead until it was just below a jetting stream. Then in one smooth motion, grunting with the exertion, he pushed the point of a plug into the hole and held it there with one hand while he grabbed the sledge from between his knees. He rapped the plug hard with the sledge and hit it again, two solid blows. He got another plug out of the bag and Grilley heard him curse and saw the sledge moving in short arcs.

DeLucia backed out from between the torpedo tubes, the sledge tucked under one arm, the orange bag dragging behind him. As he moved a bright stream of arterial blood splashed on the deck plates.

"Let me see that!" Grilley said, and DeLucia held out his left hand. Blood was pouring from a hole in the palm of his hand, a hole that went completely through the hand.

"I slipped a little," he said ruefully. "Son of a bitchin' water is strong at that pressure!"

"We'll get the Pharmacist Mate back here," Grilley said. "That has to be taken care of."

"Nah!" DeLucia said. "The Old Man ain't gonna let anyone open and close all them water-tight doors for a scratch like this!" He wrapped a handkerchief around his hand and made a fist, closing the fingers tightly. "This will be all right for a while. That last charge musta busted the After Trim tank. You'd better tell the Old Man that it was sea pressure comin' in through them blown grease fittings."

Bob Edge leaned over the hatch to the Control Room, his face worried.

"The periscope is stuck, Captain. Won't come down!"

"What do you mean, won't come down?" Mealey snapped. "Didn't you lower it when we started deep?"

"No, sir," Edge said. "That is, Botts didn't lower it, sir."

"Try again," Mealey said. He turned to Simms. "Allow for the drag of the periscope on your dive angle."

"Ain't no drag, Captain," Dick Smalley said as he grunted and strained at the big brass wheel that controlled the bow planes. "Feels natural, just as if the 'scope were housed, sir."

"Try it again," Mealey ordered. He waited, listening to the two men in the Conning Tower talking in low voices.

"Won't budge, sir," Edge called down.

"Get an electrician and an auxiliaryman to look at it," Mealey said to Sirocco. "The depth charges must have jammed something. Nate, what do you hear?"

"Three sets of twin screws well aft of us, sir, milling around." He paused as a series of rumbling explosions shook *Mako* slightly. "Those are the single screw ships up ahead of us, sir. They're dropping charges out there."

"Let 'em drop!" Mealey grunted.

The minutes wore on. The air in *Mako*'s hull grew more fetid. Men gasped for breath after the slightest exertion. Then the pinging started again, slowly.

"I think you sank his best sound man," Cohen said to Captain Mealey. "This one doesn't get on us nearly as quickly and he doesn't fasten to us like they were doing early. But the *gonif* has got us now!" The pinging increased in rapidity and Cohen raised his voice slightly.

"Here they come again, sir!"

The explosions battered at *Mako*, thundering through the thin hull. Men flinched at each crashing sound. Captain Mealey stood at the gyro table, where he had stood during most of the depth charging attacks, his face set and grim, his eyes studying the chart.

"We're going to keep on taking it!" he said to Sirocco. "It's what, three hours to full dark? We've got about four hours left in the batteries so there's nothing else to do!"

An hour went by and the tension in *Mako*, long since near the point of being unendurable, rose even further. In the Forward Engine Room a sweating machinst mate, his eyes blank with utter terror, reached into a tool box and grabbed a ball peen hammer and began to beat on the deck.

"Come and get us, God damn you!" he screamed. The hammer drummed on the steel deck. "Come and get us! Come and get us!"

John Barber whipped a 12-inch crescent wrench out of his hip pocket and swung it. The man went down, blood pouring out of his nose and one ear.

"Drag him up forward by the evaporators," Barber said. "Any more you clowns want to tell those people topside to come and get us, tell me first."

Watching the stylus on the bathythermograph scratch gently against the smoked card, Aaron saw the needle move sharply to one side.

"Layer!" be breathed and then louder, "Layer! Sir!"

Captain Mealey pushed against Sirocco in his eagerness to get to the bathythermograph. He watched the needle.

"Thank God!" he breathed. Aaron's broad face brightened and he smiled gently.

Another hour went by with no sound from the enemy. Twice during the hour the needle of the bathythermograph began to move back toward its previous even curve and twice Captain Mealey changed course and depth to keep *Mako* within and beneath the layer of colder, saltier, water.

Another two hours slipped by. Cohen had long ago lost contact with the enemy ships. Captain Mealey stood at the gyro table, the sweat dripping from his chin. *Mako* continued to plod through the sea, her crew near physical collapse.

"What time is it?" Captain Mealey asked.

"Twenty-one hundred, Captain," Sirocco said.

"How long since we lost contact, Nate?"

"Almost three hours sir. No, sorry, almost four hours."

"How much have we got left in the battery?" Mealey said to

Sirocco. He waited while Sirocco talked to Chief Hendershot, his eyes taking in the scene in the Control Room.

Sirocco, standing waiting for the answer to his question, looked to be physically ill. His big frame sagged and his craggy face seemed to have acquired deeply graven lines.

Lieut. Peter Simms was in a state of near collapse, hanging on to the Conning Tower ladder for support. His eyes were closed and his chest was heaving spasmodically as his lungs fought for air in the fetid heat. Under foot the deck was greasy with sweat and there were puddles of condensation that seemed to reappear magically as soon as they were wiped up. Mealey looked at the thermometer. It read 115 degrees. Alongside it the humidity indicator read 100 percent.

"The Chief in Maneuvering reports that at this speed we've got maybe an hour, probably less, before we run out of power," Sirocco said slowly. Captain Mealey nodded and his right hand went up and his forefinger brushed his mustache.

"If we go, we go fighting!" he said. He nodded at Sirocco.

"Pass the word to open the water-tight doors. Open the tube outer doors at one hundred feet. Stand by for Battle Surface action! Stand by to surface!"

The telephone talkers repeated the order and *Mako's* crew began to stir, to come alive, moving slowly, fighting for breath in the oxygen-depleted air. The deck gun crews crowded into the Control Room with the machine gunners. Captain Mealey climbed into the Conning Tower.

"Surface! Surface! Surface!"

The men on the bow and stern planes threw their weight against the heavy brass wheels, sobbing with their effort. In the Maneuvering Room a haggard, sweat-drenched Chief Hendershot husbanded the fading storage batteries as *Mako* slanted upward through the sea. The bridge broke water and Captain Mealey opened the hatch and fought his way to the bridge through a rush of water. Three lookouts followed him and climbed up into the periscope shears. They began to report almost immediately, all clear to port, starboard, astern and forward.

Captain Mealey looked around. The night was pitch black and a very light rain was falling.

"Secure Battle Surface stations," he said. "All main engines all ahead full. Shift to hydraulic power on the helm. Executive Officer to the bridge!"

Sirocco climbed wearily up to the bridge, relishing the gush of fresh night air that was whipping down the hatch as the four big diesels roared into life and began to pull a suction through the after end of the ship.

"That's why we couldn't raise or lower the periscope," Captain Mealey said. He pointed and Sirocco saw the long, slim, attack periscope bent over in an almost 180 degree angle, its lens face down near the main deck on the starboard side.

"Bridge!" The after lookout's voice was high, excited. "Bridge, we ain't got an after deck gun!"

Mealey edged back on to the cigaret deck and went to the rail and looked down. Where the squat 5.25 gun had stood was a gaping hole in the wooden deck. He dropped down on the deck, followed by Sirocco and the two men knelt at the edge of the hole. They could see the heavy steel bracing that had supported the gun. The braces were torn and bent.

"My God!" Sirocco said. He hoisted himself back up on the cigaret deck and Mealey followed him.

"Captain!" Don Grilley's voice was strangled, almost unintelligible. Mealey rushed to the small bridge. Grilley was pointing down at the forward deck, his arm and body shaking violently.

There, sitting squarely on one of its flat ends near the forward deck gun, was a Japanese depth charge.

It was Dusty Rhodes who finally figured out what to do with the depth charge. After following Cohen's suggestion that a careful copy be made for Naval Intelligence of the characters on the face of the depth charge exploder plate, Rhodes got a small rubber boat that was stowed in the after end of the Forward Torpedo Room bilge. The boat was unrolled and laid beside the depth charge and then Rhodes and Ginty lifted the heavy charge and placed it carefully on its side in the fabric and rubber folds of the boat and inflated the boat. They lashed a dozen turns of heaving line around boat and depth charge and, standing knee-deep in water as Captain Mealey flooded down forward, they gently pushed the rubber boat and its deadly load off the ship after Rhodes had carefully made two small holes in the boat's fabric.

As the boat drifted away, the air hissing slowly out of the two small holes, *Mako* raced away from the area.

Later that night *Mako*'s message to the submarine command at Pearl Harbor caused a duty officer to begin making telephone calls and a hastily arranged-for Staff breakfast meeting was held. On those submarines at sea on patrol where the message was intercepted and decoded there was joy and, inevitably, some envy. It read:

Please give kudos to those people who sent us the *Kongo*. BB arrived on schedule at northeast entrance, Truk.

Mako dove under twelve destroyer escort and fired ten repeat ten torpedoes at BB, scoring six repeat six hits. When last seen target had large fires forward and what appeared to be a substantial explosion in that area, with heavy list to starboard, but still under way slowly on one screw. Believe her captain may have been trying to beach his ship on the reef. *Mako* does not further report on target because of enemy retaliation which was of unprecedented ferocity.

Mako endured ten hours of repeated depth charge attacks. Near end of period *Mako* surfaced to periscope depth and fired one torpedo at *Fubuki*-class destroyer, hitting it amidships and breaking it in two. Unable to stick around for second look but heard unmistakable breaking-up noises on sonar.

Mako regretfully reports death in action of Machinist Mate Third Class Joseph P. Richards, who was thrown against the starboard engine in the forward engine-room, fracturing his skull. The remains were buried at sea in the traditional service.

Mako reports sustaining considerable and severe materiel damage. Attack periscope is bent over until it touches deck. After deck gun has disappeared from its mount. Much of main deck has been torn away. Exhaust line welds in both engine rooms have been shattered. Starboard propellor shaft believed bent. After Trim tank ruptured. *Mako* is returning home for repairs.

Two nights later as *Mako* plowed steadily toward Pearl Harbor at a steady 18 knots Lieut. Nathan Cohen came to the bridge and handed Captain Mealey a message. Mealey held the message up in the bright moonlight so he could read it.

To U.S.S. *Mako*
From COMSUBPAC:
Well done *Mako* and well done again. Intelligence reports that *Mako* scored seven repeat seven hits on target. The target is now aground on the reef east of the Northeast Passage, Truk, and considered to be out of action for at least two years. Casualty list given as three hundred seventy-five dead. *Mako* also gets confirmed sinking of a *Fubuki* destroyer with all hands.

COMSUBPAC congratulates Captain Mealey on his aggressive patrol and his fourth gold stripe. We are waiting to welcome all hands. Again, a hearty well done to *Mako*'s Captain, Wardroom and crew.

Captain Mealey handed the message to Joe Sirocco, who had followed Nate Cohen to the bridge. Sirocco read the message and then stuck out his big hand.

"Congratulations, sir, on your promotion. You've earned it."

"Thank you, Joe but damn it, she didn't sink! They beached her on the reef. With seven fish in her she should have sunk!"

"She's out of commission for two years, Skipper. We had our cake and paid for it and you can eat it with a good appetite. Hitting a battleship guarded by twelve destroyers, hitting it seven times and putting it out of commission and sinking a *Fubuki*, that's a whole plateful of cake!"

"I suppose you're right," Mealey said slowly. "But this means that I go ashore! They don't put four-stripe captains in command of a submarine."

"There's that," Sirocco agreed. "But at least you can be in a position to tell others how to do what they're supposed to do. And I'm glad that you decided to say the cause of Richard's death was due to battle action, sir."

"Against my better wishes, Mister," Mealey said shortly. "I shouldn't have let you and Grilley change my mind!"

CHAPTER 20

Lieut. Comdr. Arthur Hinman's eyes opened slowly and he rolled his head on the soft pillow, trying to remember where he was. He lay quietly for a moment, thinking. Then he smelled the faint odor of the sea and a harbor mixed with the reek of auto exhaust fumes coming through the opened window and the foreign scent of a woman's perfume.

San Francisco.

He turned his head and looked at Joan Richards. Her crisp black hair was slightly tousled. Her eyes were closed and her full breasts were rising and falling slowly and evenly under the sheet and light blanket. He studied her face in the morning light. Without make-up her skin was clear with a rosy tint underneath. Her full lips were parted slightly, showing her front teeth. He reached out and very softly touched her hair. Her eyes opened and closed and then opened again and she smiled, a slow, soft smile.

"You're staring at me," she said.

"Not staring, adoring," he said. "Did you know that you have flawless skin? It's marvelous!"

212

"Of course." She covered her mouth with one hand and yawned hugely. "You've been telling me for a week that I'm perfect so I guess I am. But is that all you're going to do, just lie there and stare at me? Does a woman get a cup of coffee in this miserable life or has the war stopped room service and morning coffee?"

"I'll call right now," he said, throwing back the covers. He stood up beside the bed and her eyes widened.

"Forget the coffee for a little while! This woman can't ignore a challenge like that! Get back in here, man!" He looked down at himself and grinned and got back into bed.

"Not heavy, romantic love," she murmured as she rolled onto her side facing him. "Just fun and games on Saturday morning in old San Francisco, okay?"

"You're the Captain," he said, fitting himself to her. "You give the orders and I'll obey them."

"Now hear this!" she said. She put a leg across him and reached downward with her hand. "You've got the right angle on the bow and the range is right and you can load and fire that torpedo when ready! How's that? Am I learning your submarine talk?"

"You're doing fine," he said. He moved in response to her guiding hand and then moved strongly and smoothly and as she gasped and closed her eyes he put his hand around her buttocks and drew himself deep into her.

Later they lay side by side, her head on his muscled arm.

"It was never like this before," she said softly. "All week long it's been so good! So absolutely wonderful!

"Women, girls too, dream, you know. They dream of the man who truly cares about the woman, the man who cares enough to make sure that the woman's every need is satisfied. But that dream hardly ever comes true. Now it's come true for me." She sighed and let her fingers trail across his shoulder. She turned her face to him, her dark blue eyes almost black in the light.

"I want you to believe that, I truly want you to believe it!"

"I do believe," he said gravely. "Simply because it has been the same for me. In all honesty, it was good before, with Marie." He said the name of his dead wife with ease. "It was good. But it was different. Not like it is with you. And now it is my turn to tell you something and I ask you to believe me." He looked at her, his eyes questioning. She nodded.

"I used to lie in my bunk on *Mako,*" he said, "remembering, after she was gone. I'd remember every detail of how it was with her, every detail. Now I can't remember those details. It's all fuzzy. Each day it gets more and more blurred. Now it's just a warm and pleasant memory, no details at all. That's because of you and what you mean to me."

She reached over, squirming, and kissed his stubbled chin.

"That is a very beautiful thing to say to a woman," she said softly. "It's something I don't think I'll ever forget. But if you don't get me some coffee I'll die! And I get to use the shower first!" She got out of bed and went to the door of the bathroom, her firm buttocks jiggling slightly. He put his arm in back of his head and grinned at her as she stopped at the door and looked back.

"You have got the finest ass this side of the Pecos River," he said lazily. "Now get it in the shower while I call down for coffee. Then we'll go down below and I'll feed you."

"It's 'down stairs' here on land, sailor and I want orange juice, a stack of wheat cakes and a yard of pork sausage and then I'll be ready to eat breakfast!" She closed the door to the bathroom behind her and he heard the water in the shower begin to drum.

The romance between the two had been slow to start. During the first week of the tour Hinman had resented Joan's impatient coaching, her cirticisms of his diction and delivery. When he would flare up against her criticism she had shrugged, lit a cigaret and changed the subject. When he had cooled down she would begin again, never wavering in her determination to make his delivery natural, his handling of reporters, friendly and hostile, smoother. It was during the second week that he realized that she was a polished professional in her own line and that her advice was sound. He realized as well that she was more than just a woman in a Navy uniform doing a job. He saw in her the deep, bubbling sense of humor that he had seen in Marie, the clear distrust of anything phony or artificial and the obvious zest she had for life itself.

One evening, a few days after he had begun to appreciate Joan

Richards for the singular person she was, they dined in his hotel suite after a banquet at which each had only nibbled at the salad. He finished a piece of chocolate cake that was dessert and at the motion of her fork reached over and appropriated her piece of cake. As he ate it he began to talk.

The words poured out of him. He told her about Marie, about his courtship of the tall, angular girl-woman, about their marriage and about her death and the terrible emptiness it had left in him. She listened, speaking only enough to keep his narrative going, filling his coffee cup, lighting a cigaret for him. And then he had stopped, his face stricken. She reached forward and touched his hand.

"Don't! It was something you had to do sooner or later. I'm glad you did it, I'm glad you told it to me!"

"I don't know what got into me," he mumbled.

"You've got it backwards," she said gently. "It was something that was in you already and had to come out. You can't keep something like that inside you and bottled up forever. It has to come out, one way or another it has to come out and it came out as it was, as something fine and decent and good. You were a very lucky man. She was a lucky woman. You were lucky to have each other."

"The reminiscing of an old man!" he said in a low voice.

"Old? Thirty-seven is old? You're young! You've got a lifetime ahead of you and it will be a better life now, for you, for those around you who care about you."

"How do you know?" he stared at her.

"Because I'm a woman, that's all. Because I think I know how Marie felt about you. And because I think I know that it makes me happy that she was happy and that you were happy.

"Because I know that if you had not found someone to talk to, to tell about the two of you, that what you kept inside of you would eventually change and corrode and when that happened you would begin to change and dry up inside. I don't want you to change, not a little bit."

He looked at her, his eyes veiled. "The Chaplain at Pearl is a wise man. He said almost the same thing but he used some different words. You are a wise woman, Joan Richards."

She smiled and her face was gentle. "If you say so. Me, I think

I'm wise enough to leave you now." She picked up her clipboard and
her handbag.

"I'll put in a call for seven tomorrow morning," she said. "For
both of us. We'll have an early breakfast and hit the bricks again.
Another day, another dollar. We hit two factories tomorrow morning
and then a luncheon speech. Do you know that as of the last account-
ing you've raised more money for War Bonds than anyone except
Marlene Dietrich? How does that grab you?"

He smiled at her and she left his room, her head high. She did
not, he noticed, swing her hips.

The evening talks in his hotel suite became a regular event.
Hinman told Joan of his boyhood, his life at the Naval Academy and
his fondness for practical jokes and how that fondness had stunted his
career until his marriage to Marie, an Admiral's daughter. He told
her about submarines and the men who sailed in them. And he spoke
freely about Captain Severn's scathing denunciation of himself and
Mike Brannon. He told her how Ben Butler's idea about the War
Bond tour had saved his career and that of Mike Brannon as well.

Joan said little, only enough to keep him talking. When he
asked, she told him about Ben Butler, the respect he was given by his
peers in the newspaper business for his honesty and his ability. Once,
when he asked, she talked briefly about her own brief marriage and
why, although her husband was handsome and on his way to success
in the advertising field, she had decided that it was better to be out of
the marriage and happy than married and unhappy.

The lid blew off in Los Angeles. The day's schedule had been
crowded; a breakfast for a group of businessmen and a short speech, a
tour of a war plant and a short speech and then a luncheon in front of
a Rotary group, two afternoon appearances before women's groups
and a formal dinner hosted by the Mayor in the evening.

Joan nudged Hinman on the arm as they walked across the hotel
lobby to the ballroom where the dinner was to be held.

"You're edgy, boss," she said quietly. "It's been a heavy day, too
heavy. Calm down and take it very easy." He nodded.

The press hadn't been around during the daytime appearances
but they were out in force for the Mayor's dinner, which the City
Council was co-hosting. By this time, three weeks into the War Bond

tour, every newspaper had a fat envelope on Lieut. Comdr. Arthur Hinman, U.S.N. and what he had said in a score of speeches and press conferences. Now the task that faced the press was to get Hinman to say something new or at worst, say what he had been saying in a different form so it would read like news, to come up with new questions that would draw answers that would make good copy.

Hinman, carefully briefed by Joan Richards, tried to cooperate, to vary his answers to the stock questions and to parry the pointed questions of those reporters whose publishers were strongly opposed to President Roosevelt's international policies and the entry of the United States into the war.

One of those reporters, a lean man with a sharp nose and an irritating voice, went after Hinman in the question-and-answer section that had become a feature of his luncheon and dinner appearances. The reporter's nagging questions and his caustic references to the low intelligence level of anyone who would be "deceived" about President Roosevelt's "real reasons" for the American entry into the war had finally broken through Hinman's composure.

Hinman gripped the edge of the lectern with his hard hands and looked out over the dinner audience for a long moment, his face grim. Then he looked straight at the reporter.

"Sir," he began in a quiet voice. "I am getting damned sick and tired of you people who keep saying that I am a fool for fighting President Roosevelt's war! I am damned sick and tired of it! And I am damned sick of you and everyone like you!

"If you think the other side is so great why in the hell aren't you over there on that side? I happen to believe that if the other side wins we will lose every freedom we have and I am not going to let that happen as long as I am alive, not to me and by God, not to you!"

The man waved his pencil and started to reply but Hinman cut him off with a raised hand and the harsh ring of command in his voice.

"No, I will not let you speak, sir! I did you the courtesy of hearing you out and you do me the same courtesy!" He pointed his finger at the reporter.

"If you really think that this war we are in is not our war then, damn you, go out to Pearl Harbor and look at the remains of the

United States Navy! There are more than two thousand dead men under the water of that harbor! Men who died without a decent chance to defend themselves! Men who were killed in a sneak attack that was timed," his voice rose, "a sneak attack timed to catch those men as they were on their way to church service!" He leaned over the lectern, his eyes boring into the reporter's eyes.

"My wife, God rest her soul, was on her way to church, to the chapel at Hickam Air Base in Pearl Harbor.

"She was in a car with the wives of two other officers. A Japanese pilot with a wealth of military targets in the harbor and on the Base machine-gunned that car with three women in it! He caught them fifty yards from the church!

"I don't want your wife or anyone here to die like that! And I won't let it happen as long as there is blood in my body, as long as the citizens—I said citizens, mister—as long as the citizens of this country give us the weapons we need to fight this 'someone else's war' you talk about! And if you don't like my attitude or what I say, mister, I'll go out in the alley with you right now and you can do your damndest to change it!"

For a long moment there was a dead silence in the hall and then the diners surged to their feet applauding, stamping their feet. A reporter for *The New York Times* sighed and looked at a reporter for the *Chicago Daily News*.

"I think *The New York Times* is entitled to make an editorial comment for all of us," he said. In full view of the diners and the speaker's table he walked over to the reporter Hinman had blasted and politely turned him half-way around and then kicked him as hard as he could. The audience began to laugh and applaud and Joan Richards nudged Hinman.

"Make your regrets to the Mayor and let's get the hell out of here," she whispered. He nodded and said a few words to the Mayor, who clapped him on the back and started for the door. A radio reporter with a microphone stopped Hinman and Joan Richards.

"I have Captain Hinman right here, folks. You just heard him on this network. Captain, will you say a few words?"

Joan pulled on his arm but he stopped and bent to the microphone the man held up to his face.

"I would be happy to do that, sir," he said slowly. "If I offended any of your audience with my sea-going language, I apologize. I do not apologize for what I said. I think it's time someone stood up and said it. We are in a terrible, a bitter, vicious war with an implacable and determined enemy. We are going to win this war come what may and when we do I hope it will be the start of peace for generations to come. Thank you."

"That was an exclusive statement from Captain Hinman, the submarine hero of the Navy, ladies and gentlemen, an exclusive report on this network . . . ." the radio reporter was still babbling into his microphone as Hinman and Joan left by a side door.

An hour later, sitting in his hotel suite with his tie off and his shirt undone at the neck, Hinman looked at Joan.

"Well, lady, I guess I blew it! You might have to cancel the whole last week of this tour."

"You don't know very much about public relations, do you?" she said. "By noon tomorrow I'll have at least a hundred requests for a speech by you!

"You were great! Absolutely great! And for your information, by tomorrow morning there will be pictures and a front-page story in every newspaper in the country! No, don't get angry at me, I don't mean that what you did was good because the story will get a big play.

"I mean that what you did was good because it was time someone told off those creeps! And about two thousand people sitting there listening and watching you do it approved. Didn't you see them stand up, didn't you hear them applaud? Didn't you see Joe Edson of *The New York Times* walk over and kick that bastard square in his ass?"

He shook his head. "I don't know. You may be right. But I think now that I should have kept my head. I should have kept my answer impersonal, not dragged in that stuff about Marie and the other two women and the church."

"Who has a better right?" she said softly. He nodded and stood up.

"Joan, lady, I think I'll hit the sack. I want to think about tonight, about a better way to handle those bastards."

She rose. "May I use your bathroom?" Without waiting for his assent she went in the bathroom and closed the door. She came out five minutes later dressed in a sheer nightgown that ended half-way between her hips and her knees.

Hinman's eyes widened as he saw the roseate nipples of her full breasts through the sheer material, the bold triangle of black pubic hair, the slim legs and bare feet. He drew a long, shaky breath.

"Do you always carry your nightgown in your handbag?"

"It's a habit I started four days ago," she said calmly. "Nightgown and toothbrush. I told you and Ben Butler in Washington that I thought a woman had the right to ask to be loved by a man. This is how I choose to ask. Now give me your answer."

"I don't have the words," he said simply. He held out his arms and she moved into them with a fluid motion, pressing herself against him, holding him tighter as she sensed and then felt his arousal. They clung together, his face in her crisp black curls, nuzzling her ear and neck, feeling the heat of her body, smelling the womanly aroma of her arousal. He slid his hand down her smooth back and she gently separated herself from him and walked over to the bed and got in and smiled at him.

CHAPTER 21

Hinman was standing at the half-opened window in the hotel room in San Francisco, listening to the muted rumble of traffic down in the street when he heard the bathroom door open. He turned as Joan came out of the bathroom, a towel wrapped around her that covered her breasts and barely covered her thighs. He poured coffee for both of them.

"Now that's what I call class, lady," he said with a grin. "The girl comes out of the shower covered up. Any other woman as beautiful as you are would be sitting here drinking coffee in the raw."

"My mother brought me up to be a lady," she said with a wicked grin. "And one of the things she taught me was to never take my clothes off in front of a sailor. All sailors are sex maniacs, thank God for that!" He drained his coffee cup and stood up and she let out a small shriek.

"My God, man, you were sitting there starkers! Talk about class! You have no class at all, you darlin' man! Get your fanny into that shower while I get dressed and then we'll go down and have some breakfast."

"Well, it's over," she said as she mopped up the last of the syrup on her plate with a forkful of wheat cake. "Today is a free day and tomorrow we go back to Washington. You are scheduled to see the President and the Secretary of the Navy the day after, at ten in the morning." She looked up as the hotel manager walked up to their table.

"You'll pardon me, Captain, Lieutenant," the man said. "This telegram, priority delivery, came for you sir."

"Thank you," Hinman said. "Won't you have a cup of coffee with us? I want to tell you what a fine hotel you have here."

"Well, that's very nice of you," the hotel manager said. "If you'll excuse me while I take care of one small matter. Be right back."

Hinman ripped open the telegram envelope and read the page swiftly. Then he read it again, slowly. He looked at Joan, his face beaming.

"It's from Bob Rudd, Commander Rudd in Pearl Harbor. No, by God, he signs himself Captain Rudd! Must have got his fourth stripe! He says orders have been cut for me and I'll pick them up in Washington. I'm to return to Pearl as soon as possible! That means I'm going to get a ship, Joan! I'll have another submarine!"

"But you won't have the thirty days' leave they promised you," she said. "Is that what that means?"

"I'm afraid so."

"Well," she said with a small shrug. "That's the way of a sailor with a girl. It's off to sea again while the shy maiden sits at home and wonders about all the other women the sailor is romancing in all the other ports."

"Maybe you wouldn't wonder about things like that if you were Mrs. Arthur Hinman," he said. She looked at him, her eyes widening.

"Oh, damn it! I bungled it!" he blurted. "I wanted to do it the right way, get down on one knee and ask for your hand in marriage and now I've ruined it!" He hung his head.

She sat without moving, her eyes closed.

"You left something out," she said in a half whisper. "You left out something you've been saying the last few nights in such a low voice that a girl strains her eardrums to hear you. Now say it out loud!"

"I love you," he said. "Yes! I love you!"

"That's better! I'll marry you! But when? We'd have to get a license, maybe blood tests. Those things take time."

"I've learned a few things from you," he said. He stood up as the hotel manager approached.

"Sit down, sir," Hinman said. "I apologize, I don't know your name, sir."

"No reason you should, Captain. A good hotel manager is never heard and seldom seen. I'm Steve Lewis and we're honored to have you with us."

"Well, Mr. Lewis, it's been wonderful for us. You run a very efficient hotel. Your people have made us very comfortable." He poured coffee from the carafe.

"I hate to impose on you for anything more but we need some information. I just hate to ask you for any more favors."

Lewis looked at him and smiled. "I was in Los Angeles the other night, Captain. I was invited to that dinner and I accepted because I was tied up here and wouldn't be able to hear you when you were speaking this week. I don't think you can ask me for any favor that would be too large."

"I'm ordered back to sea," Hinman said, "and Joan, Lieutenant Richards here, and I want to get married. Time is so crucial, sir, I thought, hoped, that maybe you could give us a suggestion as to how we could get around the formalities of license, the waiting period I mean. Is there any way around that?"

The hotel manager smiled. "If I may suggest it, sir, the Mayor has the power to perform marriages and if you don't object, our hotel lobby would be a rather nice setting for your marriage. I personally extend my invitation to you to accept the hotel's offer to be your host at your wedding supper this evening."

"I wouldn't put you to that trouble," Hinman said slowly. The manager rose.

"Trouble, Captain? No trouble at all. Please check with me after lunch. By then I will have everything arranged." He was almost trotting when he left their table.

"You've learned a few things about public relations, haven't you?" Joan said with a wide grin. "You wouldn't know that an event like this will put this hotel on the front page of every newspaper in the country or at worst, on page three. You wouldn't know that the Mayor of San Francisco loves good publicity. You wouldn't know anything about things like that, would you!"

"Oh, I've learned a few things about public relations from you," he said airily. "Learned a few things about pubic relations, as well."

"Not half of what you're going to learn," she said. "Now let's get out of here and go and do whatever soon-to-be-married couples do while they're waiting for the knot to be tied."

"Go to bed?" he asked innocently.

"Save it! I'm a hellion on a wedding night!"

The scheduled half-hour with President Roosevelt and the Secretary of the Navy, Frank Knox, a Chicago newspaper publisher, lengthened into an hour. Knox, a big, bluff, jovial man shook his thick forefinger at Joan.

"When I knew you in Chicago, young lady, you never gave any sign of having this much sense! When this war is over you bring this man of yours to me and we'll find some work for him to do so he can support you in a style you'd like to get used to."

"When this war is over she'll probably go with him to some God-forsaken submarine base out in the Pacific," the President said. "You keep your hands off my officers, Frank! I don't want you seducing them with offers of good jobs!"

Later, at the Navy Department, a gray-haired Chief Yeoman, who wore the silver dolphins of the qualified submarine man on the breast of his jacket, took them into his small office and seated them in hard chairs in front of his desk. Hinman noted the six diagonal gold stripes on his left sleeve, "hash marks," each standing for four years of honorable service. He made a guess that the Chief was on shore duty because of his age and length of service.

The Chief Yeoman was succinct. No, Lieutenant Richards now Lieutenant Hinman, could not be assigned to Pearl Harbor in any capacity. WAVES did not serve outside of the continental limit of the United States. Sorry about that, sir.

Yes, Lieutenant Commander Hinman's promised thirty-day

leave had been canceled. Captain Rudd's orders were quite specific: Lieut. Comdr. Arthur Hinman would report to Pearl Harbor at once for reassignment. And then the Chief Yeoman had turned and looked out of his office window for a long moment.

"Sir," he said, turning back to face Hinman and Joan, "as of today the aircraft assigned to you for the War Bond tour has been returned to regular duty.

"I can offer you a courier flight to the West Coast where you will have to wait seven days for a flight out to Pearl. I cannot offer that to Lieutenant Hinman, sir, there is no room on this flight, which leaves in one hour from now.

"Or, if you have to see other people here at the Navy Department and cannot make that flight all I can do is to offer you a courier flight to Chicago that leaves at fifteen hundred hours this afternoon. You will have to find something to do in Chicago for six days, sir; a courier flight will leave from Chicago six days from now for the West Coast, arriving in time to connect with the flight to Pearl." He looked down at his desk. "There is room on that flight for Lieutenant Hinman, who will be assigned to duty from Mare Island Navy Yard, sir." He looked away again, his hand resting lightly on Joan Richards' service jacket, which was lying on his desk.

"I had to make the entry of marriage in Lieutenant Richards' service jacket, sir. I noticed that her place of residence before enlistment is Chicago."

"Do I understand that there is room on the fifteen hundred flight to Chicago for Lieutenant Richards?" Hinman asked.

"Yes, sir, there is."

"I do want to see some people here," Hinman said slowly. "I don't see how I can do that and still pack and make that flight to the West Coast in one hour."

"I can understand that, sir. Very hard to do."

"Is it possible to get orders cut to ride that courier flight to Chicago?" Hinman kept his voice neutral.

The Chief Yeoman opened his desk drawer and took out two thick envelopes. "Here are your orders and Lieutenant Hinman's orders for the courier flight to Chicago, sir, and for the flight from Chicago to the West Coast and your orders for Pearl. Lieutenant

Hinman's orders to report to Mare Island Navy Yard for assignment
are included in the Lieutenant's orders."

He grinned. "Appreciate what you said to that dope out in L.A.,
sir. We've got quite a few of that kind here in Washington. They've
been pretty quiet since you sounded off!"

"You're a good man, Chief," Hinman said. "Do you miss the
Boats?"

"Yes, sir, I do. I had to put in for shore duty four years ago. My
wife had a bad heart attack. Hell of a place for a submariner to be, in
an office ashore. My battle station used to be the bow planes." His
face became wistful. "I was a very good bow planesman, if I do say it
as shouldn't."

"I'm sure you were," Hinman said.

The Chief Yeoman stood up in back of his desk. "I don't want to
keep you from your appointments, sir." He grinned. "Have a good
honeymoon!"

"Are all submarine men like that?" Joan said to Hinman as they
walked down the hall of the Navy Department building. "I mean,
that whole thing was like a charade! He had the orders cut all along,
in his desk!"

"I know," Hinman said. "But you have to follow the rules, you
know. Are all submariners like that? Pretty much so. They take care
of each other, they stick together. It's a camaraderie you won't find
anywhere else in the service except maybe in the aviation branches.
Have we got a place to stay in Chicago?"

"Any hotel will do," she said happily, squeezing his arm. "I've
got to store up enough memories of you to last me until I see you
again!"

Captain Bob Rudd met Hinman at the airport in Pearl Harbor.
Hinman nodded at the gold eagles that were pinned to Rudd's shirt
collar tabs.

"On you they look good, sir. Congratulations."

"War is no respecter of ability, Art," Rudd said. "They make
anyone who's alive and breathing a Captain. Or an Admiral. Severn
got his big stripe. He's gone back to Washington after some quote
unquote well-earned leave. I've got his job. How about that, hey?"

"I want a ship, sir," Hinman said. "With all due respect, I want a ship and the sooner the better!"

"We have to talk about that," Rudd said. "Later. Right now there's something I want you to see before we talk about giving you a ship. Things aren't like they used to be, you know." He motioned to his driver who opened the rear door of the Staff car.

"Son," Rudd said, "take us to where I told you to take us."

The car stopped at the land end of a pier in the Submarine Base and the car's driver half-turned in his seat.

"Can't go down on the pier, Captain. That sign warns us off. Cranes are working down there, sir."

"We'll walk," Rudd said. He got out of the car and with Hinman walked down the length of the pier to where two cranes were trying to pull the periscope out of a submarine. Hinman looked at the faded number painted on the submarine's battered Conning Tower.

"My God, it's *Mako*!"

"Yup," Rudd said. "Got in day before yesterday. Mealey had himself one hell of a patrol run! Dove under a screen of twelve tin cans with aircraft overhead and slammed seven fish into a *Kongo* class battleship. Took an awful pasting! Japs just kicked the shit out of them! Propellor shaft on one side, port I think, is bent a little but the Yard has a spare. You can see what happened to the attack 'scope. After Trim tank is ruptured and a lot of little stuff, busted welds, things like that. They ain't got one light bulb left in that thing, not one gauge glass that wasn't shattered! Come on aft, here, look there! Damned five-inch twenty-five deck gun got blown right off its mounts! The Yard people can't figure out how that could happen without tearing a hole in the hull but it did."

"Did he sink the battleship?"

"Not quite. Battleship's skipper beached the thing on the reef at the Northeast Entrance of Truk. Intelligence intercepted the damage reports on the battleship. Her ammunition lockers for the forward turrets exploded. Killed about three hundred of their people. The ship's out of commission for two, three years. He only gets credit for severely damaging the ship. But old Stoneface Mealey got himself rightly pissed off because they were dropping so much stuff on him that he went up during the attacks and sank a *Fubuki*, busted it right

in two with one shot! You know, that cold-blooded old bastard went in
to seven-hundred yard range on that wagon? I never liked old Mealey
very much before but he's one hell of a submariner!"

They walked the length of the submarine along the pier and
Hinman noted the torn wooden decking, the deep dimples in the
submarine's pressure hull.

"God, she took a beating! Any casualties on our side?"

"One man, youngster, machinist mate named Richards, that the
right name? You should remember, he was part of the original crew.
Got thrown against the engine in the Forward Engine Room and
fractured his skull. He was buried at sea."

"Anyone write to his parents?" Hinman asked.

Rudd nodded. "Joe Sirocco took care of that. Wrote a hell of a
nice letter. Joe took Mike Brannon's place as Exec. Hell of a man!
Reservist but just one hell of an Executive Officer. Old Mealey said
he's one of the best men he ever sailed with and when Mealey says
that about a feather merchant that is one hell of a feather merchant!
You'll like him."

"Like him?" Hinman's voice faltered slightly.

"By golly, I forgot to tell you." Rudd's face wore a broad grin.
"Mealey got his fourth stripe, he's a Captain now. They posted
him as my Number One Boy, my assistant. I had to find someone to
take the Mako, son of a bitch of a ship is all busted up and no other
officer would want her so I figured on giving her to you!"

Hinman wiped the tears from his eyes with no attempt to conceal
the act. "Don't you ever gig me again about playing jokes on anyone!
You dragged me away from a bride and a honeymoon, you canceled my
leave and you never said anything about this!"

Rudd shrugged. "Makes up for some of the lousy jokes you
played on me when I was your Skipper," he said happily. "Now I
suppose you want to go through her, check everything?" Hinman
nodded eagerly.

"Okay, let's get that over with," Rudd said. "Then I'll drop you
at the BOQ with your bags and you'll have time enough to get a
shower and get into your dress canvas before I come by to pick you
up. We're eating at Captain Mealey's house. Tomorrow or the next
day you can go out to the Royal Hawaiian and see the crew. They got

word out there today that you were coming back as the Skipper. I'd make a bet that the biggest beer bust in the history of the United States Navy is going on out there right now!"

"How is Dusty Rhodes, Barber, Ginty, the others?"

"Fine," Rudd said. "I talked to Dusty when they got in. He told me Mealey ordered a reload of the Forward and After Room tubes to begin while he was still firing, if you can picture that! Dusty said that Ginty was opening the tube outer doors and closing the outer doors with only one hand on the Y-wrench! I didn't think anyone was strong enough to do that!"

The two men picked their way down *Mako*'s shattered decking.

"They'll never get this ship ready for sea in under three months!" Hinman muttered.

"Oh yeah?" Rudd replied. "You don't know this Navy Yard! You're scheduled to go on patrol in just a little under four weeks from today, Art! This is one hell of a Navy Yard! Bring 'em back a periscope and I think they could build you a submarine under the periscope in two months!"

CHAPTER 22

The *Mako* plowed westward across the Pacific, her bull nose throwing up twin sheets of spray that glistened in the bright moonlight. Joe Sirocco had the bridge watch and Captain Hinman was at his usual night station, aft of the bridge on the cigaret deck.

Sirocco leaned his elbows on the bridge rail and studied the ocean. The immensity of the Pacific never failed to fascinate him when he had the bridge watch. The Pacific, which covers one third of the Earth's total surface, had impressed seamen for centuries. Those intrepid South Pacific islanders who had set out to sea in their outrigger canoes, armed only with their knowledge of the course of the stars and the habits of migratory birds, their familiarity with wind and current, had been so awed by the great ocean that they gave it status as a god, a natural force beyond understanding.

Sirocco turned to look southward. Somewhere out there, far below the horizon, sprawled the island groups of Melanesia, Micronesia and Polynesia; scores of islands, many of them populated by people whose cultural levels ranged from the aboriginal to the surprisingly sophisticated. A sprawling anthropological paradise that was now threatened by a war between races of people the Islanders did not know. A war that would bring to the Islanders all the benefits of higher civilization; food in cans to take the place of the food that grew so readily on the fertile mountainous upthrusts of drowned continents and the fish in the sea. War, conducted with weapons that could kill from afar, a war that would make no sense for the Islanders who waged war only for important reasons, the taking of women to revitalize the blood of the tribe or war for land on which to grow more food.

The war would bring to these people the ultimate in higher civilization—change. The invaders would bring medicines to heal the sick. The tribal wise men, who for centuries had healed with no more than a few herbs and the power of their minds, a power largely lost by more civilized peoples, would be cast into disrepute.

The white invader and the yellow, each in his own way, would rule and, in ruling, downgrade those native rulers who were descended from centuries of rulers.

The religious men among the invaders would heap their scorn on the tribal wise men who, when faced with problems they could not solve or with crises beyond their powers to confront, would sit and meditate and their souls would depart their bodies and travel great distances to consult with those long dead and bring back their wisdom.

Sirocco stared out across the trackless waters over which his navigational skills and instruments would bring *Mako* to her patrol area at the southern end of the Philippine island of Luzon. He would use the same stars the ancient navigators had used in their fearless voyages across the great waters but Sirocco needed a sextant and books of mathematical formulae to determine *Mako*'s position north or south of the Equator and an accurate chronometer set at Greenwich Meridian Time to tell him his distance west of Greenwich.

Captain Hinman was lost in his own thoughts as he stood on the cigaret deck. He felt at peace with himself. *Mako*, repaired and refitted, was solid beneath his feet. His ship. The ship he had midwived and had baptized in action against the enemy.

The crew, for the most part, was his crew. Men he had trained. He sensed a difference that hadn't been there before. Although he had been *Mako*'s Captain when she was blooded in action against the enemy there had been no retaliation from that enemy. During his absence another Captain had taken *Mako* into action against the enemy and had sunk and damaged ships. Under that other Captain *Mako* and its crew had been scourged in the flame and thunder of depth charge attacks. *Mako*'s crew had had an experience that Captain Hinman had not known and he could detect the slight, subtle difference in the crew. They had matured in small ways and each of them carried a vast respect for the enemy and the knowledge that they had been afraid and had endured the fright, which is perhaps the most maturing agent of all in a man's coming of age.

He didn't think about Joan during the long night hours on the cigaret deck as *Mako* worked its way westward over the long sea miles. He saved the thoughts about Joan for the time when he went to his bunk and as he waited for sleep to come he savored each detail of their last few days together.

He was thinking, this night, of the dinner he had gone to with Bob Rudd at CaptainMealey's quarters on the Submarine Base.

He had known Arvin Mealey casually for years. He had never liked the man very much. Mealey was known as a loner, a man who did not seek out the company of his peers and who discouraged any social contacts by those junior to him. Mealey was known as a strict disciplinarian, a man with little tolerance for the weaknesses of sailors ashore. Hinman was gregarious and he accepted the fact that a sailor ashore was a man bound for trouble. When Mealey's crewmen got into trouble ashore he investigated and if the man was at fault, he ordered court-martial. When Hinman's crew got into trouble on the beach he immediately defended his men against all criticism and if possible, let the man off with a warning.

The dinner with the Mealeys had surprised Hinman. Agnes Mealey, a tall, handsome, regal woman had embraced Hinman warmly and kissed him on the cheek, congratulating him on his marriage. Captain Mealey, in the role of host, was relaxed and on one or two occasions had let a small smile show beneath his mustache, belying the nickname of "Old Stoneface" that he had carried for years. After dinner they had moved to the screened lanai for coffee and Mealey had recounted in detail the action against the battleship and the subsequent depth charging. When he finished he turned to Hinman.

"I owe you my thanks and appreciation, Captain. You gave me a fine crew to go to sea with, very well trained. For the most part, very good men."

"Thank you, sir," Hinman replied. "But I think it's a shame they're giving you a severely damaged on the battleship and not a sinking. If she's on the reef, out of service for two or more years, she's as good as sunk."

Mealey nodded gravely. "Naval intelligence said their reports of intercepted messages show that it will be at least two years before they get her ready for sea again. I am content with the success of the attack. But speaking of damage, sir, there is a man in your Wardroom who in my opinion is damaged and should be transferred at once. I would have done so had I stayed aboard. I am talking about Lieutenant Peter Simms."

Hinman's eyes narrowed slightly.

"The man is flawed," Captain Mealey said. "There is a dry rot within him. It will spread inside him and it will spread to others I assume you heard what the electricians did to him?"

Hinman nodded. Bob Rudd had told him the story on the way to Captain Mealey's quarters, howling with laughter as he told it.

"From what I have heard the electricians had provocation, sir," Hinman said, choosing his words carefully.

"Provocation, imagined or real, should be dealt with through the proper channels," Mealey said. "What happened in this case was that a man or men, enlisted man or men, made what amounted to a physical attack on the person of a U.S. Naval officer. That, sir, as you know full well is a major offense! If there had been sufficient evidence to present at a General Courts-Martial I would have requested such a courts-martial!"

"I trust Mr. Simms has learned his lesson, sir?"

"That's not the point," Captain Mealey said. His mouth under the white mustache was grim. "After the incident Simms just avoided going aft of the engine rooms. Of itself that was stupid. He was afraid to go farther aft! I recommend you transfer him!"

"I appreciate your advice, sir," Hinman said. His mouth was set as grimly as Mealey's. "I'd like to think about it, talk with Simms, talk with Dusty Rhodes and Chief Hendershot."

"There's the problem with Mrs. Simms," Agnes Mealey said.

"Problem?" Hinman said.

"Before you returned from your last patrol, before Arvin took over the *Mako*, it was common knowledge among the O-wives that Mary Simms had, shall I say, a boarder? A civilian engineer who had been sent out here to figure out how to right the *Oklahoma* and the other sunken battleships. I am told she was very careful. She sent her small daughter to stay with Gloria Brannon while she entertained, I hope that's the right word, words and their meanings change so much these days, while she entertained her boarder."

"Simms found out about it," Mealey said. "He asked me for permission to stay aboard *Mako* during the refit, that was on the day you left for the states. I refused and he went to the BOQ."

"And now?" Hinman asked.

"Mary Simms and her daughter left for the States before *Mako* returned from this patrol," Agnes Mealey said. "There had been a lot of talk that the civilian was married with four children. That was wrong, he's a widower with two children, teenagers. I have heard that Mary Simms is filing for divorce and will marry the civilian as soon as the divorce is final."

"I didn't know that!" Bob Rudd said, his eyes opening wide in his beefy red face.

"You have to go to the weekly tea parties at the O-Club, the cat-fights as Arvin calls them, to find out what's going on," Agnes Mealey said, smiling.

"Maybe that will solve his problem," Rudd said.

"I don't think so," Captain Mealey said. He frowned. "It could destroy what little self-confidence the man has in himself. It isn't the most comforting thing to know some civilian has crept into your bed while you're at sea and your wife prefers the civilian!"

"Oh, Arvin!" Mrs. Mealey said. "From what I've heard about Peter Simms I don't think he's without blame." Then, with the finely honed sense of a senior Naval officer's wife, she deftly steered the conversation into safer channels. The evening ended pleasantly and as Mealey walked Rudd and Hinman to their car he put his hand on Hinman's arm.

"I read your patrol report very carefully. I followed your lead on the exploders; I helped Chief Rhodes and Ginty modify them. What an incredible animal that man Ginty is! I also allowed for a deeper run on the torpedoes than the depth settings would show. You'll find all that information in a sealed envelope in your quarters, sir." He touched his white mustache.

"We're going to find out how much deeper the fish run," Rudd said. "I wanted to use *Mako* for those tests but Mealey has smashed the old bucket up so badly that we can't do that as soon as I want it done. *Plunger* is due in, in a few days. We'll use her for the test firings."

Driving back to the BOQ where Hinman was quartered, Bob Rudd turned to Hinman.

"I'm afraid that this time you're in Pearl it's going to be hello and goodbye, Art. *Mako* will report in to the SouWestPac command at the end of your next run. General MacArthur wants to get his island-hopping campaign in high gear and he's made a strong case for more submarines to operate out of Australia."

"I hate to leave your command, Bob," Hinman said.

"I don't like to lose you. But we're going to have to do a lot of talking about certain things. I'll give you the broad picture right now; don't modify any exploders unless you put them back the way they were before you bring any fish in to Australia. The command down there is run by old Gun Club boys and they think that exploder is holy! They'll have your ass in ribbons if they find out you've touched the exploders! If it were me, and it isn't, I know, I'd modify the damned exploders and if I had to bring any fish back I'd change them back and not say one word!"

"That would defeat the purpose, wouldn't it?" Hinman said. "If I modify the exploders and get results and bring back fish with the exploders back as they were and say nothing, then those people down there will have a stronger case than ever for not even touching those exploders. Does that make sense to you?"

"No," Rudd said, "but it protects your ass, friend. We're doing our best here to put pressure on them. If Nimitz wasn't so busy, he's on our side I think, if he wasn't so busy we could end this damned argument in a month. Just be patient.

"Another thing; when you tie up at Brisbane or Freemantle, whichever, you'll be tying up in a political hornet's nest. Don't, for Christ's sake, get caught up in that meat grinder or you'll wind up as two pounds of hamburger! Keep your patrol reports as lean as you can write them, say nothing or less than that to the Command ashore and try to keep your people from talking. Now one other thing that I want to tell you.

"If you have anything to say to me, for my ears only, you put it in a sealed envelope and hand it over to a dude on the Staff down there, Lieut. Comdr. Gene Puser. He's my man, my eyes and ears down there. He's absolutely trustworthy. What I learn from him I tell to Nimitz, so bear that in mind." He stopped the car at the BOQ building.

"Keep all of this to yourself, Art. You'll be around for a while yet, gonna take some time to get *Mako* ready for the sea. We'll talk about this a lot more. When *Plunger* comes in I'd like to have you aboard as an observer when we fire some test fish through a net. I think we can end this crap about the fish not running deeper than they're set for right away if we have some proof."

Hinman yawned and looked up at the stars. They looked close enough to touch. He walked forward to the bridge where Joe Sirocco was being relieved of his watch.

"Will you send me a cup of hot coffee when you go below, Joe?" Hinman asked. "But no doughnuts or sweet rolls."

"If it's all right with you I'll bring a cup back topside and drink it with you," Sirocco said. I've got to take morning stars in an hour or so."

"Fine," Hinman said. He grinned at Nate Cohen, who had taken over the bridge watch.

"How you doing, Ears?" he asked, using the nickname the crew had given to the Communications Officer.

"Fine Captain, just fine. It's like old times with you back. I realized that when I found the rubber spider in my bunk!"

"Yeah, but you spoiled it," Hinman said. "You Reserves have no respect for Naval tradition. You're supposed to laugh when the Captain tells a joke and when you find a rubber spider in your bunk you're supposed to holler and carry on!"

"The Talmud teaches logic and reason, among many other things, Captain," Cohen said. "Both argued against the presence of a tarantula on a submarine, especially a spider with only six legs instead of the eight it should have."

Dusty Rhodes walked into the Forward Torpedo Room where Ginty had just taken over the morning four-to-eight watch at the torpedo tubes. Ginty was sitting in a canvas chair in front of the tubes, sipping at a cup of coffee.

"What the hell you doin' up, Chief? They's another chair over there outboard of that warhead. Get it out and sit a bit. Grabby Grabnas brought me up a fresh pitcher of coffee. Another cup around here someplace. Damned coffee is strong enough to kill you! I think that fuckin' cook back there makes it double strong on the morning watch so the son of a bitch can stay awake long enough to cook chow! Put this stuff in a fish the son of a bitch would run at ninety knots!"

Rhodes unfolded the chair and sat down and took the cup of coffee Ginty poured for him.

"Buncha shit, this modifying the exploders is okay if you operate out of Pearl but put 'em back the way they were if you go into Australia!" Ginty growled. "Lotta fuckin' work, Chief! Why in the hell can't those people get their heads together and say the exploders is *ding boo how* and fix 'em so they'll work?

"Hell, Grilley told me that even after Cap'n Rudd fired those exercise fish out of *Plunger* and found the fish runnin' eight to fourteen feet deeper than the depth setting, Grilley told me that those Admirals didn't believe it! Hell, any damned fool of a third class torpedoman could tell you that if you put a bigger warhead out in front of that fish that it's gotta run deeper than it would with the regular warhead on it! Those fuckin' Admirals are going to ruin this man's Navy!"

"Admirals live in a different world, Ginch," Rhodes said, his voice patient. "Any Admiral who's a member of the Gun Club, any of those people who spent any time in ordnance work, design and testing torpedoes, is going to think that whatever Newport says is the Holy Gospel. Haines, that Warrant who runs the exploder shop at Pearl, told me that Rudd is putting together so much evidence about the exploders and the deep running that pretty soon even the Gun Club will have to sit up and take notice." He paused. "I saw the Old Man up here again yesterday afternoon."

"Yeah," Ginty said. "He comes up every afternoon after he wakes up. Bullshits with all hands. Messes up my daily work routines. Tells his lousy jokes and expects everyone to laugh. He likes to keep everyone loose as a goose."

"He's got the whole ship loose," Rhodes said. "Worries me. I laid into DeLucia back aft the other day for letting stuff get adrift in his room and Hindu tells me that after I went forward the people back there started calling me 'Mealey Junior!' "

"Shit" Ginty growled. "Keep crackin' down! Some of these war-time sailors, an officer smiles at 'em and says hello and they think they can throw the soojie rag in the bucket and knock off scrubbin' paintwork! Some of these Fleet-boat sailors ought to do some time in an S-boat where you got four times as much work to do and only half as many men. The Old Man gonna stay on the surface again today? We got to be gettin' close enough to the Islands to be divin' mornings and runnin' submerged all day. They must have so many Japs in those Islands by now that there's two in every coconut tree along the beaches!"

"I hear he's going to stay on the surface as long as he can," Rhodes said. "That's a change that Captain Rudd made. Rudd says that some skippers start all-day dives one day out of Pearl and waste too much time getting on station." He stood up and stretched his arms until his big shoulder muscles cracked.

"Thanks for the coffee. You'd better check the room and tie down everything that might come loose. The Radio people say there's a big storm to the west. Someone over there, forget which boat, reported it. We might be in it in a day or two. Can't be a typhoon this time of year."

"Don't shit yourself!" Ginty said. "I put sixteen years out here on the Asiatic Station and I seen typhoons in every damned month of the year! Typhoons ain't anything to fuck with, Chief. On the S-37 we run into one had seas a hundred feet high and I shit you not! Fuckin' wind blew the wind gauge right off'n the periscope shears, musta been blowin' a hundred and twenty knots! Couldn't submerge because when we tried it we'd be at a hundred feet one minute and then we'd be down to two hundred and fifty feet. So we had to ride it out rigged for dive on the surface. You want misery you ride an S-boat in that kind of weather!"

Rhodes nodded and went aft to the Crew's Mess to see what Johnny Johnson, the Ship's Cook, had made for the morning meal. Usually the dour cook whipped up a batch of doughnuts or sweet rolls. This morning it was doughnuts. Rhodes picked up two of the doughnuts, drew a cup of coffee from the urn and went in to sit at a table in the mess room. Chief John Barber was sitting there with a cup of coffee. One of his off-duty firemen sat at another table. Barber stared at the man until he got the message and picked up his coffee cup and left the compartment.

"Get your fuel injector problem licked?" Rhodes asked.

"Yeah," Barber grunted. "You got to tell these people the same things over and over every day. And even then they'll forget to clean the fuel strainers. Gonna start kicking me some ass pretty damned soon. Damned people are getting sloppy!" He got up and drew another cup of coffee for himself.

"Wanted to talk to you before this but I couldn't find the time when we were alone," Barber said as he sat down. He dropped his voice so the ship's cook, busy in his tiny galley, couldn't hear.

"I had a pretty bad time after the last run. I hit that kid Richards a little too hard. Didn't mean to do that, no way! But when he started beating on the deck plates with that hammer and hollering for the Japs to come and get us, after all that depth charging we'd taken, it did something to me inside. I never felt that way before about anything or anyone! I hit him too hard with that wrench.

"I was pretty shook up afterward. Had bad dreams. Finally I had to tell Dottie about it and she told your wife and June came right over to the house. She asked me and Dottie to go into the bedroom with her and we sat on the bed and she sat on the floor and she never left the room or moved but she sort of went away. You know what I mean?"

"She meditates," Rhodes said. "That's what she calls it. She talks to the old gods."

"Yeah," Barber grunted. "Spooky as hell! She gets that blank look and she doesn't hear anything you say to her. Finally she got up and went out in the kitchen and Dottie made coffee and then June sat there and told me that Richards was all right. She said that what I did had been planned that way, that Richards was supposed to go back to wherever he came from and that I was the one who was supposed to send him back. Dusty, that's spooky!

"Then she got up and she put her hands on my head and she said I wouldn't have any more dreams and by God, I didn't have any of those dreams any more! How does she do that?"

"I don't know," Rhodes said. "All I know is that what she does is called 'Kahuna,' and it's very, very old. Her people have been doing it for hundreds and hundreds of years. She's been able to do it since she was about ten years old.

"Now let me tell you something. The day we got in from the last patrol she met me at the dock, you were there. When we got home and I'd seen the kids she took me out in the kitchen.

"Just remember, I hadn't told her one damned thing about the patrol and you know they kept everyone away from the dock when we came in because we were so badly busted up. So she didn't see the ship. And she took me out in the kitchen and pointed at the calendar on the bulkhead and there was a red crayon circle around the day we hit the battleship!

"She said that she knew that on that day we had been in great danger but that she didn't worry because the old gods told her we'd get back home safely!"

"I know," Barber said, nodding his head, "Dottie told me that story after I got home. Made me feel kind of funny inside."

Rhodes took his wallet out of his hip pocket and opened it and took out a folded slip of paper. He handed it to Barber.

"June gave me this the day before we left port," Rhodes said. "Told me to keep it with me all the time." Barber unfolded the slip of paper and read it aloud.

"*Accept what is offered even though it is not wanted.*"

"I don't get it," he said. He handed the paper back to Rhodes, who folded it carefully and put it back in his wallet.

"Neither do I," Rhodes said. "She told me that the gods told her that a time would come when this would mean something to me and when that time came I should obey what was given to her, what she wrote down."

CHAPTER 23

Mako made rendezvous with the storm in the Luzon Straits between Luzon and Formosa. As storms went in those latitudes it was not a major weather event. The winds howled at 60 miles an hour and the seas were sullen green giants 40 to 50 feet high with almost a mile of water between their tops of wind-whipped spray. Captain Hinman, dressed in rain clothes, shouted above the wind to Joe Sirocco.

"This is where we should patrol, in Luzon Strait. All the shipping going to and from Japan uses this strait. Lots of deep water. You'd get more ships here than trying to pick them off when they come out of harbors." Sirocco looked at the dark bulk of the mountain that was Bataan Island, rising more than 3,000 feet above the sea to starboard, and nodded and then grabbed at the bridge rail as *Mako* plunged her bow deep into a long, rolling sea and staggered upward, shedding the tons of water which roared down her narrow deck and broke, smashing into spray against the Conning Tower structure and soaking everyone on the bridge.

"What's our next course change?" Hinman shouted above the wind.

"We just passed Babuyan Island ten miles to port. That mountain is over thirty-five hundred feet high. When it bears two zero four degrees relative we can come left to course two three four and come down past Cape Bojeader, that's on the northwest tip of Luzon itself. Once clear of the Cape we can alter course to port again and run on down the coastline, I'd suggest about forty miles off the land."

"Very well," Hinman said. He studied the sullen gray sky.

"We'll stay on the surface today," he said in Sirocco's ear. "No sense in going down in this weather. I'm going to turn in. Call me if the weather changes or if we see anything. Keep the lookouts here in the bridge space and maintain a periscope watch."

Lieut. Bob Edge, manning the search persicope in the Conning Tower, sighted the small convoy at mid-morning.

Captain Hinman was out of his bunk at the first rap of the messenger's knuckles on the bulkhead of his tiny stateroom. He grabbed at his bunk rail to steady himself and pulled on pants and shirt and stuffed his feet into sandals.

"Can you see them yet?" he yelled as he climbed up the ladder to the bridge.

"Not yet, sir," Pete Simms shouted from beneath his rain hood.

"Chief of the Boat to the Bridge with a strong line," Hinman ordered. Dusty Rhodes came up to the bridge with a small coil of manila line over one shoulder and gasped as a sudden rain squall swept over *Mako*, soaking him to the skin.

"I want a safety line on a lookout," Hinman shouted to Rhodes. "I want to put him up in the shears."

Rhodes swiftly tied a bowline on a bight knot in the line. One of the lookouts gingerly pulled the two loops of the knot up over his legs and Rhodes tied the bitter end of the line around his waist.

"It's like a sling," he said in the lookout's ear. "If you go over the side the line won't cut you in half at the belly, it's around your legs and body." He paid out the line as the lookout worked his way up to a lookout stand in the periscope shears.

"One hand for you, one for the ship," Hinman yelled at the

lookout. "Hang on, fella!" The lookout grabbed the waist-high pipe railing around the lookout stand with one hand and raised his binoculars to his eyes with the other.

"I got 'em!" he yelled. "Three ships bearing about three two zero, Bridge. Look like two little freighters and one destroyer. Destroyer's making lots of smoke. They're headed this way!"

"Get him down from there and rig me up," Hinman said to Rhodes. "I want to get a good look."

Hinman scrambled up to the lookout stand. He clung there for a long moment, searching through his binoculars.

"Sound General Quarters!" He yelled suddenly. "Plotting Party to the Conning Tower!" He balanced himself against *Mako*'s savage rolls and pitching, raising his binoculars whenever *Mako* steadied for a few seconds at the top of a roll. He heard Joe Sirocco's voice, faint under the wind, reporting to the Bridge that he had the targets in the search periscope.

"Give me a range and a bearing," Captain Hinman yelled as he scrambled down into the bridge and stripped off the safety line.

"Targets bear three four zero, sir," Sirocco's voice came up the hatch. "Range is two five zero zero and the angle on the bow is ten starboard."

Mako rose on the top of a long wave and the people on the bridge could see the targets. Two small coastal freighters of about 3,000 tons and an old coal-burning destroyer. A bright light winked briefly on the destroyer's foredeck.

"Destroyer's opened fire with deck guns," Hinman yelled. "Lookouts below!" A gout of water shot up on the side of a long wave, far off to *Mako*'s starboard bow. "He can't hit anything with that kind of a platform, he's rolling like hell!"

"Left ten degrees rudder," Hinman ordered. "Joe, I'm going to run down the starboard flank, shoot from that side."

"That's where the destroyer is, sir," Sirocco answered.

"Affirm, Plot," Hinman said. *Mako* slid to the top of a long wave and the guns on the destroyer fired again. A shell went by high overhead, its screech muffled by the wind. Captain Hinman leaned over the hatch to the Conning Tower.

"Plot! How does it look? Are we going to get a shot?"

"Yes, sir," Sirocco called up through the hatch. "In about a minute we'll all be in the same wave trough. We can shoot then. Torpedo run will be twelve zero zero yards, sir."

"Open the outer doors in the Forward Room," Hinman called. "Here we go!"

Mako breasted the crest of a wave, spray whipping across the bridge, and Hinman saw the three ships.

"Come on!" Hinman yelled. "I've got the bastards right in front of me up here! Give me a solution!"

"Commence shooting whenever you're ready, sir," Sirocco yelled.

"*Fire one!*" Hinman yelled. The destroyer was steady on its course, rolling heavily as it tried to turn toward the *Mako*.

"*Fire two!*"

Captain Hinman saw the first torpedo leap clear of the water far short of the target. The torpedo tail-walked for a few brief seconds and then plunged back into the water, turning to the right; it was porpoising in and out of the water and headed in a long, curving course back toward *Mako*.

"*Right full rudder!*" Hinman screamed. "The fish is running wild! Close the tube doors!"

"Fish is running well aft of us, Bridge!" Hinman looked upward and saw Grabby Grabnas, the seaman who had grown up in the Southern Florida shrimp fleet, clinging to the periscope shears like a big monkey, his eyes on the porpoising torpedo.

"Bridge! We're gonna be pooped!" Grabnas' voice was a high scream.

"*Rig for dive! Close the main induction!*" Hinman's bellow was a split second behind Grabnas' warning as he looked aft and saw what every seaman dreads, a great wave towering over the stern of his ship, running at the ship with hundreds of thousands of tons of water.

"*Hang on!*" Hinman yelled and slammed the hatch to the Conning Tower closed and flung himself down on it, twisting at the hand wheel to dog it tightly closed.

The wave, inexorable, unstoppable, overtook *Mako*, burying the periscope shears and the bridge under 20 feet of solid green water. The ship staggered sluggishly under the great weight and then, with all four main electrical motors driving the screws full astern on Sirocco's order, *Mako* began to back out of the wave.

Captain Hinman was conscious of bodies on top of his own as he was flattened against the hatch cover. He held on to the hand wheel on top of the hatch, holding his breath, trying to stem the panic that rose within him, waiting for the upward surge of the ship under him that would tell him that *Mako* had recovered from the over-run of the great wave. The weight on him eased and he felt the ship surging upward. He opened his eyes and then gulped in air and scrambled to his feet.

"The lookout!" he croaked. He looked upward and saw Grabnas, his arms and legs wrapped around the periscope shears.

"Get down from there, you damned fool!" Hinman yelled.

"Bridge!" Sirocco's voice over the bridge speaker was tinny. "We're going all full astern on the motors! You all right up there?"

"Open the hatch," Hinman ordered and the quartermaster squatted and spun the hand wheel and opened the hatch. Sirocco came up the ladder until his broad shoulders were in the bridge itself.

"We'll have to come around again if you want to get another crack at them," Sirocco said. "We're on the motors, sir, going all full astern."

"Very well," Hinman said. "They get the main induction closed in time?"

"Checking now, sir," Sirocco said. He looked down as a hand plucked at his leg.

"Main induction is dry, Bridge," Pete Simms said from the Conning Tower.

"Rig for surface," Hinman ordered. "All ahead two-thirds. How do we look on the plot, Joe?"

"We're turned around, sir," Sirocco answered. "We'll have to start over to get a position."

"Get me a bearing and range on the periscope," Hinman ordered. Sirocco dropped down the hatch into the Conning Tower. Hinman looked around and then called down to Sirocco.

"We're coming up on the crest of a big one, keep your eyes open, you might be able to get a good look."

"I've got his smoke, Bridge," Sirocco called out. "Bearing is one eight five. Looks like he's headed away from us."

"Aircraft! Broad on the port beam! Low down!" Grabnas' immersion had not hurt his voice.

Hinman took one quick look and saw the dark shape to port.

"Clear the bridge!" he shouted and squeezed to one side as the lookouts and the quartermaster plunged down the ladder into the Conning Tower. He looked again to port and slammed the heel of his hand against the diving alarm.

"*Dive! Dive! Dive!*" He yelled as he went down the hatch, pulling on the hatch lanyard to close it.

"Three hundred feet!" Hinman ordered as he stood in the Conning Tower. "I don't think he can get anywhere near us. He's coming across that wind and he'll never be able to hold a fix on where we were." He cocked his head as two dull explosions rocked *Mako* slightly.

At 300 feet *Mako* was still at the mercy of the great waves that rolled by overhead. The needle on the depth gauge gyrated wildly, showing 260 feet one minute and then dipping below 300 feet as *Mako* rolled heavily in the seas. Captain Hinman dropped down the ladder to the Control Room and studied the chart.

"Joe," he said to Sirocco, "let's get back on course to the patrol area. Where's Don Grilley? Don, I'd like a reload of those two empty tubes forward if you think it can be done."

"I think we can do it," Grilley said. "But if Ginty says he doesn't want to try it maybe we'd better hold off a while."

"I'll go up and help out," Hinman said. "I don't want those two tubes empty any longer than they have to be. Joe, we'll stay at General Quarters until the reload is completed and then we'll secure and eat the noon meal."

"You gave me bad torpedoes," Captain Hinman said to Ginty as he walked into the Forward Room. "Mr. Cohen said the first fish ran out of the tube and then I saw it jump out of the water and start a circular run. I saw the second one come straight up out of the water and then do a nose dive!"

Ginty flushed, his face angry. "Sir," he said in a cold voice, "them fish went out of the tubes and they both ran hot, straight and

normal, Mr. Cohen said that! You can't fire torpedoes in seas that big!
Fish runnin' at forty-five knots starts up the slope of a big wave and
it'll get airborne and when it comes down it can go in any direction!
The gyro in the fish tumbles and the depth mechanisms get all
messed up!" His eyes were hot, his face stern and set.

"It was my fault then, Ginty," Hinman said with a broad smile.
"I had to kid you a little, fella! I want to reload those two empty tubes
if you think it can be done. She's not a very steady platform, not even
down this deep."

"I can do it," Ginty said evenly. "All's I need is for the officers to
get out of the way because this ain't no place for an observer if the
Divin' Officer don't keep the ship's bow up and a fish starts to run
into the tube too fast."

"I thought you might need some muscles on the tagle," Captain
Hinman said. He grinned at the big torpedoman.

"Sir," Ginty said, his voice still cold, "I think you'd better let
these here people I've trained do that work." He turned away and
vented Number One tube and opened the inner door. He touched the
telephone talker on the shoulder.

"Tell the Divin' Officer we're about to start a reload on Number
One," he said. "And say please when you ask him to try to give us a
half degree up bubble if he can." He walked back along the length of
the torpedo, still held in its rack by a heavy metal strap fastened with
a large brass nut and bolt.

"If you don't mind, Captain, Mr. Grilley," he said evenly, "I
need some room to work. I got to get a snubbin' line on the tail of this
fish so it can't go out through the outer door if we take a big down
angle." He caught at the torpedo skid with one hand as *Mako* rolled
and nosed downward. "Like now!" His big, deft hands threw a
bowline knot into the end of a piece of stout line and he made a noose
and slipped it around the torpedo's tail. He handed the end of the line
to Johnny Paul.

"Take a turn around the end of the skid," he growled. "We take
another one of them down angles and if you lose this fish don't let go of
the line. Go out the fuckin' outer door with the fish because you'll be
safer out there in the water than in here with me!" He picked up a

wrench and carefully loosened the nut that held the belly strap tight around the torpedo.

"Take a light strain on that tagle, shitheads! When I get this strap off ease her in a little at a time, just like you put it in your old lady the first time! Keep your fuckin' eyes on me and your ears open!"

Captain Hinman and Don Grilley watched Ginty start and stop the torpedo on its way into the tube, sensing the motion of the ship through his feet and legs, using all the skills he had learned in years of muscling torpedoes in other Torpedo Rooms. When he had closed the inner door and engaged the gyro and depth spindles he turned to his talker.

"Tell Control that Number One tube is reloaded, gyro spindle engaged, depth set four feet, depth spindle disengaged. And tell 'em we're starting the reload on Number Two." He turned to the reload crews. "Now lay out that tagle, you cowshit kickers and see if we can do this one half-way right!"

Captain Hinman ducked through the low water-tight door and went into the Wardroom. Grilley followed him and the cook put fresh cups of coffee in front of the two officers.

"The American submarine sailor is an amazing individual," Hinman said. "Just amazing! Take Ginty; I doubt that he had a high school education. His service record is full of incidents of trouble he's been in. He's been reduced in rank three times. Always for fighting while on liberty. He came to us because he got in a fight with British and French sailors in Hong Kong and the skipper of his S-boat figured that if he didn't transfer him he'd be court-martialed again and get an Undesirable Discharge."

"He's never been in trouble on *Mako*," Grilley said.

"That's due to Dusty Rhodes," Hinman said. "Ginty's the strongest man I've ever seen but he respects Rhodes."

Sirocco had come into the Wardroom while Hinman was talking.

"Tubes forward are reloaded, we're secure from General Quarters and steady on the course to the patrol area, sir," he said. "The last weather report we got before we dove indicates the weather front is moving past us and we should be clear of it by nightfall. We'll be off Luzon by morning."

"Very well, Joe," Hinman said. He yawned. "I'm going to get some sleep. Call me an hour before dark."

Mako plowed on beneath the sea, rolling heavily from time to time. Dusty Rhodes drew a half cup of coffee from the urn in the Crew's Mess and made his way forward.

"Heard you had some high-priced help up here on the reload," he said. Ginty scowled at him.

"Fuckin' gold braid! Why can't they stay the hell out of a sailor's way? Ain't no call for the Old Man to come up here and want to pull on the tagle! That's my work! He's gold braid, he oughta keep himself apart from the troops.

"You give me a choice and I'll take that miserable fuckin' Mealey any time over these buddy-buddy fuckers, even if Mealey did turn the water off in the showers! That son of a bitch of a Mealey, he knew he was the Captain and he let you know it! He knew his place and he knew my place and he knew the place of every shithead aboard! Fuckin' Navy's gettin' too soft! For a while there after this Old Man's old lady got creamed at Pearl he was like a regular Navy officer. Bite your ass off if you looked at him sidewise. Now he's back like he was when I come aboard, grab-assin' around all the time.

"Shit, he even put a rubber spider in the Jew-boy's bunk! Anyone puts rubber spiders in any bunk in my Room and they'll have that spider up their ass, believe you me!"

"I know how you feel, Ginch," Rhodes said gently. "Do me a little favor, huh? Don't tell anyone else how you feel. You have to understand, Ginch, that the Old Man was hit real hard when his wife was killed. Now he's got a new wife and he's as happy as a clam in muck. But because he's happy and plays a little grab-ass doesn't mean he isn't a good submarine man or a good skipper."

"Fuckin' Japs don't play no grab-ass!" Ginty muttered. "He was over in the States when we found that out, Chief. He don't know what those depth charges sound like yet.

"Another thing; the people in the Radio Shack say that Pearl's been tryin' to raise two boats out here for the last five days and they ain't gettin' no answer to the calls. That only means one thing, Chief, fuckin' Japs have got those boats! Ol' Jap don't play grab-ass, we both know that."

Rhodes nodded, making a mental note to tell Lieutenant Cohen to tell his people to keep their mouths shut about things like lost submarines. He touched Ginty lightly on the shoulder.

"Hell of a job on the reload, Ginch. I don't think there's another Forward Room could have done it, rolling and pitching like we were. If you want to sound off, do it to me. I've got good ears and what they hear doesn't go out of my mouth."

Mako surfaced at full dark in seas that were still long and rolling but without the wind that had torn spray from the wave tops and hurled it like buckshot. Lieutenant Cohen took a position report and a contact report on the small convoy into the Radio Shack. An hour later Cohen came into the Control Room.

"Captain on the cigaret deck?" he asked Sirocco, who nodded.

"We've got a special mission," Cohen said in a low voice as he climbed the ladder and went up to the bridge.

CHAPTER 24

"Welcome to General Douglas MacArthur's Southwest Pacific Submarine Navy!" Captain Hinman said to his officers who had gathered in the Wardroom. He put his hand on the message Nate Cohen had given him earlier.

"Our orders have been changed," Hinman continued. "We are not going to our patrol area. We are ordered to proceed to Subic Bay, south of Manila, and there contact some Army people who must have escaped from the Japs after the surrender at Marveles. These Army people, they're apparently a guerrilla force, have found a Scotch missionary and his wife and their two small children in the jungle. We are to make contact, pick up the family and take them to Brisbane."

"Sounds interesting," Pete Simms said. "Go in to the beach, rescue people! We'll have to make up a landing party, sir. I'd like to volunteer to lead it!"

"That won't be necessary," Hinman said. "The message says the Army people have a boat and will bring the people out to us."

"If I may, sir," Don Grilley said slowly, "I don't quite understand the part about 'General MacArthur's Submarine Navy.' "

Hinman looked around the table.

"As most of you may know," he said, "I don't like politics in any form. Apparently the submarine command in Australia is one big pot of politics. It boils over constantly, I am told. One of the more influential politicians down there is the Commanding Officer, SouWestPac. He's reputed to be a very close friend of Dugout Doug, or to be formal, General Douglas MacArthur.

"Captain Rudd filled me in on a lot of this before we left Pearl. He told me that submarines operating out of Australia do an awful lot of special missions because MacArthur wants them to do those missions. It follows, or this is the way I see it, that when a submarine is on special mission it isn't shooting torpedoes at the enemy, damn it! The situation down there, I'm speaking of the political situation now, is so bad that a number of officers, including one Rear Admiral, have offered to resign their commissions!

"Captain Rudd told me something else. The submarine command officers in charge down there are all old Gun Club boys, people who were assigned to Newport and to torpedo and exploder work at one time or another. They all think the Mark Six exploder is sacred. You can modify the exploder if you're working out of Pearl but if you're working out of Brisbane or Freemantle and they catch you doing that you're in deep trouble. So I want you to tell your people that they should keep their mouths shut when we get in. The less you say, the less any of us say, the better." Hinman pushed the message over to Joe Sirocco.

"Lay out our course, Joe. I'd like to arrive in the area during daylight, submerged of course, so we can look it over. I am not going to commit this ship to an operation like this without knowing what the place looks like, how many fishing vessels there are in the area, if the area is patrolled." He shook his head.

"Good God! One of the children is aged three and the other is less than a year old! Babies on a submarine! Anyone got any suggestions on where we'll put them?"

"Why don't you give that problem to Chief Rhodes," Sirocco

said. "I'm sure he'll come up with the only good place, the CPO quarters. There are four bunks in there."

Hinman nodded. "Put it to him, Joe. Nate, you'd better have Doc start reading up on child care if he's got any books on that. And how to treat malnutrition, jungle rot or whatever other diseases these people might be expected to have. The message says they've been running from the Japs, living in the jungle, for over a year. That means that the baby must have been born out in the jungle!" He looked at Cohen, a small smile on his face.

"This is a Scotch missionary family—at least the man is, so I presume he's a Presbyterian. You could exchange theological theories."

Cohen smiled shyly. "I don't know, sir. Missionaries are very dedicated people. He might try to convert me."

Viewed through the periscope, Sampaloc Point, the entrance to Subic Bay, looked peaceful enough. There was a stretch of white sand fronting the wooded point. There was no sign of life anywhere. In subsequent messages received by *Mako* the Command in Australia had pointed out the importance of the mission; the missionary's wife was a distant relative of Prime Minister Winston Churchill and the Staff in Australia had already sent a message to London saying that the rescue would be effected. Hinman read the message and ground his teeth together in exasperation.

"Damned politicians! Trying to make Brownie points before we've ever had a chance to make contact! If we don't get these people we'll be crucified. If we do get them the Staff will get all the credit. And I don't have to be told to extend every courtesy and hospitality to people who have been living in a jungle for more than a year! What do they think we are, animals?"

Mako spent hours cruising off the point of land, watching through the periscope. Twice they saw a figure come out of the woods and walk down and sit beside a boat that was drawn up on the sand. Just before dusk Joe Sirocco, who was manning the persicope, saw two figures move out of the woods. As he watched he saw the two figures stretch some white cloth across the bushes.

"Captain to the Conning Tower," he said crisply. Hinman came up the ladder.

"They've made the signal, sir," Sirocco said. "A white cloth spread on the bushes." He stood to one side and Hinman put his eye to the periscope.

"It could be a trap!" Hinman said. "I'm not going to go up until after full dark."

"That's an hour from now," Sirocco said.

"I want both deck gun crews in red goggles," Hinman said. "Put the machine gunners in red goggles. We'll go to Battle Stations Surface when we go up."

"We don't have that many pair of red goggles, sir," Sirocco said. "I tried to draw some but they didn't have them at Pearl. We've only got eight pair."

"Black out the Control Room and get the people in there now," Hinman said. "I don't want to put anyone topside with their eyes unadjusted to darkness. I don't like this operation, Joe! We haven't seen a single fishing boat all afternoon! The only damned thing we've seen is a guy come out of the bushes and walk down the beach and sit down by that little boat and then he goes back up in the bushes. There should be fishing boats around, something should be moving in the area." He swung the periscope around and studied the horizon. "Empty sea! It's unreal!"

Mako surfaced after full dark, the gun crews tumbling over the bridge and down to the deck. The machine gunners set up their 50-caliber guns on special stanchions set in the deck near the Conning Tower. Dick Smalley, the Gunner's Mate, adjusted the broad strap of the twin 20-mm machine guns around his buttocks and leaned back, his hands on the cocking levers of the guns.

"Both deck guns manned, sir. Breeches open. Standing by to load both deck guns." Chief Rhodes' voice from the deck was calm.

"If we have to open fire I want you to lay your rounds into the tree line," Captain Hinman called down to the gun crew forward. He turned and spoke to the lookouts in the periscope shears.

"Keep your eyes in your own sectors! Don't look around to see what's happening! The biggest danger we face is being surprised by some patrol boat or aircraft!" He turned to the quartermaster.

"Make the identification signal."

The quartermaster raised the signal gun to his shoulder. He

aimed the signal gun at the white blur of the cloth and began to pull the trigger, sending three sets of dot-dash-dot, "R" in the Morse code. There was no answer from the beach. He sent another group of three signals. A small light blinked faintly on the beach, a series of three short blinks, "S" in Morse and then a long blink repeated three times, "T" in the code.

"They answer the right way, sir," the quartermaster said.

"Small boat under way from the beach," Grabnas sang out from his position in the port lookout stand.

"Load deck guns!" Hinman's voice was sharp. "Machine gunners, load and cock! Stand by on deck to receive the party!"

"Standing by on deck, Bridge," Rhodes answered. Ginty, a strong line tied around his waist and fastened to the base of the deck gun, was down on the swell of the pressure hull, waiting.

The boat drew closer, a long, narrow fishing canoe with one outrigger. Captain Hinman, his binoculars at his eyes, saw two people in the forward part of the canoe, each holding a child. Two men were paddling and a large man with white hair that shone in the moonlight was at the steering oar.

The boat came alongside *Mako* and Ginty, with Rhodes belaying his safety line, leaned outward.

"Gimme the kids first," Ginty said. He handed the two children up to the deck and then picked the woman bodily out of the canoe and handed her up to the deck. He gave his hand to the man, who stumbled and slipped on the wet pressure hull and then gasped as Ginty grabbed him and pushed him up over his head and back to the crew members in the deck party.

"They're all yours, Navy," the white-haired man said. "I wrote a report and gave it to the Reverend. Will you see that it gets to General MacArthur for me?"

"Will do," Captain Hinman called down. "Can I have your name, sir? You've done a good job."

"Master Sergeant Peter McGillivray, U.S. Army, sir. Now the commanding officer of McGillivray's Raiders."

"Anything you need that we can give you?" Hinman asked. "Food, clothing? If we've got it and you need it it's yours."

"I could use some sulfa powder if you've got some, sir. I can steal what we need from the Japs but they're as short of medicine as I am."

Hinman turned and spoke briefly to Nate Cohen. He handed the box over the rail.

"Here's five pounds of sulfa powder," he called to the man in the boat. "That help?"

"That's a Godsend," McGillivray said. "See you around, Navy. I've got to get the hell out of here!" He raised a hand in salute as his two paddlers shoved the canoe away from *Mako*'s hull.

"Secure deck party," Captain Hinman ordered. "All hands except the watch get below. Let's get the hell out of here ourselves!"

Once safely out to sea with regular sea watches set, Captain Hinman turned the deck over to Don Grilley and went below. He went into the Wardroom and sat down.

"Where are the people we picked up?" he asked Thomas T. Thompson, the black Officers' Cook who held sway over the small galley next to the Wardroom.

"Well, Captain, it's like this," Thompson said. "The lady's clothes are in rags, so bad that she can't hardly be decent in front of other people. So Johnny Paul, he ain't too big you know, he's given her some dungaree pants and a shirt and she's in the Officers' shower right now, cleanin' herself up. They're dressing her husband in dungarees and a clean shirt and sandals and they're tryin' to find some sandals small enough for the lady. Mike DeLucia took the little boy back to his torpedo room to clean him up and Ginty is taking care of the baby girl."

"Ginty? Ginty? Taking care of a baby girl?"

"Yessir," Thompson said with a broad grin. "Old Ginch has got that baby girl up there and he's givin' her a bath in a bucket!"

"I've got to see this!" Hinman said.

"Uh, uh, Captain. I wouldn't if I were you. Ginty rigged some sheets around the shower in the Forward Room so the lady could have some privacy when she come out of the shower and he closed the water-tight door to the Wardroom so no one could bust in on her. If I were you I'd just sit tight and have some more coffee. When the people get the visitors all cleaned up they'll bring 'em here."

"Sailors!" Hinman said.

An hour later the missionary and his wife, each dressed in clean dungarees and wearing submarine sandals, lightweight shoes with perforated leather tops and a strap to hold them on, pushed their plates back in the Wardroom.

"That all you gonna eat?" Thompson said from his galley.

"My dear man," the missionary said. "You cooked a superb meal! Just marvelous! Roast beef and Welsh rarebit!"

"I didn't cook none of it," Thompson said. "I just sort of supervised. Couldn't get no haggis for you. Had to make do with the Welsh rarebit. How about more tea?"

When Thompson had cleared the table Captain Hinman turned to the missionary.

"I'd like you to meet my officers now." He nodded at Thompson and in a few minutes the off-duty officers crowded into the Wardroom.

"Gentlemen," Captain Hinman said from the head of the table. "Meet the Reverend Lucius Shrewsbury and Mrs. Shrewsbury and their two children, Ronald and Deborah." He introduced each of his officers.

"Amazing people you have, Captain. It is Captain, is it not?" the Reverend Shrewsbury said. He indicated the Forward Torpedo Room with his hand. "That huge man up there almost scared Mrs. Shrewsbury to death, y'know! Took the baby right out of her arms and told her to get in the shower and get cleaned up!"

"His name is Ginty," Hinman said. "He's a very good man."

"Indeed he is," Mrs. Shrewsbury said in her soft voice, lisping through the gap where her front lower teeth were missing. "After I had dressed in these nice clothes I went up there by all those shiny brass things and that huge man had Deborah in his arms and she was all washed and clean and he was singing to her! And some nice man has cut Ronald's hair."

"The barber would be Mike DeLucia, the man in charge of the After Torpedo Room," Captain Hinman said.

"And this kind gentleman, here," the Reverend said, pointing to Lieutentant Cohen, "this gentlemen took charge of us and showed us everything. He made us welcome and oh, that wonderful hot water shower bath! And the clothes! A most Christian thing to do, sir!"

"Lieutenant Cohen is Jewish, Reverend," Hinman said.

"So was Jesus!" the Reverend said. "A habit of speaking one gets into, you know. No offense intended, none taken, right, sir?" He looked earnestly at Nathan Cohen, who smiled gently.

Mako twisted her way southward through the islands of the Sulu Sea, running at full speed on the surface during the night hours and submerging by day. The children adapted well to the submarine. The boy, Ronald, was everywhere. Deborah, the small girl, was a toddler and couldn't negotiate the high sills of the water-tight doors, but a sailor always seemed to be loitering nearby to lift her over the sill. In the galley Johnny Johnson and his crew worked overtime trying to concoct meals that would stun the passengers and did amaze the crew.

Four days after the passengers had come aboard Dusty Rhodes went to Joe Sirocco.

"Sir, we've got to talk about something," Rhodes said. Sirocco nodded.

"Some of the crew got together," Rhodes said, "and they decided that the reputation of the *Mako* is at stake, sir."

"In what way?" Sirocco asked.

"They decided that we can't turn those people we've got over at the dock looking like, well, sailors. Someone, I don't know who, salvaged the lady's torn dress from the GI can. They took it aft and they broke out the bolt of white linen we use to clean the deck guns and they cut out a new dress. Someone else chipped in with a pair of blue trousers and they made piping for the edges of the dress and the arms, the edges around the sleeves.

"A couple of Chief Barber's people have got some civilian clothes aboard, I know it's against regulations but I'm not going to hit them for that. Anyway, they've done some eyeball tailoring and they've got a pair of trousers, a clean shirt and a tie and a jacket that they think will fit him. Chief Hendershot, he hasn't got any hips or ass in any case, he found a pair of swimming trunks that are too small for him and DeLucia did a tailoring job on those, cut them down for the boy and he made him a shirt out of an undress white jumper. And a dress for the baby."

"Is that all?" Sirocco asked.

"No, sir, they used some of the cowhide we carry for chafing gear and they're making sandals for the two kids."

"My God!" Sirocco said.

"That's not all," Rhodes said patiently. "There's a little gift package goes to the lady with the dress. Four pair of nylon stockings and a bottle of perfume and some lipstick!"

"Where in the hell did they get nylon stockings and perfume and lipstick?"

"I don't ask questions like that, sir," Rhodes grinned.

"I won't either. When do they want to give these gifts to the passengers?"

"The day before we get in, sir. If the Captain will allow it."

"You know he will! He'll want to thank every damned man on the ship for this! I think it's marvelous!"

"I think Ginty wants to adopt that little girl," Rhodes said. "He spends most of his time off watch holding her. Yesterday he was giving her a bath and one of the people standing around made some remark about the baby's private parts and Ginty clouded up and said he was going to break arms and legs if he heard any more talk like that around a lady! I've got two boys of my own but I never would have thought that Ginty would have any liking for kids."

"Nor would I," Sirocco said. "But you never can tell, can you?"

The message diverting *Mako* from Brisbane came while the ship was running down the length of Makassar Strait. The message instructed *Mako* to cross the Java Sea, traverse Lombok Strait between the islands of Lombok and Bali and go to Exmouth Gulf on the northwest coast of Australia. An official welcoming party would be on hand to take the passengers to Perth and the Navy would send a PBY aircraft bearing two torpedoes and food for *Mako*. A Staff officer of ComSubSouWesPac would be on the PBY to hand deliver new patrol orders to *Mako*.

"Exmouth Gulf?" Hinman said as he studied the chart. "Why, there's nothing there! It's nothing but a fueling station!" He turned to Cohen.

"Nate, get a message off to Staff. Request that *Mako* be sent enough beer so the crew can unwind. Damn it, if they're going to rob us of a regular R and R the least they can do is send us some beer for the crew!"

The ceremony at which the *Mako* took leave of her passengers was brief. An Australian Colonel and two Majors, one a physician, welcomed the Shrewsburys. The Colonel drew himself and saluted Captain Hinman.

"Damned good job, sir! I admire the tailoring job your chaps did. Mrs. Shrewsbury just told us about it. Good chaps you have, sir, damned good chaps!"

He beamed proudly as the Shrewsburys walked down the line of *Mako*'s crew, speaking to each one. When Mrs. Shrewsbury came to Ginty she reached upward with her hands and pulled his scarred face down to hers and kissed him on the lips.

"Mr. Ginty," she lisped through the gap left where her husband had pulled her teeth with a pair of pliers. "I want to thank you for the love and care you have given Deborah. She will miss you and so will I. You're a very dear man!" She kissed him again. Ginty stood rigid, a deep blush crawling up his thick neck.

"Well, ma'am," he finally said. "When that little lady grows up some and anyone bothers her you get in touch with me. I'll pull their arms and legs off like they was a fly!" He scowled fiercely and she giggled.

The Reverend Shrewsbury said goodbye to Nathan Cohen. "I'll write to you, my friend. There are some points of Christian theology you really should be put straight on." He looked earnestly at Cohen. "You won't be offended?"

"Of course not," Cohen said. "But before we get to arguing by mail why don't you ask a Rabbi to get you a copy of the Talmud? I think you'd enjoy the lovely logic and reasoning in it. Our people have scholars who devote an entire lifetime to the study of that great work and never begin to understand all the wisdom that is within it." The Reverend Shrewsbury nodded. "I will do that. Fair is only fair, I always say. The Christian thing to do!" He chuckled and Cohen laughed with him.

The Australian Colonel turned to Captain Hinman.

"Once again, old chap, His Majesty's Government thanks you and your crew. We'll board our aircraft now. The High Command wallahs are quite excited at seeing these people you pulled out so neatly. I'm told your own people will arrive shortly with food and other things for you. Just hope you don't think it's bad manners to shove away and be off but I do have a wallah back there with pips all over his bloody shoulders who will crawl right up my back if I don't get back!"

"I understand, Colonel, we have that kind at Staff ourselves. But I'm a bit disappointed you didn't want to see the inside of *Mako*."

"Love to, old chap, love to! It's this bloody leg! Cork, you know, in a manner of speaking. From the thigh down. Bloody German got me with a burst from a Schmeiser at close range, over in Crete. Went into their bloody lines to kill some of their top wallahs and got caught. Stupid! Gives me a spot of trouble going up and down ordinary steps to say nothing of your vertical bloody ladders! When you come down to port where we are maybe we could get a bloody crane, lower me down and pick me up, eh?" He grinned and walked away and Hinman marveled that he walked as well as he did.

The Navy PBY landed an hour later and a Lieutenant Commander in rumpled khakis climbed down the plane's short ladder and went over to Captain Hinman and Joe Sirocco.

"I'm Gene Puser, Captain," he said.

Hinman nodded and introduced Joe Sirocco. "We have a mutual friend, sir," he said to Puser.

"Yes," Puser said with a grin. "Glad you remembered the name. Saves all that business of introduction and other stuff." He handed Captain Hinman a thick envelope.

"Your patrol orders, sir. I'm afraid you have another special mission to perform first, then you get a quite good area." He turned and motioned to a short, barrel-chested Australian Major who had followed him off the PBY and had been loitering about out of earshot. The Major had a bright red face and a huge, sweeping mustache at least eight inches from tip to tip.

"This is Major Jack Struthers, His Majesty's Australian Army, Captain Hinman," Puser said. "Major, Captain Hinman." The two men shook hands.

"This is my Executive Officer, my second in command, sir."
Hinman said to the Major.

"Big lad, aren't you?" Struthers said as he took Sirocco's hard
hand in his own muscled paw. "Bloody big man, I'd say!"

"Did you bring me any torpedoes?" Hinman said. "And if you did,
how in the hell do we get them aboard? They don't have a torpedo
carrier truck here, you know."

"Know that, sir," Puser said. "They didn't send any. They're a
bit put out that you fired two fish in heavy seas. Actually, one of the
calmer heads said you could do quite well with only twenty-two fish
instead of twenty-four. I did stretch my warrant, as the Major here
would say, and smuggled enough beer aboard the plane to keep your
crew happy for a few hours."

"Smuggled?" Hinman asked.

"The Admiral doesn't approve of sailors' drinking beer, Captain,
but that doesn't matter. What does is that we have enough beer. It's
Aussie beer, strong enough to knock a horse down! I've got the cases
packed in ice but it won't hold for too many more hours so if you want
to get a working party over to the plane we can get that stuff off. I've
got some other stuff, the Major's gear that has to be off-loaded as
well, sir. We're going to be here for two days."

"Let's go down to my Wardroom," Hinman said. "There are
some things I don't understand and I'd rather talk down below than
up here." He motioned to Dusty Rhodes and gave him orders to get
the Major's gear off the plane and on to the dock and to supervise the
beer party.

Lieutenant Commander Puser opened his briefcase and spread a
small chart on the Wardroom table.

"I'm sorry this is the best chart we could find. Actually, it's a page
out of an atlas but it does show the area for this special mission."

"That's what I want to hear about, this special mission,"
Hinman said, his face grim.

"Well, in a nutshell, sir," Puser began. "And mind you I'm only
the messenger. Some of the idea people in Australia thought that if
ships in quote unquote safe Japanese harbors could in some way be
sunk, not one ship but a half dozen or more at one time, that it would
upset the Jap very greatly.

"Everyone seemed to think that it would upset the Jap. The next problem was to figure out how to get into a quote unquote safe Japanese harbor. That's when they called in Major Struthers, who is a veteran commando specialist. He came up with an idea. Build a little boat that could be disassembled and reassembled very quickly and without tools. Someone else thought of a version of the Eskimo kayak for the boat.

"The Major thought that two men could carry ten-pound limpet mines into a harbor from a submarine and place them on the ship's hulls at anchor. With a timing device the mines would all go off after the infiltrators had left the harbor."

"What in the hell is the sense of that!" Hinman snapped.

"Don't look at the Major, sir," Puser said soothingly. "He was asked how it could be done. He didn't originate the idea of the mission."

"Crazy bloody scheme, I call it," the Major said softly. "Mind you, it can be done and not very hard to do, either. Dress a man in black, dye his face and hands black and in that little boat you can go right up to a ship in harbor without being seen."

"That's hard to believe," Hinman snorted.

"I hate to say this," Puser said, "but the Major took his little boat, as he calls it, and paddled under the stern of the *Isabel*, the Admiral's yacht in the Swan River in Brisbane. He went up over the stern, knocked out the watch, broke into the Admiral's quarters and gathered all the Admiral's papers into a pile and then set them afire and left!"

"Didn't hurt the bloke I knocked about," the Major said apologetically. "Never do to hurt the Allies, would it? Gave him a bit of a sock with sand in it, was all."

"If the operation is a success," Puser said slowly, "the Staff thinks it could be repeated at intervals, odd intervals of time so as to keep the Jap off balance. The net effect is likely to be that the Jap will have to strengthen his garrisons in harbors all through the territory they occupy and to assign more destroyers escort to those harbors, leaving the sea lanes a little freer of Jap ships for submarines."

"And if it is known that the Japanese have assigned additional troops to known areas that would make it easier for General MacArthur when he begins his promised return to the Philippines. Isn't that so?" Hinman was staring at Puser.

"Sir, I ventured no such opinion but I am happy to say that you have a decisive mind, sir," Puser's voice was patient.

Hinman sat and thought for a long moment. Then he looked straight at Puser.

"I don't have any choice, do I!"

"I'm afraid not, sir," Puser said. "But from what Captain Rudd has told me about you I think you can pull it off. The Major shares my opinion. I've shown him what Captain Rudd wrote to me about you, sir."

"As I said," the Major said, "I don't like the bloody show!" He squeezed his eyelids closed and when he opened them the bright blue eyes were snapping at Hinman.

"Mind you, Captain, done a lot of bloody chores in my time, I have. This one could come off smooth as taking off a sheila's panties in the dark! All it needs is a man with cold steel in his guts on the ship at sea and a good man to go with me, your best man!"

" 'Sheila'?" Sirocco said.

"That's Aussie slang for girl," Puser said.

"Why two men?" Captain Hinman said.

"Because you can't maneuver the kayak to place a mine down just below the water, takes one man to lean the other way to sort of counterbalance the little boat," the Major explained. "Bloody mines weigh ten pounds with their magnet to grip the hull. Got two dozen of them with me but I don't think the little boat will carry more than a dozen. That's why we want to do a day or so of practice here, try it in daylight and then at night. With some luck we shouldn't be in the harbor more than an hour or two, and then we'll come out."

"Very well," Hinman said slowly. "Let's have some coffee and take this thing apart, step by step." He looked at Puser.

"Is this special mission the whole patrol?"

"No," Puser said slowly. "Once this thing is over you'll have one hell of a patrol area. You'll probably scare Major Struthers half to death!"

Hinman looked at the Australian Major, whose bright blue eyes were merry beneath sun-bleached eyebrows.

"Somehow I doubt that Major Struthers will be scared of anything we do on a submarine," Hinman said.

CHAPTER 25

The *Mako* crept cautiously down a channel at the southern end of the fiddle-shaped island of Bougainville. Captain Hinman was on the cigaret deck aft of the bridge. Major Struthers stood beside him, his short legs braced against the slow roll of the ship. Hinman lowered his night binoculars and let them hang from the neck strap.

"Can't see a whole lot out there with no moon. The land looks to be low, very little elevation. Probably swampy."

"If so, full of the little buggers that give you the malaria," Struthers said cheerfully. The port lookout cleared his throat and the people in the bridge tensed.

"Light bearing dead abeam to port, Bridge. On that little island over there. The light flickers like it might be a small fire."

Hinman raised his binoculars. "Mr. Grilley," he called to the OOD. "Ask the navigator for that island's name."

Joe Sirocco, working at his charts on the gyro table in the Control Room, heard the request and shook his head in frustration. There were no proper navigation charts for the part of the Solomon Islands where they were. He picked up a magnifying glass that Gene

Puser had been thoughtful enough to bring with the page from an atlas that showed the island of Bougainville and studied the atlas page.

"Ask the Bridge for permission for me to come topside, please," he said to the Chief on watch in the Control Room.

"Permission granted," the OOD said into the bridge microphone and Sirocco climbed up to the bridge.

"There's no name for that island, Captain," Sirocco said. "All it shows on this atlas page is that it's there." He pointed out to the starboard side of the ship.

"When the end of this point of land bears one four zero degrees, sir, we can come right to course three one six degrees. That will put us on a course across the mouth of Tonolei Harbor. As far as I can guess we'll have about three miles from where we turn to the center of the harbor mouth or to either side. I'd like to take fathometer readings to find that out, to find out how fast it shoals."

"Very well," Hinman said. Sirocco went back below and Hinman moved back to his station on the cigaret deck.

"Bit chancey, is it?" Major Struthers said. "No bloody charts. Bloody Limeys took over this part of the world after World War One. They should have made some charts."

"It wasn't important to them commercially," Hinman said. "Australia took this area over right after that; why didn't your people make charts? You can't blame the British for everything, you know."

"Why not?" Struthers said. "Bloody Pommey bastards!"

The *Mako* swung to starboard as Grilley ordered the course change Sirocco had suggested and Captain Hinman turned to Struthers.

"Now we find out if the Japs have got night patrols out across the harbor mouth." He turned toward the bridge.

"Mr. Grilley, order the machine gunners to the bridge with weapons. Deck gun crews to stand by in the Control Room. All lookouts to keep a very sharp lookout. If we're detected in here I'm going to run for it on the surface."

Grilley's repeat of Captain Hinman's orders was followed by Joe Sirocco's laconic voice over the bridge speaker.

"Your course out of here will be three zero one, Captain."

"Very well," Hinman said. "Make turns for one-third ahead, Bridge." He turned to Struthers.

"That bloody big man as you called him, Joe Sirocco, doesn't miss a thing. He had the escape course ready. He's a hell of a lot better Executive Officer than I ever was."

"Would have liked to have him with me on this little walkabout," Struthers said. "Not that I object to Chief Rhodes. He's a rare man, too."

Hinman nodded. He had suggested to Sirocco that he might like to go with the Major but Sirocco had looked at him with his steady eyes and shook his head. When Hinman had tried to explore the subject further Sirocco had stopped him, saying that if he insisted he'd be advised to check with Washington first. Then he turned away.

The *Mako* crept across the mouth of the harbor, wallowing in the ground swells. The harbor was quiet, wrapped in the stillness of night.

"Advise reversal of course, Bridge," Sirocco's voice came over the Bridge speaker. "Advise the Captain that the fathometer shows steady shoaling. We're past the center of the harbor and the ship channel is on the south side of the harbor entrance."

"Very well," Captain Hinman said. "Mr. Grilley, come left and make one more pass across the harbor mouth." He turned to Major Struthers.

"I think this is about where we'll drop you and Chief Rhodes, tomorrow night. You'll have a good mile and a half to paddle to get into the harbor itself."

"Not to worry, sir," Struthers said. "The Chief is a very strong man on that two-ended paddle. We'll do fine from here."

The port lookout cleared his throat and Hinman tensed.

"From this angle I can see a lot of big dark shapes in the harbor, Bridge. Looks like a lot of ships anchored all in a row."

"Very well," Hinman said. He smiled at Struthers. "Looks like the ship watchers up in the hills were right about there being targets in this harbor. You'll have good hunting! Mr. Grilley, please carry out the orders in the night order book and let's get out of here, we've seen enough." He listened to the quiet reply to his order and felt the vibration in the deck as *Mako* picked up speed.

It was pitch black the following night as *Mako* crept slowly toward the center of the harbor entrance. Major Struthers and Dusty Rhodes, dressed entirely in black with black stocking caps on their heads and their faces and hands dyed black, assembled their small kayak on the deck forward of the gun. Captain Hinman had the bridge and as the *Mako* swung slowly in the ground swell at the harbor entrance he leaned over the bridge rail.

"This is where you get off, men," he called down. And then, in a voice too low to be heard on deck but heard clearly by the quartermaster, he said,

"Go with God."

The small black kayak rode low in the water under the weight of Struthers and Rhodes and a dozen 10-pound limpet mines. Hinman saw a paddle blade flash briefly at the side of *Mako* and then the kayak and its two men were lost completely to view. Hinman turned to Grilley and Joe Sirocco, who had climbed to the bridge.

"Take over the deck, Don. Joe, I want to know where we are every minute in relation to the launching site. If everything goes well they should be back in four to five hours. I want the lookouts on half-hour shifts, Don, keep the relief lookouts in the Conning Tower in red goggles." He punched his right fist into his left palm.

"Now comes the hard part, the waiting."

The kayak paddled easily, even with its heavy load. Rhodes, sitting in the front seat hole of the tiny craft, suddenly stopped wielding his paddle.

"Ship dead ahead," he whispered. "Big one!"

"Good-oh, mate," Struthers answered in a whisper. "Under the stern we go!" Working their paddles underwater they eased forward until the kayak was under the overhang of the ship's stern. Rhodes reached out a black hand and took hold of the ship's rusty rudder post. They sat listening, hardly daring to breathe.

The ship was quiet. They could hear the splashing of water from an engine room pump on the starboard side. Rhodes pointed his hand at that side and Struthers gently paddled in that direction as Rhodes fended the kayak's bow away from the hull. They reached the sluggish stream of engine room discharge water and Rhodes raised his hand. Struthers stopped the kayak. Rhodes reached down between his legs and got a mine.

He balanced the mine on the wooden rim that ran around his seat hole and carefully turned a knob that wound the spring-loaded timing mechanism of the mine's detonator. He took a deep breath, picked up the mine in both hands and carefully placed the top edge of the round mine against the side of the ship and then pushed the mine as far down under water as he could reach, as Struthers leaned the other way to balance the narrow kayak. When he had reached the limit of his arms Rhodes carefully let the mine rest against the ship, feeling the magnets on the mine's underside grab at the steel hull. He sat up and the two men backed the kayak under the ship's stern. The second ship was barely 200 yards away. The kayak moved across the dark water toward the next target.

Rhodes was soaked with sweat as he finished placing the mine on the eleventh ship, a long vessel with high cargo booms that stood out against the black night sky. They were deep in the harbor now, three miles from where they had left the *Mako*. The Major gently sculled the kayak back under the ship's stern and Rhodes clung to the rudder, breathing hard.

"I can see three more ships, mate," Struthers whispered. "Take a breather, cobber, and then we'll decide to take the next in line or give all a look and pick the biggest. Should have brought more bloody mines!"

Before Rhodes could reply there was a muffled explosion down the harbor toward the sea, followed by two more explosions and then another. A siren on a ship began to blow and then other sirens began to wail. They heard a rush of feet on the deck of the ship above them. Struthers leaned forward.

"Bloody mines must be going off! Fucking timing devices must be crook!" His whisper sounded loud to Rhodes.

A searchlight from one of the ships that had been mined flared into bright light and began sweeping the sky. Struthers whispered, as he leaned forward in the kayak.

"Bastards think it's an air raid!"

"Let's get the hell out of here!" Rhodes whispered. "If we can get over next to the beach we can paddle back down the length of the harbor and get out to the ship."

"No bloody chance of that!" Struthers whispered. "The little bastards will have boats all over the harbor in minutes! Best thing to do is head for the beach and go ashore, they won't look for us there." As they began to paddle toward the low beach they heard another explosion and felt a shuddering shock through the kayak's thin canvas skin.

"That's the one we just mined!" Struthers hissed. "We're for it now, cobber!" They heard sharp cries on the ship back of them. "Keep it slow and steady," Struthers muttered. "Bastards can't see us unless we make a lot of fuss!"

The kayak's bow slid into soft muck 50 feet from the shoreline and the two men eased themselves out of the small craft and pulled it up into the shelter of some small bushes.

"Stay here!" Struthers ordered and disappeared. He was back in five minutes.

"Big thorn bush up there a way. We'll hole up in the bush. Good hiding place. Stay there the rest of the night and tomorrow. I hid in thorn bushes in New Guinea when I was running from the bloody Jap. Safe place to be if it's big enough and this one is bloody big from what I could tell. Let's break down the boat, can't leave it here." They worked swiftly in the dark, disassembling the small craft and stowing it in a bag of the kayak's canvas skin.

The thorn bush was huge, covering almost an acre of ground. "On your belly, mate," Struthers said. "Use the elbows and don't raise your fucking head or the thorns will take your ruddy eyes out!" They wormed their way deep into the thorn bush, dragging the kayak behind them. After twenty minutes of crawling Struthers stopped.

"Far enough, this," he said. "We've got a bit of an opening here, can sit up and stretch a bit without getting all bloody. You still got that bloody mine that was left over? Make sure that damned thing won't go off, will you?"

"I made sure of that when we left the last ship," Rhodes said. "So what do we do now?"

"First things first," Struthers said. "Wait a bit here while I go back and make sure our tracks are swept away so no idle bastard of a Jap sees them and starts to wonder what kind of an animal crawled in here." He left, elbowing his way along the ground.

He was back in a half hour, dragging a branch from a bush behind him. He lay on his back, breathing deeply in the humid air.

"Now, cobber, nothing else to do but sleep a bit. Bloody Jap isn't likely to poke his head into a thorn bush without cause. Safe enough to sleep if you don't snore. Tomorrow night we'll take a walk down the beach a bit, put the little boat back together and go for a ride back to your comfy ship. Tra la la and all that sort of shit!"

Rhodes nodded in assent. He felt bone weary and assumed that part of the terrible weakness and exhaustion he felt was due to excitment and shock. He looked at the Australian, who was curled up in a fetus-like ball, his head pillowed in the crook of his elbow so that his nose and mouth were almost covered. Rhodes lay back on the soft leaf mold and listened. The guns they had heard earlier in the harbor had stopped firing. He could hear the distant sounds of men shouting, of boat engines badly in need of mufflers. Struthers had been right, the Japs had put small craft in the harbor. They wouldn't have had a chance had they decided to make a break for the open sea. The Australian's plan had merit. The odds were that they could walk nearly to the harbor mouth the next night and then launch the kayak. He rolled over and tucked his nose and mouth into his arm as the Australian had done and waited for sleep.

He dreamed, an odd, mixed-up two-dreams-in-one. He dreamt that he was eating breakfast, plump pork sausages and scrambled eggs and at the same time he dreamt that he was home in Pearl Harbor, in bed with June, whose slim leg was across his two legs and whose hands were gripping his face and chin in a tightening grip. The grip on his chin began to hurt and his eyes opened.

"Don't you move one fucking muscle!" Struthers hissed in his ear. "Don't close your mouth when I let go of your face, don't move your tongue!" He felt Struthers' leg move off his legs and the terrible grip on his face and chin was suddenly gone. He moved his tongue tentatively and felt the smooth skin of a pork sausage between his lips. Struthers' hand gently opened his mouth wider and he felt something granular, sandlike, being sprinkled into his mouth and there was a strong, salty taste. Struthers' hands pulled his head sideways as he started to convulse in reflex against a flood of blood that suddenly filled his throat.

"Let it spew out, spit! Quietly, you bastard!"

Rhodes tried to clear his mouth, shuddering at the coppery taste of fear and blood. Struthers' hands continued to press his face to one side.

"Bloody big leech right in your mouth, cobber!" Struthers whispered. "Saw him when I wokened up. Didn't want you to bite down on the beggar or try to yank it out. The beggars leave their little teeth in you if you pull 'em off or kill 'em." He released his grip on Rhodes' face and Rhodes sat up and rubbed his forearm across his mouth.

Struthers handed him a khaki handkerchief. "Wipe out the inside of your mouth and keep it. Had one of those grab me by the tongue one night in New Guinea. Like to vomited my asshole up! Got a packet of salt from your cookie before we left. Like to have a bit of salt with me when I go walking about in this country. Salt makes the buggers disgorge and they don't leave their teeth in you. Gives you a hell of an infection, do those teeth. Don't know why. That bloke in your mouth was a feeder! Looked like a thing your Red Cross ladies sell at their place in Perth, what do you call 'em? Ah, hot dogs or something like that. Awful things!" He shook his head as Rhodes suddenly retched silently. "Forget it, cobber. No harm done. Sunup in a bit so we can see where we are."

The sun came up with a rush, bathing the island in a strong, white light. Struthers reached out and gripped Rhodes' arm with a hard hand.

"Look!" he whispered.

The two men were sitting in a small clearing in the thorn bush, barely five yards from a wire fence. Through the thin fringe of vegetation they could see a large clearing on the other side of the fence. There were a number of buildings in the distance. Close to the fence, only a dozen yards from it, there was a small structure not more than five feet square and raised on stilt legs that made the floor of the structure about four feet above the ground. A flight of six wooden steps led up to the structure, which had an open doorway. As they watched, two Japanese soldiers, each with a shoulder stick and two buckets of water, neared the small structure. Struthers and Rhodes edged backward, deeper into the thorn bush.

"I know what that bloody shack is," Struthers whispered. "Saw one just like it when I was a prisoner in New Guinea."

"That's a ruddy shower bath! No running water in this place, I reckon. Soldier climbs that ladder leaning against the shack and takes up a bucket of water. Inside the shack there's a big can hung with holes in its bottom. Soldier on the outside pours water into the can and the man under it gets a shower bath." As he spoke one of the soldiers climbed up the ladder and the other soldier handed up a bucket of water.

Two Japanese came out of the building nearest to the shower. Each was naked except for a white breech clout. The younger of the two, a flat-bellied man, bowed politely as the other man, paunchy with spiky gray hair, slipped off his getas and climbed the steps into the small shack. The soldier at the top of the ladder began to pour water slowly. They could hear the splashing of the man bathing inside the shack. The portly man came out, slipped on his wooden clogs and walked away. The other man went up into the makeshift shower.

"Five thirty ack emma on the dot when he walked into that bloody home-made shower bath," Struthers whispered. "Odds are they take their shower every morning at the same time. The Jap is a very orderly person, you know." They watched the two soldiers gather up the buckets as the second man came out of the shower and walked toward the building he had come from.

Struthers stroked his mustache, his bright blue eyes distant. "When the light is a bit better, we can find a place in this bush where we get some good light, do you think you could have a go at finding out what went wrong with the fucking timing devices on those mines? If it was the timing devices? I've got an idea in mind. That is, if you don't need a bloody tool kit to get into the bastard."

"I've got a Swiss Army knife with me," Rhodes whispered. "It's got a good screwdriver in it and the timing device is held on to the mine with four screws. What's your idea?"

"Learned a thing or two running from the Jap in New Guinea." Struthers whispered. "Learned that the Jap likes to do routine things in the same way at the same time each day. Like taking a morning bath.

"Bath house looks like it's made of mostly tin. If you can find out what's crook with the mine and fix it we might be able to leave our calling card. Might get ourselves a good bag. Fat boy must be a Colonel. Love to do in a Colonel! The natural enemy of a Major, d'ya'see, no matter what flag he's under!"

Rhodes grinned and crawled toward the fence to take a look inside the Japanese area. Soldiers were milling about in a big clearing, forming up into lines. Struthers crawled up beside him.

"Bloody place is a full-bore army camp!" he whispered. "Must be thousands of the fuckers! Linin' up for their chow. With all those bastards there fat boy might be a General. I hate the Generals worse than I do Colonels! Let's get well back in the bush, cobber, no sense in takin' chances."

When the full glare of the midday sun was filtering into the thron bush Rhodes carefully removed the timing mechanism on the mine and inspected it. He gave a little grunt of satisfaction and pointed with the screwdriver blade of his knife.

Thorn

"Found out what was crook?" Struthers asked. Rhodes nodded and pointed with the screwdriver blade of his knife.

"The rate of the spring unwind is regulated by these three metal gates," he whispered. "Whoever put this one together put the spring through only one gate. That would let the spring unwind a lot faster than it should have and it would trip the detonator as soon as it was unwound. Maybe all the others were the same."

"Can you check if you're right?"

Rhodes nodded. "When this spring is unwound it releases this other spring and that drives this detonator pin here down against a shotgun shell that's in the mine itself and that discharges the explosives. All we have to do is check how long the spring takes to unwind when it's threaded through all three gates. We can set it for two hours and time it. If it moves the detonator pin at the right time we've fixed it."

"Bloody genius I'm with!" Struthers said.

"No genius," Rhodes whispered. "Most explosive devices are pretty simple. Except torpedoes. Working on a torpedo is like working on a watch." He set the timer for two hours and wound the spring and put the mechanism in his pocket and checked his watch. An hour and fifty-five minutes later he took the mechanism out of his pocket and laid it on the leaf mold in front of him, his eyes on his watch. The mechanism functioned at two hours and five seconds.

Struthers nodded in satisfaction. "Let's crawl out to where we came in last night, cobber. I want to take a look-see at the ground we'll be walkin' over tonight. Don't fancy barging off into the dark over ground I haven't seen. Done that too many times in my life, it scares me."

They crawled on their bellies under the thick thatch of thorns until they came to the place where they had entered the thorn bush. They looked out through the leaves at the harbor.

There were small boats milling about in the harbor, moving back and forth between several ships that appeared to be very low in the water. The first ship that had been mined lay on its side, its rusted bottom gleaming in the sunlight.

"I count eight of the ships down low in the water, they must be sitting on the bottom," Rhodes whispered. "And that first one that rolled over. The other two we mined don't seem to have any damage."

"Nine of eleven is a bloody good score!" Struthers said in a low voice. "Hard to see how a little mine like that could do so much damage."

"It's a hydraulic principle," Rhodes whispered. "You can't compress water to any measurable degree. When the mine goes off it blows a hole about a foot in diameter in the ship's hull. At the same time it blows a bunch of water back from the ship.

"When the water rushes back it's like a big hammer or a can opener. It opens up the hole the mine made, opens it up to maybe six feet wide."

"What do you suppose our other mine will do to our fat friend?" Struthers staring blue eyes were sparkling with glee. "Open up his bloody bowels, that's what!"

The *Mako* had just completed a turn to make another run past the harbor mouth when the first muffled *crump* of an explosion was heard on the bridge. Captain Hinman jammed his binoculars against

his eyes with such force that the rubber eyepieces collapsed and the
adjusting screw opened a cut on his nose. The soft Southern voice of
Grabnas on the stern lookout reached down to the bridge.

"Saw white water bubblin' in the harbor, Bridge. More of that
white water, fathah in, suh." As he spoke the faint sound of a
half-dozen explosions reached across the water.

"Now I can see some flashes in the harbor, Bridge!" Grabnas'
soft voice had sharpened. "Looks like gunfire to me, Bridge!"

The sharp, barking sound of distant guns reached the *Mako*.
The Gunner's Mate, pressed into service as an extra bridge-level
lookout, cocked a professional ear.

"Anti-aircraft fire," he said. "Three-inch stuff."

Captain Hinman had come forward to the bridge. "You sure of
that, Guns?"

"Yes, sir," Dick Smalley said. The steady bark of the guns was
plainer now. Hinman steadied his elbows on the bridge rail and
looked through his night binoculars. He could see the flashes of the
guns plainly. The loudspeaker on the bridge rasped.

"Does the Captain want a course into the harbor?" Joe Sirocco's
voice was calm.

"I want it but I'm not ready to commit yet," Hinman snapped.
He swung his glasses around as a battery of guns, much closer to
Mako, began to roar.

"Five-inch stuff, Captain," Smalley said. "Over on that point,
there, south of the harbor."

"Can they depress those guns for use against surface ships?"
Hinman asked.

"Most five-inch batteries are dual purpose, sir," Smalley said. "I
think they'd be able to do that. They must think they're bein' hit by
an air raid over there."

"Do you think the mines went off, that they think they might be
getting an air raid?" Hinman said to Grilley. "I can't believe that!"

"It could be," Grilley said. "They don't know we're here. What
worries me is why the mines are going off. They were set to go off at
five in the morning."

"How about that, Smalley?" Hinman said.

"We were ordered not to mess with the timing devices, sir,"

Smalley said. "The mines could have prematured. If they did the Jap would have a helluva time figuring out what was happening. They sure as hell are shooting the sky full of holes so they must think they've been hit by an air raid."

Grabnas spoke up from his stern lookout. "Ah see small craft lights in the harbor, Bridge. Lots of small craft."

"Where in the hell are our people?" Hinman snapped. "Damn it to hell, they should be on their way back if the mines prematured! They'll have no chance at all if there's small craft in the harbor!"

"Maybe they hid themselves," Smalley said.

"Where the hell do you hide in a harbor, man!" Hinman's voice was harsh. "Use your head!"

"Maybe they headed for the beach and hid themselves," Smalley said stubbornly. "I talked to that Major's sergeant back in Exmouth Gulf, the guy who brought the Major's gear along.

"That Major is one tough son of a bitch. He was in a prison camp in New Guinea and he strangled a guard and went over the fence carrying his skipper on his back. His skipper was sick. Japs hunted them for three weeks. The Major stayed in back of the Japs instead of in front of them. He lived on their garbage and he carried his skipper across the Owen Stanley mountains on his back and into Port Moresby. His sergeant says he's one smart bastard. He might have headed for the beach and hid out."

"I hope so," Hinman said. "That would be the only chance they'd have. They couldn't escape from that harbor now."

The *Mako* patrolled off the harbor for the rest of the night. As dawn neared the big submarine made its way out into deep water and submerged. As soon as the ship had settled down into the routine of the all-day dive Captain Hinman called his officers into the Wardroom.

"From what we could see from the bridge," he began, "it appears that our people got the mines in place but they began to premature. The harbor was alerted. God only knows where our people are right now. We hope they got ashore and are hiding somewhere.

"But that's only a guess. But if they did get ashore they'd expect that we would be here when they come back out. And we will be here! I'll stay here for a month if I have to!

"Until we know what happened, until we have to give up hope, I want you to take evasive action no matter what you sight, on the surface or submerged. As long as there is hope that our people can get back I don't want to risk being discovered out here. Pass that word to your people. Tell them we aren't going to abandon the Chief of the Boat and the Major come hell or high water! And impress on the lookouts the need for sharp eyes. God knows what the Jap will send here once he figures out what happened in that harbor."

The afternoon hours ground by slowly for Rhodes and the Major, deep in the thorn bush. As evening neared they saw and heard the Japanese troops forming up for their evening meal.

"I could do with some of that grub," Struthers said. "I like that rice they eat."

Night descended with the abrupt suddenness that is common in the tropics. When it was full dark and the camp was quiet Rhodes and Struthers made their final preparations. Struthers held a tiny pen-sized flashlight, hooding its flow in his hand so that Rhodes could set the timing device on the mine. Then they moved toward the fence.

"Let me go first," Struthers said. "My sort of game, you know. I'll dig under and go inside and look about. Then I'll come back and you come through."

"Better check that fence to see if they've got it wired," Rhodes said.

"Haven't a bloody meter in your pocket have you?" the Major whispered. "Chances are it isn't wired. This place was probably an old coconut plantation, lots of those hereabouts. Grew the nuts for the copra, the husk, you know." He dug at the edge of the fence. "Leaf mold, easy to move aside." He began to dig with his hands. Then he wriggled under the fence and disappeared. He was back in ten minutes.

"Did a bit of a recon," he whispered. "All's as quiet as the bloody grave! Going to be a piece of cake, this! Follow me. I'll go under and then you hand me the bloody mine and come along." Rhodes nodded and squirmed through under the fence. He got to his feet and moved to the dim bulk of the bath house and went underneath where the

Major was waiting, the mine in his arms. Rhodes reached up and very gently scratched at the floor of the bath house.

"It's tin or some kind of metal," he whispered. "Give me the mine and I'll activate it. When I get ready to put it up you put your fingers under the edge of the mine in case I slip. I don't want it to bang against the metal when the magnet takes hold."

"Put it over near the door," Struthers whispered. "Bit harder to see there." They placed the mine carefully, both of them holding their breath and freezing, almost motionless, as the mine made a slight click against the metal flooring. They crouched beneath the bath house, searching the compound with their eyes. Then they drifted back to the fence, two dark shadows in the night. Rhodes backed through the trench Struthers had dug and the Major followed him, smoothing the leaf mold back into the trench as he backed through.

They crawled through the thorn bush, dragging the kayak with them, until they reached the place where they had entered the bush the night before. Struthers went outside of the bush and lay quiet for five minutes, his sharp blue eyes studying the area. Then he stood up and waited, searching for some evidence of movement in the area. He reached down and touched Rhodes.

"Nothing stirring that I can see," He whispered. "But as my little Ghurka friends used to say, 'Notwithstanding, we'll go as quietly as death.' "

They moved down the beach toward the mouth of the harbor, keeping close to the edge of the scattered bushes that grew along the long spit of land. When they had gone more than half-way to the harbor mouth Struthers stopped.

"Might as well turn this show over to you, cobber. The going is getting muckier by the yard. Might as well be paddling as trying to walk in this shit." They crouched and swiftly assembled the kayak. As they carried the small craft out into the water the Major grinned.

"Think that bloody captain of yours will be waitin'? If he isn't we've a long paddle to New Britain and I don't want to go there at all!"

"He'll be waiting," Rhodes said.

"Wish I had as much confidence in my senior officers," the

Australian said as he settled himself in the kayak's rear seat and took hold of his double-ended paddle. "I always considered the buggers to be a bit daft, you know. You're the sailor, your show now, which way do we go?"

"I'd like to hug the shoreline until we get to the harbor entrance," Rhodes said. "Less chance of being seen, less chance of being set off course by currents or tides. Once we get near the harbor entrance we can cut over and head out and see if we can find the ship."

At the entrance to the harbor Rhodes changed course and the kayak steadied on a heading where he thought the *Mako* might be. He reached under the front edge of the seat hole he was sitting in and unclipped a small battery-powered light with a hooded red lens. He fastened the light into a fitting on the rim of the seat hole and turned it on.

Fifteen minutes later the port lookout in *Mako*'s superstructure called out.

"Bridge! Red light! Very dim, low down to the water!" Captain Hinman scrambled up to stand alongside the lookout.

"Where, son?" He focused his glasses as the lookout pointed out the light. "Mr. Grilley, it's them! Pass the word below that we have our people in sight!" He scrambled down to the bridge level.

"I'll take the deck, Don. Get your party ready to take them aboard. Be careful in case they're hurt." He bent to the bridge speaker.

"This is the Captain. We are going to pick up our people. Ginty and Aaron to the deck with Mr. Grilley. Machine gunners to the bridge with weapons. Deck gun crews stand by in the Control Room. Mr. Sirocco, flood bow buoyancy and stand by to blow!"

Rhodes heard the long sigh of air leaving the bow buoyancy tank before he saw the *Mako*'s dark bulk against the moonless sky.

"Skipper's flooding down forward so we can paddle aboard," he said over his shoulder. "Told you the Old Man would be here!"

They paddled the kayak up to the forward gun sponson and Struthers jumped in surprise as a roar up forward indicated that bow buoyancy tank was being blown dry to raise the deck above water.

The two men packaged the kayak and Struthers hoisted it to the cigaret deck.

"Take good care of this beauty, mate. Fine little boat."

Captain Hinman shook both men's hands as they climbed over the bridge rail.

"Damned glad to have you back, fellas. Now we can haul ass out of here."

"Beggin' pardon, sir," Struthers said. "Is it possible to stay here in this place for a bit, say until about five-thirty ack emma or shortly after? We left a surprise package for the Jap and we'd like to see if he opened it."

Captain Hinman looked at the Australian and then at Dusty Rhodes, who nodded slightly.

"Maybe you'd better tell me what this is all about," Hinman said.

"Happy to do that," Struthers said cheerfully. "Do you think we could do it over a spot of tucker and some hot tea? Been a good while since we had our last bread and water, so to speak."

"I'm sorry," Captain Hinman said. "Mr. Grilley, secure the deck crew and the gunners, resume regular sea detail, resume the Night Orders until you hear from me. All lookouts maintain a very sharp lookout." He followed Rhodes and Struthers down below.

Tommy Thompson had a platter of sandwiches on a tray and pots of steaming coffee and tea set out on the Wardroom table.

"You eat in here, in the Wardroom, Chief," Captain Hinman said. "I'm not going to stand on custom after an operation of this sort. Tom, will you please ask Chief Maxwell to come in with his notebook? After you've eaten you can talk out the operation."

He waited patiently, sipping at a cup of coffee and talking genially with John Maxwell, the Chief Yeoman. When Tom had refilled the cups for the third time Hinman leaned back in his chair.

"Suppose you start from the time you left the ship," he said. "As the ranking officer, Major, you make the report. Chief Rhodes is privileged to break in any time, make any corrections or amendments to what you say. Is that all right with you?"

"Too right, Skipper," Major Struthers said. He reached over and took one of Joe Sirocco's cigarets and lit it and then be began to talk. When he had finished the part about mining the bath house Captain Hinman looked at him, a tiny grin playing around his mouth.

"Biggest practical joke I ever heard of!" he said admiringly. "But I have to think of this ship, Major." He turned to Maxwell. "Stop writing, Chief. I'll tell you when to start again."

"You must be a little crazy, Major! God only knows what the Jap has got on the way here, after all the damage you two people did in that harbor! I might get caught in this harbor mouth, have you thought of that?"

"Thought that if you didn't get us back this night, sir," the Major said pleasantly," that you'd be here tomorrow night and the next night ad infinitum, no matter what the Jap sent here. Was I wrong?"

"No," Hinman said slowly. "If you hadn't come back tonight I'd be here tomorrow night. You have a point, Major."

The Major sensed his advantage and pressed it.

"Look at it this way, Captain." He caressed his mustache lovingly. "Every time you sink a bloody Jap ship you paint a little flag on the side of your Conning Tower, don't you? Plain white flag with a red ball in the center for a merchant ship, Rising Sun flag for a warship? Got two of each up there right now, right?"

"Well, we put nine ships down last night. Eight flat on the bottom with their decks just above the water, one over on its bloody side! So by rights you can paint nine flags on your bleedin' Conning Tower. Bloody coup, that! Nine ships in one action!

"If the bloody bath house blows up you can paint a bath house on the bloody Conning Tower! Be the envy of the whole submarine Navy!" He sat there, his staring blue eyes dancing with delight. "If you'll do the talking for me, sir, my good cobber and me will go with you up to Japan and we'll go ashore and knock off a railroad train! Alongside of the bath house you'd be the darlin' of the bloody Fleet, you would!"

Captain Hinman shook his head and refilled his coffee cup.

"What the hell do I tell the Squadron Commander when I get back to port? I've got no business staying here."

"Never tell a senior officer anything," Major Struthers chuckled. "That's my secret of success, never tell 'em a bloody thing. Demand things from them! Keeps them wary of you. First off, send the buggers a bloody message demanding that some artist in port whip you out a stencil of a bath house!"

Hinman looked at the Australian and then he sighed. He reached for the telephone on the bulkhead.

"Bridge? This is the Captain. Remain on station. Dive the ship at zero four thirty." He turned to the officers who were crowded around the small table.

"I think you'd better pass the word to your people, tell them why we're sticking around. They deserve to know." He turned to Chief Maxwell.

"We'll resume the de-briefing, now. Major, after you had mined the bath house. Start from there."

At five-fifteen that morning Captain Hinman climbed the ladder into the Conning Tower. Rhodes and Struthers, standing in the Control Room, heard the whine of the electric motor that raised the periscope.

"He's using the search periscope," Rhodes said to the Major. "That one has a larger lens, you can see more with it."

At five-twenty Captain Hinman's voice came down through the hatch.

"Forty feet, Control. Hold her at forty feet."

Rhodes stared at his wrist watch. Five-thirty-five came and passed and suddenly they heard Captain Hinman's feet shifting in the Conning Tower as he swung the periscope in short sweeps.

"Damned if they're not firing those guns again!" Hinman said in a voice loud enough to be heard in the Control Room. The Major turned to Rhodes, his red face beaming.

"I do hope the fat one was washing his balls when the bloody mine went off! Proper way for a man to go is with his cock in his hand! Jap or no Jap!" Captain Hinman came back down the ladder.

"Sixty-five feet," he ordered. "We'll leave the area now. Joe, set a course." He turned to the Major and Dusty Rhodes.

"I could see the guns firing. I guess we'll paint a bath house on our Conning Tower!"

Struthers grinned.

CHAPTER 26

Captain Hinman's message detailing the results of the special mission arrived at a bad time in Brisbane. The Submarine Staff had just gone through a period of celebration over the successful landing of 11,000 U.S. Marines on Guadalcanal and the capture there of the new airport the Japanese had built and a landing on nearby Tulagi Island, where front line reports said heavy resistance to the Marines had developed but was being overcome.

Hard on the heels of the good news had come the reports on the Battle of Savo Island. A Japanese cruiser force, striking boldly from Rabaul, on New Britain Island, had routed an Allied cruiser fleet inflicting terrible losses. Four Allied heavy cruisers had been shot to bits and sunk; the H.M.A.S. *Canberra* and the *Vincennes*, *Astoria* and *Quincy* of the United States Navy. The U.S.S. *Chicago* had been badly damaged by shell fire and its Captain a suicide. More than 1,500 officers and men of the Allied naval force were dead or missing.

The defeat, the worst in American naval history, hung over the Staff at Brisbane like a pall. It was all too clear that the Japanese admiral had out-maneuvered the American ships and the Japanese gunners had been far more accurate than the famed American gunners. Now, with Japan in control of the Solomon Sea, the U.S. Marines fighting for their lives on Guadalcanal would face even greater odds as the Japanese rushed reinforcements from Rabaul.

When Captain Hinman's message was read at the staff meeting in the Submarine Command, Southwest Pacific, there was a silence. Lieut. Comdr. Gene Puser broke the silence.

"Well, that's one piece of good news. Hinman got into the harbor and his people carried out the special mission successfully."

"If you can believe him!" the Operations Officer said with a frown. He looked down at his copy of Hinman's dispatch.

"I refuse to give him nine ships sunk! Not in a shallow harbor, not from ten-pound mines! Those ships can be repaired, will be repaired probably in a matter of days. I'll give him credit for damaging nine ships, no more.

"As for this nonsense about having a staff artist design a stencil of a Japanese bath house, my God! What we should do is to have a stencil made for *Mako*'s Conning Tower that reads quote Obey your patrol orders unquote! His patrol orders didn't call for him to tell his demolition squad to go frolicking about on the beach blowing up shower baths or whatever they said they blew up!"

Gene Puser looked up from his note pad.

"*Mako* has twenty-two fish left, sir. Hinman's not far from the sea route between Rabaul and Guadalcanal and Tulagi. He might be able to shoot down some of the troop transports they will probably be running down there to reinforce Guadalcanal."

"I'm aware of that," his senior officer snapped. "Send him a priority message to cancel his present patrol orders and to patrol off the mouth of Rabaul Harbor until further notice.

"Specify that these orders do not call for beach parties or the ambush of Japanese officers going to the latrine!

"I suppose you had better send him some latitude and longitude coordinates; there are no charts of that area worth a damn. Hell, when Intelligence told us the Japs were building a new airfield on Guadalcanal we couldn't even find the place on the charts we had!

"While you're at it, tell Hinman we are giving him credit for possibly damaging nine ships. Those damned Pearl Harbor Captains are all alike; they're very good at screaming about defective torpedoes and exploders and at claiming sinkings that never happened!"

The message, sent that night, stunned Captain Hinman. He sat in the Wardroom sipping coffee, reading the message over and over while Joe Sirocco worked at his charts to lay out a course for Rabaul Harbor. Major Struthers came in and added to the discomfiture in the Wardroom.

"Been listening to the Jap radio frequency, Captain, courtesy of your radio chappie. Bad news for our side."

"What do you mean?" Hinman said.

"Our friend the Nip has kicked the shit out of our combined naval forces at a big battle not far from here in the Solomons," the Major said. "Took place at a place called Savo Island. The stuff I heard was plain language Japanese, the chappie doing the talking was saying that the Jap Fleet had destroyed a major American and Australian cruiser fleet without the loss of a single Jap ship! He said at least five major Allied ships had gone down!"

"I didn't know you understood Japanese, Major," Hinman said.

"I don't read it or write it," Struthers said. He took a cup of tea from the Officers' Cook with a smile of thanks.

"I savvy the lingo. Wasn't always a bloody-handed commando, you know. Was a time, it seems years and years ago, when I taught the Romance languages at the university in Sydney. Studied Japanese as a sort of hobby. Chinese, too. Bloody army wallahs figured if I could speak, read and write a half-dozen European languages that I would be an ideal commando type!

"Must say that knowing Japanese did me some good. When our lot got captured on New Guinea a silly cow of a sentry, thinking no one could understand his language but another Jap, told his buddy to cover for him while he went off to take a shit. With him gone and his pants down, so to speak, no trick at all to strangle the other sentry and climb the fence with my Skipper on my back. Poor bastard had the dysentery so bad he couldn't walk. Would have died if he'd been left behind."

"That report you heard might have been propaganda to fool our intelligence people who monitor their radio," Hinman said.

"If so, pretty complicated propaganda, sir," the Major said.

"The bloke on the radio was addressing a message from Admiral Mikawa to the Emperor himself, telling of the victory.

"That's about as official as you can get. If he was polishing his brass, as we'd say, and he was found with the lie in his teeth he'd have to say his prayers and open his belly. No, I'd say it was the straight goods."

"What the hell is there in this area to fight a major sea battle over?" Hinman said. "Nothing out here!"

"Might be this place Guadalcanal," the Major said.

"Never heard of it," Hinman said. "Where's it at?"

"Nor did I hear of it before," Struthers said. "But I was talking to some of your intelligence types when this mission we did was being planned. They told me the Jap had built a big airfield on Guadalcanal, down at the southeast end of the Solomon Islands, east of where we're going now. Caused no end of a dust-up with your people and ours. An airfield there would control the sea lanes from the U.S. and Hawaii, I was told, as well as flank the east end of New Guinea. With New Guinea flanked it would fall and that would give the Jap a port of entry to Northern Australia."

Captain Hinman and the *Mako*'s officers listened to the heavy-set Australian, their faces intent.

"Your intelligence people said your Navy was launching a top-hole amphibious landing job, going to put thousands and thousands of your Marines ashore at Guadalcanal. Reckon the Ghurka and the American Marine are the two finest fighting men in the world, bar none, not even our own chaps. This battle the Nips are boasting about may have been the result of trying to stop the amphibious assault or it could have been an effort to throw the Marines off the island if they'd already landed."

"They never tell us anything like that in these damned messages they send," Hinman growled. "They're quick as hell, though, to tell us that those ships you put on the bottom in that harbor aren't sunk, that we quote and unquote may have damaged them!"

"To be expected!" the Major said cheerfully. "If the bloody rear echelon bastards don't do it themselves they can't see how others can do it. When I brought my Skipper out to Port Moresby, had to carry the poor fucker most of the way on my back and him shittin' all down

me all the while, the intelligence brain down in Sydney decided my
report that I'd killed thirteen of the Japs on the way out was an error.
He credited me with five, I think. Bastard sits there in a cushy office
with beer and American cigs at hand and tells me what I did! You'd
think there was a bounty on the head of the Jap and they didn't want
to pay the money!"

"Did you really kill thirteen of the Jap bastards, Major?" Pete
Simms' eyes were shining, his tongue flicking out to lick his lips.
Struthers looked at Simms for a long moment.

"I stopped counting at thirteen, sonny," he said. "I think it was
probably double that. Really doesn't make any difference, does it? You
have to put down something so the fat-asses in the rear know it wasn't
all steak and eggs. Bloody war is a bloody war, right? If you don't kill
them they kill you. That's progress, you know. Sign of an advanced
state of civilization when you can kill your fellow man before he kills
you. Look at this lovely ship of yours; beautiful piece of machinery!
Bloody useless except for legalized murder.

"Look at me! Bloody professor, I am. Spent my years trying to
teach students the mysteries of grammar and pronunciation. For
what purpose? What I should have been doing is studying the habits
and ambitions of my natural enemy, the Jap.

"If I kill enough of them and if I live and if we win this bloody
war and those are all great fucking iffffs." He drew the word out, his
sweeping mustache bobbing.

"Then, when it's all over I'll be de-mobbed and will go, hat in
hand, and ask if I can have back my old school desk. And in twenty
years some student will point me out as I go hobbling across the quad
and tell his girl that I fought in the war. And she'll say what war?
And he'll say the war against Japan. And she'll say war against Japan,
against our great friend and trading partner? So what's the sense of it
all?"

"There's sense to it if you're attacked!" Simms said.

"I grant you that," the Major said. "The attack against your
Pearl Harbor made no sense. The Jap should have invaded! If he did I
warrant he'd won that battle and where would you be now?"

"Where would Australia be?" Sirocco asked.

"Down the bloody toilet, mate, that's where! Down the bloody head, as you call it!

"Make no mistake, we know we owe our existence to date to you chaps. Without you we'd long since been in Jap prison camps. Poor bloody Pommies can't help us, they've got their hands full with Adolf. But none of that changes the fact that all war is for naught, as some old Greek once said. Forgot who said it."

"How far are we from the new patrol area, Joe?" Hinman said pointedly, anxious to end the conversation and the direction it was moving. Sirocco pricked off the distance with his dividers.

"Less than two hundred miles, sir. We should be on station before midnight tomorrow."

"I wonder why Rabaul?" Hinman said. "The message doesn't tell us what to expect there."

Another message came from Brisbane just before *Mako* dove on its patrol station off the harbor of Rabaul. The message said that Naval Intelligence believed the Japanese would make a strong effort to reinforce their garrisons at Guadalcanal and Tulagi, that *Mako* might encounter various types of small ships pressed into service as troop carriers. *Mako* should also expect these troop ships to be escorted. The message concluded, "Attacks will be made on troop-carrying ships rather than escorting warships unless necessary for survival."

"Different commands, different orders," Hinman said to Joe Sirocco in the Control Room. "In Pearl it's 'get the escort ships first and then go after the merchant ships or tankers.' In this command it's get the escort vessels last, if you can."

"Probably the special circumstances," Sirocco suggested gently. "The Marines must be hanging on by their toenails in Guadalcanal and Tulagi and if that message the Major heard was the real thing, and I'm inclined to think it was, the only thing that stands between an unopposed reinforcement of the Japanese garrisons on both those places is the submarine navy. *Flying Fish* is to the southeast of us and they're moving others in, according to the messages, but we're the first boy in the line."

"I thought sure we'd see something coming out of that harbor last night," Hinman said. "Place was black as pitch all night long, not a light anywhere. That would mean to me that the Marines still hold the airfield at Guadalcanal and Rabaul is afraid of air raids." He yawned hugely. "I'm going to sack out. If we don't see anything moving today I want to patrol closer in to the harbor tonight. Make the patrol courses two miles from the harbor mouth."

Mako surfaced after full dark and began running back and forth across the harbor lanes. It was Grabnas' sharp eyes that picked up the sudden blacking out of a star by a ship's masts. Captain Hinman scrambled up into the lookout stand beside the gangling seaman.

"Nice going, Grabby," he said softly as he leveled his binoculars. He stared for a long moment, moving the binoculars back and forth.

"I see four of them, do you?" he said to Grabnas.

"Yes, sir, three small ships and what looks like a tin can way out ahead there. It was his mast I saw cut through the starlight."

Hinman dropped back down to the Bridge. "Control!" he said into the speaker. "Get the Executive Officer to the Conning Tower!"

Sirocco's voice came up through the hatch.

"I'm here, Bridge. What's cooking?"

"Run the search scope up, Joe," Hinman called down the hatch. "Bearing two seven zero and sweep aft about twenty degrees. Tell me if you see something. We've got ships out there!"

He watched the thick-necked search periscope ascend and begin its search. Then Sirocco's voice came up the hatch, an edge of excitement in his tones.

"I've got four of them, sir! Looks like a destroyer escort out in front and then three small ships behind in a line."

"Sound General Quarters!" Hinman snapped. As the gong began to sound throughout *Mako* Hinman clapped Nate Cohen on the shoulder. "I'll take the deck, Nate." He leaned over the hatch to the Conning Tower.

"Plotting Party will work in the Conning Tower," he called down. "Joe, I want a course to close on the last ship in the line. Then put me on a parallel course to the convoy, make the course seven hundred yards to the convoy's starboard side. I'm going to run along beside these ships for a while, I don't think they can make too much speed, they look too small. We'll see what the escort up ahead does. If he doesn't pick us up we'll set up to shoot at the last ship in the line. Set torpedo depth two feet. Repeat two feet." He waited while Sirocco worked out the plot and then grabbed at the bridge rail as *Mako* went into a sharp turn that would bring it parallel to the line of ships.

"Moon's coming up," he called down the hatch. "In our favor! The targets are between us and the moon! Another five minutes and you should be able to get a real good look through the periscope."

"Bearing. . . . Mark!" Sirocco's voice came up through the hatch to the Bridge clearly in the quiet of the night.

"Target bears three three zero, Bridge. That's the last ship in the line, the one closest to us. Destroyer up ahead bears zero five zero. Range to the last ship is estimated at nine hundred yards. Target has very stubby mast, hard to figure height. Range to the destroyer is seven thousand yards. Convoy speed estimated to be eight knots. Parallel course to the convoy is one three eight, sir. We can come right to one three eight now and we'll be seven hundred yards away."

"Very well," Hinman said. "Steer course one three eight. Make turns for nine knots. We'll overhaul and see what the escort does. Keep an eye on him, Joe."

Mako moved silently through the calm sea, pacing her speed to the speed of the convoy that was ahead of her and off her port bow. The moon crept higher in the sky and Hinman could see the outlines of the three ships clearly and the destroyer escort out ahead of its flock.

"Destroyer has started a turn to starboard, Bridge!" Joe Sirocco's voice was urgent. Hinman leaned his elbows on the teak bridge rail and studied the destroyer. It was turning, showing a small feather of white at its bow.

"Range to the destroyer is six thousand yards, Bridge. Angle on the bow now nine zero starboard. He's in a definite turn! Sound reports twin screws picking up speed, Nate thinks it must be the destroyer, sir!"

"Open tube outer doors," Hinman sang out. "If he comes for us we'll give him four down the throat! Start the plot on the destroyer! I want to swing my bow five degrees to starboard if he comes at us head

on and take him with a spread of four fish running across his track!"
He felt light-headed. He could feel the adrenaline coursing through
him like a big surge of power, the same sense of elation he had felt in
his first and only surface engagement with the enemy in Makassar
Strait. As he shivered in anticipation he realized that what he was
feeling now he had felt when he made love to Joan. He shook his
head.

"Let me have some information, damn it, Plot! Keep feeding
me!"

"Range to the destroyer is four zero zero zero yards, sir. Angle on
the bow is zero! He's coming right at us. All torpedo tube outer doors
are open, depth set two feet, spindles disengaged. Target speed is
sixteen knots and increasing slowly. . . . Range to the target is three
five zero zero . . . speed seventeen knots."

"Give me a solution for shooting at twelve hundred yards range to
the target," Hinman said. "We'll shoot a spread of four from the
forward tubes and then swing ship to bring the after tubes to bear in
case we need them."

"Aye, aye, sir," Sirocco said. "Angle on the bow of the target is
still zero zero zero. Range is two five zero zero yards. Speed is
eighteen knots. He is shooting!"

Hinman saw the flash of a gun on the dark bulk of the destroyer's
foredeck as Sirocco shouted. The shell screamed by, far overhead.
There was another flash and the shell passed by above them and to
one side.

"He's trying to drive us down," Hinman shouted. "How do we
look, Plot!"

"Coming up to a solution, sir. Recommend we swing five degrees
to starboard now . . . range one five zero zero yards!"

"Stand by Forward!" Hinman shouted. "Give me a solution!"

"You can shoot!" Sirocco called out.

"*Fire one!*" Hinman counted down from six to zero.

"*Fire two!*

"*Fire three!*

"*Fire four!*

"*Right full rudder! All ahead flank! Stand by aft!*"

Mako's first torpedo ran ahead of the target. The second slammed into the destroyer's bow and the third, six seconds behind, exploded with a huge roar at the destroyers' engine rooms.

"*Joe!*" Hinman screamed. "Get up here! Confirm this!"

Sirocco scrambled up the ladder to the bridge and saw the bow of the destroyer, torn apart by the first torpedo, sticking out of the water. The stern reared high out of the water, seemed to reach higher and then began to slide under the sea.

"One down!" Hinman yelled. "Now we'll take those other three! It's going to be like shooting fish in a barrel! I want a torpedo track of seven hundred yards, Joe. Bring me up so I can run head on to the targets and shoot. One fish for each one should be enough!" Sirocco nodded and dropped down the hatch.

Mako raced after the ship closest to it, a long, lean shark coursing after its prey. The range closed and *Mako* turned to deliver the death blow to the target.

"You can shoot, Bridge!"

"*Fire five!*"

Captain Hinman felt the slight jolt under his feet as the fist of compressed air hurled the torpedo out of the tube. At 700 yards the torpedo run to the target would be less than 30 seconds.

"Torpedo is running hot, straight and normal," Nate Cohen's voice floated up to the bridge. "Torpedo has run through the target bearing! It's still running!"

"You've got a solution, Bridge!"

"*Fire six!*"

Hinman watched, counting down slowly. The target was trying to zig zag but it had insufficient speed to make the maneuver effective.

"Torpedo is running through the target bearing!" Cohen called out. "It's still running!"

"Bridge!" Sirocco's voice was loud in the night. "Suggest the fish are running underneath the target!"

"Bring me around for a set-up on the after tubes!" Hinman yelled down the hatch. "Set torpedoes at zero depth! Repeat, zero feet depth!"

Mako heeled over as the rudder was put hard right and Hinman waited for Sirocco to tell him the torpedo problem was solved.

"You can shoot, Bridge!"

"Fire seven!"

He watched from the side of the bridge, straining to see the torpedo as it ran. There was no sign.

"Torpedo is running through the target bearing," Cohen's voice was faint. "It's still running!"

"Close the outer tube doors!" Hinman snapped into the bridge microphone. "Plot! Bring me around so my port side is parallel to the target. I want six hundred yards range. Stand by to go to Battle Surface as soon as the outer doors are closed!" He heard Sirocco's rapid orders to Bob Edge on the TDC and to the helmsman and the rush of feet passed the word to stand by for a battle surface action. *Mako* swung in a wide arc and began racing up a course parallel to the ship he had fired three torpedoes at and failed to hit.

"Battle Stations Surface!" Hinman yelled and stood to one side in the small bridge as the gun crews climbed out of the hatch and climbed down the side of the Conning Tower, racing to the two big deck guns.

"Range is now six zero zero yards, sir," Sirocco called out.

"Deck guns manned! Breeches open! Standing by to load, Bridge!" Dusty Rhodes' voice was loud from the deck. "Fifty calibers manned and loaded and locked!"

"Load deck guns!" Hinman shouted. "Pointers, set sights for range of six zero zero yards! I want to hull this bastard, gunners!"

"Ready fore and aft on deck, Bridge!"

"Commence firing!"

The forward 5.25-inch deck gun roared first and Hinman saw a gout of water soar skyward, short of the target. The after gun bellowed and another spurt of water went up, also short of the target. The second round from each gun would reach farther as the gun barrels heated up and the powder in the shells burned faster. The forward gun roared again and Hinman saw a bright red burst on the side of the target ship.

"Now pound that bastard!" he yelled as the after gun roared.

"Bridge!" Grabnas' voice from the port lookout stand was almost lost in the roar of the deck guns. "Bridge! I can see a lot of people and looks like trucks on the deck of the ship!"

"Machine gunners open fire! Sweep the ship's decks!"

Behind him on the cigaret deck the twin 20-mm guns began to pound viciously and Hinman watched the tracers reach out across the water, arcing lazily, tiny balls of fire that found the target ship and then probed upward on the hull and began to sweep across the target's deck, a molten scythe of death. Below him on the deck the 50-caliber machine guns, mounted on special stanchions, were pounding the target's bridge structure. There was a sudden burst of bright fire from the target's main deck as the 20-mm shells found the gas tank on a truck and blew it up. There was a cheer from the forward deck gun as a sudden gout of white steam rose in the moonlight and the bright red flames of an explosion within the ship's midsection.

"*Cease fire!*" Hinman yelled. "I think we got his boiler rooms! He's sinking, he's sinking! Plot! Put me on the next target!"

"Bridge!" Rhodes' voice from the deck was sharp. "Bridge, we need more ammunition on deck. Request below-decks ammunition party begin supply."

"Very well, Chief," Hinman passed the order down to the Conning Tower. "Damned good shooting, gunners, damned good!" *Mako* was turning, picking up speed, running down the second ship.

"Same setup!" Hinman yelled down the hatch. "Six hundred yards is a good range!" He looked at the target ship, now off his port bow. Down below him on the forward gun he heard the angry voice of Officers' Cook, Thomas T. Thompson.

"Chief, I'm the first loader on this damned gun and ain't no one else gonna be the first loader so leave me alone!" He listened, wondering what Thompson could be arguing about with Dusty Rhodes. The two men were good friends and Rhodes was not one to tolerate an argument in a Battle Stations situation or any other situation. He started to lean over the bridge rail and stopped as he heard Sirocco's voice.

"On range now, sir!"

"*Commence firing!*" Hinman yelled. Both deck guns roared in unison. Hinman could feel the excitement mounting in him, the crazy feeling that time had run backward and that he was on the deck of a frigate with all sails set and the guns roaring out in broadsides and then crashing back against their restraining tackle. He could hear, somewhere in his mind, the yells of the sailors and the cries of the gunners as they sponged out their gun barrels, the yells of the gun captains as they pulled the guns back into position in the ports and then the long, rolling broadsides. This was the traditional way of warfare on the high seas, with guns roaring and the smell of cordite sharp in the nose, the yells of the gunners as they served their weapons.

"Good shot!" He screamed as he saw bright orange burst at the target's water line. He saw the lazy tracers of the machine guns reaching for the target, searching out the windows of the ship's bridge, sweeping across the decks. And then he saw other tracers arcing toward him, heard the clang of bullets striking metal around him and he realized that the target, hopelessly outgunned, was shooting back at him.

"Get that machine gun on that ship!" he yelled at Dick Smalley on the 20-mm guns. He watched as Smalley's tracers walked in at the source of the other tracers and then steadied and hammered on the other gun station.

"Target is down by the bow!" Dusty Rhodes' bellow could be easily heard above the roar of the deck guns.

"*Cease fire!*" Hinman yelled. "A case of beer to the gun that puts him under. *Commence slow fire!*" The forward gun barked and Hinman saw a burst of fire near the water line of the target's bow. The after deck gun bellowed and there was a burst of flame at the target's exposed hull aft and then a muffled explosion and the ship jerked sideways and broke in two.

"After gun gets the beer!" Hinman yelled. "Plot, where in the hell has that third ship gone to?" He turned to climb up in the periscope shears and stopped as he saw the dark rivulets running down the mottled camouflage paint of the periscope shears. His eyes followed the dark streams upward and he saw Grabnas hanging like a limp rag doll over the pipe railing of his lookout stand.

"Doc to the bridge!" Hinman yelled. He scrambled upward to Grabnas, lifting the man's limp upper body, and as Grabnas started to slide out of the lookout stand, Hinman heard Major Struthers' voice below him.

"I've got him, Skipper. Let him go. I've got him." Hinman eased Grabnas' sagging head by the rail of the lookout stand and felt the man being taken from him. He scrambled down to the bridge.

"No need for your medico," Struthers said slowly. "The man's had it. You want me to hand him down to someone?"

"Where's he hit?" Hinman said, his breath coming in huge gasps. "How do you know he's had it, damn it!"

"Captain!" The Australian's voice was hard, flat. "The man's been cut near in half!" He put his hands under Grabnas' armpits and with one foot kicked Grabnas' limp legs into the hatch opening.

"Below there, mates! Take this chap!" Joe Sirocco reached upward and let the limp legs fall against his chest and took the burden. He turned to the Control Room hatch.

"Below, there! Take Grabnas, will you, Pete?"

"I've got him, sir!" John Barber's voice was steady. Sirocco released the body and spun back to the periscope and began a search for the third ship. He swung the periscope around in a complete circle once, then twice.

"Can't see the other target, sir. He must have hauled his ass out of here while you were taking care of the other two!"

"Lots of Japs in the water, Captain," Major Struthers was unsnapping the flap on his pistol holster. "Mind if I pot a few of the bloody bastards? I've got a lot of good chums dead at the hands of the Jap! Wouldn't do for this lot to get picked up or to swim to one of those bloody islands and live to fight another day!"

Hinman stood, his eyes closed tightly. Then he opened his eyes and looked at Struthers and up at the dark traces of blook on the periscope shears.

"Deck guns, secure and get below. Fifty-caliber machine guns switch stations to the bridge stanchions. Smalley, begin firing at the targets in the water! Major, pick your own targets!"

Mako moved slowly through the flotsam of the two sunken ships, the machine guns hammering steadily at the men in the water. A flash off the port bow caught Major Struthers' eye.

"Ah, you bastard!" the Major said genially. "Shoot back at us, would you? Poke your bloody head up for another look-see!" He steadied his heavy pistol on the bridge rail and aimed carefully. The pistol roared and bucked upward. "Got you! Just like shooting 'roos in the outback!"

"Aircraft!" Smalley's scream cut through the noise of the guns. Hinman looked aft and saw Smalley swing his twin 20-mm guns upward and begin firing a long burst out to the starboard side. Then he saw the plane, a black bulk against the starlit sky, saw it suddenly soar upward as the tracers reached toward it, saw two bulky black objects fall from the plane and tumble toward the water. The bombs hit well out to starboard and exploded with a huge roar squarely in the middle of a huge cluster of swimmers.

"*Clear the bridge! Down periscope! Dive! Dive! Dive!*" Hinman's voice was a roar. "Major, damn you, get down the hatch!" He shoved Struthers toward the hatch and waited until the lookouts and the machine gunners had hurled themselves down through the hatch, not bothering to use the ladder, depending on the big hands of Joe Sirocco to catch them and spin them toward the hatch to the Control Room. Hinman slammed the diving alarm twice with his hand and dropped through the hatch.

"One hundred feet!" he snapped as he slid down the ladder to the Control Room. "Get some down angle on her, damn it! There's a plane up there!" *Mako* knifed downward. Far off to one side they heard the crash of two more explosions.

"Make it one hundred and fifty feet," Hinman said. He stood, panting, watching the long black needles of the depth gauges move around the dials of the gauges in front of the bow and stern planes.

"That'll do it. Level her off." He turned around to Aaron, who was standing quietly by the gyro table.

"Where's Grabnas?"

"In the Forward Torpedo Room, sir," Aaron replied. Hinman nodded and ran forward. Ginty was standing by the torpedo tubes.

"He's in Number One tube, sir," Ginty said, his voice a low growl. "Doc made sure nothing could be done for him. I thought the tube was the best place for him, until you give some orders."

"Very well," Hinman said. He stood, staring at the shiny brass face of the torpedo tube door, tasting the bile that had risen into his throat. Then he turned and went back to the Control Room.

"Stand easy on Battle Stations," he said to Sirocco. "Tell the galley to serve coffee to all hands and ask Tom to bring me a cup, please."

"He can't, sir," Dusty Rhodes said. "Tom took a bullet through the neck from that first ship. He wouldn't go down below when I told him to go. He's in the Crew's Mess, Doc is working on him."

"Oh my God!" Hinman said. He ran aft to the Crew's Mess. Thompson was laid out on a mess table surrounded by crew members.

"How is he, Doc?" Hinman demanded.

"I think he's gonna be okay, sir," the Pharmacist's Mate said. "He took one right through his neck. Good thing he's got such a big neck! Lots of room in there for something to go through. There isn't any arterial bleeding so I figure the bullet didn't hit anything serious. What I'm worried about is infection. I heard the Japs rub garlic on their bullets. That would cause infection."

Hinman looked down at his cook. Thompson's normally coal black, smiling face was ashy in color.

"How you feeling, old friend?" Hinman said.

Thompson opened his eyes. "Fine, sir. Doc's gonna fix me up just fine."

Chief John Barber came into the Crew's Mess carrying a pair of long-nosed pliers, an alcohol torch and a piece of stiff wire 18 inches long. He put the torch on a mess bench and, using the pliers, he bent one end of the wire back to form a smooth, blunt end. Then he formed a larger loop at the other end. He stuck the pliers in his pocket and lit the alcohol torch and passed the flame up and down the wire several times. He handed the torch to one of his machinist's mates and held the pliers in the flame.

"That ought to sterilize it," Barber grunted. He held the wire in the pliers, the larger loop toward the Pharmacist's Mate.

"Okay, now thread your gauze through that loop and then I'll crimp it closed so it won't slip out." The Pharmacist's Mate put a half-dozen six-inch long pieces of cotton gauze into the loop of wire and Barber carefully squeezed the loop tightly closed. He handed the wire to the other man, who dipped the gauze into a bottle of iodine.

"This is gonna sting you some, Tom, so hang on." The man on the table rolled his eyes and then closed them and his big hands clamped down on the edge of the mess table.

"Someone hold his head steady," Doc Whitten said. Chief Rhodes moved around to the end of the table and put his big hands on either side of Thompson's face.

Doc Whitten crouched down until his eyes were on a level with Thompson's neck and carefully pushed the bare end of the wire into the small black hole in Thompson's neck. He pushed gently, feeding the stiff wire into and through the man's neck until Barber, standing on the other side of the table, grunted and reached down and got a grip on the end of the wire with his pliers.

"Pull it through very slowly," Whitten said. "I want that iodine to touch everything in there." Barber nodded and began pulling on the wire. The iodine-soaked gauze disappeared into the hole in Thompson's neck and the big man on the table gasped and Rhodes clamped his hands tightly on Thompson's face. Barber began to pull on the wire and a low moan came through Thompson's teeth.

"My fucking oath!" Major Struthers said.

Johnny Johnson, the ship's cook, handed Whitten a coffee cup. "I mixed as much sulfa powder in that vaseline as it would take," he said. Whitten nodded his head and picked up a wooden spatula and began packing the sulfa-loaded vaseline into the holes in each side of Thompson's neck. When he had finished he put a square of gauze over each hole and strapped the squares down with tape. Thomas opened his eyes.

"You're one hell of a surgeon, Doc," Thompson said. "Next time I have to cut my toenails I'm gonna have you do it. Now lemme get up from here because I have to feed my people."

"No you don't!" Captain Hinman said. "You're going to get in your bunk and stay there!"

"Captain," Thompson said, sitting up on the mess table. "Ain't no itty-bitty Jap bullet make me flake out in my sack!" He swung his legs off the table and stood up, moving his head from side to side gingerly.

"Don't hurt hardly none at all," he said. "This old Doc has fixed me up just fine!" He smiled and started to walk and then suddenly collapsed in a heap on the deck.

"Shock," Doc Whitten said professionally. "Had to hit him sooner or later. Nothing to worry about. After we get him in his sack I'll give him a shot to knock him out and he'll sleep for about twelve hours. After that he should be okay if there's no infection inside there."

Hinman walked back to the Control Room and stood beside Joe Sirocco. "I've got to come to a decision on Grabnas," he said. "Barber just told me the temperature of the injection water, the temperature of the sea water outside, is ninety-six degrees! We can't keep Grabnas' body in that torpedo tube very long; it's too hot. I can't put him in the freezer locker, no one would want to eat any of the food."

"Burial at sea, sir?" Sirocco said gently. "It's been done for centuries."

Hinman nodded.

The following midnight John A. Aaron, Radioman Second Class, USNR, preached a short sermon over the ship's communication system. The body of Andrew F. Grabnas, Seaman First Class, USNR, aged twenty-two, was carried topside encased in the heavy plastic cover from his bunk with a bar of lead lashed to his feet.

As the officers and Chief Petty Officers of the U.S.S. *Mako* stood at attention on the main deck Captain Hinman read the traditional words that have been used to bury seamen far from home. When he had finished with a soft "Amen" Ginty and DeLucia slid the body over the side as Lieut. Nathan Cohen, standing on the cigaret deck, softly chanted the *Kaddish*, the Jewish prayer of mourning.

CHAPTER 27

The message ordering the *Mako* in to Brisbane for refit and a period of rest and relaxation came a week after the deck gun actions against the Japanese ships. There were no expressions of joy from *Mako*'s crew when the news came that the patrol was over and they were heading for port. The death of Grabnas had sobered the crew. The soft-spoken Floridian had been popular with his fellow crewmen. Tribute was paid to him in small subtle ways that only the men who knew and served with him appreciated. Ginty summed up the crew's feelings in the Crew's Mess, his deep growl dominating the compartment.

"That Greek kid, that Grabby Grabnas. Called hisself a 'Conch' because he was born in Key West. He was proud of being born in Key West. Lousiest submarine base in the Navy to do duty in, I heard! What the hell is there to be proud of, born in a lousy place to do duty? I'll say this for the bastard; he never came forward to my Room what he didn't bring fresh coffee for the man on watch and a doughnut or a sandwich. Never shot his mouth off to no one. I'll say another thing and any you poges want to call me wrong stand up; that son of a bitch wasn't no 'Conch' or whatever he wanted to call himself. He was a submarine sailor! Coulda served on S-Boats with me and that's something I wouldn't say about very many of you bastards!"

Two Australian Navy gunboats met *Mako* at sea off the Great Barrier Reef and escorted her into Marston Bay, where a uniformed pilot came aboard, and then into the mouth of the Swan River. On the way up the river the port lookout leveled his glasses at the shore line.

"Someone over there on top of that little white building is sending us semaphore flag signals, Bridge! It's two broads!" The off-duty crew members on deck enjoying the unaccustomed sunlight came alert.

"Better see what they want, Bradshaw," Captain Hinman said. The quartermaster climbed up into the periscope shears and squeezed himself in beside the port lookout.

"Gimme your white hat," he said to the lookout. "I'll use my hat and yours for flags. God knows where our flags are stowed." He held a hat in each hand and answered the girls on the small building. One of the girls began whipping her semaphore flags rapidly.

"What's she saying?" Hinman called up.

"Meet . . . you . . . at . . . gate . . . sixteen . . . hundred," Bradshaw yelled out. "Hey, that second one is going now and she's too fast for a Chief Signalman on a battleship to read! Man, can she go!"

"Never mind that crap," a voice yelled from the deck. "Just tell them we'll be there with bells on!"

Captain Hinman laughed and turned to the Australian Navy pilot.

"I've been in a lot of ports in my life but I've never seen anything like that before."

"This is your first trip here," the pilot said. "Brisbane is a lonely city for women. You won't see a man in civilian clothes on the street between the ages of seventeen and fifty unless he's lost an arm or a leg or is blind."

"Why?" Joe Sirocco asked.

"Our men made up most of the famous Ninth Divvy, the Ninth Division of the Australian Army," the pilot said quietly. "The bloody British threw our men in against Rommel, in Africa. Rifles and flesh and blood against tanks! Rommel's tanks cut our boys into ribbons! They've been overseas since late Thirty-nine and this city is a lonely place for women."

The official welcoming party at the New Farm Wharf lacked the enthusiastic celebration that the Submarine Staff at Pearl Harbor usually gave a returning submarine, but it was warm enough. A working party from the submarine tender brought aboard crates of tropical fruits and eight sacks of mail. As the crew spread out on the deck, chewing at fruit and reading their mail, Captain Hinman and his officers went up on the Wharf to meet and shake hands with the Submarine Staff officers. A tall, slim, Australian General stepped out and shook hands warmly with Major Struthers.

"First things first, Captain Hinman," the Operations Officer of the Staff said. "We are pleased to credit *Mako* with four ships sunk in the special mission at Bougainville. Four.

"In all fairness I will say that we could not give *Mako* credit for any sinkings until Intelligence had confirmed the actual results. That confirmation has come in. The Japs have written off four of the ships as a total loss. Three other ships are badly damaged, engine rooms flooded, that sort of thing and you are credited with damaging those ships. Two other ships have been repaired so we cannot give credit for those." He paused and nodded his head at a junior officer, who stepped forward and handed Captain Hinman a large, flat manila envelope.

"Open it, Captain," the Operations Officer said.

Hinman opened the envelope and pulled out a stencil of a bath house on stilts with a Japanese Rising Sun flag painted on its side.

"Naval Intelligence also reports the Japanese Command at Bougainville reported that a Major General, a full Colonel and two enlisted men were killed in what was described as the explosion of a probable aircraft bomb during an air raid while they were taking their morning shower on the date," he paused and allowed a small smile to cross his face, "on the date *Mako* reports that the shore party had mined a bath house within the Japanese Army camp!

"In view of the fact that both the Japanese officers were known to be experts in jungle warfare and inasmuch as the U.S. Navy's Marine Corps is now engaged in a bitter battle to hold on to Guadalcanal, it has been officially decided that the, ah, mining of the bath house was a heavy loss to the enemy and *Mako* is hereby given credit for sinking one, ah, Japanese bath house!"

"Bloody good show!" Major Struthers bellowed. "Our turn now?" He looked at the Australian General, who nodded.

Major Struthers executed a smart left face, took two steps and did a right face and cracked his boot heels together. He put his riding crop under his left arm and snapped off a smart salute, his right hand quivering at his hat brim in the Australian Army style. The Operations Officer returned the salute and Major Struthers held out his hand. The General stepped forward and gave him a manila folder, one of two such folders the Major had handed him when he walked up on the Wharf.

"It is my privilege to present you with this copy of my report to our General Command, sir." He handed the folder to the Operations Officer.

"I will summarize the contents for the benefit of those here and for the benefit of the U.S.S. *Mako*'s Captain and officers who have not seen the report," Major Struthers went on.

"I have detailed the special mission from start to end with my own estimates of damages inflicted on the enemy.

"I have strongly endorsed what I assume you know already, gentlemen, that Captain Hinman is a courageous, aggressive, highly skilled Naval officer with a fine crew." He drew a deep breath.

"Further: I have made a strong recommendation that Captain Hinman and Chief Torpedoman's Mate Gordon Rhodes be awarded the Order of the British Empire for gallantry in action in the face of the enemy!

"I have strongly recommended that the Submarine Command, United States Navy, serving in Australia in the common effort against the enemy, be commended by His Majesty for their daring use of the submarine as a diversified weapon and that the U.S.S. *Mako* and each member of its crew be commended by His Majesty for gallant service!" He stepped back a pace and saluted again.

The Australian General cleared his throat.

"We are most happy to forward Major Struthers' recommendations, gentlemen. I might add that the Major's recommendations will carry great weight. Recommendations for the award of medals for gallantry and for commendations for gallantry which come from a holder of the Victoria Cross with a bar for a second Cross are most seriously considered."

There was a dead silence on the Wharf. Joe Sirocco nudged Don Grilley slightly. Grilley nudged back to let Sirocco know he understood. The Major had taken no part in the Wardroom discussions about defective torpedoes and the political bickering in the Brisbane Submarine Command. But he had, by his résumé of what he had put in his official report, effectively spiked the guns of those who might have intentions of reprimanding Captain Hinman for his prodigal use of torpedoes.

The Australian General cleared his throat again.

"I might add this to the Major's report, gentlemen. Major Struthers is a very dangerous combat man. He has been threatening for a long time to bag a General. Now that he has done so I think I can sleep safely of nights!" A gust of laughter swept the Wharf.

"The buses will be here at fourteen hundred hours, Captain." The Operations Officer was talking to Captain Hinman. "You'll have to warn your men to be on their best behavior. The Canberra Hotel, where they'll be quartered, is a temperance hotel, that is, there is no drinking allowed. We have no separate accommodations for your Chief Petty Officers but the good people of this city beg us to quarter Americans in their homes. The Chiefs will be billeted in private homes if they so desire. Officers will be housed in homes we have leased for the duration. My aide will get together with your Executive Officer and take care of the details. If you don't mind, I'll send a car for you and your Executive Officer at fourteen hundred so we can get the de-briefing over with today. I'll have read your report of the patrol by then."

"This place don't allow no liquor or beer, that right, Pops?" Ginty growled at the one-armed elevator operator in the Canberra Hotel.

"Matter of speaking, that's the way it is," the old man said. "But us old sojers stick together. I lost my left flipper in the first Big War, at the Dardenelles. All you have to do is let me know what you want. Same price as you'd pay in the pub."

"You wouldn't have a girl up that empty sleeve, would you?" Ginty grinned.

"I'm past the time for that, bucko," the old man said. "But you'll not want for girls. All you have to do is stand on the street corner and look lonesome. There's women so starved for a man in their bed in this city they'll fair kidnap you!"

"God!" Mike DeLucia said from the back of the elevator. "We've all been killed and gone to Heaven!"

"My first reaction to your patrol report," the Operations Officer said to Hinman and Sirocco, "is that your tactic of a night surface torpedo attack on the convoy you sighted was wrongly conceived. You wasted four torpedoes on a destroyer escort. We are very short of torpedoes, Captain! One would have been enough. Two at the most."

"I felt I had to fire the spread of four, sir," Hinman said. "It was a down-the-throat shot, sir."

"If you had made your initial attack against the troop-carrying ships, as ordered, the odds are you might have had a much more advantageous firing angle, sir," the Operations Officer said. "One torpedo fired at the first two troop-carrying ships, one torpedo at each ship, would have brought the destroyer escort back to his charges and you could have picked your firing angle. If you had been submerged, as you should have been, the DE wouldn't have had a chance! You stayed on the surface and enticed the DE!"

"Sir," Hinman's voice was stubborn, "I fired at the DE in what I thought was the best action I could conceive. Once the escort vessel was out of the way I could set up and fire one torpedo at each troop-carrying ship at leisure, take my time, get my hits.

"I did that. As I noted in the patrol report, I fired at seven hundred yards. I made each set-up very carefully. The torpedoes ran too deep! My sound man, there isn't a better officer in the whole of the submarine Navy than Lieutenant Cohen, heard the fish run through the target bearings, sir! Even when I set the depth at zero feet on the last torpedo it ran under the target!"

"Captain, the torpedoes do not run deeper than the depth setting! I should know, I spent two years working on torpedo depth setting and performance! You missed!"

"Sir," Hinman said, "with all due respect, sir: Captain Rudd
fired three torpedoes out of *Plunger*'s forward tubes before I left Pearl.
Fired them through a net. Each torpedo ran much deeper than set to
run. One fish ran almost sixteen feet deeper than it was set to run!"

"Three torpedoes fired in a hastily contrived operation do not
constitute a body of proof," the Operations Officer said calmly.
"Show me the results of three hundred torpedoes fired in a carefully
supervised test at a proper test range and I'll consider the evidence of
those tests and evaluate them. You Pearl Harbor Captains are very
good at complaining about your torpedoes, sir. All of the senior
officers in the South West Pacific Command are torpedo experts;
we'll all worked on them at the range in Newport. Your complaints
about torpedoes will get no ear in this command, sir! As for the rest of
your patrol, I congratulate you.

"The special mission to rescue the missionary and his family was
carried out very well. The way your crew treated those unfortunate
people has been noted and will undoubtedly be noticed by Sir
Winston Churchill. It will help cement better relations between our
two nations. This last special mission at Bougainville, very well done,
sir!" He paused, his eyes distant.

"This Major Struthers—a most peculiar man."

"I found him to be a delightful man to have aboard ship, sir.
Very cooperative, very pleasant."

"The Australian military people are very peculiar," the Operations Officer said. "Not long ago a troop transport loaded with Australian troops from Africa docked at Freemantle, over on the other side
of the continent. All the officers commanding those troops had been
killed in action or wounded and invalided home.

"A group of English officers was waiting on the dock to take
command of the debarking troops. Those Australian troops literally
drove the English officers from the dock with a hail of pennies! The
Australian penny, Captain, is a very large coin. Thrown with great
force it can damage anyone it hits. They threw so many pennies,
aimed them so well, the English officers ran in retreat! And the
Australian High Command ignored the incident!"

He stood up. "Well, I don't want to interfere with your rest and
relaxation, Captain. I congratulate you on the recommendation for a

medal for gallantry by Major Struthers. Our own recommendation will, of course, be filed. I'll see you here in my office when your ten days are up."

"I thought we were getting two weeks, sir."

"Ten days. I'm very sorry but we need submarines out there who can and will fight, sir. As it is I'm stretching it to give your crew ten days."

Later, sitting over a glass of strong Australian beer, Lieut. Comdr. Gene Puser said, "Captain, there is no way you are going to change these old Gun Club boys. You're just going to have to grin and bear it."

"My God!" Hinman said. "How can they discount the evidence? How can they sit there and say that we are missing our targets when I know I didn't miss?"

"The first thing you have to recognize, sir, is that when you say the torpedoes are faulty you are criticizing all of them. But to be fair, and God knows I don't want to be, you should see the condition some of the torpedoes are in when some submarines arrive here after patrol. They haven't been routined, some of them have air flasks with only a half an air charge in them, I've seen water scoops plugged up with filth, I've seen the air line that goes to the combustion flask so badly misthreaded that it was hanging on the flask by one or two threads. It would blow off the minute the torpedo was fired and the fish wouldn't have run!

"I've seen torpedoes with no alcohol in the alcohol tanks, fish so filthy that I know the screws wouldn't have turned because the bearings had never been taken care of. So these people do have some basis in their assumption that you people out there are missing the targets, because they're sure that the torpedoes are so badly cared for that they don't function.

"And that's only half of it, the lesser half. What's worse is the political situation here. Admirals are feuding with other Admirals. General MacArthur, who is the best politician of all of them, takes one side and then the other, playing our people off one against the other so he can get what he wants. It's a damned wonder that anything gets done at all!"

"Why do you stay here and put up with it?" Hinman's tone was blunt.

"I owe a hell of a lot to Bob Rudd. He asked me to be his eyes and ears. I hate being a tale bearer but I rationalize it by saying to myself that it's for the good of the Service.

"And I can see some good coming of it. Captain Rudd is putting enormous pressures on Washington and the torpedo experts there and in Newport.

"The fact that they admitted that you had sunk those ships in the harbor would not have happened six months ago. Six months ago they wouldn't have asked for an Intelligence evaluation of your contact report! Six months ago they would have put you on the carpet for even admitting your shore party had mined a Japanese bath house! But when they asked for an Intelligence report on that I knew it was a sign that what I do for Captain Rudd, what he's doing from his end, is getting results."

"Hell of a thing," Hinman grinned. "Painting a bath house on the Conning Tower! Major Struthers wanted me to go up to the Empire and put him ashore so he could blow up a train and we could paint a train on our Conning Tower! He's a character!"

"One to be a friend with, not an enemy," Puser said. "He's one of the few around who are living who's got two Victoria Crosses. That's the British equivalent of our Congressional Medal of Honor, you know."

"He never even hinted at it when he was on board," Hinman said. "What did he get them for?"

"I only know about one," Puser said. "British Intelligence got word that Rommel was going to host a dinner party for his top commanders in Bizerte, in Tunisia. The Major parachuted into the outskirts of the city and walked into the General Staff Headquarters building, and God knows how he did that!

"Then he walked up, nice as you please, and rapped at the front door. When the German sentry opened the door he cut the man's throat! He walked into the building, found the room where the dinner party was going on, kicked the door open and Sten-gunned the whole dinner table! Rommel wasn't there but he killed a lot of top German brass!

"Then he ran out of the building, it was built up on stilts like so many desert buildings, and went under the building and jumped into the cesspool that the building's toilets emptied into! He stayed there all that night and the next day and then he climbed out the following night and walked out into the desert to a prearranged place and was picked up by a light plane. I'm told that the plane's pilot put in for Hardship Discharge, said the Major's stench had ruined his nose and eyes for life!"

Hinman toyed with his empty beer glass. "He's a strange man but a good one. He's properly trained for his work. We're not. The Japs are much better at anti-submarine warfare than we are. We were never trained properly to attack enemy ships. We don't know much about their mast heights, their silhouettes, their speeds. But the Jap knows how to fight us! Bob Rudd told me that we're taking very heavy losses in the submarine force."

Puser nodded assent. "I'm sure you're right. Some of our submarine skippers are far too timid. You didn't mention that but you could have because I'm sure you know it. We get patrol reports in here from a Captain and then we hear a request for a transfer from his Executive Officer and you wouldn't think the two men had been on the same war patrol! We've got younger officers accusing their Captains of outright cowardice! Not one, quite a few! It's shocked the Command here almost into a coma, they don't want to believe that Academy officers are cowards, some of them.

"I'll say this to your face, sir; there aren't very many Art Hinmans around and there are damned few Arvin Mealeys! Which reminds me, there's another thing I want to tell you.

"You read Mealey's report on the patrol he made with *Mako*? He went into great detail about the tenacious and skilled attacks made on him by the Japanese. Intelligence has found out who was directing those attacks on Mealey. His name is Captain Akihito Hideki. He used to run the anti-submarine warfare school for the Japanese Navy. His nickname in the Japanese Navy is 'The Professor.' Not many anti-submarine people know as much as that fellow does and Mealey was lucky to get away from him. Just hope that you don't ever meet up with him!" He drained his glass.

"Now, if you want to know about Brisbane's night life, which isn't much, or about the ladies of Brisbane, and there are lots of them, let me know."

Hinman shook his head, grinning. "I got married just before I left the States. I'll stick to the zoo and the botanical gardens and write letters. But thanks for the offer."

"No reason you should spend all your time alone," Puser said. "I happen to be single and I'm sort of going with a very lovely girl. You could be a third at dinner any evening you want some company." He smiled at Hinman.

"Your crew won't have any trouble finding someone to give them a back rub! You might not be able to find more than half of them when it comes time to go back to the ship. That happens in Brisbane!"

CHAPTER 28

Dusty Rhodes and John Barber spent the better part of two days trying to find *Mako*'s crew in Brisbane with little success. Here and there, in a neighborhood pub or a small restaurant, they'd find one or two men. When they did they delivered their message: a party for the crew this coming Friday evening. Be there. Finally they went back to the Canberra Hotel to see if anyone had gone back there. John Aaron, his Bible beside him, was writing a letter to his wife at a writing table in the lobby.

"Where is everyone, John?" Rhodes said as he sat down at the writing table. Aaron looked up and smiled slowly.

"I guess you could say that most of them have found sort of temporary homes. I haven't seen very many of the fellows since the second day, Chief. This is a very nice hotel, nice people, good food. Where are you and Chief Barber staying?"

"We're quartered with a family, man named Emil Masters. He lives out in the suburbs, Toowoomba. Older guy. Manager of a bank. Very nice home, nice garden. You haven't seen Ginty, Hendershot?"

"No, I haven't, but you might ask the elevator operator, that old man with one arm. He seems to know everything that's going on around here and all over town."

The elevator operator took note of four blue hashmarks on Rhodes' jacket sleeve, his rating insignia and the billed Chief's hat.

"And a good day to you, First Sarn't," he said pleasantly. "What can I do for you?"

Rhodes described Hendershot and Ginty to the man.

"The big man you talk about, I saw him last night with the Bluey," he said with a smile, showing stained teeth. "The other one, ladies' man he is, wearing a uniform like yours, he was with one of the Bluey's friends."

"Bluey?" Barber said. "Who or what is a Bluey?"

"In our lingo it's a person with red hair, First Sarn't. Don't ask me why we call red-headed people 'Bluey' but we do, just as we call a pal a 'cobber.' "

"And who is the Bluey, who's he?" Rhodes asked.

"Not he, she. Was a time, before the war, when the Bluey ran the fanciest whorehouses in all of Australia. Had three of them here and I'm told some in Sydney. Beauty, that woman! Used to come in here to take her lunch in those days.

"But with the war and all and no men about and the good women of the city goin' crazy in their empty beds her business has gone to the dogs if you know what I mean. I hear now that she's very big in the black market. Has lots of friends, you know, big businessmen, local political wallahs."

"Does she have an address?" Rhodes asked.

"Just tell any cab driver I told you that you wanted to see the Bluey," the old man said. "He'll take you straight there, right enough and I thank you First Sarn't." He pocketed the pound note that Rhodes slipped to him.

The house the cab driver took them to was on the outskirts of Brisbane, a low, sprawling house on at least two acres of lushly landscaped land, surrounded by a low stone wall. Rhodes rang the bell at the gate. A young aborigine woman came out of the house and walked down a curving path to the gate.

"Madam isn't receiving," she said.

"Madam will receive me," Rhodes said. He opened the gate and walked by the girl and went up to the house. A long, screened porch spanned the entire front of the house. Rhodes knocked briskly on the edge of the screen.

"Who is it?" Ginty's growl was like the rumble of thunder.

"It's me," Rhodes said. "I want to see you, Ginty."

"One second, Chief. Lemme get some pants on." He came to the door and opened it. He was dressed in a pair of dungaree trousers and nothing else. He scratched his massive hairy chest.

"Well, come on in," he said. "Have a cold beer." He led the way into the house and Rhodes blinked his eyes at the opulence of the huge room into which they walked. Ginty waved him to one of the three sofas in the room. He sat down and sank in to his hips in the soft cushioning. In front of the sofa there was a long table, low, its legs carved caryatids. The sideboard against one wall was an antique, Rhodes guessed. On it was a collection of polished brass and pewter mugs. A Persian rug was on the floor and its muted colors complemented a shaggy white bearskin that was spread in front of a fireplace. Above the fireplace a shield hung, its face dented. Crossed beneath the shield there were two broadswords.

"Real," Ginty said pointing at the shield and swords. "Old as hell." He raised his voice. "Get yourself decent, woman, and come on in. We got company from the ship."

The Bluey swept into the room a moment later, a tall woman whose red hair was piled on her head in a heavy, regal coil. Her lush figure was barely concealed by a flowing, lacy peignoir that was cut low in the front to reveal the cleavage of her big breasts. She walked with a flowing stride, her long legs moving gracefully. Ginty made the introduction after Rhodes had struggled to his feet from the soft confines of the sofa. The serving girl brought in a silver tray with four bottles of beer and four glasses on it. She put the tray on the table in front of the sofa where Rhodes was sitting and Rhodes saw the lettering on the rim of the tray. It was the name and number of a U.S. destroyer that had been lost in action early in the war. He looked at Ginty.

"Don't worry, Chief," Ginty said. "I checked it out the day after I saw it. The Bluey here bought the whole Wardroom silver service off'n that destroyer about four years ago. Some snot-nosed Ensign ran out of money and peddled it to her for twenty pounds. Then he told his Exec. that the stuff had been stolen. I called a yeoman I know on the tender, old China hand, and he said the tin can was here four years ago on a good-will cruise. She's even got a recipt for the damned stuff!"

The red-headed woman had said nothing. She cleared her throat.

"Is Arnold in any sort of trouble, Chief?"

"Arnold? Oh, Ginty. No, ma'am. We're trying to round up as many of the crew as we can. The people we're staying with out in Toowoomba are throwing a party this Friday for the crew. They're very nice people and I wanted to get as many people there as I could."

"What are the names of your hosts?" she said.

"Mr. and Mrs. Masters, Emil Masters," Rhodes said.

"I know Emil," she said, a faint smile crossing her lips. "A very nice man. No children. I understand Mrs. Masters is a very lovely woman."

"She is," Barber siad. "We don't like to break in on you like this but we're having trouble finding the crew."

"I'm not surprised," the Bluey said. "There's a shortage of able-bodied men in Brisbane you know, it's been a long drought."

"She picked me up right outside the hotel," Ginty said. "I was standin' on the sidewalk and she drove up in a car and ordered me to get in!"

"The usual approach, I am told," the Bluey said, "is for a lady to ask a sailor how long it's been since he had a good home-cooked meal. If he responds as he should," the full, ripe lips curved in a smile, "nature takes its course.

"I wasn't that subtle with Arnold. When I saw the size of this lovely man I was overcome! I just leaned out the window of my car and told him to get in! He's a very obedient sailor." She turned her head and grinned wickedly at Ginty. "He does everything he's told to do over and over and over and over!"

"I'm sure he is," Rhodes struggled to his feet. "The party is for nineteen hundred day after tomorrow, Ginty. Be there!" He turned to the red-headed woman.

"We'd like to extend an invitation to you, ma'am."

"I appreciate your gallantry," she said, rising from her chair in an easy graceful motion. "But I think all the good and true husbands of that area would run for the Outback if they saw me come in the door! I'll deliver Arnold to the party and pick him up and I do thank you for being so nice."

"Hendershot?" Rhodes said. "You seen him around?"

"Yeah," Ginty said. "He's with a girl friend of this ugly old woman. I'll bring him along. I know where all my gang is and I know where DeLucia is. He should know where most of his people are. I can round up maybe thirty guys if this old woman will have her chauffeur drive me around. You ought to see this guy, Chief, both legs off at the knees and only one arm yet he drives like he had everything he was born with."

"He's my first cousin," the Bluey said softly. "He has a wife and two children and there are very few jobs for a man with two artificial legs and one arm. I'll make sure that we find at least half of your crew, Chief. There's not much that goes on in Brisbane that I don't know about. It's been a pleasure meeting you and if either of you are lonely . . . ." She let the sentence hang in midair.

Rhodes smiled. "John and I are married. We can wait. We know our wives wait."

"You are four very lucky people," she said. "Would you accept an invitation to dine with us Sunday? Fourteen hundred, as your charming Navy puts it? I'll expect you both."

The party was held in the gymnasium of the local school. The ladies of the suburb outdid themselves in decorating the gym and provided huge platters of sandwiches and freshly baked cakes. The men of the community made a fruit punch in an enormous cauldron. Ginty, immaculate in his white uniform, tasted the mixture and made a face.

"No stick in this crap," he growled to Johnny Paul. "You get your ass outside and tell that one-armed dude who drove us over here to take you back to Bluey's house. I seen a couple of empty cases of Coke bottles out back of the house and I stowed two five-gallon cans of alky in her kitchen. Fill a dozen, fourteen of them Coke bottles with alky and get back here in a hurry." Paul nodded and ran off to do the errand. When he got back he found Ginty waiting outside.

"I got some pitchers in the place where we stowed our white hats," Ginty said. "Put them Coke bottles in your belt, as many as you can, and go in and fill a couple of pitchers. Stow the rest of the bottles under the hats."

Emil Masters was standing nearby when Ginty poured two big pitchers of the 180-proof torpedo alcohol into the punch.

"Diluting our mixture with water, are you?" he said.

"Have to, sir," Ginty replied. "You people kinda forget that a submarine sailor doesn't get any fresh fruit at sea. This stuff is so strong that I'll break out with pimples or something! Thought I'd weaken it a little. Otherwise the men won't drink it and your people would feel bad."

"Never thought of you chaps not having all the fruit you wanted. Yes, what we're used to would seem a bit rich for you."

"You take me," Ginty said, stirring the punch vigorously with a big ladle. "I never eat no salads. Don't like that green stuff. I'm a meat and potatoes man. But when we got in from this war patrol I found myself buying a whole head of lettuce and I ate it like a big green apple, walking down the street. Lady I met who knows about things like that said it was something I couldn't help, that my system demanded green stuff."

"My word," Masters said. "It's a very difficult subject, isn't it, diet? Never thought about such things. But I can see the sense of her words. Yes."

The high point of the party was a "sing-song" in which the partygoers sat in long semi-circles on the floor of the gymnasium and sang songs, led by two of the women of the suburb.

The curved lines formed, each *Mako* sailor flanked by two civilians, arms stretched out and embracing their neighbors' shoulders. As they sang the lines rocked from side to side. Ginty and Johnny Paul kept themselves busy carrying pitchers of the spiked punch to the singers, filling glasses and joking. After a half-hour of vigorous singing and drinking the choristers got to their feet to rest bottoms unaccustomed to sitting on hard wooden floors. One matron in a flowing dress of bilious green with a necklace of sea shells resting on the shelf of her bosom took a deep draught from a glass Ginty had filled for her.

"You know," she confided to Ginty, "I always say you can have
· ever so much fun without boozing. Don't you agree?"

Ginty looked at the rivulets that her perspiration had carved
through the layer of powder on her neck and bosom and nodded his
head in agreement. She belched deeply and smiled, wholly unaware
of her social gaffe. Ginty patted her large fanny with a meaty hand
and she giggled.

"You make me feel like a young girl!" she lisped, her rouged
Cupid's-bow mouth forming what she thought was an attractive pout.

The party rocked on but no one bothered to get down on the hard
floor to sing. They gathered together in small groups, each intent on
singing its own songs, breaking the singing for frequent trips to the
punch bowl.

At eleven in the evening the school's janitor began blinking the
lights as a warning that the party had to break up. Dusty Rhodes and
John Barber, both of whom had correctly assessed the reason for the
excessive conviviality of the party, stood to one side, watching, as the
guests streamed out. Four of the husbands couldn't find their wives
and Rhodes wondered which of his crew had gone off with the
missing women.

Sitting in the Masters' neat kitchen the next morning, Rhodes
waited while John Barber boiled a kettle of water and poured it over
the Nescafé crystals he had put in two cups. Barber reached over to
the sideboard of the kitchen sink and picked up a Coke bottle with a
half-inch of clear alcohol in it. He carefully divided the alcohol
between the two cups and filled the bottle with water from the tap
and stood it beside another Coke bottle full of alcohol and corked.

Rhodes sipped his coffee gently. "After last night a little stick in
the java tastes good," he said. "Where'd they hide the stuff?"

"Under the white hats in the cloakroom," Barber said. "One
bottle had that little bit in it, the other one is full. Wonder how many
bottles they dumped in that punch?"

"Enough to liven up the party," Rhodes yawned. "Some of those
people are going to wake up this morning and wonder what the hell
hit them!" He turned as Emil Masters came into the kitchen dressed
in a bathrobe, his thin gray hair standing up in a ruff at the back of
his head.

"You chaps did something to the punch, didn't you?" he said, grinning.

"Coffee, sir?" Barber said, his voice innocent of guile. "I went out to the ship yesterday and brought back a case of Nescafé, since you and Mrs. Masters like it. Thought it was the least we could do in return for your hospitality."

"You're very generous," Masters said. His eyes glistened merrily. "But you did do something to the punch, didn't you? I've never seen the pastor's wife in such a festive mood!" He lowered his voice, nodding his head at the ceiling. "I saw her patting one of your big bucko sailors on his rear end! Those tight white trousers you chaps wear! I bet she hasn't patted the Reverend on his bottom in ten years!"

"Well, yes," Barber said. "We did do a little something to the fruit punch. Spiked it with a little American Indian whiskey." He raised the Coke bottle he had emptied of alcohol and filled with tap water and took a long swallow. He put the bottle down and reached for the Coke bottle that was full of alcohol and pulled the cork.

"Let me put a drop of this stuff in your coffee, sir," he said. He poured a scant quarter inch into the coffee and put the bottle down on the table. Masters reached out and picked up the Coke bottle.

"Just a nip to clear the passages," he said. Rhodes and Barber stared in horror as Masters tipped the Coke bottle and took a mouthful of the pure alcohol.

Rhodes was the first to move, bolting around the end of the table to catch hold of Masters as he staggered, coughing, gasping for air, his eyes wild and frightened. Barber grabbed a dish towel and held it to Masters' mouth as Rhodes pounded him on the back.

"Spit it out, man!" Rhodes rasped in Masters' ear. "Get rid of it!"

They sat him down in a chair when he had stopped retching and Barber gave him a glass of water to rinse out his mouth, holding the towel so he could spit out the water. He sank back in the chair, his hands massaging his throat. It was several minutes before he could speak.

"Oh, bloody Yanks! Japs will never beat a people who can drink whiskey that strong!"

Ginty was the last of the *Mako*'s crew to report back for duty. He jumped out of the Bluey's car as it rolled to a stop on the pier and bolted down the gangway and into his place in the morning quarters line with seconds to spare.

"Glad to see you, Ginty," Captain Hinman said cheerfully. "Glad to see that you have a driver to help you make quarters." He looked up and down the line of *Mako*'s crew.

"Well, you all look rested and relaxed. Shows you what going to the zoo and taking daily walks in the park will do for you!" He grinned as a ripple of laughter went down the ranks.

"Fun and games are over," Hinman said. "We're going back to sea. Two section liberty from now on, Chief Rhodes. Liberty to be granted only if the Division officers and the Chief Petty Officers of the division agree that you can be spared to go ashore.

"If any of you have contracted a venereal disease tell Doc Whitten at once. No one is going to court-martial you for anything like that but for your own sake, I don't want to take you to sea with something we can't treat correctly.

"Division officers will meet with their people right after quarters and with me in the Wardroom in one hour. Now I have some changes and promotions to announce." He turned to Chief John Maxwell, whose dark eyes were completely rimmed by bruised-looking flesh after nine days with the buxom wife of an Australian Lieutenant who was stationed somewhere in North Africa. Maxwell handed Captain Hinman a sheaf of papers.

"I don't much like reading this first item," Hinman said slowly. "Lieut. Comdr. Joseph J. Sirocco, USNR, you are hereby detached from duty aboard the U.S.S. *Mako* and transferred to Pearl Harbor for further assignment." He looked at Sirocco.

"I'll say this in front of all hands, Joe. You are the very best Executive Officer a submarine Captain could ever have! I'll miss you. Chief Maxwell has your travel orders.

"Lieut. Peter Simms, USN, you are hereby promoted to Lieutenant Commander and will take over as Executive Officer. Pete, my congratulations." Simms grinned, unable to conceal his joy.

"Lieut. j.g. Nathan Cohen, you are hereby promoted to full Lieutenant. I congratulate you, sir, you earned it.

"Gordon L. Rhodes, Chief Torpedoman's Mate, USN, you are hereby promoted to the rank of Lieutenant, Junior Grade, by the order of Admiral Chester Nimitz. The rank is temporary for the duration of the war. Mr. Rhodes, Chief Maxwell has your orders. You will report to Captain Mealey's staff in Pearl for duty.

"John R. Barber, Chief Machinist Mate, USN, you are hereby promoted to the rank of Lieutenant, Junior Grade, by order of Admiral Chester Nimitz. The rank is temporary for the duration of the war. Mr. Barber, Chief Maxwell has your orders. You will report to Captain Mealey's staff in Pearl Harbor.

"Arnold Samuel Ginty, Torpedoman's Mate First Class, you are hereby promoted to Chief Torpedoman.

"Michael P. DeLucia, Torpedoman's Mate First Class, you are hereby promoted to Chief Torpedoman. My congratulations to both of you new Chief Petty Officers." He went on, noting a number of other promotions for members of the crew.

"That's it, gentlemen. Carry on the ship's work. I want to see Mr. Sirocco and Rhodes and Barber in the Wardroom at once. Chiefs Ginty and DeLucia, stand by to see me later this morning."

Sitting in the Wardroom over coffee Captain Hinman looked at Sirocco, Rhodes and Barber.

"It goes without saying that I hate to see you guys go. I never served with three better men, I mean that. Here's what happened.

"Captain Rudd has been detached to work on a project he has been trying to do for a long while—develop a method of using our submarines in groups. The Germans do this. They call their group operations 'Wolf Packs.' It should work for us.

"Captain Mealey has taken over Bob Rudd's job." Hinman looked at Rhodes and Barber. "It was Captain Mealey who made the recommendations for your promotions. He beat me by about two months, I guess. I wanted to do the same thing and keep you aboard. He wants you on his staff. Dusty, he wants you to take over the torpedo problems and he wants you, John, to take charge of engine room refits."

"Is there any chance of refusing this, Captain?" Barber asked. "I just don't see myself as an officer doing shore duty in a war. I don't think Dusty does either, although we haven't had a chance to talk about it, so I'll let him speak his own piece."

"I think you could refuse the promotion," Hinman said. "But if you did it wouldn't sit well. I might be able to keep you aboard for one more patrol run but once that was over you'd probably find yourself assigned to Alaska or Iceland for the rest of the war." He leaned back in his chair. "You've both got close to twenty years in, haven't you?"

"Yes, sir," Rhodes said. "Let me explain something that John didn't make clear. What John said doesn't reflect on either of you, you know that. It's just that we've been working stiffs all our lives, white hats and then Chiefs. It's pretty hard to imagine ourselves as officers."

"Why don't you talk it over and come back in half an hour?" Hinman said. "You can do me one more favor, Dusty." He dropped Rhodes' nickname casually. "If you decide not to take the jobs I've got to get rid of Ginty and DeLucia. Can't carry even two Chief Torpedomen aboard on a patrol. If you do decide to take the promotions would you give me your thinking on which one I should make the Chief of the Boat? Not that anyone could take your place but someone has to take the job."

Rhodes thought for a moment. "Ginty is a marvelous torpedoman. He knows this ship from stem to stern. DeLucia is a damned good torpedoman, one of the best, just not as good as Ginty. He knows the boat as well as Ginty does. But I think DeLucia has the edge on Ginty in organizing and managing ability. If it were up to me I think I'd give the job to DeLucia."

"I don't want to hurt Ginty's feelings," Hinman said.

"Let me talk to him," Rhodes said. Hinman nodded.

Rhodes found Ginty in his Forward Room, checking the work he had asked be done on his torpedo tubes.

"Damned relief crew bastards don't do nothin' right," he growled. "Can't even grease things right! Look at the gobs of guck hangin' off'n these fittings!"

"You should be up on the tender buying yourself a Chief's hat and some khakis," Rhodes said. "Let the other people worry."

"Whaddya mean, let other people worry? This is my fuckin'

room, Chief! I mean Mister Rhodes! This is my room! If I don't do it who the else fuck is goin' to do it right?"

"If I decide to take the gold you'll have a lot of other things to worry about if the Old Man makes you the Chief of the Boat," Rhodes said. Ginty whirled around and stared.

"That's the last fucking thing I want! I ain't no Dusty Rhodes, mother hen to all the fucking chickens!

"I'm Arnold Samuel Ginch Ginty of the Asiatic Submarines! The Old Man gives me your job and I'll go ashore and that red-head will hide me where no Shore Patrol will ever find me. She already told me that!"

"No profit in thinking like that," Rhodes said. "But you're putting the Old Man in a bind. He's been thinking about putting DeLucia in charge of both rooms." He let his voice trail off.

"The Old Man wants his torpedo rooms run right, he wants fish that run hot, straight and normal every damned time, tell him to put me in charge!" Ginty's voice was belligerent. "I ain't taking nothin' away from Mike DeLucia. He's damned good torpedoman. One of the best. But he ain't as good as I am just like I'm not as good as you are.

"DeLucia wants to be Chief of the Boat, for Chrissakes! He studied you all last run, you know what? When you cracked a whip on someone he'd go around day or so later and try to find out how the people felt who got nicked by the whip. Shit, he pure wants that nose-wipin' job! He ain't gonna be one, two, three after you but I'll help him out all I can!"

"I'll suggest that to the Old Man," Rhodes said. Ginty caught his arm in an iron grip.

"Chief, Mr. Rhodes, dammit it's hard to say that! You do more than suggest it! You tell him this is the way it has to be! He'll listen to you, he always listens to you. You do this for me, you hear?"

Rhodes went into the Wardroom where Captain Hinman sat with Pete Simms.

"If you get Ginty and DeLucia in here for a talk, sir," he said, "if you suggest to Ginty that you need the best man you can get to take charge of both Torpedo Rooms, put that first, sir, he'll jump at the chance to do that rather than be Chief of the Boat. DeLucia will do a good job as Chief of the Boat and Ginty will help him all he can. But you'll save face for Ginty and Mike if you work it so Ginty thinks he should be in charge of both rooms." Hinman grinned and nodded his head.

"I'd appreciate it, Dusty," he said, "if you'd talk with Barber about your own situation. I hate to crowd you but if you both decide to refuse the commissions I'm going to need all the time I can get to get you transferred back aboard.

"The trouble is, the Staff doesn't like Pearl Harbor boats or captains. And they might cross me by letting you stay Chief and putting both of you in the relief crews. I don't think either of you want that."

"I'll let you know in half an hour, Sir," Rhodes said and went in search of Barber.

He found the balding man sitting on a bollard on the dock, morosely watching the men he had been in charge of rig the fuel oil lines to fill *Mako*'s fuel oil tanks with 125,000 gallons of fuel oil.

"They doing it right, John?"

"Of course," Barber answered. "I taught them how to do it. Dusty, I don't much like this idea of taking the gold. How do you feel about it?"

"I didn't think about it too much at Quarters," Rhodes said. "It was too much of a shock. Since then I've been thinking a lot about it. I don't much like the idea. All I ever wanted out of this Navy was to be Chief and to do a good job and get my twenty in and then get a good job in the Yard, so I could put the boys through college and so I could be with June all the time. This doesn't change things all that much, we'll both revert back to Chief when the war's over and this means we'd both be home every night in Pearl."

"Means we'd be moving into Officers' Country to live," Barber said. "A lot of officers got no use for a Reserve, got no use for a Mustang who's come up out of the ranks. Got to think of that, got to think about a lot of things. They don't give you enough time for the thinking."

"As long as we're chewing things over," Rhodes said. "If we say no we might be going back to sea with Pete Simms in Sirocco's job. That doesn't make me turn somersaults with joy."

"The son of a bitch has got a screw loose, somewhere," Barber growled. "Old Man came to me before the start of this patrol. You know what Mealey told the Old Man to get rid of Simms? Thought you did. Old Man says he wants to keep him aboard, this was in Pearl, because he said Pete Simms had good stuff in him and that he'd been kicked in the balls by his wife and needed another chance. Shit, the only kick in the balls he's had is the one old Hindu gave him in that head back in the Maneuvering Room!"

"Maybe the Old Man was right," Rhodes said slowly. "Simms did a pretty good job this patrol. He didn't fuck up any."

"How could he fuck up? The engines ran good. Hindu takes care of the electrical stuff like it was a baby. We didn't have any hard things to get over. Outside of Grabby Grabnas' gettin' killed and Tommy takin' that slug through the neck in that silly damned deck gun action we didn't have a tough patrol."

"But the whole idea of taking the gold doesn't sit right, does it?" Rhodes said softly. "It doesn't sit right because it doesn't feel right. It isn't something we wanted. I was up in the Forward Room, talking with Ginty a while ago and that feeling was nagging me when Ginty apologized for calling me Chief. And then I remembered this." He took out his wallet and pulled out a slip of paper and unfolded it.

"Remember this? I showed it to you on patrol. The paper June gave me." He squatted beside Barber and read the words on the paper aloud in a soft voice.

"Accept what is offered even though it is not wanted."

"I remember that," Barber said. "You think what she wrote down was meant for something like this?"

"All she told me was that it would mean something at the right time and I should follow it, that I'd know when the right time was," Rhodes said slowly. "I keep getting a feeling that this is the time her old gods told her about."

"Well, if you take the gold then I'll take it," Barber grunted. They both turned as they heard footsteps.

"How about getting your flat asses up to Ship's Service on the tender and buying yourselves some collar bars and hats so I can take you to lunch at the Officers' Club downtown?" Joe Sirocco said.

"That is, if you don't mind eating in the presence of some people who are pretty stupid, as a rule. Not like the Chiefs' Club, I'm told."

"Heard that the food isn't that good, either," Barber said. "When we get back to Pearl you come out to my house for dinner. That Dottie of mine puts out a meal would make a professional cook in a fancy hotel go and slit his throat!"

"It'll have to be eat and run," Sirocco said. "I think I'll only be in Pearl for a few days."

"Sir," Rhodes said, eyeing the big officer, "let me ask you something straight out. No offense in the asking. None taken if you tell me to mind my own business."

"Go ahead," Sirocco said, grinning.

"You're not a regular officer," Rhodes said slowly. "You might be a Reserve, you might not. But there's something different about you. I'd like to know what it is."

"What gave you that idea?" Sirocco said. He was still smiling.

"Ginty noticed it first, I think," Rhodes said slowly. "The way Captain Mealey treated you. Captain Mealey doesn't like any Reserves. He's Old Navy. You know that.

"Putting you aboard as Exec. when Pete Simms rated the job on the basis of his patrol runs, his time in rank. To quote Ginty: You're too smart for a Reserve, too smart for a regular Navy officer. Too many people higher than you in rank treated you with too much respect. For my own part, I like the way you operate. You're one hell of a man."

"I must have slipped up," Sirocco said slowly. He looked at Rhodes and Barber.

"I'm doing what I shouldn't do," he said. "But I trust you two. Implicitly.

"Yes, there's something different. I'm Naval Intelligence. A Reserve, that's true enough. I was put aboard the *Gudgeon* as a sort of training period. They put five of us aboard submarines so we could get qualified as submarine men. Three of the five were Chiefs, by the way. Just so we'd have the experience.

"Then the war broke out so they left me aboard *Gudgeon* and I made two war patrols. The *Gudgeon*'s Captain didn't know my status. After two runs on *Gudgeon* I went to the Staff at Pearl. Bob Rudd knew about me but no one else other than the Admiral, Nimitz. The reports came in about defective torpedoes, defective diesel engines, lots of those, John.

"Washington thought it was a long-range sabotage plan that was being put into operation. So they sent me to sea on *Mako* with Captain Mealey. To check out the torpedoes. Admiral Nimitz and Bob Rudd figured that Mealey was a hard enough case so that he'd make an aggressive patrol. There were two other submarines closer to Truk than we were, did you know that? They could have taken the assignment but they wanted Mealey to do the work."

"I'll bet Captain Mealey let you know how he felt about having you aboard," Rhodes said. "He isn't the sort of man who would keep that kind of thing to himself."

"What he didn't like, really, was the idea that if there was something wrong with the torpedoes, the exploders I mean, that his word wouldn't be good enough, that I had to be there as an observer and to confirm his report. But he's a hell of a man, you know. He treated me better than I expected and I learned a lot from him."

"And what did you learn about the things they wanted you to find out about, the exploders?" John Barber asked.

"Nothing that you regular Navy people didn't know," Sirocco said. "But that's the way it goes in any bureaucracy. Now I'm going back to Washington for reassignment with a few days off in Pearl. That reminds me, speaking of Pearl: I went up to the Squadron office and fixed things so we don't have to leave here until after *Mako* leaves on her next patrol. I sort of wanted to watch her go to sea and I thought you'd like to do that, too."

"You were assuming we would take the gold?" Rhodes said.

"I didn't assume anything," Sirocco said with a wide grin on his craggy face. "I knew what the plan was.

"If you refused the promotions, either one of you, they were going to fly you back to Pearl, let you have one night with your wives and then march you up in front of Admiral Nimitz to tell him why you preferred to be a Chief in Iceland for the duration of the war to being a Lieutenant in Pearl Harbor, doing important work and being at home every night!"

CHAPTER 29

Dusty Rhodes tried to swallow the lump in his throat and failed as he stood on the New Farm Wharf in Brisbane and watched the U.S.S. *Mako* maneuver in the Swan River to begin the trip downriver to the sea and her fifth war patrol. The *Mako* was the only ship that Rhodes had ever put in commission and, he feared, the last ship that he would love as a sailor. John Barber stood beside him, his face dour.

"She's making too much smoke out of number two engine," Barber grunted. "Damn fool on watch isn't taking care of things like he should."

Rhodes nodded. His eyes were on Ginch Ginty, his new Chief's hat already battered and "seagoing," as he secured *Mako*'s topside for sea. Ginty paused in his labors and *Mako* finished her turn in midriver and his eyes searched the wharf. He raised a hand shoulder high in salute to the two former Chief Petty Officers and then he turned his back on the wharf and went back to his work. Lieut. Comdr. Joe Sirocco, standing a yard or so away, moved up beside Rhodes and Barber.

"Hurts a little, doesn't it?" Sirocco said softly.

"Too damned much," Barber grunted. "That bastard on watch in the Forward Engine Room is letting that number two engine smoke too damned much!"

"It's like watching a daughter get married, I guess," Sirocco said. "No matter how nice the new son-in-law is, you know that he's not good enough for your own flesh and blood." Barber looked at him and then nodded his head and turned away as *Mako*, still trailing a thin plume of smoke from her number two engine exhaust, moved down the river, the pilot boat trailing astern.

Rhodes turned to Sirocco.

"What time does our plane leave, sir?"

"Eighteen hundred," Sirocco said. "They'll send a car for our gear at sixteen hundred. We'd better figure on eating an early lunch and an early dinner or else eat a late lunch and take along a box lunch or something. It's a long way to Pearl."

"How come Ginty's doing topside?" Barber asked as the three men walked down the wharf toward the submarine tender. "De-Lucia's Chief of the Boat, isn't he? Captain didn't change his mind, did he?"

"No," Rhodes answered. "DeLucia's smart. He knew that Ginty wanted to do the topside work, Ginch is a damned good all-around sailor, so DeLucia asked him to take topside. It makes Ginty feel important and it puts him in DeLucia's corner." He looked at Sirocco.

"How long you going to be in Pearl? Long enough for you to come out to the house and meet our families, have dinner with us?"

"Oh, yes, long enough for that. Probably a week or more and then I'll go back to Washington for de-briefing and write reports for about a month and wait for my next assignment."

"I'd hate like hell to have your job," Barber said. "You're a hell of a good sailor, hell of a good submariner, why'd you want to be a damned undercover agent?"

"You make it sound like something dirty," Sirocco said. His big, battered face was grinning. "I didn't ask for it. You know how the military is, you join up and say you're an expert cook and they put you to driving a truck or something. I'm a mechanical engineer. So they made me an intelligence agent. I don't like it, I never wanted it but I do it because they told me to do it. All I can say is that the two patrols on *Gudgeon* and the two on *Mako* made it worth while." The three of them walked by an American Red Cross booth where coffee was on sale and on down the wharf to the Salvation Army booth where coffee and doughnuts were free. Each of them dropped a pound note in the bowl the Salvation Army girl had put at the end of the coffee bar for contributions, accepted their cups of coffee and doughnuts and walked out onto the wharf and stood in the sun.

"What did she draw for a patrol area?" Rhodes asked around a mouthful of doughnut.

"Luzon Straits," Sirocco said. "The stretch of water just north of Luzon Island and south of Formosa. Good water, deep as hell in most places, up to three thousand fathoms if I remember the chart. Lots of small islands to hide behind. The Straits are funnel for all the Jap shipping moving between the Philippines and the Empire; in fact everything going to and from Japan goes through the Straits."

"Sounds like a good area," Rhodes said.

"I'd say choice," Sirocco answered. "I heard there was some bitching from older captains when *Mako* was given the area. A lot of the older guys are still virgins, haven't sunk a ship yet. They want lots of targets so they can collect their medals and get a boost in rank. Before I forget it, I saw a ship movement memo in the Squadron office yesterday. *Eelfish* is over in Freemantle, getting ready to go out on her first patrol. Mike Brannon's her skipper."

"Good man," Rhodes said. He chewed slowly on a piece of doughnut. "Damned good man. *Mako* was lucky. We had Brannon as the Exec. for two runs and then we had you for two runs. I don't know about now, with Pete Simms riding as Number Two."

"He might be all right," Sirocco said slowly. "The Chaplain and the Squadron legal officer were waiting for him when we got in from the last patrol. His wife's divorce went through while we were at sea. The legal officer had all the papers. Pete seemed kind of relieved that it was all over."

"How about their little girl?" Barber asked.

"I don't know," Sirocco said. "Pete said something about being able to see her any time he was in the area as long as the war is going on. Once the war is over there's some sort of an arrangement drawn up so he can see her at regular intervals."

"Damned shame he's such an asshole," Barber said. "That is a nice little kid. His wife is a nice woman, ex-wife I mean. But he's an asshole!"

"You can use that kind of language when you're an enlisted man," Sirocco said with a broad grin. "But officers don't talk about fellow officers in quite that way. You have to say he's a gold-plated asshole."

Chief Torpedoman Ginch Ginty stood in the middle of the *Mako*'s Forward Torpedo Room, his Chief's hat pushed back on his head, his meaty fists on his hips.

"Johnny Paul Shithead," he rumbled. "You seen me get this room ready for a war patrol four times now and by now you should know what you gotta do! I put in for you to get bumped up to First Class and you better by-God do your damned job and do it right or I'll bust your ass down to Second Class again! They's some clothing adrift in that upper bunk aft, they's a thirteen-fourteen tool layin' on the work bench space up for'd and you'll be lookin' for that damned tool in the bilges once we take the first sea outside of the reef. The fuckin' deck outboard of the port sound head is crummy. Do your fuckin' job, sailor!" He turned and stomped out of the Torpedo Room, heading aft. Johnny Paul reached for the sound-powered telephone and dialed the After Torpedo Room.

"He's comin' aft and he's breathin' fire!" he said into the telephone. "Start heavin' around before he gets there!"

Mako dropped her pilot with a wave from Captain Hinman and turned north, her bull nose meeting the first deep swells of the sea, splitting the green water and sending a clean drift of spray out to either side as *Mako* settled down to the long run to her patrol area. In the days that followed *Mako* moved northward through the Coral Sea and then west past Cape York on the northeastern tip of Australia and into the Arafuro Sea. Then she pushed on through the southern edge of the Banda Sea, through the Flores Sea until finally she turned northward. Pete Simms came to the bridge and looked up at the moon, half-covered with clouds, and then walked back to the cigaret deck where Captain Hinman stood.

"We're steady on course three four zero, Captain," Simms said. "We should be abeam of Makassar to starboard in an hour."

"Very well," Hinman said. "When will we be off Balikpapan?"

"Day after tomorrow, roughly," Simms said. "We should be running by on the surface at night. I'll set the course as soon as you tell me how close you want to go into the land."

"The *Permit* cleared the area three days ago," Hinman said. "She's been off the port for the last two weeks. Her Captain's report that we picked up the other night said she'd made some good contacts but couldn't close to fire." He shook his head. "I can't understand that; if they're there you go after them!"

"The *Permit* isn't the *Mako!*" Simms said jovially. "If they're there we'll shake 'em up!"

"Depends," Captain Hinman said. "*Permit* might have made them gun shy. I'm not going to waste any time off the port, just go on by. If something's there we'll attack but I want to get on to our patrol area. It should be a honey! Luzon Strait is the crossroad for everything going and coming to the Empire. You're going to have to be damned careful with your navigation, Pete; the twenty-first parallel of latitude is the dividing line for the Pearl and the Australia boats. We have to be sure to stay well south of the parallel."

"Got it marked with a double red line, sir," Simms said. "Damn it, it's good to be back at sea! Good to get away from all those civilians and those shore sailors!"

"Everything all settled on your legal problems?" Hinman said in a low voice.

"It's over," Simms said. "Over and done with and I'm glad. Never marry a civilian, sir. Civilian women don't know anything about how to keep a house shipshape or how an officer's lady should act."

"I'm sorry it happened, Pete. Sorry for you. Sorry for her and I feel real sorry for your little girl."

"I'm not," Simms said in a thick voice. "From the way her mother acted I'm not sure the kid is even mine!"

Captain Hinman turned his back on Simms and raised his binoculars to his eyes and began to search the horizon to starboard. Simms stood there for a long moment and then he shrugged his shoulders and went forward to the bridge and down below decks. After he had gone Hinman lowered his binoculars and let them hang from the leather thong around his neck. He tipped his head up and watched the SD radar element making its slow circles on top of the radio mast.

He had argued for hours in Brisbane for a new radar, the SJ type, to be installed on *Mako* rather than an old SD type set. The SD was strictly an aircraft warning radar, useless against surface ships. The Staff Communications officer had listened to his arguments with a straight face and then had suddenly smiled at Hinman.

"Captain, you've already demonstrated that you can see ships at night! You don't need this new equipment nearly as bad as some of our Captains who can't seem to see ships in the daylight! Those are the people who need the SJ to convince them they can get into position to attack at night or in a fog. When you come back from this patrol I give you my word I'll have a brand new SJ radar set here for you and we'll install it. And by the way," he paused and began to draw a series of circles on his desk pad with a pencil, "I ordered the sonar gear moved out of the Control Room and back up into the Conning Tower where it was designed to go. I can't understand why the Navy Yard where the ship was built ever shifted that gear down into the Control Room."

"They did it, sir, because I asked them to do it," Captain Hinman said. "I convinced them the Conning Tower was too crowded for that gear up there, that it could be put in the Control Room where it would be close to the Plotting Party. With all respect, sir, I wish you had notified me you were going to do this."

"I didn't think it was necessary to do that," the Staff Communications officer said. "The blueprints show the sonar gear should be in the Conning Tower. I didn't want to bother you on your R and R time for something so trivial."

Lieut. Nathan Cohen shrugged his shoulders when Captain Hinman told him that his sonar gear and dials would be in the Conning Tower. Cohen made some measurements and then took his stool to the ship's carpenter on the submarine tender and had the man cut several inches off each leg of the stool and fasten a battery-powered light to the stool seat so that he could see his dials if a depth charge attack shattered the lights in the Conning Tower, as had happened during the attack on the battleship at Truk.

Captain Hinman walked over to the port side of the cigaret deck and looked forward, seeing the long stretch of water that was now flooded with moonlight. Somewhere out there ahead was the area where he and *Mako* had made their first contact with the enemy. He smiled to himself. The chances he had taken! Altering the sacred torpedo exploders, making a night attack on the surface, broadcasting his defiance of Staff orders to the submarines in the area. He shook his head, smiling gently to himself. He had been bold, almost too bold. But he was still taking chances; the exploders on the torpedoes he carried on this trip had all been modified on his orders. Chief Ginty would have to put them back the way they had been if there were any still left aboard when the war patrol was over. But the risk was worth taking, he felt confident that the exploders would work, he was sure he would have targets. He relaxed, yawning, his hip resting comfortably against the cigaret deck railing as he watched the play of the moonlight on the calm water, listening with half an ear to the muffled conversation between the Officer of the Deck and the quartermaster.

Forty miles astern of the U.S.S. *Mako* the U.S.S. *Eelfish* was plowing northward on almost the same course. Captain Mike Brannon was standing on the cigaret deck, his binoculars hanging from a leather strap around his neck. His Executive Officer, a tall, lean man whose pale blond hair and bright blue eyes marked him as of Swedish descent came back to him.

"What do you have on *Mako*'s position?" Brannon asked.

"We should have them on radar before we dive, sir. We can overhaul and speak to them not long after we surface tonight."

"Thank you, John," Brannon said. "*Mako*'s a fine ship."

"You were Exec. in her, weren't you?" Lieutenant Olsen said.

"Yes, under Art Hinman. They detached both of us after her second run. I was sent to take over our ship and Captain Hinman went on a tour selling war bonds. When that was over they gave the

Mako back to him. I understand she was in a hell of a shape after Arv Mealey took her against that battleship and the destroyers."

"I talked to a guy in Perth who was aboard," John Olsen said. "Old mustang named Botts. He said he couldn't figure out yet how the ship stood up to the depth charging she took. Told me that the depth charges blew the after gun right off the ship and that the attack periscope was bent down at right angles with the lens down near the main deck. Must have been a hell of a thing to go through."

"She's a hell of a good ship," Brannon said. "The people who built her and our ship did a good job." He smiled broadly in the dark. "I wonder what Captain Hinman will say when we speak to him tonight!"

"I hope he doesn't set up and shoot at us!" Olsen said. "I'd better go below now, got some work to do." Brannon nodded and lounged against the quadruple 1.1 pom-pom gun that had been mounted on the *Eelfish's* cigaret deck in place of the 20-mm gun most submarines carried. The 20-mm gun was now mounted on a small bulbous swelling out in front of the bridge and below it. Brannon rubbed his chin. If Hinman agreed perhaps the two ships could run in tandem up to the point where each had to split off to go to their respective patrol areas. If they came across any targets they could mount a twin attack, the sort of thing he and Captain Hinman had spent hours talking about during their first two war patrols. The Germans were very efficient in their use of submarine wolf attacks but the Staff Commanders in Australia and Pearl Harbor had not yet decided whether it was an acceptable form of attack. If he and Hinman could work together on such an attack maybe it would jar the Staff commands into action. He took a deep breath of the humid night air and smelled the faint trace of land in the offshore breeze that was just beginning to ruffle the surface of the ocean. He smiled in the dark as he heard the punch line of a long, very dirty story that the quartermaster was telling to the Officer of the Deck. *Eelfish* was his ship, a good ship with a fine crew. He'd driven them without mercy in the few short weeks he'd had after the ship was commissioned and on the long haul from the East Coast through the Panama Canal and out to Western Australia. In those weeks of endless drills he'd seen the crew change from a group of inexperienced men into a close-knit group of team players, each man knowing his own job and the job of those around him. He was satisfied they could respond to any demand he could make of them, any crisis the enemy could bring. He relaxed against the gun mount, turning his head slightly as he heard the mewling cry of a lone sea bird.

CHAPTER 30

Shortly before midnight *Mako*'s stern lookout drew in his breath in a gasp that was audible down on the cigaret deck. Captain Hinman looked upward.

"Light back there bearing one seven zero, Bridge! The light is blinking on and off, looks like he's sending code!"

"Sound General Quarters!" Hinman barked. "Open doors on all torpedo tubes! Quartermaster, get up in the shears and see if you can read him. He might be a Jap ship and if it is he might think we're one of his navy!"

He heard the rush of feet below decks as *Mako*'s crew went to their Battle Stations and then the voice of Pete Simms came up through the hatch.

"All Battle Stations manned, Bridge. All torpedo tube doors open. Request depth settings for torpedoes, Bridge."

"Set depth two feet on all tubes," Hinman ordered. He was watching the quartermaster squeeze in beside the stern lookout.

"He's sending code, sir. Wait a minute . . . he's saying *Mako* over and over, sir!"

340

"Bridge, get a signal gun up here on the double," Captain Hinman ordered. He waited until the signal gun was handed up from the Conning Tower and passed to the quartermaster.

"Give him an acknowledgment that you read him," Hinman said. "Ask him who he is." He listened to the quartermaster clicking off the code signals with the trigger of the signal gun. The light on the ship aft of them began blinking slowly.

"R . . . E . . . Q . . . request . . . P . . . E . . . R . . . permission to . . . come . . . along . . . side . . . signed . . . Mike. He sent 'request permission to come alongside' and signed it 'Mike,' sir."

"My God, it's the *Eelfish!*" Hinman cried. "Tell him to close, quartermaster, close on our starboard side. Bridge, make turns for one-third speed." Hinman raised his voice.

"All lookouts, keep a very sharp watch in your sectors!" He strained his eyes, searching for the dark bulk of the other submarine and then he saw it, a dim shadowy bulk against the dark horizon.

"Submarine in sight, bearing one six zero, Bridge," the stern lookout said.

"You're not very sharp up there," Hinman snapped. "I saw him thirty seconds ago. Keep your eyes open!"

The *Eelfish* closed rapidly as *Mako* slowed and then slid up alongside *Mako*, barely 50 yards off *Mako*'s starboard beam. Mike Brannon, leaning both hands on the cigaret rail, took a deep breath and yelled.

"*Mako*, ahoy! Is Captain Hinman on the Bridge?"

"I'm here!" Hinman yelled. He turned to the OOD. "Don, take me in closer, I can't yell that far, damn it!" The *Mako* wallowed and began to edge to starboard and then straightened out parallel to the *Eelfish* and a scant 30 feet away. Hinman could see Mike Brannon clearly in the dim moonlight.

"Damned good to see you, Mike! How's everything?"

"Fine, sir. Family is fine, I've got a good ship and a good crew. Congratulations on your marriage. I have a proposition to make to you, sir."

"Go ahead," Hinman said, "but before you do let's get to the important things. They gave us Klim back there in Brisbane instead of ice cream powder. Can you spare us some ice cream powder?"

"Sure thing," Brannon said. The two Captains watched as crew members of the two ships exchanged a heaving line and hauled two 10-pound cans of ice cream powder mix over to the *Mako*.

"How about a fair exchange?" Brannon yelled. "Got any good boogie-woogie records?"

"Nope," Hinman replied. "Now what's your proposition?"

"I'd like to run north with you, if I may," Brannon said. "If we see anything we could attack in tandem. Like we used to talk about in your Wardroom, the first two war patrols, sir."

"Roger," Hinman said. "I'd love to do that."

"I've got a new SJ Radar," Brannon said. "Picked you up way back there. You're senior, sir, but if I may suggest, I could take the van and use my SJ. If we pick anything up you give the orders."

"Agreed," Hinman said. "Take position on my starboard bow, distance one thousand yards. Make turns for fifteen knots. Course will be three five five for the present. When we dive I'll drop back to three thousand yards. Make two knots submerged. We'll surface tonight thirty minutes after full dark. Okay with you, Mike?"

"Aye, aye, Captain," Brannon replied. "We'll take position one thousands yards ahead on your starboard bow. Course three five five. Make turns for fifteen knots. You'll drop back to three thousand yards when we dive. Make turns for two knots submerged. Surface thirty minutes after dark, sir."

"Very well," Hinman yelled across the water. "Where you going to, Mike? We're headed for Luzon Strait. I'm going up the eastern coast of the Philippines."

"We're going to Leyte Gulf," Brannon answered. "Talk to you some more tonight. Nice to see you again, sir."

Captain Hinman watched as *Eelfish* dropped astern of *Mako* and then swung off to starboard and began to pick up speed. He moved to the speaker on the bridge and pressed the transmit button.

"This is the Captain," he said. "We have the *Eelfish* on our starboard bow. She'll travel with us for a few days. Her skipper, for all of you *Mako* plank owners, is Mike Brannon." He paused for a moment. "Secure from General Quarters. Close tube outer doors.

Resume normal watch standing." He punched Don Grilley lightly on the arm and went back to the cigaret deck.

The two submarines moved northward through the Makassar Strait and then angled eastward across the Celebes Sea. They saw no targets. *Eelfish*'s radar twice picked up medium-sized fishing boats as the two ships entered the Celebes Sea and the two submarines had changed course to avoid on Captain Hinman's orders—despite Pete Simms' pointed suggestion that they should go alongside one of the fishermen and board, on the off chance that the boat could be harboring a Japanese naval officer with a powerful radio set who just might be reporting the passage of American submarines.

Five days after the two ships joined forces they passed the southern tip of Mindanao and began a passage north along the east coast of that island. On the night of the fifth day, shortly after the two ships had surfaced, the *Eelfish* requested permission to drop back near *Mako*.

"I have to break off now, Captain," Mike Brannon yelled. "My orders are to proceed through Surigao Strait to my patrol area. Best of luck and good hunting!"

Hinman made the appropriate reply and watched as *Eelfish* dropped astern and then turned to port and was lost to view.

"Alone again, Don," he said to Grilley, who had the deck watch. "Kind of nice thing, having Mike close by for a few days." He went back to the cigaret deck and stood by the after rail, staring out to the port side. Somewhere out there Mike Brannon was making his approach to enter Surigao Strait and go on up to the waters of Leyte Gulf. An hour later the port lookout spoke.

"Ship! Bearing three five zero, Bridge! I can see more than one ship out there!"

Hinman swung himself up into the periscope shears and leveled his binoculars. He jumped back to the cigaret deck and ran forward to the Bridge.

"Sound General Quarters! Plotting Party to the Control Room. Open torpedo tube outer doors and set depth on all torpedoes at two feet! Executive Officer to the search periscope! We've got a convoy out there! Mr. Cohen, get a message off to *Eelfish* that we've picked

up a convoy of at least seven ships and invite him to join the party!"
He listened to the reports coming up to the Bridge in response to his
orders. Pete Simms' voice came up through the hatch.

"Bridge! I have the targets! Five, six, no by God, eight ships out
there! There's two in line and then two abreast and two more abreast
and looks like two more in line back of those ships! Look like small
freighters to me, sir. Estimated range is four zero zero zero yards!"

"Very well," Captain Hinman said. "Don, go below, I'll take
over the bridge. Take charge of the Plot in the Control Room. I'm
going to go in on the surface." He turned and bent toward the hatch
to the Conning Tower.

"Pete, give the periscope to Nate Cohen, we won't be using any
sound bearing in this attack. You come up here and take over the
After TBT station." He waited until Simms had climbed to the
Bridge.

"Take station back there, Pete. If you have to, fire at will but let
me know if you start shooting. There's a lot of ships out there and I
don't want to waste fish." He bent his head as the bridge speaker
rasped.

"Plotting Party is ready, Bridge," Grilley reported and Hinman
heard Nate Cohen feeding the Plotting Party a stream of bearings. He
grinned to himself. It was like the other attack he had made in
Makassar Strait on his second war patrol. Below him he could hear
the voices of Nate Cohen rattling off ship bearings and Bob Edge
repeating them as he fed the bearings into the TDC. Then he heard
Cohen's normally gentle voice sharpen slightly as he spoke to Lieut.
Ronnie Burns, a new officer *Mako* had taken aboard in Brisbane.

"Damn it, Lieutenant, don't just stand there! It's easier for me if
you read the bearing ring when I give you a mark! The Old Man will
tell you when to push that damned shooting key!" Captain Hinman
bent to the hatch.

"Belay that conversation down there! Start feeding me some
data, damn it! I just can't eyeball it up here, there's too many damned
targets!"

The intricate terpischorean ritual of death by torpedo had begun
in *Mako*'s Conning Tower and Control Room. On the Bridge Captain

Hinman fidgeted, waiting until the Plot brought him close enough to begin the attack.

"Damned shame Mike isn't here," he said to himself. He eyed the enemy ships, black splotches against the dark background of the mountains of Mindanao. He searched the line of ships with his binoculars but could see no escort vessels. Maybe they felt safe, this close to Mindanao.

"Bridge! Range to the leading ship in the convoy is now three zero zero zero! Angle on the bow is two zero port. We've got a constant shooting solution from now on, sir!"

"All ahead full!" Hinman barked into the bridge transmitter. "Plot—I'll close to one zero zero zero yards and then begin to shoot! Order of targets will be the first ship in the line and then the second. Then I'll take the inboard ship in the brace of two that follow those first two. After that it's going to be everyone for themselves! We'll get what we can!" He felt *Mako*'s deck quiver under his feet as the ship picked up speed.

"Here we go!" Hinman sang out. "The wolf among the sheep! Give me some ranges, God damn it!"

"You can shoot, Captain!" Bob Edge's voice was high.

"*Fire one!*" Hinman yelled. He felt the shock under his feet as a fist of compressed air shoved the torpedo in Number One tube out. He counted down from six to one.

"*Fire two! Right five degrees rudder! Stand by . . .*

"*Fire three!*"

A mushroom of fire bloomed at the waist of the first ship in the line of enemy ships.

"*Hit! Hit on the first target! Give me more speed, damn it!*

"*Fire four!*

"*Right ten degrees rudder! More speed! Pour on the coal!*"

"*Hit! Hit on the second target!*" Simms' scream came from the cigaret deck aft.

"*Meet your helm right there, damn it! Stand by forward!*" Captain Hinman was braced in the small bridge structure, his binoculars clamped to his eyes. He lowered the glasses and let them hang by the neck strap and gripped the teak edge of the bridge rail.

"Give me a set-up on the next target!" he yelled down the hatch. "We're closing fast, damn it! Look alive down there! Meet that helm, damn you! Meet it right there!"

"You've got a solution on the next target!" Lieutenant Edge's voice from the Conning Tower was high, excited.

"*Fire five!*

"Belay the set-up on the fourth target, he's too small! *Right fifteen degrees rudder!* I want to run down between the third and fourth targets, down the starboard side of that fourth target to the next two targets."

"*Tin can! Tin can!* The other side of this ship to our starboard!" The starboard lookout's voice was a high yell. Hinman spun to his right in the small bridge, searching with his binoculars.

He saw the high bridge of a *Fubuki* destroyer-leader on the far side of the small freighter whose bow was drawing even with *Mako*'s bow. The *Fubuki* and the freighter were on an opposite course to *Mako* and the small freighter was screening *Mako* from any gunfire from the *Fubuki*. He took a quick look ahead at the two ships he had picked out as his next targets. They were at least 1,500 yards distant, he had plenty of time to dive and run submerged under those two ships before the *Fubuki* could work its way clear of the two ships he had hit and the small freighter and get back to him.

"*Close torpedo tube outer doors!*" Hinman yelled the order down the hatch to the Conning Tower. He waited calmly, gauging *Mako*'s speed and the speed of the small freighter that was now almost abeam of *Mako* and barely 50 yards away. He gasped in disbelief as he saw the starboard side of the freighter suddenly blossom into flame as a dozen or more heavy machine guns opened fire. Above him a lookout called out and then moaned as a hail of machine gun fire swept through *Mako*'s bridge structure. Hinman felt a heavy fist slam into his right shoulder and then another fist drove him back from the bridge rail. Instinctively, he slammed his left hand down on the diving alarm and then hit the alarm a second time. Another jolting blow savaged his rib cage and he lurched to one side as the quartermaster's body fell against him. He tried to draw a deep breath to yell the order to clear the bridge but something was blocking his throat.

He opened his mouth and tasted the blood that filled his throat and mouth. As he sagged he reached for the latch that held the hatch to the Conning Tower open and tripped it. The weight of his body forced the hatch closed.

The gunfire that riddled *Mako*'s bridge echoed in the Conning Tower and was heard in the Control Room. When the diving alarm went off Chief Mike DeLucia reacted, yanking the lever on the hydraulic manifold that opened the vent on bow buoyancy tank and then pulling the levers that vented the main ballast tanks. Lieut. Don Grilley moved over from the plotting desk on top of the gyro compass to stand back of the bow and stern planesmen.

"Hard dive!" he said. "There's trouble up there, get her down fast!" He heard a voice yelling faintly over the bridge speaker as *Mako* sliced downward under the sea. He took a quick look at the men in front of him and at DeLucia and then he moved back to the chart table and swiftly marked in *Mako*'s position at the time of diving. That done, he moved back to the bow and stern planes.

"Sir," Dick Smalley on the bow planes half turned toward Grilley. "Sir, what depth do you want?" Grilley suddenly realized that no order had been passed down for a depth. He looked at the depth gauge in front of Smalley. The long black needle was passing 200 feet.

"Ease to a five-degree down bubble," he ordered and went up the Conning Tower ladder until his head and shoulders were in the Conning Tower, bracing himself on the ladder against *Mako*'s diving angle. He saw Nate Cohen standing at the persicope, running the long tube downward. Cohen turned to face him and Grilley saw that Cohen's normally dark face was ashen.

"Where's the Skipper?" Grilley asked.

"No one got off the bridge before we dove!" Cohen said, his voice almost a whisper. "Someone up there started shooting at us. It sounded like they got a lot of hits on the bridge. I heard someone yell and then the diving alarm went off and the hatch was closed from topside. When we went under, when the bridge went under water, the hatch started to leak. Chief Maxwell went up the ladder and found that the hatch was only caught by its latch, it wasn't dogged

down. When he tried to turn the hand wheel I had to hold him on the
ladder so he could use both hands. That's why I was late in getting
the periscope down."

"I think someone was laying on top of the hatch, sir, on top of
the hand wheel on the other side of the hatch," Maxwell said. "At
least that's what it felt like, sir."

"Sir," Mike DeLucia's voice from the Control Room was insis-
tent. "Sir, we're passing three hundred feet with a five-degree down
angle and going all ahead full!"

"Level off at four hundred feet, all ahead one third," Grilley
called down to DeLucia. He looked at Cohen.

"Did you hear the Skipper give the order to clear the bridge,
Nate?"

"No, sir," Cohen said. "We heard a lookout yell that he saw a tin
can, a destroyer, and then the gunfire started. We were awful close to
that one small ship on the starboard side. I had the 'scope turned in
that direction and I could see a big destroyer beyond the small ship
right next to us. The next thing that happened was the diving alarm
went off and there was an awful lot of gunfire and then the hatch
closed. And then the other . . . " his voice trailed off.

"What other?" Grilley asked.

"When I was holding the Chief so he could dog down the hatch
Pete Simms yelled into the bridge transmitter."

"What did he say?" Grilley's voice was patient.

"He was saying 'No! No! No!' " Cohen whispered. "Just that,
over and over!" He looked at Grilley.

"I think you're the senior officer aboard, sir," Cohen said softly.
"You're the Captain!"

"Come on down in the Control Room, Nate," Grilley said. He
waited beside the plotting table until Cohen joined him.

"I'd like to go back up and see if we can pick up our people,"
Grilley said. He looked at the plot.

"There's a destroyer up there, Captain," Cohen said. "I saw the
destroyer. Big ship. I don't imagine we'd have much of a chance if we
stick our head out up there." He hesitated, eyeing Grilley.

"You're the Number Two man in the Wardroom after me,"
Grilley said softly. "I value your thoughts, Nate." He picked up the

phone and dialed the selector switch so he could speak to all compartments.

"Now hear this," he said calmly. "This is Lieutenant Grilley speaking.

"We were attacked by heavy gunfire while we were on the surface, a few moments ago. Captain Hinman sounded the diving alarm and we believe he closed the hatch in the bridge. We don't know because none of the people topside got down below." He waited, listening to the dead silence in the ship.

"I'd like to tell you that we're going to go back up there and get our people back," he said slowly. "But I cannot. There is a big destroyer up there, it was seen by a lookout and Lieutenant Cohen also saw it through the search periscope. We believe the destroyer was the ship that opened fire on us. If we went up there now it might . . . it probably would . . . mean the end of the *Mako* and the death of all hands!

"We don't know if the gunfire hit any of our people or not. I have to assume that some people were hit. Mr. Cohen heard some yelling that indicated someone was hit. All our people topside have on Mae West life jackets and as soon as we can shake this destroyer, or as soon as we can get into a position where we can attack it and sink it we'll go up and start searching for our people.

"Until we have further information, as senior officer aboard I am assuming the duties of the Commanding Officer. Mr. Cohen, as the second senior officer, will act as the Executive Officer." He paused and lifted his thumb from the transmit button and turned to Nate Cohen.

"Did you get the message off to *Eelfish* that we had sighted this convoy?"

"Yes, Captain. We got an acknowledgment that he had the message and that he was coming at top speed to join the attack." Grilley nodded and pressed the transmit button again.

"Mr. Cohen has just told me that Captain Hinman's message to *Eelfish* that we had a convoy in sight was received and that Mike Brannon, the captain of *Eelfish* answered that he was coming at top speed to help in the attack. So let's all do our duty and if *Eelfish* gets here within the hour, as it should, we can have some revenge!"

Cohen stood with his head bowed for a moment and then he looked at Grilley.

"Do you want me on the sonar gear, Captain, or do you want to put Aaron on the gear?"

"I'd rather have your ears, Nate, if you don't mind," Grilley said. Cohen nodded and climbed the ladder into the Conning Tower.

"Four hundred feet, Captain," Chief DeLucia said. His calm brown eyes looked at Grilley.

"Do you want me to go through the ship, sir, talk to the people?"

"I don't think that's necessary, Chief. I appreciate the offer." He turned his face toward the Conning Tower hatch.

"Mr. Cohen, give me all the bearings you can get, please."

He stood at the plotting chart, marking in the bearings that Cohen fed down to him.

"That single-screw stuff, the slow ships we shot at, are breaking off in all directions, sir," Cohen said. "Here's what I've got." He rattled off a half-dozen bearings.

"There's a solid twin-screw bearing that I think is the destroyer the lookout sighted and I saw," Cohen said. "It now bears two seven five and I've picked up one other twin-screw beat. It's up ahead of us and it bears three five zero, sir. I think that we have two destroyers—repeat two destroyers up there!"

Grilley marked in the bearings on the plot, chewing his lip reflectively. Apparently the Japs had sent the convoy down the coast of Samar with the escort vessels trailing, hiding astern of the small convoy, inviting an attack.

The twin-screw ship bearing three five zero is picking up speed, sir!"

A metallic *ping* rang through *Mako*'s hull and then a series of *pings* hit *Mako*'s hull.

"Ship bearing two seven five is pinging on us, Captain!" Cohen's voice was calm.

Lieut. Don Grilley stood at the chart table, staring down at the plot he had drawn. *This is where Captain Mealey had stood when the Japanese destroyers attacked Mako at Truk. This is what they meant when they taught you in Officer's Candidate School that command is the loneliest job in the world. It was up to him to make the decisions that would result in* Mako's *outwitting and escaping the enemy or being overcome. There was no one to turn to for advice. The ship, the lives of almost seventy men, rested on his shoulders.*

He looked at this wrist watch. It would be at least forty to forty-five minutes before *Eelfish* could reach their area. Cohen's voice came down through the hatch.

"The two ships out ahead of us are beginning to increase speed, Captain. I think this is an attack run!"

"Rig ship for depth charge attack," Don Grilley said to Chief DeLucia.

Mako waited.

CHAPTER 31

Captain Mike Brannon leaned over the chart in the Control Room of *Eelfish* and looked at the plot his Executive Officer had drawn in.

"I think we left him too damned soon, John," Brannon said. "Art Hinman always did have luck! How far are we from him?"

"Twenty-one miles, sir," Lieutenant Olsen said. "An hour and five minutes if we push it." He pointed at the chart. "We can cut across the corner, sir. Plenty of water out here. This is the edge of the Philippine Trench. There's over fifty-five hundred fathoms of water in this area."

"We'll push it," Brannon said. "Damn it, I don't want to miss out on the fun! Let's send the crew to General Quarters now." Olsen pushed the General Quarters alarm button and Brannon waited until the gong had stopped ringing and the reports had come in that the crew was at Battle Stations. He picked up the telephone.

"This is the Captain speaking," he said. "Our friends on the *Mako* waited until we'd left and then they picked up a convoy! They were good enough to tell us about it and we're going over and join their party. It will be an hour or so before we get there so stand easy on Battle Stations. The galley can serve coffee in the next fifteen minutes and all hands cross their fingers and toes and hope that Captain Hinman doesn't sink all the ships before we get there!" Brannon turned to John Olsen.

"Set the course and let's get going," he said. "Doggone that Art Hinman, he always was a lucker sucker! I'm going topside, John. When you've got the plotting party organized come on up. If I know Art Hinman he's going to attack on the surface and we'll do the same. I'll need you on the After TBT. We might be able to knock off one or two of the convoy if they're running from the attack."

Captain Brannon climbed up to the bridge and repeated what he had said on the telephone to the bridge watch and the lookouts. As he went back to the cigaret deck he glanced upward and saw the SJ Radar turning above him.

"Fifty-five hundred fathoms, you said?" Brannon said to Olsen. "God, that's deep! Wonder if you'd have any layers in water like that?"

"I doubt it," Olsen said. "The chart shows a strong current running there."

"I wonder what that convoy's doing, running without escorts," Brannon mused. "Seems odd."

"They're pretty close to our patrol area, Leyte Gulf," Olsen said. "Maybe they felt safe this close to a major port."

A half hour went by and then the port lookout spoke up.

"Bridge! I can see a flickering red light bearing three five zero! Looks like a little fire, sort of!"

"Try and get a radar bearing!" Brannon said. He turned his head upward and saw the radar settle on the lookout's bearing.

"No contact, Bridge," the radar operator sang out. "Maybe the ship is below the horizon or maybe it's too small to pick up at this range, sir."

"Very well," Brannon said. "Keep trying." He walked back and forth across the small cigaret deck, waiting.

"Got me another little flickering light!" the port lookout called out. "Two flickering lights, Bridge!"

"Radar contact bearing three five zero!"

"All ahead flank!" Brannon ordered. He went to the bridge and bent his head to the bridge transmitter.

"All hands, this is the Captain. We've got two ships up ahead of us that appear to be on fire and we've got radar contact. *Mako* must have hit some targets. Now it's our turn! We're going to go in and get 'em! All hands stand by for a surface attack with torpedoes! I'll slow down to let you open the outer doors when the time comes."

"Plot is running, Bridge," the voice came up through the Bridge speaker. "We're on an intercept course with the contacts."

"Very well," Brannon said. He turned to the Officer of the Deck. "Go below, Jim. I'll take over now. Stand by to dive if we have to do that."

"Bridge!" the radar operator's voice was sharp. "I've got a lot of small blips up there and one pretty big blip! Bearing is zero zero one!"

"Keep the bearings coming," Brannon said. He raised his binoculars. The flickering lights the lookout had reported were within his sight. He turned his face upward toward the lookouts.

"Can you see what kind of ships are burning?"

"Looks like two kinda small ships, sir," the port lookout answered. "I can see some other small ships now, little ships they look like. They bear from dead ahead to three four five degrees, sir."

An echoing boom rang across the water and then another and another.

"Depth charges!" Lieutenant Olsen called out from his post at the Aft TBT. "Those sound like depth charges, Captain!"

Fleet Captain Akihito Hideki of the Imperial Japanese Navy put a bathrobe on over his pajamas with a word of thanks to the seaman who had brought him the robe. He rubbed the sleep from his eyes and turned to the commanding officer of the *Fubuki* destroyer-leader that was designated *Eagle*.

"Please bring me up to date."

The *Fubuki*'s commanding officer pointed out to the port side where the flames from two ships were clearly visible.

"The two lead ships, loaded with lumber as you know, were attacked by a submarine on the surface. Both were hit. The fires are now under control. The submarine then attacked the inboard ship of the next two. They were in formation side by side. The torpedo missed and the submarine then ran down between our two ships. The captain of the outboard ship reports that he opened fire on the submarine with all his machine guns and that he scored a great many hits on the submarine's bridge."

"They always say they hit the target," the Professor said.

"The range was only about forty-five meters, sir."

"Hm, in that case maybe they did hit what they shot at. When they opened fire did the submarine return the fire?"

"No, sir. It dove immediately."

"Not because of any damage, I'd bet," the Professor said. "The vulnerable part of a submarine is not its bridge, you can wipe that off the ship and not hurt it greatly. They should fire at the pressure hull!"

"Contact!" the telephone talker on *Eagle*'s bridge raised his voice. "We have a contact . . . zero five zero . . . range two zero zero zero yards."

"Depth charge settings?" the Professor asked quietly.

"As you ordered sir; the Y-guns are set for four hundred feet. The charges on the racks are staggered from two hundred to six hundred feet, sir."

"Signal *Eagle*'s Feather One to make an attack down the target's track. We'll follow to the starboard of the track." The *Eagle*'s commanding officer said a few words to his telephone talker and then raised his arm. He dropped it and a signalman on the wing of the bridge aimed his light at Eagle Feather One.

The first attack on *Mako* went awry. *Eagle*'s Feather One dropped its charges too quickly and *Eagle,* following to starboard, dropped its charges too late. Even so the heavy charges, many of them exploding at depths greater than *Mako* was cruising, shook the submarine heavily. In the Forward Torpedo Room Johnny Paul turned to Chief Ginty.

"God damn it," he said in a half-whisper, "we got a feather merchant playing Captain and we're gonna get the shit kicked out of us!" He winced as Ginty's massive hand closed on his upper arm.

"Shut your fuckin' trap, sailor!" Ginty rasped in Paul's ear. "You're in charge this fuckin' room! The people here look up to you so don't go bad-mouthin' Grilley! Do your fuckin' job, man!" He turned and started for the after end of the room. A member of the reload crew stopped him.

"Captain's dead, Chief?"

"Either dead or swimmin,' " Ginty answered.

"Looks pretty bad, hey? No Captain?"

"What's bad?" Ginty grunted. "You're makin' your first war patrol and you sit here bellyachin'! Them topside people is either dead or they're being picked up by the Jap ships or they're swimmin' and the beach is fuckin' miles away! Which is worse off, them or you?

"You heard Captain Grilley, *Eelfish* and Captain Mike Brannon is on the way. Fuckin' Jap is gonna get a big surprise!" He reached for a dog on the water-tight door and swiveled it around and reached for a second dog. A series of *pings* echoed through *Mako*'s hull. Ginty dogged the door down tight and went back to the forward end of the torpedo room. He turned and faced the people in the room.

"Alla you people with nothin' to do and that means all of you, you get in bunks and hold on and don't make no noise! Ol' Jap has got a bearin' on us and he's gonna drop some shit on us! For you people ain't heard no depth charges, don't shit your skivvies! What you hear ain't gonna hurt you!"

In the Maneuvering Room just forward of the After Torpedo Room, Chief Hendershot cocked his head upward as he heard the sound of the Japanese sonar.

"Told me when I shipped in this Navy," he said to the man sitting beside him in front of the control console, "told me that joining the Navy was like getting married. It was for better or for worse and son of a bitch if this isn't one of the worse parts comin' along now!"

The second attack on *Mako* was coordinated precisely. The two destroyers under the command of the *Fubuki* destroyer-leader called *Eagle* wheeled and formed up and ran down *Mako*'s track, one on each side. The Y-guns roared, sending their charges far out to each side, the depth charges tumbling awkwardly through the air before hitting the water with a great splash and sinking downward. On the narrow sterns the depth charges rolled off the racks and plunged straight downward. *Mako* shook and rolled, groaning under the heavy pounding of the explosions. Don Grilley, holding on to the chart table for support, looked at Aaron at the bathythermograph. Aaron's wide blue eyes narrowed slightly and then he shook his head. No layers.

"He twists and turns oddly," the Professor said to the *Fubuki*'s commander as the two men studied the neatly drawn plot of *Mako*'s movements. The Professor looked up at the taller, younger officer. He tapped the plotting paper with a bony forefinger.

"I see what you mean, sir," the *Fubuki* commander said as he looked at the plot. "The target is behaving as our targets used to act in your school. He's predictable. He turned toward the attacking ship's track to avoid the spread from the Y-guns and continued his turn full circle to get away from the charges dropped in the attacking ship's wake." He shrugged.

"Maybe he is not very experienced," he said slowly.

"Would an inexperienced submarine captain carry out such a bold attack on the surface? I find that hard to believe." The professor shook his bald head.

"A number of American submarines have attacked on the surface in recent weeks," the *Fubuki* commander said. "Our intelligence reports show that. Perhaps it is now one of their new techniques."

"We'll see," the Professor said. He picked up a pencil and drew three lines on the plot.

"There: *Eagle*'s Feather One will come down here, on this side of the target. The target, if he acts as he has done, will follow this line and we will be here. We will not fire the Y-guns but we will drop two charges and then slow to listen. If he turns into the first attacking ship's track and continues his turn, as he has done before, then we will come," his finger snapped down against the paper. "We will come here, turning with him and intercept him!" He grinned at the younger man.

"Now, let's get a solid bearing on this fellow and we'll see if this tactic works!"

Nate Cohen pushed his left earphone pad up on his temple and listened as *Mako*'s hull rang under a barrage of sonar searching beams. He leaned toward the Control Room hatch.

"Two ships doing all that pinging, Captain. I'd bet a bagel with lots of lox and cream cheese that we're going to catch a good one!"

"Very well," Grilley said. He turned to DeLucia.

"When Nate gives us the word the attack run has started take me down to five hundred feet. They know by now that we've been steady at four hundred, so now we'll mess up their depth charge settings." He stood at the chart table, looking at the plot, wishing that Captain Mealey—or Captain Hinman—were there.

"Here they come!" Cohen's voice carried from the Conning Tower.

"Five hundred feet! Ten degree down bubble!" DeLucia said.

"First ship is coming up our starboard side!" Cohen said. "Coming fast! Second ship is astern of the first one and off to our starboard."

"Right full rudder!" Grilley ordered. *Mako* banked slightly as she turned and drove deeper under the sea. A depth charge exploded with a shattering roar, breaking light bulbs and showering the interior of the ship with shattered cork insulation. Another depth charge crashed and *Mako* shook violently.

"Six hundred feet!" Grilley ordered. He held on to the chart table with both hands as *Mako* shuddered under a string of heavy explosions that seemed to be all around the ship. He looked down at the plot and then let go with one hand to sweep the bits of cork from the paper.

"Left full rudder!" Grilley said suddenly. "We turned full circle the first time. This time we'll only go half way. Steer course one seven zero, helm."

"Second ship is starting its run, Control! Coming like a bat out of hell!" Grilley looked upward as the distant drum of the *Fubuki*'s twin screws cut through the turbulence left by the depth charges.

"He's dropping!" Cohen said. "I think he's off the track, Control, he's out to starboard!" A series of explosions shook *Mako* but not as violently as the others had done. Grilley swiftly drew in the lines on the plot.

"Steady on course one seven zero, sir," the helmsman said.

"Very well," Grilley said. He smiled inwardly. How easy the

jargon of command came to his lips! If only the ability to outwit a destroyer commander would come as easily. He sighed and stared down at the plot.

"He fooled us!" the Professor said. "He did not complete his turn as he had done before!"

"You sound almost pleased!" the *Fubuki* commander said.

"Not pleased, but maybe a little gratified. We are true professionals. It does us no honor to defeat an amateur!"

"Contact!" The telephone talker on *Eagle*'s bridge sang out. "*Eagle*'s Feather One has the target bearing two four five, depth six hundred feet, sir."

The Professor bent over the plot, his pencil darting. "This and then this, do you see? Form our ships up so, and so, and then . . . "

The sound of the depth charging was clearly heard on the bridge of the *Eelfish* as she raced toward the action.

"Secure the radar," Brannon ordered. "I don't want one of their radio operators to pick it up." He braced his elbows on the bridge rail and held his binoculars to his eyes. Up above him the port lookout spoke.

"Bridge! I've got two ships, dead ahead! I can see a lot of white water shooting up, too!" The sullen roar of exploding depth charges rolled across the black water.

"Plot!" Brannon barked. "Give me a set-up on those two ships dead ahead. Conning Tower, give me a range!"

"Range is five zero zero zero yards to the nearest of the two ships, Captain."

"Clear the bridge!" Brannon shouted. He stood to one side as the lookouts and then his Executive Officer plunged down through the hatch. He took one last look at the two ships ahead of him, dark shapes against the rising moon. He punched the diving alarm twice and dropped through the hatch. *Eelfish* slanted downward.

"I want to run right in on them, John," he called down the hatch to Olsen. "They're busy as hell giving *Mako* a working over. I'll give them something to think about!" He stepped over to the periscope and waited until *Eelfish* had leveled off at periscope depth. He caught the handles of the periscope as it rose and snapped them outward.

"Sixty-five feet," he called down the hatch. He steadied the cross hairs in the periscope on the two ships.

"Mark!"

"Bearing three five zero," the assistant TDC officer said.

"Range is four zero zero zero yards," Brannon said. He looked toward the hatch.

"Give me a course to the target bearing," he said calmly. "Open all torpedo tube outer doors. Set depth on all torpedoes at two feet. Repeat: two feet." He put his eye to the lens again.

"All tube doors open. Depth set at two feet on all fish, sir."

"Very well. Let's start the shooting run, Plot. Stand by . . . Mark! Range is three five zero zero. How does it look?"

"What range do you want to shoot, sir?" the TDC officer looked at him.

"One thousand yards," Brannon said. "I want to be sure of hitting the bastards!"

"If the targets don't move away we'll be in shooting position in twenty-two minutes, sir."

"They'll move," Brannon said dryly, "They're maneuvering all over the damned ocean out there. Stand easy, they're about to start another run on *Mako*. Plot, let's go to full speed for a few minutes, I want to close the range and be ready for them when they form up for the next run on *Mako*." He felt the deck vibrate under him as the screws bit into the water.

The young officer at the TDC was deadly serious. "At this speed now, sir, you should be able to shoot in thirteen minutes."

"Don't solve the problems before we know what the other guy is going to do," Brannon said softly. "Just stand easy." He ordered the periscope run down and stood patiently, looking at his watch from time to time. He signaled to the assistant TDC officer to raise the periscope.

"We can slow down now, Plot," he called out. He put his eye to the persicope and the people in the Conning Tower saw the muscles under his shirt bunch.

"Stand by. . . . Mark! Range to the nearest target is . . . two zero zero zero! Angle on the bow is zero six zero starboard! Start the problem! As soon as this guy commits himself to his run I'm going to give him three from the forward tubes and then try for a set-up on the other target. The second target is out beyond our first target."

"Surface ships are speeding up, sir," the sonar man said.

"Stand by . . . stand by. . . . Mark! Range is one two zero zero yards . . . angle on the bow is zero five zero . . . "

"You can shoot, sir! We have a solution!"

"*Fire one!*" Brannon began counting down from six to one.

"*Fire two!*

"*Fire three!*" Brannon turned the periscope to the second target.

"Mark! This is on the second target! Mark! . . . Range is one eight zero zero . . . angle on the bow is zero nine zero starboard . . . no . . . Hold everything! He's turning away and speeding up. Keep me on this course, Plot. We'll catch him in a minute!"

The first two torpedoes fired by *Eelfish* missed astern. The third torpedo slammed into the stern of *Eagle*'s Feather One and the combined explosive force of the torpedo and the score of depth charges on the stern racks erased all of *Eagle*'s Feather One from the stern to the bridge. The *Eagle*, trailing its sister ship and to its port, shook violently in the huge explosion.

"*Eagle*'s Feather One!" The *Fubuki*'s commander stood, shocked. "Her depth charges exploded! Come right, helm, head for her!"

"Alter your course to her course and proceed with the attack!" The Professor's voice was cold, distant. "We can do nothing for her or her people. Attack the target!"

In *Mako*, six hundred feet below the surface, Nate Cohen's keen ears picked up the high whine of the torpedo screws. His eyes widened as he heard the thrashing scream of the high-speed torpedo screws and then he shook his head in pain as the explosion that blew *Eagle*'s Feather One to bits blasted through *Mako*'s sound heads.

"I heard torpedo screws, two or three of them!" Cohen yelled down the hatch to the control Room. "I heard the screws just before that big explosion! I know that was a torpedo hit, sir, I know it! The torpedo screws went right in the bearing of the ship I was tracking!"

"Left full rudder," Grilley ordered. He looked at Chief DeLucia. "If Mr. Cohen is right, and he is almost always right, that means that Mike Brannon is close by! Nate, where did the torpedo screws come from, did you get a bearing?"

"Came from starboard and aft, sir. The ship I was tracking had just started to speed up. It bore one nine zero, sir." He waited, knowing that Don Grilley would be marking the bearings in on the plot.

"I heard the torpedoes running from starboard to port, well aft. The submarine that fired them has to be somewhere out there on our starboard quarter!"

"Rudder amidships," Grilley ordered. "Meet her right about there!" He looked from the gyro compass repeater to his plot. If he could maneuver *Mako* a little farther in this direction then the remaining Japanese destroyer would be between *Mako* and *Eelfish*. He chewed his lip reflectively. Should he go up to periscope depth and join in the attack on the enemy destroyer or should he stay down at this depth and let *Eelfish* deal with the destroyer? If he went up would he interfere with Mike Brannon's attack strategy? What would Mike Brannon expect Captain Hinman to do? Brannon and Hinman had talked for hours in the Wardroom on the first two war patrols about the advantages of two submarines attacking a target. Captain Hinman would go up and join the fight. He turned to DeLucia.

"You're the Diving Officer, Chief. Take me up to sixty-five feet!" He reached for the telephone.

"This is Captain Grilley. *Eelfish* has arrived! The last big explosion we heard was a torpedo from *Eelfish* hitting one of the destroyers that have been attacking us! Mr. Cohen heard the torpedo running, he heard two or three torpedoes running and he tracked one of them right into the enemy bearing! We're going up and get into the fight and get that other bastard up there! All hands stand by, we'll open the torpedo tube outer doors at sixty-five feet . . . correction . . . make that open the torpedo tube doors as we pass ninety feet on the way up." He reached over to hang up the telephone and was thrown to his knees by two tremendous explosions. Dimly he heard Cohen shouting that the second destroyer had begun its attack. Two more gigantic explosions shook *Mako,* rolling the ship to starboard forty-five degrees. As *Mako* rolled back another depth charge exploded close aboard and Chief DeLucia's grip on the Conning Tower ladder was broken and he hurtled across the Control Room. He scrambled to his feet and collapsed on the deck. As Grilley watched, DeLucia crawled back to the Conning Tower ladder, his right leg beneath the knee sticking out at a sickening angle.

"I think my fucking leg is broke!" DeLucia grated as he hauled himself upright against the ladder. "Watch your God damned bubble, Smalley!"

"Damage reports," Grilley said to the telephone talker.

"Oil! Big bubbles of oil bearing two nine zero!" The port lookout on *Eagle's* bridge raised his voice in a triumphant yell. The Professor and the *Fubuki's* commander rushed to the wing of the bridge, their eyes following the lookout's pointing arm. The oil was clearly visible in the moonlight.

"We've hurt him!" the Professor said. He smoothed his goatee. "A very nicely executed attack, sir." He walked back to the plotting board. "Let's get a bearing on him as quickly as we can. Then we'll finish him off!"

"Torpedo! Torpedo!" The wailing cry came from the starboard lookout. "Torpedo passing ahead!"

"From that side?" The Professor stared down at the plot. "Impossible!"

"Contact!" The telephone talker's voice was high, excited. "Sound Room reports submarine contacts bearing two nine five and zero four zero!"

"Fifteen degrees right rudder, all ahead flank speed!" The *Fubuki's* commander snapped out the order and the *Eagle's* bow reared and then settled as her powerful screws roared to full speed.

"Two submarines!" The Professor looked at the *Fubuki's* commander. Then he bent over the plot, his small bony fingers holding a pencil swiftly traced the *Eagle's* change of course and marked in the bearing of both submarines. He laid the pencil down and belted his bathrobe tightly about his waist.

"I will take charge, Isoruko," he said quietly. "Left full rudder.

Drop two charges from the stern racks as we are well into the turn."
He looked down at the plot and then at his former student.

"The second submarine will expect us to attack him so he will go
deep, too deep to fire torpedoes. We will not follow his expectations!"
He cocked his head as the explosions of the two depth charges roared
in the night. "Reduce speed to one-third, please. Get me a bearing on
the target, the first target! We will finish him off with this attack and
then we will have a second submarine for an encore!"

"First target bears zero one zero, sir!" The telephone talker on
Eagle's bridge spoke up.

"All ahead full," the Professor said calmly. "Captain, you will
signal the dropping pattern, please." The *Fubuki*'s commander nodded and raised his right arm. Then he brought it down with a swift
motion. The big Y-guns roared and sent their charges tumbling
through the air and on the stern of the *Fubuki* the gunnery ratings
began to release the depth charges.

Eelfish was passing 150 feet when the young sonar man reported the attack run had begun on *Mako*. The sailor's eyes widened
as he listened.

"Explosions all around out there, sir. Worst noise I ever heard,
sir!"

"The son of a bitch is a professional," Mike Brannon said. "He
wants his first target! Blow Safety! Blow Negative! Open the outer
tube doors at one hundred feet! Stand by to flood Negative, John, I
want to show my bridge to that son of a bitch! Maybe that will draw
him off of *Mako*. Come on, get me up! He can't hear anything out
there with all that noise! I want that son of a bitch to see us! Then I'll
take him!"

Mako twisted in the wracking explosions, her hull groaning and
creaking. In the After Torpedo Room the lights blew out and the
one-inch thick steel holding pins on a torpedo rack holding a 3,000-
pound torpedo sheared off and the rack slammed across the room and
crushed a reload team member.

The Control Room telephone talker turned to Captain Grilley.

"Maneuvering Room, Chief Hendershot, reports that the starboard propeller shaft started to run wild and he's shut down that
screw, sir! The Chief says we might have lost the wheel, sir!"

DeLucia leaned over from his position at the ladder and tapped the stern planesman on the shoulder.

"You still got stern planes?" The man nodded.

"If we lost a wheel, sir," DeLucia said, "we'd probably lose the stern planes too. Must have been the shaft, is all."

"Very well," Grilley said. "Helm, we've only got one screw turning, port side. Compensate for that." He turned his head toward the Conning Tower hatch as Cohen spoke.

"He's turned and he's coming back, Control! He's coming fast!"

A series of heavy explosions shook *Mako*. DeLucia fought back the desire to yell with pain as he was knocked to the deck. He held on to the ladder, his right leg sticking out at an odd angle.

"Two hundred feet, sir, five degree up bubble!"

"Keep her coming," Grilley said.

"After Torpedo Room is flooding!" The telephone talker's face was white in the light of the emergency lanterns. "After Room reports they've got a split in the After Trim bulkhead between the tubes an inch wide! Room is flooding, sir!"

"Order the Maneuvering Room to open the salvage air valves to the After Room," Grilley snapped.

"Hard to keep her ass up, sir!" The stern planesman had his planes on full rise. Grilley felt the deck under his feet tilt as *Mako*'s stern sank.

"Blow Number Seven Main Ballast!" Grilley ordered. His mind was sorting out the factors. The After Torpedo Room held almost 140 tons of sea water if it were flooded completely. The Number Seven Main Ballast tank held 39 tons of sea water. If they could get enough air pressure into the After Torpedo Room to hold the water in check before the tonnage of flood water outweighed the water he had blown out of the ballast tank, there was a chance *Mako* could be kept on an even keel.

"Number Seven is blown dry, sir," the auxiliaryman said. *Mako* sagged, her stern down, her bow rising.

"Blow Main Ballast Six Able and Six Baker!" Grilley said. He waited as the high pressure air roared through the manifolds, blowing dry two of the four tanks in the Number Six Main Ballast group. *Mako*'s stern began to rise slightly.

"We're gonna broach!" DeLucia yelled. "Forty feet and going up fast! We're gonna surface, sir!"

The lookout stationed on the port wing of the *Eagle* saw *Mako's* bow burst through the surface of the dark sea. His yell brought a calm response from the *Fubuki's* commander.

"Right ten degrees rudder! Gunnery officers—your target is a submarine bow! Commence firing!" He watched, not bothering to use his night binoculars, as the shell splashes neared *Mako's* bow.

"Submarine! Submarine bearing zero nine zero!" the starboard lookout yelled.

"Blow Main Ballast Six Charlie and Dog!" Grilley ordered. "Let's see if that won't get this damned up angle off her! He whirled as a giant hammer blow rang through *Mako's* hull.

"What the hell was that? Get me a report!"

Chief Torpedoman's Mate Arnold Samuel "Ginch" Ginty died as he had lived for the better part of the past sixteen years, standing in front of his torpedo tubes as a five-inch shell from the destroyer burst through the *Mako's* hull just aft of the tubes. Four of the reload crew escaped the hail of shrapnel that riddled the Torpedo Room and drowned as the last of Number Six Ballast Tank blew dry and *Mako's* bow came down to an almost even keel. The flooded Forward Torpedo Room dragged *Mako's* bow downward and the ship began a long slide back down into the sea from which it just burst.

"Can't raise the Forward Room, sir!" The Control Room talker clutched at the chart table as *Mako* began her descent.

"Blow Bow Buoyancy!" Grilley snapped.

"Blowing bow buoyancy tank, sir!"

"I don't have a reading on bow bouyancy vent, sir!" The auxiliary electrician who had taken over Chief DeLucia's Battle Station at the hydraulic vent manifold rapped his knuckles against the indicator panel that showed with lights whether the vents and flood valves were open or closed.

"I got no light at all, no red and no green on bow buoyancy!"

"Keep blowing!" Grilley ordered. "Telephone, try the Forward Battery, see if Thomas can tell us what's wrong up there!"

The telephone talker hunched over his mouthpiece. Then he raised stricken eyes to Don Grilley.

"Tom says he looked through the bull's-eye glass in the water-tight door. He says all he can see is water!"

"Passing one hundred feet Captain," DeLucia said from the deck beside the ladder.

"Blow all tanks! Blow everything!" Grilley snapped.

"Stand by forward!" Mike Brannon ordered. "He's shooting at our bridge! Son of a bitch has seen us! Turn, you bastard, turn! Mark! Range is one three zero five! . . . angle on the bow is thirty port! . . . stand by . . .

"*Fire five!* . . .

"*Fire six!* . . . *Left full rudder . . . stand by aft!*"

"Torpedoes running hot straight and normal, sir!" The sonar man's voice was low but intense, charged with the excitement he felt.

Mike Brannon's eye was glued to the periscope lens as he twisted the periscope around. He saw the *Fubuki*'s high, knife-like bow plainly in the bright moonlight and then he saw a dull orange flower at the destroyer's midsection that changed to bright red.

"*Hit!*" Brannon yelled. "*Hit!*"

Another bright flash enveloped the side of the *Fubuki* just below its bridge and Brannon saw the entire bridge rise up in the air as the ship's boilers exploded.

"Got you, you bastard!" Brannon yelled. "We've got him! Now where the hell is *Mako*?" He swung the periscope savagely, searching the sea.

"Start a sonar search!" He said to the sonar operator.

"Lots of noise out there, sir, have to wait a minute . . . "

"To hell with the damned noise! Start the sonar search! That destroyer was firing its guns at something on the far side from us. Had to be the *Mako*! Stand by to Battle Surface! He jammed his hand down on the klaxon horn button three times and the *Eelfish* surged upward, its gun crews fighting for balance as they raced to the Control Room and up the ladder to the Conning Tower.

Mike Brannon opened the bridge hatch before the bridge had drained itself of water, fighting his way upward through the solid

12 FINAL HARBOR

wall of water that came pouring through the hatch onto him.

"Left ten degrees rudder!" he called down as the gun crews went over the bridge rail and down to the deck. He raised his glasses and began to search the sea beyond the flotsam of the blasted *Fubuki*.

"Meet your helm right there, all ahead one third, Mr. Olsen, get up here!" He pointed out to port as Olsen stood beside him.

"That's where the destroyer was when we hit her," he said. "She was heading, oh, her bow was pointed right at about where we are now and she was firing to port. So *Mako* must have been out there, somewhere. She must have come up to help us and then went back down when the destroyer opened fire."

"Contact!"

"Give me a bearing, Sonar!"

"Contact bears zero one zero, sir."

"Get on the sending key!" Brannon yelled. "Tell *Mako* to come on up, the party's over!"

The pulsing beam of the sonar from *Eelfish* rang against *Mako*'s hull. Aaron, standing at the bathythermograph, listened intently.

"Code, sir," he said to Don Grilley. "He listened to the long and short sounds hitting *Mako*'s hull.

"He says to come up, the party is over. Signed *Eelfish*"

Grilley looked at the depth gauge. It read 150 feet. *Mako* was slowly, inexorably, sinking.

"Aaron," Grilley said, "Get up there beside Mr. Cohen and get on the sending key. Tell *Eelfish* we have both torpedo rooms flooded, one screw out of commission and sign my name."

"Tell him to blow everything! Blow every damned thing he's got!" Brannon called down the hatch after *Eelfish* had received *Mako*'s message. Brannon waited.

"He says he's tried that, sir," the sonar man called up. "He can't blow his fuel oil tanks, the vents must be wide open and he can't close them. He's at two hundred feet and sinking slowly!"

"Oh Jesus!" Brannon said. "Tell him I want to talk to Captain Hinman, son."

Brannon and Olsen heard the sonar man as he repeated the *Mako*'s message to the quartermaster of the watch in the Conning Tower. "Captain Hinman and Pete Simms and all topside party lost in deck gun fire from freighter. . . . Lieutenant Grilley has assumed command . . . *Mako* is at four hundred feet."

"Oh, God!" Brannon said. "What the hell can we do?"

"Not much," his Executive Officer said slowly. "Not much except pray!"

There was a strange, eerie calm within *Mako* as the ship slowly sank downward. Chief Mike DeLucia looked at his twisted leg and half-smiled. "You won't hurt for very damned long," he said softly. "That's for damned sure!"

In the Forward Battery Compartment Chief Officer's Cook Thomas T. Thompson drew a cup of coffee from the urn in his tiny serving galley and took it into the Wardroom and sat down and began to sip slowly from the cup.

In the Conning Tower Aaron, sitting beside Nate Cohen, prayed, his voice soft in the quiet Conning Tower. When he had finished his prayer Nate Cohen began to chant softly in Yiddish.

Mako continued to sink.

"She's at five hundred feet, sir!" the sonar man reported to Captain Brannon. "Five hundred feet and sinking slowly!"

Mike Brannon wiped his eyes with the back of his hand.

"Tell them," his voice broke," tell them we are praying for them. Tell them that!" He turned away, sobbing.

He waited, the tears streaming down his cheeks, listening to the measured pulses of *Mako*'s response. The sonar man in the Conning Tower called out each word to the quartermaster and on the bridge, Captain Mike Brannon and John Olsen heard each word:

"The Lord is my Shepherd . . . I shall not want . . . He maketh me to lie down in green pastures . . . He leadeth me beside the still waters . . ."

There was silence.

"Sir," the sonar man's voice was small, hardly audible. "Sir, transmission stopped and I heard a big crunching noise!"

Brannon looked at his Executive Officer, his eyes streaming.

"My God, John, the water is six miles deep here!"

John Olsen nodded and in a soft voice finished the words of the Twenty-Third Psalm.

Epilogue

The story of the life and death of the U.S.S. *Mako*, Fleet Submarine, is fiction.

Here is fact: A very small group of submarines waged a bitter war against Japan, sinking more than 1,000 Japanese merchant vessels and a considerable portion of the Imperial Japanese Navy, including one battleship, eight aircraft carriers, three heavy and eight light cruisers, many destroyers and a large number of Naval auxiliary ships.

The stunning impact of this war within a war led a great many experts to express the postwar view that the U.S. Submarine blockade against Japan had been so effective that the invasions of the Philippine Islands, Iwo Jima, Palau, and Okinawa, the dropping of the atomic bombs on Nagasaki and Hiroshima, were unnecessary. The submarine war had already drawn the noose so tightly around Japan's neck that it could not survive as a nation.

The price the American submarine force paid for waging this war was expensive. Twenty-two percent of the 16,000 men who went to war in U.S. submarines died in action. In terms of the percentages engaged that was the highest death toll of any branch of the U.S. Armed Forces. Some of those deaths, perhaps many of them, could be laid at the door of the U.S. Navy itself. The Navy's prewar training for submarine captains was poorly conceived and ineffective. It sent submarines to sea with defective torpedoes, defective torpedo explosers and diesel engines that would not run properly.

For all those who went to sea in submarines and never came back:

Requiescant in pace.